What the critics wrote about *Different Class*

'A magnificently plotted and twisty journey to the heart of a 24-year-old crime . . . darkly humorous . . . constantly wrongfoots and misdirects . . . up to a satisfyingly eccentric conclusion.'

Observer

'A long way from *Chocolat*, Joanne Harris's reinvention as a writer of psychological thrillers continues apace . . . delivers it beautifully.'

Mail on Sunday

'Slowly, Harris reveals tiny clues, withholding full explanations until the startling denouement. Classy writing, sensitive and moving.'

The Times

'Harris pulls off an impeccable thriller denouement . . . consistently entertaining.'

Sunday Times

'A cracking psychological thriller that drips with menace . . . tightly plotted and completely engrossing.'

Good Housekeeping

'Harris magnificently manages every minute thread of the story, and even makes us laugh along the way . . . exquisitely sinister . . . Part black comedy, part thriller, and totally enjoyable.'

Daily Mail

'Crime novel or literary novel? Categories really don't matter; readers will find themselves comprehensively gripped.'

Independent

Fiction by Joanne Harris

THE *CHOCOLAT* NOVELS

CHOCOLAT

Vianne Rocher arrives in the French village of Lasquenet and opens a sinful chocolate boutique, directly opposite the church.

'Mouthwatering . . . A feelgood book of the first order'
Observer

THE LOLLIPOP SHOES

Seeking refuge in Paris with her two daughters,Vianne encounters a dangerous adversary.

'*Chocolat* was a hard act to follow but Harris has managed it in style'
Daily Express

PEACHES FOR MONSIEUR LE CURÉ

When Vianne Rocher receives a letter from beyond the grave, she must follow the wind back to Lansquenet.

'Immerses the reader in a bath of seductive imagery'
Sunday Times

Psychological thrillers

(*THE MALBRY CYCLE*)

GENTLEMEN & PLAYERS

At St Oswald's, a Northern boys' grammar school, a dark undercurrent stirs, of obsession and revenge.

'A gripping psychological thriller . . . with pace, wit and acute observation'

Daily Express

BLUEEYEDBOY

A dark tale of a poisonously dysfunctional family that makes creative use of all the disguise and mind games that are offered by the internet.

'Delivers an almighty twist in the tale . . . heartbreaking'

The Times

DIFFERENT CLASS

After thirty years at St Oswald's, Latin master Roy Straitley has seen all kinds of boys come and go. But there's one boy that still haunts his darkest dreams.

'A masterpiece of misdirection'

Val McDermid

Other novels

BLACKBERRY WINE

A bottle of home-brewed wine left to Jake by a past friend provides the key to a terrible secret.

'Touching, funny and clever'
Daily Telegraph

FIVE QUARTERS OF THE ORANGE

A tragic childhood in Occupied France comes back to haunt a secretive widow.

'Vastly enjoyable, utterly gripping'
The Times

COASTLINERS

Mado returns to her Breton island after a ten-year absence, to fight the tides and bring a dying community back to life.

'A writer of tremendous charm, who creates a winning blend of fairy-tale morality and gritty realism'
Independent

HOLY FOOLS

In seventeenth-century France, Juliette takes the veil, only to find that that a man from her past returns to haunt her behind the convent walls.

'With this bold, inventive book, Harris confirms her position as one of Britain's most popular novelists'
Daily Mail

SLEEP, PALE SISTER

A blackly gothic evocation of Victorian artistic life.

'A hauntingly evocative laudanum-dream of a novel'
Time Out

THE EVIL SEED

Joanne Harris's haunting debut novel.

'A dark, gothic romance filled with mystery, jealousy, and violence . . . a thrilling read'
Style

SHORT STORY COLLECTIONS

JIGS & REELS

'Tantalising and suggestive, and leave us wanting more'
Sunday Times

A CAT, A HAT, AND A PIECE OF STRING

'A moreish collection . . . comical, scary, sad and surreal'
Independent

FANTASY NOVELS (AS JOANNE M. HARRIS)

RUNEMARKS

An epic tale set in the world of the Norse gods.

'If you liked Philip Pullman's *Northern Lights*, try this'
Heat

RUNELIGHT

Two girls. With new runes. And the end of the world is coming. Again.

'Wonderful imagination showcased to great effect'
Sun

THE GOSPEL OF LOKI

The rise and fall of the Norse gods, led by the world's ultimate trickster, Loki.

'Should beguile the fans of Neil Gaiman'
Metro

Different Class

JOANNE HARRIS

BLACK SWAN

TRANSWORLD PUBLISHERS
61–63 Uxbridge Road, London W5 5SA
www.penguin.co.uk

Transworld is part of the Penguin Random House group of companies
whose addresses can be found at global.penguinrandomhouse.com

Penguin
Random House
UK

First published in Great Britain in 2016 by Doubleday
an imprint of Transworld Publishers
Black Swan edition published 2017

A CIP catalogue record for this book
is available from the British Library.

ISBN 9780552777018 (B format)
9780552777025 (A format)

Typeset in 10.5/13.5pt ITC Giovanni by Thomson Digital Pvt Ltd, Noida, Delhi
Printed and bound by Clays Ltd, Bungay, Suffolk

Penguin Random House is committed to a sustainable
future for our business, our readers and our planet. This book is
made from Forest Stewardship Council® certified paper.

MIX
Paper from
responsible sources
FSC® C018179
FSC
www.fsc.org

To my Brodie Boys:
You know who you are.

Prologue

1

September 1981

Dear Mousey,

Fun Facts About Murder: Use Coca-Cola to clean up blood spills. The combination of ascorbic acid and carbonated water actually digests the blood, leaving no trace of evidence.

Not that I'm planning a murder. But it is an interesting subject. Unlike most of the subjects I will be studying this term – Maths; Latin; English; French. Actually I *do* like English. But the reading list is awful. *To Kill a Mockingbird;* Chaucer; Barry Hines. And Shakespeare. Always Shakespeare. Why can't we read something *fun*, for a change? Something with a bit of bite?

Still, you'd have been proud today. I didn't give myself away. Never tell tales, never cry, and never give yourself away. That's what it takes to do well at school. That and being cool, of course. Which is why no one will ever suspect that I am writing this diary. A diary isn't cool. Diaries are for sissies and girls. A diary gives *everything* away, which is why I'm going to write my thoughts in a place my parents will never look. My new St Oswald's Prep diary, handed out this morning on the first day of the Michaelmas term. Hiding my story in plain sight, like a corpse at a graveside.

They never look at my schoolwork, except for the bit in red at the end. AAA: the row of tents. As long as those tents are there, it's fine. And my form-master will never look. I can tell that already. Mr Straitley, Quaz to the school. That's short for Quasimodo, because he looks like a gargoyle and lives in the Bell Tower. I *think* that's supposed to be a joke. It doesn't seem very funny to me. In fact, Mr Straitley scares me a bit. I don't think I'm going to like him.

Back at my old school, Netherton Green, my teacher was Miss McDonald. She was blonde, and pretty, and young, and wore Indian skirts and ankle-boots. Mr Straitley wears a cape, like all the other teachers. But his is dusty and covered in chalk. He calls us by our surnames. We all go by our surnames here. It's one of those St Oswald's rules, like not running in corridors, and never leaving your shirt untucked.

They tell me it's important to follow *all* the rules this time. St Oswald's is a *New Start*, far away from Netherton Green. A new start. No trouble; no pranks. No hanging around with the *Wrong Sort*. No sharp objects. No rough games. And always follow *all* the rules.

Of course, I don't *know* all the rules. That's part of being a Seventh Term Boy. Seventh Term Boys have a whole two years to catch up, including schoolwork, making friends, joining teams and learning *The Ropes*. That's a nautical term, by the way. Dad likes nautical terms. He'd have liked me to join the Navy one day, but I can't, because of *My Condition*. (That's what they call it. *My Condition*, Mousey.)

My Condition means that there are things they'll never let me do at home. My Condition determines the friends I make, the games I play, even the school I attend. That's why

Dad chose St Oswald's. St Oswald's is a Church school, with a *Rigorous Moral Code*. That's what I need, apparently. Well, maybe there's some truth in that. After all, there's no fun in breaking rules unless they really *mean* something. Running in corridors doesn't count. You need to see past the trivia before you can reach for the fun stuff.

Oh, and *Never Get Caught*, of course. *That's* the most important thing. Breaking rules is only fun if you get away with it. That means not telling anyone, even your best friend – assuming I had one, which I don't. Not any more, anyway. Perhaps that's why I'm telling you all my secrets, Mousey. Imaginary friends – like dead ones – don't talk. They never give the game away. Still, it might be nice to find someone who shares my interests. Someone who likes to break the rules. Someone to share in the fun stuff. The fun stuff, like at Netherton Green.

The fun stuff. Like murder.

Part One

Agnosco veteris vestigia flammae.

(Vergil)

1

St Oswald's Grammar School for Boys
Michaelmas Term, September 7th, 2005

Ah, yes. There she blows. St Oswald's, a metaphor for eternity if ever I saw one, heaving into view like something from a boys' adventure book – a Jules Verne, perhaps, as the mysterious island peers over the horizon. Or a Rider Haggard, in which sinister natives cower and lurk at the gates of the Forbidden City. You can see the Bell Tower from the road, the peaked turret that has never housed a bell a haunt for pigeons – and lately, mice. And behind it, the long spine of the Middle Corridor, mullioned with light, and the illuminated front of the Chapel, the rose window casting its fugitive gleam across the walk of lindens.

Home at last, I tell myself, and the thought is at the same time a benediction and a curse.

Silly old fool, comes my silent retort, in a voice eerily like that of my colleague and long-time adversary, Dr 'Sourgrape' Devine. I'll be sixty-six on Bonfire Night, with a hundred and two terms under my fast-expanding belt – what will it take to keep me away?

Good question. It's a drug, of course. Like the occasional Gauloise, taken in secret behind the door of my office, it helps to keep me going. And my ticker pills, of course, prescribed for me by my doctor after last year's little incident – along with a good deal of unwanted advice on smoking, stress and pastry.

My doctor is an ex-pupil of mine (the Village is full of them nowadays), which makes him hard to take seriously. He means well, for all that, and I do try my best to humour him. But stress is a part of the job, and besides, what would the old place become without me? Thirty-four years I've served on this ship. I know it from every angle. Master and boy; teacher trainee; form-tutor; Head of Classics; and now, Old Centurion. Might as well try to knock the gargoyles off the Chapel roof as dislodge old Straitley, and if the management don't like it, at least they have the sense to keep quiet on the subject. I did the School a service last year – the year that, after a promising start, became our *annus horribilis* – besides which my Latin results were the best we've had since '89. At the time, I'll admit it, I was close to giving in. But murder, scandal, deception and fraud have driven the old ship on to the rocks. How could I leave St Oswald's to the scavengers and the wrecking crew?

So here I am again, two days before the official stampede, watering the plants, clearing my desk (well, I aim to) and generally planning next year's campaign with the cunning and precision of a Marcus Aurelius. Or so I hope my colleagues will think, when they arrive this afternoon for the ritual pre-term staff meeting to find me already installed in my room in the Bell Tower, smoking a quiet cigarette and fully conversant with the new term's class lists, timetable, gossip and dirt, the stuff on which St Oswald's dines like the graveyard kings of old.

I owe much of my insider information to a single source. Jimmy Watt. My secret weapon. Reinstated after last year and promoted to the position of Assistant Porter. No intellectual, but sound, and good with his hands – besides which Jimmy owes me a favour or two, and through him I hear much of what is denied my more elevated colleagues.

'Morning, boss.' His face is round and good-natured, lit now with a brilliant smile. 'Good holiday?'

'Yes, thank you, Jimmy.' I try to remember the last time I went on holiday. Unless you count that School trip to France in 1978, when Eric Scoones took the boys on foot to see the Sacré-Coeur by night, blissfully unaware that the famous basilica sits in the middle of the most notorious red-light district in Paris.

I suppose I must have *had* a holiday – if you can call it that, with its burden of wasps and cricket and bare midriffs and unseasonal rainstorms, with tea in the afternoons and the mantelpiece clock ticking away the long and somnolent summer days. *Gods*, I think, *it's good to be back*. But how long for? A term? A year? What next? What then?

Holidays, I suppose. Leisure activities. Novels. An allotment, perhaps, somewhere up by the Abbey Road estate, where I will grow rhubarb and listen to the wireless. Hobbies. Pub quizzes. Sudoku, whatever *that* is. All the things I postponed in the name of duty, back in the days when such things were still to be desired. Depressing prospect. A St Oswald's Master has no time for frivolities, and it is far, far too late for me to develop a taste for them now.

'Yes, back in the jug for another stint,' I told Jimmy, with a smile so that he would know that I was joking. 'You'd almost think I *liked* it here.'

Jimmy gave his honking laugh. I suppose it must seem strange to him; but then, of course, he's still young. He has his pastimes – such as they are – and the great white whale of St Oswald's has not yet consumed him entirely.

'Any sign of the new New Head?'

'He's in his office. I've seen his car.'

'He didn't introduce himself? Pop into the Lodge for a cup of tea?'

Jimmy grinned and shook his head. I expect he thought I was joking. But a good Headmaster knows his staff before he takes the helm of the ship – and that means the cleaners, the Porter *and* the ladies who make the tea. A good Head values the rank and file at least as much as the officers. But since his appointment in early June, sightings of the new New Head have been infrequent, to say the least. We know him by name and, to some extent, by reputation. But only a privileged few have seen his face. Rumours abound, however. Meetings held behind closed doors; whispers of insolvency and academic failure; all compounded by a far from friendly School Inspection which, added to the most appalling set of exam results in St Oswald's memory, has brought us to this all-time low; a Crisis Intervention.

The dreadful events of last year; the murder of a schoolboy, the stabbing of a member of staff and the scandal that split the Common Room still reverberate, even now, and there have been many casualties. We lost our Second Master, Pat Bishop, as a result of those events, and since his departure there has been unrest, unease and downright rebellion among the rank and file, while Bob Strange – the Third Master, a clever administrator, but with no flair for people – tried to keep the old galley from sinking with the help of computers, management courses and internal assessment.

It didn't work. Our Captain, the erstwhile New Head, unaccustomed to command, began to flounder. There were mutterings in the ranks; some staff deserted (or walked the plank) and finally, in June, came confirmation from the Governors of what they called an 'emergency management restructuring'. In layman's terms, the hemlock bowl.

Not that I cared much for the man. Suits come, Suits go, and in sixteen years he'd achieved little for us, and still less for himself. St Oswald's tradition dictates that a Headmaster shall always be known as the *New Head*, until he has earned the respect of the crew. The *old* New Head never managed this. A state-school man in shades of grey, whose tendency was to dwell on the smaller transgressions of St Oswald's dress code rather than turn his mind to the general health of the *corpus scolari*.

The new man, rumour tells us, is very different. A Super-Head, trained in PR – and *sound*, according to Bob Strange, which makes him eminently qualified to take the helm of our leaky old ship and to steer us triumphantly into happier waters. I personally doubt this. He sounds like another Suit to me – and his absence throughout the summer term, when he could have been getting to know his staff, suggests that he will be one of those men who expects the menial work to be done invisibly, by others, while he enjoys the benefits; the publicity and the glory.

His name, we know, is Harrington. It happens to be the name of a boy I once disliked very strongly: not the new man's fault, of course, nor is it such an uncommon name, but I can't help wishing that his name had been Smith or Robinson. We know little else about him, except that he is a guru of sorts, having already saved two failing schools in Oldham and in Milton Keynes; is a prominent member of Survivors, a charitable organization dealing with child abuse, and has an MBE from the Queen. We also know, thanks to Jimmy Watt, that he is young, good-looking, well dressed and drives a silver BMW (a fact that already ensures him Jimmy's wholehearted support and admiration).

'That's what St Oswald's needs,' says Bob Strange. 'A new broom, to sweep away the cobwebs.'

Well, I, for one, *liked* the cobwebs. I suspect that to Strange I am one myself. But our Bob has hopes of promotion. At forty-six he is no longer a Young Gun, and his flair for technology, which might have been unusual twenty years ago, is now the norm for the new generation. Failing the Headship, he covets the post of Second Master – and with reason; he's been doing Pat Bishop's job since Christmas. Of course, a post at St Oswald's is always more than the sum of its parts, and the things that made Bishop a success – his heart, his humanity, his genuine affection for the boys and for the School – had nothing to do with his job description. Strange has never quite grasped this, and the rest of us have long since given up hope that he might emerge from his cocoon of paperwork as a flamboyant Second Master. On the other hand, it could be that the new man will need inside help; someone to show him the ropes, perhaps, and to give him the dirt on his pirate crew.

Strange most certainly fits the bill. His glaucous eyes see everything: who is late for lessons; who has trouble with the boys; who steals the Common Room copy of the *Daily Mail* to read in his form-room during Prep. He keeps to his office most of the time, and yet his ears are always open. He has his spies among the staff (some even suspect him of using hidden cameras), and as a result he is respected and feared, though seldom actually liked. He runs the timetable, and those unfortunate enough to be out of favour get more than their fair share of Friday afternoon cover and lower third-form sets. A sneak, in short. A management stooge.

This morning as I made my way up the stairs to my form-room I wondered – with some small apprehension – what the coming term might bring. So many things have changed since last year; so many colleagues reshuffled, or gone. Bishop; Pearman; Grachvogel; the Head – and, of course, our own Miss Dare. I could have been among them – in fact, I fully intended to retire – but for the state of the dear old place, and the gnawing conviction that the moment I left, Bob Strange would delete my subject from the curriculum.

Besides, what would I do without the perpetual soap opera of St Oswald's to sustain me? And my boys – my Brodie Boys – who else but I could look after them?

The scent reached me as I opened the door. *Eau de Room 59*, a blend so familiar that for ten months a year I barely notice its presence. And yet here it is again, as nostalgic as burning leaves; a comforting scent of wood, books, polish, geranium, mice, old socks and perhaps a hint of illicit Gauloise. I lit one in celebration, knowing that when Dr Sourgrape Devine – Head of German, Head of Amadeus House and (more's the pity) Health & Safety Officer to St Oswald's and the world – made his entrance, such luxuries as a quiet smoke, a pasty or even a Liquorice Allsort (of which I have a small supply hidden in my desk drawer) would be once more forbidden to me.

Speak of the devil. Damn and blast. He must have got in early this morning, because I'd barely blown out the match when I heard a sound of footsteps at my door and glimpsed the end of Devine's sharp nose behind the panel of frosted glass.

'Morning, Devine!' I disposed of match and cigarette under the lid of the Master's desk.

'Morning, Straitley.' The nose twitched, but refrained from comment.

'Good holiday?'

'Yes, thank you.' He and I both know that Dr Devine hates holidays. On the other hand, as a married man, he has, I suppose, some responsibility to Mrs Devine, and so grudgingly, once a year, he packs off to the French Riviera and spends two weeks planning lessons in the shade while his wife – a well-preserved fifty – sunbathes, plays tennis and goes to the spa. 'And you?'

'Oh yes. Great fun. Been here long?'

'Been coming in since last week,' he said, with a casualness that filled me with suspicion. 'Things to do. You know what it's like.'

I certainly do. Any excuse to get back to St Oswald's. He's an ambitious chap in spite of his age (sixty, damn him, and looks younger), and he must have guessed that there might soon be a Third Master's job going begging, or if not, some new and highly paid administrative post. Besides, the New Head will surely need a friend on the ground, and Devine sees no reason for Bob Strange to be the only contender.

'Inducting new staff?' I said slyly.

I know that this year, appointments have been mainly overseen by Bob Strange, the New Head and the Bursar; and that as Head of German, Devine feels that he should have had a more central role in the department's restructuring. Kitty Teague's promotion to Head of French, for instance, he feels to be inappropriate, and he is aggrieved at the fact that two new appointments have already been made, largely at her discretion. For myself, I'm rather fond of Miss Teague, whom I've known since she was a teacher trainee. I think she'll make a splendid Head of French, and I suspect old Devine knows it too.

As for his own department – well. The new German Master, his protégé, already strikes me as dubious. His name precedes him – Markowicz – though apparently his busy schedule means he won't be in School until next week. I know that kind of member of staff – the sort who puts administrative work before the lowly business of actually teaching his subject – and I'm not sure his appointment will reflect well on his Head of Department.

'I've not seen much of the new staff,' said Devine in a frosty voice. 'Even the New Head—' He sniffed. Some say the eyes are the mirror of the soul, but in Devine's case it is the nose that expresses most fully the hidden emotions. His had turned pink, like an albino rabbit's, and twitched resentfully.

'Have a Liquorice Allsort,' I said.

He looked at me as if I'd offered him cocaine. 'No thanks,' he replied. 'I don't indulge.'

'A pity,' I said, selecting a yellow one. 'I've always thought a little indulgence would do you the world of good.'

He gave me a look. 'You would,' he said. 'Have *you* seen him? The New Head, I mean?'

'I'm beginning to think he's the Invisible Man. Still, he'll be here at eleven o'clock for the Headmaster's Briefing. I imagine everyone's curious to see how he's going to handle the situation. It's not every day you get to meet a Super-Head.'

Devine gave a percussive sniff.

'I take it you've met.'

'We exchanged a few words.'

It struck me then that there was something distinctly odd about his manner. Dr Devine has never been the most outspoken of people, especially where criticism of the management is concerned. I wondered what the new man had said to him to provoke such a reaction.

'And?' I prompted.

But Devine had regained his usual composure. His allegiance to the management means that whatever his personal dissatisfactions, he does not discuss them with the baser element. 'You'll see,' he said, and left the room, leaving in his wake an unmistakable odour of sanctity.

I spent the following couple of hours going over my records, writing in my diary and enjoying the occasional Liquorice Allsort. St Oswald's has its own diaries, distributed to boys and staff. The boys use theirs for class notes and Prep; the staff, for planning lessons. Or rather, they *did*, until three years ago, when the Bursar decreed that the expense was too much of a burden. One more of our traditions gone, although I have kept a small supply of diaries, for personal use, in my stockroom. It's not the expense I begrudge, but the fact that, on my shelf at home, I have a neatly matched set of thirty-odd School diaries, with our crest in blue and gold, and the School's motto beneath it. It seems somehow immoral now, at the end of my career, to adopt a new design. The boys may choose what they like, of course, but I'm old-fashioned enough to believe that Prep belongs in a Prep diary, not in a Filofax, or (in the case of my boy Allen-Jones) a shocking-pink notebook with *Hello Kitty* on the cover.

Tomorrow, the boys return to School. It's the moment for which I've been waiting all summer. Unlike Devine, who has been known to say, without a trace of irony, that the School would be far more efficient without a single boy in the place, I'm very fond of my boys, which is why I have always refused to take on extra administrative tasks, preferring to teach in room 59 rather than push papers in an office. This year, however, the first day of term will mostly serve as a vehicle for various Briefings, plus as a time to digest (and dispute) aspects of the timetable; including cover, free periods and extracurricular duties.

My new timetable is unusually sparse, I notice with disapproval; only twenty-one periods a week compared with the usual thirty-five. Of course everyone knows that Bob Strange (a physicist) views Latin with suspicion, and would like nothing better than to see it vanish from the timetable. So far, however, I have managed to keep control of my one-man department, and in defiance of probability, the results have remained consistently good. Still, this year I see that (no doubt with the help of the New Head), Bob has finally managed (using the National Curriculum as his low excuse) to relegate Latin to an optional subject, and moreover, has placed it in direct competition with German, which means that the serious linguists – those who want to read Languages at A-level and beyond – will have no choice but to opt for German as their second language, and either delay their study of Classics until the Sixth Form (absurd), or (worse still) choose to study Latin at lunchtimes, as an extracurricular activity.

Extracurricular! There was a time in St Oswald's history when *everything* was conducted in Latin, including Break, and boys were caned for getting their cases wrong. Rather before my time, I'll admit. Nevertheless, how dare they?

I spent the next few minutes cursing both the New Head and Bob Strange in Latin, Greek and Anglo-Saxon. Then I cursed Dr Devine, who doubtless will benefit most from the decision, and who has resented my subject since the day he arrived. Devine and I go back a long time – thirty-four years, to be exact – and during that time he has made it clear that he considers Latin obsolete and possibly subversive, interfering as it does with his Teutonic ambition. He is, if not a *friend* of Strange, at least a fellow-traveller; and I suspect that this relegation of my subject to the option pool is at least partly due to his influence. Still, *id imperfectum manet dum confectum erit*, as I think Clint Eastwood may have said. There may be one more showdown before either of us hangs up his guns.

At twenty to eleven, I collected my gown from its brass hook at the back of the stock-cupboard door. Twenty years ago, all members of staff wore gowns in School. Now I am more or less alone in continuing the tradition. Still, an academic gown conceals a multitude of sins – chalk dust, tea stains, a copy of Vergil's poetry set aside for the more tedious meetings. Not that *this* one would be dull, I thought as I slung on my battered old gown and made my way down to the Staff Common Room in good time for tea and a chocolate biscuit before the Headmaster's first Briefing of term.

To my surprise, I found the Common Room already crowded. Curiosity, I suppose – besides which there's not a lot of space when all the staff get together, and, today of all days, no one wanted to miss the chance of a ringside seat.

My favourite chair was unoccupied. Second from the left, under the clock, at a comfortable angle of sixty degrees. Years of judicious lounging have moulded that chair to my exact measurements, and it will take more than a change of Head to affect its contours. I poured a cup of tea from the urn and settled in happily.

Eric Scoones was already there. My colleague for over thirty years, and a friend since childhood, he has the same concerns as I – except that, being a Modern Linguist, he is considered more of an asset to the department, and therefore feels himself to be in a superior position to mine – a fact he likes to emphasize when he is feeling insecure, which, to be fair, is most of the time.

'Morning, Straitley.'

'Morning, Scoones.'

The years have left their mark on us all, but on Eric Scoones they have settled like barnacles. The boy I knew at eleven years old – small, clever enough to have been put up a School year, mischievous and quick to flee in the face of trouble – has become a brontosaur; a large, slow half-Centurion with a drinker's nose and an alarming tendency to wheeze when climbing stairs. The mischievous boy has become a man who sees every setback as a direct blow from the Almighty. A bitter man, who believes that Life has robbed him of pleasures as yet unspecified, and looks upon the success of his friends as a personal defeat. And yet, I'm fond of the old ass, as I believe he is fond of me.

'Good holiday, Straitley?'

Even after so many years, he calls me by my surname, just as he did when we were boys, more than fifty years ago.

I gave a noncommittal shrug. 'I'm not sure holidays are my cup of tea. Too stressful.'

Eric gave me a look of weary superiority. 'I wouldn't have thought *you* could ever be stressed. Not with *your* workload.'

Eric sees my timetable, with its small class sizes and emphasis on the Upper School, as a kind of hobby; a pleasant escape from the realities of teaching Modern Languages. Thus, Eric maintains a pretence of being perpetually overworked, in spite of the fact that he has no form, and therefore claims five extra hours a week to himself, while I have to cater to the needs of my boys, their work and their parents. Having been an indifferent form-tutor for the first ten years of his career, Eric now refuses to have a form, and rather despises, I suspect, the affection in which I hold my boys – a sentiment he feels to be undignified, inappropriate, and which will one day lead to trouble. In spite of this, he has a warm heart, which he hides (rather badly) beneath a façade of gruffness.

'Spotted any newbies yet?'

This was not an idle question. We lost quite a few people last year, including our Head of Department. This has left the Languages Department sadly depleted, with only the League of Nations (a husband-and-wife team of almost unbearable smugness), plus Eric, Devine, Kitty Teague – and, of course, myself – to man the departmental cannons.

Eric huffed. I took this as an expression of general dissatisfaction. I suspect he had his eye on the Head of Department's post – in spite of the fact that he ought to be planning his retirement. But Eric is one of the old school, and the promotion of Kitty Teague seems to him unnatural. In our day, women were secretaries, or dinner-ladies, or cleaners. For one to be his superior now goes against every principle.

'It might as well be a girls' school,' Eric said morosely. 'Two more women appointed for French. That's what you get when you appoint one as Head of Department.'

I drank my tea and forebore from comment. Male Languages graduates are like hens' teeth in the teaching profession, and I'm sure Kitty's judgement is perfectly sound. Still, I'm afraid the appointment of two women to our department is likely to result in a spate of ribaldry from certain of our colleagues – and I don't expect the Bursar (who considers himself a wit) to refrain from comment.

'What about the Germans?' I said.

'Haven't seen the new man yet. Apparently, he's on a course. Won't be here for another week.' Eric's voice was listless. His opinion of members of staff who choose to go on courses, rather than stay in the classroom, is both salty and well documented.

'What about the New Head?'

Eric shrugged. 'Not seen him yet. No one has, except the Inner Circle.'

'What about Devine?' I said, thinking back to the morning's brief, uneasy encounter.

'Oh, he's over the moon, of course. He thinks the Crisis Team walks on water.'

I shook my head. 'I saw him today. He seemed a bit – preoccupied.'

'You mean, he was nosing around again. Sucking up to the Crisis Team in the name of Health & Safety.' Devine and Eric have never been friends. Eric holds Devine responsible for his own lack of promotion, and Devine considers Eric to be moody and inefficient.

'Not this time,' I told him. 'I got the feeling that somehow Devine wasn't too impressed with the New Head.'

Eric looked sceptical. 'Oxbridge man; education guru; charity worker; Superman. What else does he want?'

What else, indeed?

'Of course,' said Eric mournfully, '*some* might think that a Head should have spent at least a few years in the classroom. *Some* might question the wisdom of letting a state-school Yes-man into a place like St Oswald's.'

I could see his point, of course. A Head starts out at the chalk-face; not in some PR hothouse. And yes, St Oswald's traditions are not those of the state sector. But crisis measures (and their Heads) are usually short-term investments.

St Oswald's has stood for five hundred years. State-school man or not, I thought; how much damage could he do?

By now it was time for the meeting to start, and yet the famous Super-Head still hadn't made his appearance. What was the fellow waiting for? I suspected a showman, and, pouring myself another cup of tea, I settled into my armchair and prepared to watch the show.

Five minutes later it began. The door opened; silence fell; a phalanx of Suits entered the room in arrow formation. Bob Strange was among them, his face oddly expressionless, flanked by Devine and the Bursar; but no one paid them much attention. Instead, all eyes were on the newcomers. Two men and one woman – all three smart and so well pressed you could have cut yourself on the creases. The New Head was at the tip of the arrow (I assumed the other two Suits were his Crisis Team), and I had time to take in the cut of his suit, the shine on his shoes and a smile that would have made a piano keyboard look narrow before recognition surprised me into a muffled oath and the contents of my teacup soaked my trouser leg and began to trickle inexorably towards my shoes.

A Master never forgets a face, though boys' names often come and go. I'd put down the name to coincidence – in over forty years of teaching, one tends to encounter most names more than once. But as soon as I saw his face, I knew that my instinct had been right.

Because I knew the man, you see. Dr Harrington, MBE – Johnny Harrington of 3S – returned after twenty years' absence to inflict fresh misery. There was no chance he wouldn't recognize me; as he scanned the little crowd our eyes met and his smile broadened still further. He gave me a nod, as if greeting an old friend, and my heart sank like a doomed frigate.

Johnny Harrington, ye gods. My nemesis; my *bête noire*; the boy who almost cost me my job and cost the School a whole lot more. And now he's a Headmaster, forsooth – not just a Head but a *Super*-Head – and I could almost find it in me to regret the *old* New Head, brittle and ineffectual as he was, because a weak Head can easily be carried by a competent deputy or two, but a Super-Head allows no one to be his bearer. A Super-Head follows through. A Super-Head steers his own ship – proudly, yea, even unto the rocks.

And unless young Harrington has changed beyond all recognition over the past twenty years, my guess is that those rocks are precisely where we're heading.

2

Michaelmas Term, 1981

Dear Mousey,

So this is St Oswald's. Can't say I'm impressed. Everything's so *old* – the desks, the Honours Boards, the gym, even the staff are all ancient. It's like being in a museum full of dusty old stuffed animals. Mr Scoones, who shows French films at lunchtimes and probably thinks he's *très cool*. Dr Devine, who never smiles. And Mr Straitley – the worst of them, with his Latin jokes and his sarcasm. I wish I was back at Netherton Green. I wish I was in a different class.

So many people are animals, under the skin and the uniform. A pig, an elephant, a dog. With his big head and curly hair, Mr Straitley's a pantomime lion, playing to the gallery of all his baying sycophants. Mr Scoones is a bullfrog, full of air and pompousness. Dr Devine is a mantis, all brittle and righteous. Most of the boys are dogs, of course. Running in packs, begging for scraps, yapping '*Yes sir, no sir.*' I used to have a dog, you know. Not for long. I hate dogs.

The Head of St Oswald's is Dr Shakeshafte. He looks like a pig. Small eyes, big nose. The other boys call him 'SS'. At first I thought that this was because he was a German teacher, but now I think it's something rude. I don't like him either. On my first day he yelled at me for going the wrong way down South Stair. *South Stair*. In the singular. That's what they call it here. In fact, there are forty-three (plural) *stairs*, but apparently St Oswald's rules override the rules of grammar.

And St Oswald's is a maze. There's the Bell Tower, of course. That's where my form-room is. I'll be running up and down stairs all day. Then there's the Upper Corridor that runs across the top floor. Below that, there's the Middle Corridor that connects it with the ground floor, and finally the Lower Corridor at the far end of the building. On either end, there's a flight of stairs.

This is where it gets complicated. According to St Oswald's rules, Lower and Middle School boys can only go *up* North Stair, and *down* South Stair. This is to *Ease Congestion*, says Dr Shakeshafte. Out of bounds to Lower and Middle School boys are: the Upper School Common Room, the Sixth Form Common Room, the Staff Common Room (of course), the Quiet Room, the Chapel (outside of services), the boiler room, the Porter's Lodge and pretty much *all* form-rooms unless a master is present. (That's what we call them here. Masters. Does that make us all dogs?)

Then there are the *other* rules I am somehow expected to know. Line up outside your classroom. Stand up when a master comes in. Always say *Sir* when you're talking to a master. Say *Sir* to prefects, too, and make sure you do what they tell you. Don't take your blazer off unless the Head announces *Shirt Sleeve Order* in Assembly. Don't eat in the corridors. Always keep your shirt tucked in. Don't bring your own books into the library. Always keep to the left-hand side. Already I've been shouted at a hundred times. *New Boy, don't do that! New Boy, walk on the left!* How hard is it to remember a name? Maybe I'll change mine to New Boy.

I sometimes try to tell myself that I'll only be here for five years, max. That will make me eighteen. I'll be practically old by then. Sometimes I already feel old. If the average life is seventy years, then I have fifty-six years left. Fifty-six more years. That's all. And five of them will be wasted here. That leaves me with just fifty-one. Fifty-one years of existence. It makes me shiver all over to think that people will be alive when I'm dead. People who haven't been born yet; people who've never heard of me. Kids who are younger than I am now, with more of their lives ahead of them.

I know I shouldn't think about that. It doesn't help My Condition. But it's like scratching a midge-bite. It hurts a bit, but it feels good, too. Besides, I know how to deal with that now. I'm in control of it, Mousey.

My new form is 3S. There are two other New Boys there. You can tell by their blazers. Everyone else's blazer is worn shiny at the elbows. The rest of the uniform may be new, but blazers are expensive. Parents like to make them last, at least until the fourth year, when you have to go from a plain blazer to one with a blue trim. Only a New Boy's parents would buy a blazer for just one year. And only a New Boy's parents would buy him a briefcase so shiny and new that it actually *creaked* when he opened it. That shine; that creak. Those are the signs of a New Boy.

Anyway, those two New Boys. Nothing special, either of them. One of them is a golden retriever, well fed and well bred. The other's a nicely clipped poodle, not big enough to be scrappy, but one that might give you a bite on the leg if it thought you weren't looking. No one has said much to me up to now. The New Boys are trying to play it cool. Or maybe no one's interested. Unless you want to join a team, a Seventh Term Boy is surplus. My House Master, Mr Fabricant, came into the form-room the other day at lunch break, trying to sign me up for the School Orchestra, but I told him I couldn't spare the time.

He gave me a kind of sad-doggy look. 'Well, *that's* disappointing,' he said. 'I would have thought you'd be happy to join. Make friends; contribute to the House.'

(That's right, we're in Houses. Mine is Parkinson House, which means that I get to wear a red tie if I earn a hundred House Points. I doubt I will. Still, Mr Fabricant doesn't know that. To him, I'm an unknown quantity, all bright and new and shiny.)

I gave him my brightest New Boy smile. 'I'm awfully sorry, sir,' I said. 'It's just that I'm waiting to see how much work I have to do before I catch up with the other boys. I hope it won't be *too* much. But until I know for sure, I can't afford to take on any extra commitments.'

Mr Fabricant looked happier. 'Oh, well, I suppose that's all right. It's nice to see you taking it so seriously. Maybe once you've settled in—'

'I'll be sure to tell you, sir.'

I noticed Goldie and Poodle watching me as they ate their lunch.

'What did you get?' said Poodle.

I always get the same thing. Same sandwich, same piece of fruit, same kind of snack at Break. No sweets, no crisps, no cake, nothing my mum would think common. Like I'm going to be judged, somehow. As if a healthier diet could cure me of My Condition.

'We could share, if you like,' I said.

So we pooled our resources. Three sandwiches – one ham in a bap; one cheese and pickle on brown; one peanut butter on Mother's Pride – two bags of salt and vinegar crisps; half a pork pie; two Mr Kipling's Bakewell Tarts; a quarter of Yorkshire Mixture; a Blue Riband bar; a Wagon Wheel; some sweet cigarettes; some Lucozade and a satsuma. Goldie's mother always gives him money to buy whatever he likes. Poodle is hyperactive, and isn't supposed to eat chocolate. (Of course, he took the Wagon Wheel. I pretended not to care.)

After that, we talked a bit. I learnt that both of them go to our Church. Neither have brothers or sisters. We don't have much in common, except for those brand-new blazers, but I can't afford to be choosy. If I'm to fit in here, I'll need some friends of the kind my father would approve.

After a bit, Poodle spoke up. 'We don't have to stay here at lunchtimes,' he said. 'We can go to Mr Clarke's room. He plays records and everything. He's way cooler than Straitley.'

Mr Clarke is Poodle's English master. He has a fifth-form, and his room is just above Mr Straitley's. Mr Straitley's classroom is a lot like Mr Straitley; messy and covered in chalk dust. There are wooden desks with inkwells, and a squeaky old blackboard. But Mr Clarke's room is a little glass room built a bit like a greenhouse, with plastic desks, big windows, and posters on the ceiling and walls.

Mr Clarke isn't my teacher, worse luck. He teaches the other group. Mr Fabricant teaches ours, and although I haven't been here long, I can already tell that he's no fun at all. Mr Fabricant is a goat, all grey-haired and straggly. But Mr Clarke is actually cool. He has a record player in his room, *and* a bubblegum machine. He doesn't mind if boys come in, even boys from another class.

'Come on,' said Poodle. 'Check it out.'

We followed him up to Mr Clarke's room. It was almost empty. Later I found that the fifth-form had their own Common Room downstairs. Mr Clarke was at his desk, going through a box of LPs, but he looked up as we came in.

'Ah, you're just in time,' he said, pulling an album out of the box. The name of the album was *Animals*. It was by a band called Pink Floyd.

I don't know much about music, you know, except for the kind my parents like. Elgar and Mozart and stuff like that. I'm not allowed to watch *Top of the Pops*, or listen to music on Radio 1. I sometimes do, though, when Dad's not there, so I know at least some of the hits. But I couldn't tell you what was so special about this music of Mr Clarke's, except that it *was* – special, I mean – like fingers playing on my spine. I didn't even recognize any of the instrumental sounds. I thought perhaps there was something in there that *might* have been a guitar, or a voice, or a synth, or some kind of animal in pain.

And all the song titles were named after animals; 'Pigs'; 'Sheep'; 'Dogs'. That one was my favourite. 'Dogs'. I felt like someone had opened up a dirty window in my mind.

'Wow,' I said, when it finished.

Mr Clarke looked up and smiled. His eyes are like yours, Mousey.

'Come on up. Feel free to browse.'

There are two full boxes by his desk, one of singles, one albums. Boys are allowed to look at them, as long as Mr Clarke's in the room, which seems to be pretty much all the time. Some of the artists I recognized; The Carpenters; Roberta Flack; Elton John; The Beatles. But there were lots of others I'd never even heard of.

'I want to hear them all, sir!'

He laughed. 'That's what I like to hear. But not so much of the *Sir*, all right?' He laughed again at the look on my face. 'You can call me Harry,' he said. 'At least when we're both off-duty.'

Well, that came as a surprise, you can guess. I've never called a teacher by their Christian name before. Not even Miss McDonald. It's something that you just don't do. But then, Mr Clarke – no, *Harry* – isn't a regular teacher. He sees things differently. He's smart. And I can tell he likes me.

Pigs. Dogs. *Animals.*

It's funny, you know. I always thought I was the only one who saw other people as animals. Turns out someone else does, too. Mr Clarke gets it. What kind of animal is Mr Clarke? A mythical beast of some kind; a unicorn, or a dragon. I mean, I know he's kind of old, but there's something in his eyes. Something different, Mousey.

After school, my dad asked if I'd made any friends yet. I told him yes. He asked me their names.

I said: 'Harry.'

'And what does Harry's dad do?'

I told him I didn't know. (It was true.)

He said: 'You've got to know these things. A man's friends say as much about him as his clothes, his job, his class.' (Dad's very big on class.)

'I'll ask him,' I said.

'You do that,' said Dad.

3

September 7th, 2005

Now I try to be fair. Really I do. I treat all my boys the same, you know; but unless you're Bob Strange, who despises all boys equally, or Eric Scoones, who has no form, and thus makes such small distinction between them that he scarcely ever remembers their names, you're bound to feel more or less affection for one individual or another.

My Brodie Boys, for instance – Allen-Jones, Sutcliff, Tayler and McNair – in spite of their propensity to wreak mayhem at every turn, hold a special place in my heart. I've always had rather a soft spot for the jokers and the subversives. But every decade or so, there's one – a smart alec; a troublemaker – a boy whose face keeps popping up in all the wrong circumstances and who, years later, can still pop up in a Master's dreams when one's dream-self, clad only in a mortar board and a pair of yellow swimming trunks, attempts to teach a subject about which he knows nothing at all to a disruptive class in which that one boy, grinning like an ape, plays the role of ringleader.

The truth is that no Master, however venerable, is ever entirely without insecurities, and there are boys – not so many of them in my case, no more than six in a whole career – who are capable of sniffing out those insecurities, of using them, of twisting them, of single-handedly making a good class into a bad class, a bad class into the stuff of dread.

Johnny Harrington was one of them. That pale-faced, bland, insufferable boy, with his impeccable uniform and his air of barely concealed contempt. How I hated him, then and now – and as he came towards me, with a smile that might *almost* have been sincere, I felt the past rush in on me like a cloud of mustard gas.

'Why, it's Mr Straitley!' he said. 'Good Lord, you haven't changed a bit. How long has it been? Twenty-four years? Don't say you don't remember me?'

I drew the flap of my gown across the tea-stained crotch of my trousers. Not quite trusting myself to speak, I gave the man a curt nod.

The smile broadened still further. 'Of course. We'll catch up later,' he said. 'Maybe after the meeting.'

Of all the boys I've watched grow up, moving from larva to chrysalis, and then to dubious butterfly, in time taking wing as accountants, bankers, journalists, researchers, soldiers – God help them, sometimes even *teachers*, which, according to Eric Scoones, rank even higher on the perversion scale than Clive Punnet, who ate his wife – none have surprised me as utterly as little Johnny Harrington.

The arrogant, sullen little boy has been reborn as a smiling, smooth-voiced politician, whose lack of essential warmth is now all too ably camouflaged beneath a veneer of surface shine. But people rarely change at heart, except in the growing sophistication of their various disguises, and it doesn't take much for me now to see beneath the surface.

Still, I have to admit that Harrington had made an impressive entrance. His opening speech to the Common Room was a kind of masterpiece; rousing; funny; articulate and shot through with that self-deprecating charm that only the most dangerous of politicians can manage. He spoke of his affection for St Oswald's; of his sadness to see the dear old place so run-down and neglected; of his hope that together we would raise the phoenix from the ashes.

'We have to think of St Oswald's,' he said. 'But not through a veil of nostalgia. There's a joke we used to tell, back when I was still a boy. *How many St Oswald's Masters does it take to change a lightbulb?*'

He gave the Common Room a smile as bright as a toothpaste commercial.

'The answer, of course, was: *CHANGE??*'

The audience laughed obediently. The New Head laughed with them. I noticed that, as he delivered the punchline, Harrington altered his posture a little, adopted a voice to match the stance, and for a moment, I was convinced that the little rat was mimicking *me*—

But Harrington had already moved on. Humour had suddenly given way to a politician's earnestness. The middle section of his speech now had a yearning quality; a dewy, romantic quality, peppered with every cliché in the orator's manual.

'Change,' he repeated. 'Change can be hard. But, like the lightbulb, change can also be illuminating. The Bursar, the Third Master and I have worked hard with my team and the Governors to put into place a number of necessary changes. Some are financial – the Bursar will explain them in greater detail later, but I'm sure you must know that St Oswald's has been living beyond its means for years. Others are domestic, and may prove the greatest challenge. But I have every confidence in the staff of St Oswald's. We have a strong tradition of battling against adversity.'

And then he looked right at me and said: 'My Latin Master taught me that, along with so many other things. *Ad astra per aspera*. The rocky road will lead to the stars. The road to recovery may be rough. But I hope we can get there together.'

And in the applause that followed that speech, perfect in its cynicism, I wasn't sure which I hated most: the fact that, for some reason, the man was trying to woo me, or that he was doing it in the language of Caesar.

Harrington beamed at his audience. I raised my teacup in tribute. The Senate – I mean the Common Room – gave him a standing ovation. Devine's expressionless features were almost animated. Even Eric said: 'Hear hear!'– a fact that depresses me more than it should – and Bob Strange looked like a schoolboy cricketer who has been allowed to carry his hero's bat.

Ye gods. Can't they *see* him? His fakery? But Julius Caesar had his charm – so, too, had Caligula. And so I prepared myself for the worst – for the Bursar's financial plan and that list of domestic changes – with a sinking, rebellious heart, as Johnny Harrington – now reborn as *Dr* Harrington, MBE – watched me with a tiny smile, almost like a challenge.

'And now for a look at the future,' he said, turning towards the Bursar. 'In his presentation, the Bursar will outline the changes that will make us more competitive, better equipped to deal with the world of business and innovation.'

Innovation. That explained the viewing screen and the laptop computer on the desk. The Bursar is much addicted to something he calls PowerPoint, a kind of electronic crib-sheet for idiots. I settled in for a little nap. As an Old Centurion of St Oswald's, there are a number of unnecessary innovations to which I will not submit. PowerPoint is one of them, as is e-mail, in spite of Bob Strange's persistence in 'copying me in' to the minutes of meetings I do not attend, or summoning me to his office by electronic messenger, as if just opening the door and calling down the corridor (or even scribbling a note to pop into my pigeon-hole) were henceforth completely impossible.

Fortunately, Danielle, the School Secretary, is rather more amenable, and for the price of a few kind words and a box of chocolates at Christmas had arranged to print out my e-mails this term and deliver them to my pigeon-hole. This was why I had been surprised to find my pigeon-hole empty this morning, even though the beginning of term is always a morass of paperwork.

The Bursar's PowerPoint soon explained the mystery. Apparently, St Oswald's is to become a paper-free office environment, run entirely online. This, according to the Bursar – a sharp-nosed Scotsman with a reputation as a wit – will make for a greener St Oswald's as well as a more efficient delivery system, and will make the old wooden pigeon-holes (which have been in use since 1904) redundant.

According to Harrington, their removal will create more space in the Quiet Room, which needs to be refurbished and supplied with staff workstations – here the Bursar paused in his speech to show us a series of diagrams to illustrate the new desks and the cubicles, each one supplied with a computer, in which we are to sit like battery hens, efficient and productive. For members of staff requiring extra training in what he calls 'developing technology', there will be an after-hours surgery with Mr Beard, the (beardless) Head of IT, to which we are all invited to bring our ideas and suggestions.

I, for one, shall not do so. I'm far too old a dog to learn that kind of new trickery. If necessary, I shall remain at my desk in room 59 during my free time, with a bag of Liquorice Allsorts and only the mice for company.

However, there was more to come from the Bursar's budget. Most of it I'd heard before – consolidating of resources; sale of School assets; streamlining of departments; maximizing efficiency – all Bursar-speak for less money and less space for some department or other. I'm used to fighting my corner, and the prospect of doing so again was, if anything, invigorating.

But it was his next statement that made me sit bolt upright, clutching the armrest of my chair with a deathly grip as he announced 'an exciting new development, which we hope may be the beginning of a long and successful partnership with our sister school, Mulberry House, and which, as you will already know, begins as of next week in Sixth Form . . .'

I said: 'Excuse me, Bursar. But what exactly are you talking about?'

The Bursar gave me a look. 'I'm talking about Mulberry House,' he said, 'and our plan to introduce a system of consolidated classes in certain subjects at Sixth-Form level.'

Consolidated classes, forsooth.

'You mean *mixed* classes, Bursar?' I said.

He gave a rather narrow smile.

'Our boys and Mulberry girls?'

'That's usually what we mean by mixed, Roy,' said the Bursar, playing to the gallery. 'Don't worry. I'm sure you're more than satisfactorily equipped to prevent any inappropriate behaviour.'

I made a sound much like the one favoured by the Old Head.

'Don't say you didn't know about this,' the Bursar went on impatiently. 'The details were e-mailed to you months ago.'

'I don't *do* e-mail, Bursar,' I said.

'Don't do female, did you say?' The Bursar was hitting his stride now, playing for laughs at my expense. 'Well, you heard the Head, Roy. We're all facing changes. Besides, with class sizes as they are, I thought you'd be grateful for the extra bodies.'

I suppose he had a point there. Last year, my Lower Sixth Latin set consisted of four boys, one of whom dropped the subject at Christmas in favour of Business Studies.

Still – girls. *Mulberry* girls. There's something about our sister school that sets the whole of my being on edge. I don't know if it's the girls themselves – the rolled-up skirts, the giggling and the look of superiority – or if it's the mistresses, most of them dowdier versions of the girls; or the current Headmistress, a bottle blonde of indeterminate age and increasingly predatory temperament, whose hemlines over the past ten years have risen in inverse proportion to her dwindling chances of snaring a man.

But in thirty-four years at St Oswald's, I've usually managed to avoid dealing with our sister school, linked as it is with St Oswald's by our own Foundation, as well as by decades of collaboration in school plays, concerts and trips abroad.

'Gods preserve us,' I muttered.

Sitting beside me, Robbie Roach gave a lecherous snigger. 'I think you're being ungrateful,' he said. 'What I'd give to have a few of those Mulberry girls in *my* class.'

Robbie teaches History – so badly that Bob Strange ensures he never has a Sixth Form. Instead he runs field trips and Scout Camp, which he enjoys enormously, whilst maintaining the pretence that this takes up a great deal of his valuable leisure time, and therefore deserves compensation.

Now he gave me a wink and hissed: *'Berry fresh, old boy. Berry fresh.'*

To hear him you might imagine an elderly roué of the kind featured in one of Eric's French films. In fact, he is harmless; all talk; unable to control his hair, let alone his classes. The idea that he, of all people, might be capable of seducing a Mulberry girl – or even getting one to hand in her homework on time – was beyond ludicrous.

I addressed the *real* enemy. 'Bursar. May I venture to ask whether *all* subjects will benefit from this proposed consolidation? Or is Classics the only area in need of – er – curricular corsetry?'

Robbie Roach sniggered again.

The Bursar gave him a sharp look.

'Just the usual,' he said. 'And the Languages Department.'

By *the usual* I guessed he meant Music and Drama, both departments which have had more to do with Mulberry House than most over the past few years. As a result, their members of staff have gone native to an alarming extent, staging productions of musicals with exclamation marks in the title, running yoga classes after School and *getting in touch with their feminine side.*

All very well, I suppose, but it's an open secret that Mulberry House wants a merger, which St Oswald's, like a cautious bachelor faced with the threat of matrimony, has so far neatly avoided.

This seemed to me the thin end of the wedge. It's not that I don't like girls, of course, but I prefer to like them from afar. I also like kittens and ice cream, but would rather not see them brought into class.

Harrington gave me a sympathetic look. 'I know this must all seem very new,' he said. 'But we must face the facts. The dinosaurs have had their day. It's time for St Oswald's to *evolve*. Survival is our priority now. And we *will* survive. Well, maybe not *all* of us—' His smile grew a little more pronounced. 'But those who face the future instead of clinging to the past. *They'll* survive. *We'll* survive. *Because we are survivors!*'

Once more, the Common Room rose *en masse*, to give him a standing ovation. I remained seated, though Eric stood, clapping furiously with the rest. Harrington accepted their tribute with an air of amusement – and maybe a hint of veiled contempt, which of course only I saw. Once more, I thought his gaze shifted to mine, as if to assess the potential threat. Is this how the snake-charmer feels, when he locks eyes with the cobra? And if so, I can't help wondering which is the charmer, and which is the snake?

4

Michaelmas Term, 2005

In every Common Room in the world, certain well-known tribes are represented. The Suit, brought into the School by chance on a plague ship during the Sixties, as exemplified by Bob Strange; the Stickler, by Dr Devine; the Old Boy, who, like Eric Scoones, can't seem to keep away from the place, and, of course, the Tweed Jacket, of which I am the prototype. Ladies are either Dragons or, most often, Low-Fat Yoghurts, a damp subspecies of female who sits in a corner, discussing by turns the latest diet, or scandal, or episode of *Neighbours*. And then there is the Snake-Charmer; a type that occurs only once or twice in a Master's lifetime. How strange now to see Johnny Harrington reborn into such a disguise; how strange, and yet I am not surprised. Haven't I always known he'd come back? Haven't I known it for twenty years?

He arrived in my life at the age of fourteen, in the autumn of '81. He was new to St Oswald's; a seventh-term boy with an impressive academic report and a flawless behavioural record. Shiny hair of impeccable (though slightly girlish) cut; a face unmarked by adolescent acne; even his uniform looked neater than the other boys', his shoes polished to an alarming gloss and his School tie knotted in just the right way—

I'll admit it: I disliked him on sight. There was something *cold* about Harrington; the same coldness, perhaps, that defines our own Bob Strange. He was polite; he was handsome; he was correct; he always said *sir*. But he had a *way* of saying it, and a way of looking at you that made you want to check whether your fly was zipped up, and made you aware of the sweat stains under your armpits and the chalk marks on your jacket and the mistake you made in Latin translation that you thought you could pass off as a joke—

His Latin, I found, was excellent. He'd been home-schooled until he was nine, after which time he had been placed in one of our local Middle Schools, and by the time he reached St Oswald's he was already more than up to standard. This pleased me at first; one of the problems of seventh-term entrants was that barely half of them had studied Latin at all, and it was my job, as the most junior Classicist, to catch them up over lunchtimes and Breaks, while Dr Shakeshafte, my Head of Department (who also happened to be the Headmaster), sat in his office, listening to the cricket and eating cheese against his doctor's advice.

Harrington, however, needed no help from me. He did his work quickly and accurately and with a look of polite boredom on his face, never volunteering answers, but never making a mistake either. He was easy to ignore in favour of those boys who genuinely found the subject taxing; my group numbered thirty-five, and although I didn't exactly neglect Harrington, I'll admit he was easy to overlook. So easy, in fact, that when the first complaint came, it took me altogether by surprise.

Remember, times were different then. Margaret Thatcher was Prime Minister. The Yorkshire Ripper had just been condemned; Charles had just married Diana. Classics still had an empire then, consisting of three Masters; an office; a section in the School Library and various classrooms, annexes and stock cupboards. At forty-one, I was at my peak; sprightly of step and speedy of brain. I was no novice, however. I'd been at St Oswald's for a decade, having taught at a couple of inferior schools before then, and I was reaping the rewards of experience. The boys knew and respected me – after all, I'd taught most of them at one time or another.

As for the staff – St Oswald's Masters tend to stay put once they have been appointed, and several of that long-ago crew are still on board the old ship today – among them, the Chaplain, Eric Scoones and even our own Dr Devine, younger and even less bearable at only thirty-six years old, with all the misplaced arrogance that usually comes with the territory. I had my own seat in the Common Room, its cushions unmarked by the passage of years, and a leonine share of the timetable that now seems impossibly generous.

Most of my colleagues at the School – many of them Tweed Jackets of the kind I was destined to become – seemed startlingly decrepit to my untutored eyes. I baulked at St Oswald's tradition by not attending Assemblies, by my unorthodox methods, and by infusing my lessons, or so I thought, with something a little more colourful than *mensa, mensa, mensam* (personally I've always found that the noun *merda* illustrates the First Declension just as well, and for some reason stays with the boys for a whole lot longer).

In those days there were the three of us in the Classics Department: Dr 'Touchy' Feeley, an irascible Oxbridge man approaching his Century; myself and the Headmaster, Dr Shakeshafte, who was Head of Department in name only, and on those infrequent occasions when the timetable required a third Classics Master to be available.

Like so many Headmasters, Shakeshafte did as little teaching as possible, leaving myself and Dr Feeley to run operations in his name, and spent the best part of his day in his inner sanctum, engaged in headmasterly activities as vital as they were unfathomable. Of course, when it came to complaints, Shakeshafte was always the first to find out, which was what happened about four weeks into the term when I was summoned (that's the only word to describe it) to his office one rainy lunchtime.

'Enter.'

The Headmaster's office was a large, brown room overlooking the Quad, with Gothic windows and a predominant aroma of leather and cheese. The Head was at his desk, apparently writing a letter, although I was sure that until he heard my knock he had been listening to the wireless as usual. A gold-nibbed pen the size of a torpedo between his large fingers, he did not acknowledge me as I came in, but ponderously finished his letter, signed it with a flourish, and then began another, as I waited in silence on the small Oriental rug in front of his desk.

That was the Old Head's style, you know. A bludgeoning rudeness permeated everything he did, and his contempt for anyone incapable of matching it was legendary. I waited for precisely five minutes, watching the rain crawl down the mullioned window, then I said: 'I can see you're busy, Headmaster. I'll try to come back at a more convenient time.'

I turned to the door. I would have left, too; and the Head must have known I'd call his bluff because he put down the torpedo, stood up and faced me with the look that had reduced so many boys to pulp and earned him the nickname of SS – or 'Shitter' Shakeshafte.

I was not a boy, however, and I was not unmanned. The Head was a bully of the old school, and the only way to deal with bullies is to face them down. It wasn't easy. There was something vaguely pachydermic about the Old Head; a distribution of his not inconsiderable weight that was more rhino than man. His eyes were small, in great, bloodshot orbs. Even the sound he made as he got to his feet – a kind of inarticulate *oof!* – put me irresistibly in mind of Ionesco's play *Rhinoceros*, which Eric Scoones's French Sixth-Form class happened to be studying that year.

'Please, Headmaster,' I said. 'Don't bother to get up on my account.'

He oofed again, and damned my impertinence. 'Suppose you think it's funny, eh? Bloody comedian. Well, we've had a complaint. *Here.*' And he flung a piece of paper in my direction, which I caught, and found to be a letter on notepaper headed *Dr R. Harrington, MA (Oxon)*.

It wasn't the first time I'd had a complaint. Of course I get more of them nowadays, because boys know their rights (or think they do), and behaviour that would have earned them a reprimand, detention or even the cane in those days has now been identified as a sign of learning difficulty, hyperactivity, dyslexia or Attention Deficit Disorder (which we, in the unsympathetic old days, used to call *Not Paying Attention*), all of which conditions deserve sensitive treatment rather than a kick in the pants.

Personally I found the old treatment quite effective (and so did the boys), but the same faction that has since believed I had a rapport with the boys in my form. I stayed in the form-room at lunchtimes; I joined in their conversations, even made the occasional joke. My nickname was Quasimodo – because I lived in the Bell Tower – and word around School was that I was mostly OK, except with bullies and homework evaders, and that my classes, though tough, were probably more fun than most.

But somehow, with Harrington, something had changed. I didn't notice it at first – he really was such a colourless boy – but it seemed to me that Michaelmas term that my form had not quite come together the way it normally did. Sometimes it happens that a form is shaped by a few dominant personalities; sometimes a rift between two rival groups can make for a form that is ill at ease. That year's 3S were a diffident lot, with heads that seemed forever bowed and eyes that refused to make contact. It took me two weeks to learn their names – as a rule I know them in a single day.

There were other anomalies, too. Usually in a class there's at least one clown; one bully; one fighter; one rebel; one butt. In September '81 there seemed hardly any definition; no one seemed to step out of line; and the faces that peered out from behind their desk-lids were bland as rows of cheeses. And yet, there was an atmosphere. Something disagreeable. Something sly, that sniggered and watched.

It took me some time to connect this with little Johnny Harrington. The boy wasn't especially popular. He didn't play to the gallery. He had no apparent interest in girls, societies or sports – although he was quite a good swimmer, and even once won a House trophy in the 100-metre crawl. He always gave in his homework on time, never even failed to hand in one of his library books. He was friendly with two other seventh-term boys; Nutter, who, despite a promising name, gave no redeeming sign of eccentricity, and Spikely, the tattletale; a neat, bespectacled little boy with a curiously alert and intellectual look, belied by his exam results.

I wondered what the three boys had in common, except for their outsider status. All came from good families; all were only children; all attended the same church, and yet they were so different. Seventh-term boys often find it hard to make friends at first, especially when they are not naturally outgoing. And yet, the three stood out as odd, even for seventh-term boys. At fourteen, the world is a fairground of ominous attractions. A time of violent enthusiasms and equally violent aversions; of poignant sorrows and terrible joys and secret laughter that wrenches the heart. Other boys played football, using their jerseys for goalposts. Other boys played Top Trumps; discovered girls or rock music. Other boys ran hell-for-leather across St Oswald's playing fields, shirts untucked and splattered with mud, with shoes that would have to be left at the door to spare the parquet flooring, and which would slowly dry and crack under their carapace of clay.

But Harrington, Nutter and Spikely never got muddy; never ran; never even untucked their shirts. Nutter was prone to allergies that made him wheeze at the slightest exertion; Harrington was too dignified and Spikely was a clumsy boy, always tripping over his feet. They rarely said very much in class, or to me, although they seemed to enjoy spending time in the room above mine, with Harry Clarke, who taught the third-form middle set. In the case of another member of staff (or another group of pupils), I might have felt a little aggrieved to see them prefer his room over mine. But Harry was a good friend – and frankly, if I'd been in their place, I would have preferred it, too.

Harry was older than Eric or I, but looked and sounded younger. A lanky, vaguely awkward man, with hair slightly longer than the regulation length and a voice that commanded attention without his ever raising it. He'd entered the teaching profession some years before, via the state sector, and was thus unencumbered by the kind of rigid academic thinking that characterized St Oswald's. As a result, he was popular with the boys – not in the style of those colleagues who never set any homework, and thereby believe that this gives them an understanding with the boys, but because he made every boy in his care feel like an individual. He was less popular with the staff. Perhaps because he made no effort to fit in, preferring to stay with his form rather than socialize in the Common Room; or because he encouraged the boys to call him by his Christian name; or because of his humble background and lack of qualifications.

Most of St Oswald's staff at that time had doctorates, or at least the kind of MA that comes free from Oxford or Cambridge. Harry had no doctorate, and his degree was from the Open University. And yet he was a natural when it came to teaching; his reading tastes spanned all genres; and he had an encyclopaedic knowledge of popular culture, which meant that a lesson with Harry Clarke might begin with a Shakespearian sonnet, segue into the lyrics of a song by David Bowie, shift sideways into an Anglo-Saxon riddle, and finish with a reference to *Private Eye* or the *Beano*. It was an unusual approach, and one which Mr Fabricant viewed with enormous suspicion; but St Oswald's had a policy of never interfering with a colleague's methods unless they affected the boys' results; and given that Harry's exam results were always well above the average, he was tolerated, if not approved, by his more conservative peers.

Harry's was room 58, the room directly above mine. The topmost room in the old Bell Tower, it was a small, hexagonal room of even more eccentric design than my own – chilly in winter, oppressive in summer, accessible via a narrow flight of uneven little stone stairs. This was where Harry spent much of his time, and at lunchtimes he would play records and talk to anyone who cared to drop by, including Harrington and his friends, who seemed to prefer his company to mine, or that of their classmates.

Two weeks had passed since my meeting with the Head, and I had obediently (though with some reluctance) excised some of the more robust items of vocabulary from my Latin lessons. But it annoyed me; made me feel like a student teacher on report. And for what? The Harringtons were members of some biblical sect that saw a devil in every bush. I knew the type, and expected the worst. As the boy's form-tutor, by then I'd already collected complaints from Harrington Senior about PE (in which he objected to the communal showers); English (in which he deplored the foul language of Barry Hines's *Kes*); Biology (which exposed the boy to the twin evils of Human Reproduction and Darwin's Theory of Evolution); French (during which Eric, a film buff, was planning to show *Les Diaboliques*); and even Geography, possibly the most inoffensive subject known to man, in which (if we were to believe Dr Harrington Senior) the teacher, Mr Mooney (a typical geographer, earnest and suited and eminently respectable), had allowed the boys access to a pornographic magazine.

The magazine turned out to be the *National Geographic*, with a special supplement on African tribes, but by the time this was made clear, Mr Mooney, a sensitive soul, was a mass of nerves and twitches, afraid for his job and no use at all when it came to teaching 3S.

'Hard to adjust? It seems to me he's finding it all too easy. Coasting his way through his lessons, complaining about all and sundry—'

Harry said: 'I heard about that. But Harrington's parents are great friends with Mr Speight and the Chaplain. All of them go to the same church. Of course they discuss St Oswald's. And Harrington's parents go through his things. They probably found his Latin notes.'

'You think the boy *didn't* report me?'

Harry shrugged. 'I don't know. But in your place, I'd give him the benefit of the doubt. I know he's not one of your Brodie Boys—'

'My what?'

'Roy, don't deny it,' he said. 'Each of us has his favourites. You have a soft spot for rebels and clowns. You like to encourage subversion. The Chaplain favours the sporting ones. Eric, the polite, respectful ones.' He saw my expression and smiled. 'It's OK. You can't like *all* the boys equally. But what we can always do is make sure that we're not being unfair.'

For a while I said nothing. Harry had a point, of course: but it rather disturbed me to think that my feelings were so easy to read.

'What would *you* do?' I said at last.

'In your place? I'd have a word with him.'

I thought about what Harry had said. Nowadays I am aware of my tendency to favour some boys above others. More often than not, I try to compensate for my partiality. Of course I was much younger then, less inclined to scrutinize my motives. All I knew was that I'd disliked Johnny Harrington from the start. Was Harry right, I asked myself? *Had* I allowed my prejudice to interfere with my judgement?

It was two weeks before the half term break. Progress tests had just finished – soon to be followed by School exams – and as I'd expected, young Harrington had scored highly in most subjects, coming joint first in Latin and taking sixth place in the form overall – an excellent start for a New Boy, though I'd seen his face as I read out the results, and I knew he'd hoped for better still.

'You're a clever boy,' I told him after Registration. 'I hear you're thinking of Oxbridge.'

He was going through his locker. In those days we still kept them in the form-rooms, and you could tell a lot about a boy from the way he kept his locker; whether it was tidy or shambolic; what pictures or stickers embellished it; whether his books were carefully backed or left to curl at the edges.

Johnny's locker was monastic. Books neatly backed with brown paper; all arranged in order of size. One pencil box of plain wood; one ruler, unadorned; a Blue Riband bar. No litter – not even a pencil shaving. Nothing to indicate the boy's personality at all – not a poster, a sticker or a drawing in sight.

'Sir,' said Harrington in his colourless voice. Hard to tell if he meant yes or no.

'You're certainly able,' I went on cheerily. 'Joint first in Latin, eh – ninety per cent – and sixth from the top in the whole form. You might even have been first if it hadn't been for that English test.'

I thought his face darkened a little. There had been nothing but trouble so far with the English Literature syllabus – *Kes* had given way to Ted Hughes, D. H. Lawrence and finally to Chaucer, none of which had been judged suitable by the Harrington parents. As a result the boy's assessment had placed him seventeenth in a middle set of twenty-one, and the report from his teacher – Mr Fabricant, a veteran Tweed Jacket with no time to waste on what he referred to as 'the sensitive brigade' – stated quite clearly that Johnny was lucky to have scraped seventeenth, and that if he didn't get his act together – and that meant actually *reading* the books and thinking about what they meant – then he'd be looking at no better than a pass in the end-of-term exams.

'I take it you're not keen on English Literature.'

'Sir,' said Harrington, closing his locker.

'It's a pity,' I said cheerily, 'as all of the *best* universities tend to take the view that a man who doesn't understand literature is generally ill-equipped to understand anything else, either.'

Harrington said nothing, but his eyes narrowed.

'Literature broadens the mind,' I said. 'And it seems to me that yours may be in need of a little broadening.'

He gaped at me, unused to such a direct approach.

I smiled reassuringly and went on. 'You'll find that School and life have a lot in common,' I said. 'If you like, School is life with training wheels, a safe environment in which to learn, not just the subjects on the curriculum, but the way to deal with people and ideas you have never met before. Now the ostrich, we're told, when faced with a new idea, simply sticks its head in the sand. This may work for the ostrich—' I looked at my watch and rose from my chair. 'But on the whole,' I said, 'you don't see many of those applying to university.'

Now Harrington was a clever boy. His face, bland as it was, nevertheless told me that he'd understood perfectly what I was trying to say. A slight flush marbled his cheek; his spine seemed straighter than ever, and his inevitable *Sir!* – when it finally came – was as cold and expressionless as a pebble.

'What I'm trying to say – as a teacher and, I hope, a friend' – it wasn't true, but I wanted to take some of the sting from my words – 'is that School isn't the place to impose one's ideas. It's a privileged environment in which you will be exposed to many, many *new* ideas – some of which will reflect your own, others not. You may reject them – but only when you have studied them. And remember, a man with his head in the sand has only one other orifice left with which to communicate with the rest of the world.'

With any other boy, that might have raised a smile. Not Harrington, though. He simply nodded as if marking me for later extermination, picked up his satchel and exited the room, leaving me to fear that, instead of making a connection with the boy, I might instead have made an enemy for life.

5

Michaelmas Term, 1981

Dear Mousey,

I don't like Mr Straitley. He doesn't like me either. He teaches Latin like it's a joke that only he can understand. Well, I'll give him *merda*. (See what I did there? *Merda. Murder.* And everyone keeps telling me I have no sense of humour.)

It's funny, since I arrived here, lots of things have been different. At home, I'm the same as I ever was. Mum and Dad aren't fans of change. They only ever notice I'm there when something awful happens. At Church, I'm patient and polite. At meetings, I try to co-operate. Sometimes I bring up sins to confess. Little sins. The rest stay put. No one wants to hear about *those*.

I've been thinking a lot about *Animals*. I've copied all the lyrics down in the back of my Prep journal. One of them uses the F-word. Harry doesn't even mind. But there's no point in me trying to buy anything like that for myself. My dad would never allow it. Quite apart from the F-word, he'd just take one look at the picture of the band and decide what kind of people they were. *Perverts*, he'd call them. *Degenerates*. To Dad, any man with long hair has to be one or the other. I sometimes wish I had long hair. When I escape, I'll give it a try. That's how I think of it nowadays. As an *escape*, Mousey.

Only five more years to go. Till then, I'm going to have to pretend. *Beg. Fetch. Roll over*. I *look* like one of the other dogs, even though I'm a wolf in disguise. No one (except maybe Harry) suspects I might be faking it.

Of all the staff in St Oswald's, there's only Harry who's OK. Mr Straitley we know about. Mr Scoones is always going on about visiting Paris, and Jacques Tati, and rotten old French films. Then there's Mr Speight, RE, who goes to the same Church as we do. In fact, I think he was the reason my parents chose St Oswald's – because they knew that Mr Speight would be there to keep an eye on me. My parents think the world of him. Mr Speight believes in happy, healthy, God-fearing boys. Of course, Mr Speight also believes in demons, that yoga and vegetarianism are 'soft gateways into the occult', and that rock music, comics and horror novels contain Satanic messages that can brainwash young people into selling their souls to Lucifer. It's pretty funny, actually.

Still, I've managed to settle in here. I think I'll be OK – except perhaps in English, where I have to sit and listen to goaty Mr Fabricant, when right above us Harry is teaching *his* group English. His lessons are fun, too. Sometimes, on a nice day, when the windows are open, I can hear the sound of his voice. Sometimes he plays music. Sometimes, they laugh. I can hear them. Once, they all laughed so loudly that Mr Fabricant closed the window.

I wish I was in Harry's class. Even their books are better than ours. They're reading *Lord of the Flies*, and *Nineteen*

Eighty-Four, and *Julius Caesar*. Ours are all rubbish, but I bet if he was teaching us, we'd enjoy them anyway. I've started reading *Lord of the Flies*. I borrowed Harry's copy. It's full of little written notes, all in Harry's handwriting. I like that. It's almost like he's teaching me in secret. As if he's sharing his thoughts with me, like a secret journal.

Mr Straitley's still being a pain. I'll never be one of his favourites. The two other New Boys don't like him either. Goldie watches him like he's something the cat dragged in, and Poodle spends his time in class drawing in his Latin book. Neither has settled in properly yet. Neither has proved to be popular. Poodle's a bit of a freak, and Goldie's a bit too full of himself to ever be one of the cool kids.

Well, we have that in common, I guess. I've never been popular. I don't run with the rest of the pack. I'm a different species. But in view of My Condition, it's not good to be seen as a loner. And, not being quite an Alpha Dog, I can't afford to pick and choose. Still, none of that matters now. Today, something happened, Mousey. Something really important. A door has opened. A page has turned. And it all began with an apple.

St Oswald's is a Church school. They're always collecting for some cause or other. If it's not poppies, it's flags, or buns. This lunchtime it was apples. Fivepence each, for charity, an apple and a sticker. Mr Clarke's room was half-full of boys – plus me and Goldie and Poodle, of course – and this boy from the Lower School came in with a box full of apples.

No one seemed too keen at first. Fivepence for an *apple*. You could get a ton of sweets for that. But Mr Clarke – no, *Harry* – said: 'Forbidden fruit. How can we resist?'

After that, everyone wanted one. So we went over to the teacher's desk and handed over our money. Everyone was milling around, putting stickers on their heads, grabbing apples from the box. And then there was this ugly one. Not bad, but smaller than the rest, and with a funny- looking wart like something on a witch's nose. And by the time we'd all chosen ours, there were only three apples left in the box: two good ones and the ugly one. And Harry chose the ugly one, and left the two good ones for someone else.

The boy who was selling the apples said: 'Sir, that one's manky.'

Harry smiled. I was standing next to him. And then he looked at me and said: 'It'll be fine on the *inside*. And that's what matters, isn't it? What it's like on the inside?'

The boy went away, looking puzzled. But *I* knew at once what Harry meant. He'd chosen the apple that no one else would. The ugly apple. The odd one out. I've always been the odd one out. Even before Netherton Green, I was always the last to be chosen.

But Mr Clarke – *Harry*'s not like that. Harry sees my potential. Harry lent me *Lord of the Flies* – his copy, with his personal notes. Harry isn't the kind of man to lend his books to just anyone. And now I go to Harry's room every Break and lunchtime. I bring him tea in the mornings from the big urn in the kitchens. I water his plants. I tidy his bookshelves. I put his records into alphabetical order. I've always liked helping out at school, and there are so many ways to help.

Miss McDonald at Netherton Green called me her Special Little Helper. OK, so that's really lame, and besides, it didn't turn out that well, but with Harry, it's different. For starters, I'm not eight any more. Harry and I have a more adult relationship. We can have conversations. We can talk about music and Life. I think he sees how mature I am, compared to the other boys in his class.

That's part of My Condition, of course. I've seen more than some of those boys ever will. Harry understands that. He knows I'm an exceptional case. And I like to think I understand him too – at least, I do a little. I can tell how much he loves his job, but sometimes he looks tired. I wonder how he ended up here, instead of at a better school. I wonder why he's still just a master, and not Head of Year or something. And I wonder why he's not married. He's clever, and kind of good-looking, and not too old for that kind of thing. Perhaps he's like me, and doesn't like to get too close to people. Perhaps, like me, he has a past and doesn't like to discuss it.

I've thought of just asking him. But no. There's an invisible chalk line that runs along the teacher's desk. Even though he's asked me to call him by his Christian name; even though he talks to me as if I were his equal. He's still a master. I'm still a boy. There's still a distance between us. But in a way, I respect him more, for keeping his private life private.

And I can wait. I'm good at that. I'm good at waiting, Mousey. I can be like other boys; at least I can on the outside. And one day, when I'm sure of him, then I'll tell him everything – Bunny, Miss McDonald, the dog; the games down by the clay pits; even you. Because you were nothing, Mousey. You were nothing, compared to me. And Mr Clarke will *understand*—

Still, there's lots of time for that.

After all, it's only September.

6

September 7th, 2005

It was, I suppose, a testament to Harrington's powers of fascination that no one noticed much at first about his two new deputies. I'd thought them just a couple of Suits, but as the New Head turned down the high beam of his boyish charm, I began to think I might have underestimated the level of menace they represent.

Men like Johnny Harrington never share the limelight. But behind every showman there has to be a couple of familiars – efficient, but not too flashy – to handle the technical side of the show.

He revealed them after the Bursar's speech, with a careless flamboyance, much as Seuss's *Cat in the Hat* unleashed his creatures, Thing One and Thing Two.

'As you know,' he said, 'recent events have brought to the attention of the Governors a number of – areas of *concern* – in the running of the School, and the role of the Crisis Deputies – a purely temporary role, may I add – is to help maintain the staff status quo whilst facilitating the transition between the old ways and the new. Tradition and excellence should be our aim. *Progress through tradition*. Over the next few days, you'll be seeing that phrase on a lot of our promotional material. As the Bursar has already explained, we need to bring customers back to the School, and that means building confidence. Together, we and the Crisis Team will build a new St Oswald's; stronger than it was before, armed with the knowledge of the past, ready to face the future.'

He paused for effect, and then went on: 'I give you Dr Marcus Blakely and Ms Rebecca Buckfast, my wonderful Crisis Deputies.'

Cue applause from the rest of the staff, led by the Head and Bob Strange, as Thing One and Thing Two took the stage. Like their Dr Seuss counterparts, they share a curious resemblance which – in the case of the Crisis Team – has little to do with their features and everything to do with a kind of corporate sameness, a suited homogeneity, as jarring as a pair of plastic chairs around a scarred oak school desk.

Thing One – Dr Blakely – forties; balding; not too tall, shaved with eye-watering closeness to a shiny plastic-pink finish. Thing Two – Ms Buckfast – a largish lady about the same age; round face; red hair in a bob; red slash of lipstick across the mouth. Both were wearing suits, of course – though not quite as stylish as Harrington's – in matching shades of charcoal, with a gold silk tie for Thing One, and in the case of Thing Two, a silk scarf in an ethnic print artfully twisted around her neck.

Harrington explained that both were experts in their fields: fundraising; image; pastoral care; gender awareness; cultural sensitivity and learning difficulties. He explained that Ms Buckfast would be in charge of the 'rebranding' of the School, and that Dr Blakely had close links with the children's charity Survivors, as well as being the creator of a national think-tank to discuss 'abuse situations', and was in the process of drafting a Zero Tolerance Policy to deal with all aspects of bullying.

'Every school has its failures,' he said. 'We must face ours with humility. Only last year, St Oswald's suffered the ultimate tragedy. We let down a troubled young man by the name of Colin Knight' – at this I thought he glanced at me – 'a young man who might still be with us today, if there had been a policy to deal with his situation.'

I suppressed an indignant *oof*. I'd like to see the policy that would have prevented what happened last year. Besides, in my experience, pastoral care and paperwork exist in inverse proportion to each other, like common sense and training.

However, once more, I forebore from comment. Suits and their policies come and go, rather like Headmasters. St Oswald's has borne such attacks before, and survived; I expect it to do so again. Still, I suspect that this will mean a tedious round of training days, organized by Thing One and Thing Two, during which such as Yours Truly will have to demonstrate awareness of such practices as cyber-bullying and internet grooming, while performing role plays, building forts from furniture and generally indulging in the kind of party games favoured by the Drama Department.

Abuse guru. Ye gods.

Certain of my colleagues, of course, will respond to all this nonsense with the enthusiasm of a group of cub Scouts gambolling around their Akela. Geoff and Penny Nation, the husband-and-wife team currently attached to the German Department, are both veterans of think-tanks and focus groups; besides which, Penny once went on a course entitled *Kids in Counselling*, which left her under the delusion that she is approachable and relates well to 'youth issues'.

For his part, Bob Strange seems impressed by the fact that, under the new regime, all St Oswald's current problems will be transferred to a series of policy documents, and will therefore completely cease to exist in the real world. As for Dr Devine, well. He must remember the Harry Clarke affair, but he never taught Johnny Harrington, or had much to do with him. Eric, too, is aware of it; but he was on the outside of events, and his involvement in that old tale is mostly mine to remember.

Still, *transit umbra*. I suspect the Crisis Team won't be here long. Word in the Common Room last term was that Crisis Teams rarely stay out the year. Once the paperwork (sorry, *computer*-work) is done, they tend to migrate to pastures new, leaving us to demonstrate how little relevance real life has to the world of their fiction.

Fiction? Well, you can't build a School on theories and think-tanks. A good schoolmaster knows that, and cuts his cloth accordingly. In the old days, we knew how to deal with the baser element. We didn't need a policy to tell us bullying was wrong, or that boys should be polite, and try to behave like gentlemen. There were no charters, no workshops, and certainly no abuse gurus – just a single Latin phrase that covered all eventualities.

In loco parentis. It used to mean 'act as a reasonable parent does'. Now hardly anyone knows *what* it means. And besides, most parents nowadays are anything but reasonable. Instead they are litigious, entitled, gullible, defensive, rude and obsessed with getting their money's worth. As the new Headmaster says: no longer parents, but *customers*.

Most St Oswald's customers will love the New Head for all the reasons I do not – his charm, his youth, his oratory, his effortless use of jargon. For myself, I'd like to see him deal with a riotous fifth-form class last thing on a Friday afternoon, but I doubt I ever will. Men like Johnny Harrington never have to roll up their sleeves or get chalk dust on their hands. Men like Harrington sit and make plans while others follow orders. And men like Harrington know how to set other men in motion; winding the mechanism, pulling the strings, setting them off in directions they *think* they have chosen for themselves—

At long last, the Briefing was over. The Head and his Crisis Deputies went off to discuss the master plan over tea and biscuits in the Head's inner sanctum. I know that sanctum very well; the last Head left it exactly as old Shitter Shakeshafte did, except that the smell of cheese has been replaced by the scent of floral air-freshener. Bob Strange followed them like an expectant basset hound, leaving the rest of us to compare notes around the tea urn. Kitty Teague passed me a biscuit.

'So. What do you think?' I said.

Kitty gave me the kind of smile she reserves for her slowest pupils. 'He seems very pro-active,' she said. 'I think he'll be good for St Oswald's. We needed a bit of a shake-up after everything that happened last year.'

'*Pro-active*. Isn't that a kind of yoghurt?'

She said: 'You don't sound very convinced.'

'I don't think he's the man for the job.'

'Why? Because he's too young? Or because he's not from a teaching background?'

Well, come to think of it, those are both excellent reasons for mistrust. St Oswald's is an old ship, requiring careful handling. One does not put an old ship in the hands of the cabin boy. Besides, although I have no doubt as to Harrington's competence in the field of Public Relations, a *real* Headmaster comes from the ranks; he serves his time at the chalk-face; he learns from ugly experience; he gets blisters on his hands. This new generation of Headmaster is a different class; computer- literate; personable, politically correct and in touch with the new methodologies – but unless he has *taught*, how can he expect to understand what we do here? How can he understand the boys? How can he understand the *staff*?

'I don't know about that,' Kitty said. 'Everything's moving so fast now. We need someone to take control, to help us compete in a changing market. I think he'll be good for all of us, Roy. St Oswald's needs a human face.'

A human face? Johnny Harrington? Gods, am I the only one he *hasn't* managed to seduce?

I noticed Kitty was wearing a suit for the first time since I've known her. That's what promotion does, I suppose. I shouldn't hold it against her. Kitty, at thirty-five, is still young, with a promising future ahead. Chances are she knows nothing of what happened here twenty-four years ago. Dr Devine is different. I expected more of him. And Eric – he was there from the first, much as he would like to forget, and those who will not remember the past must be condemned to repeat it.

But maybe I shouldn't be too harsh on my colleagues, or on myself. None of us saw the crisis approaching, back in that autumn of '81. None of us guessed how everything would spring from that first, improbable seed, like a chain of paper flowers pulled from a circus-master's hat and blooming gaudily over the years to flower again on a dead man's grave . . .

7

Michaelmas Term, 1981

Dear Mousey,

It wasn't always like this, you know. I didn't always have to pretend. My dad wasn't always this pompous, and sometimes my mother used to smile. But then we had Tribulation. That's what they call it, Mousey, with the capital letter. Tribulation is what God sends when He thinks you're not paying attention. It can be cancer; or locusts; or boils. It can be an accident. Or he can take something away. A precious possession; the use of a limb; even, in some cases, a life.

What God took was my brother.

His name was Edward, but Mum and Dad always called him Bunny. I was seven years old when he died. In fact, he was the reason I got sent to school in the first place. Till then, Mum had looked after me at home, but after my brother was born, she decided that she couldn't look after two children at once. And so I was sent to Netherton Green, while Mum looked after Bunny.

I didn't want to go to school. Netherton Green was noisy, and big, and filled with other children. I didn't like other children much. They frightened me a little. So when I arrived, I didn't speak. I barked like a dog for the first three days. I figured people liked dogs. I thought it would make them like me. Turns out it made me a weirdo. I've been a weirdo ever since.

They never told me exactly what happened to Bunny. Perhaps they thought I was too young. All they said was: *God took him*. Other people told me the rest. Bunny had been having his bath. My mother had gone to answer the phone. She'd only been gone a minute. Bunny was nearly two by then. He drowned in six inches of water.

I think that's when I first started to really be afraid of God. If He could take Bunny, then He could take me. And worse, my parents talked about it like it was a kind of treat, like maybe going to Disneyland. Except that sometimes, I could hear Mum crying in her room, and at Church I heard Mrs Plum say to Mrs Constable that Mum was no better than she should be, and that maybe now she'd understand that God doesn't play favourites.

Mrs Constable didn't like my parents, because Dad had told some people at Church that Mrs Constable's daughter was living in sin with a woman in Leeds. After that, Mrs Constable didn't talk to my parents at all, and Mr Constable started a Gay Families Support Group, which Dad said was a gateway to approving immorality. I was a bit young to understand, but Dad explained that being gay was wrong; that it was in the Bible. Of course, that was in the olden days. Now it's not even illegal. How can that be? Did the rules change? And if they did, what happened to the people who went to Hell for being gay? Do they get a free pardon? Or do they just have to stay there?

At lunchtime today the three of us went up to Mr Clarke's room again. Mr Clarke – *Harry!* – was marking books.

That's what he does most lunchtimes. The boys in his form either go to lunch, or play football in the Quad, or go to the fifth-form Common Room, or stay in and eat their sandwiches, listening to records. Sometimes Harry lets you choose. Sometimes he chooses something himself.

At first I wanted *Animals*. Goldie was already eating his lunch. Poodle didn't say anything, but just gave him his usual look, like a dog expecting a biscuit.

Harry looked at me, then took a record sleeve from the box and said: 'I thought I'd play you a classic today. Something tells me you'll like it.'

The album was called *The Rise and Fall of Ziggy Stardust and the Spiders from Mars*. It was by David Bowie. I didn't know much about him, though I'd seen his pictures in magazines. He's the kind of singer that my dad despises most of all, and that Mr Speight thinks is the devil incarnate. Hair like a girl. Face like a girl. Eyes like a kind of demon. Of course, my dad makes Mr Speight look sane when it comes to demons. He's like a sniffer dog that can sense evil. Or so he thinks. If only he knew what demons were here, hidden away right under his nose.

I wanted to look at the album sleeve, but Harry had put it aside. He dusted the record with a cloth, then checked the record player. He's always very careful like that, making sure it's on the right speed and the needle's free of dust.

I sat down next to the teacher's desk. Goldie and Poodle sat next to me. The others opened their lunch boxes. I'd swapped one of my sandwiches for Goldie's chocolate biscuit, and my Wagon Wheel for Poodle's pork pie. But somehow it didn't seem right to eat while Harry was playing his music. Harry had chosen that record for me. I owed it to him to listen. And then the music started, and I mostly forgot about eating. All I could think of was the way the music seemed to fold around me like a hand and finger its way into my heart.

I don't know too much about instrumentation: I could hear some sax, and some graunchy guitars, and some keyboards, and some voices – or was it all the *same* voice? – telling a story that I knew from somewhere, maybe out of a dream. It was amazing. It was immense. It was the biggest, most powerful thing that had ever happened to me. I sat there, holding my biscuit, listening to the music, hardly even daring to breathe. Goldie ate his sandwiches. Poodle was drawing in the margin of his Prep diary. Neither of them seemed to have realized the awesomeness of what they had just heard. To them it was just music. To me it was like a door in my mind opening into another world.

'Can we play it again, sir?'

Harry was still marking books. When I spoke, he looked up and smiled. 'Hadn't you ever heard it before?'

'My dad doesn't like rock music.'

'It's not just the music. It's the vibe. In fifty years' time, they'll remember this.'

I looked at the album cover then, which showed Ziggy, standing with his guitar on a street corner at night under a sign that said: K. WEST. It was a painting, not a photo, and you could see the way the artist had picked out the bricks in the wall and the rain shining on the pavement. There was a pile of litter and old cardboard boxes in the foreground; it looked seedy and exciting and dangerous all at the same time. And although he was the star of the show, Ziggy looked small in the picture, standing outside a closed door, with all the lights in the windows shining yellow and welcoming, and him outside, alone in the rain, getting wet and not giving a damn.

It struck me then that Harry looks a little bit like Ziggy. Older, of course, and with glasses. Ziggy with experience.

In fifty years' time, I'll remember this.

That would make me sixty-four. Six years to go till I'm seventy. Funny, how death steps into my mind, even at the best of times, like a dog that won't stay away. Still, I knew that Harry was right. I'll remember this moment till I die.

'I wish life was like a record, sir. I wish we could start all over again.'

He put down the pen he was using. 'Why?'

'Well, sir,' I said. 'Because it feels it's all going by too quickly. Like there's no time to get it right. Like it's all been decided, and there's nothing we can do to change.'

I felt a bit embarrassed then. I hoped I didn't sound like a spaz. (It *was* a spazzy thing to say.)

But Harry wasn't laughing. He said: 'Life is a gift from the universe. We're all of us free to do what we want. We can all be who we want to be. We can all change, if we want to change. All it takes is courage.'

'Courage,' I said.

'That's right.' That smile. His eyes go Chinese when he smiles. 'A little courage is all it takes. After that you can be free.'

'Do you really believe that, sir?'

'Of course I do,' he said. 'Don't you?'

8

September 7th, 2005

Word in the Common Room so far is that the New Head is sound. Dr Devine is too dignified to share his views with the hoi polloi. Eric is also lying low. His shameful, toadying applause in the wake of the Headmaster's speech means that he is avoiding me. But everyone else is already sure that Harrington will be good for us. Dr Burke, the Chaplain; Bob Strange; Robbie Roach, the hopeful historian, who still hasn't quite recovered from the exhilarating prospect of Mulberry girls in the School. Of course, Roach is an idiot; Strange, a management toady; and the Chaplain lives in a world of his own where reality seldom penetrates – but I'd thought that Eric, at least, would show a little loyalty.

I poured a final cup of tea and prepared to return to the Bell Tower. Suddenly, the bright new term seems rather less promising. Passing Bob Strange's office, I heard the sound of raised voices and glanced through the half-open door, to see Devine at Strange's desk.

He was standing half turned to the door, and his nose was pink with emotion. His voice, too, registered an unusual degree of animation as he said:

'Roy Straitley knows—'

Then he saw me and stopped. For a moment our eyes met. I saw the nose twitch once, and then he closed the office door in my face, leaving me outside in the hall, trying to make sense of what I'd heard.

Roy Straitley knows. Knows what? That Latin is under threat from the National Curriculum? That he shouldn't eat Liquorice Allsorts? That his days are numbered?

Arriving in room 59, I found a young man in overalls, standing on a school desk, dusting the top of the doorframe. Thirties; slight; sharp-featured; blue hooded top; blue overalls. One of the new cleaners, no doubt: all part of the Bursar's new money-saving initiative. Hence, Mary, our elderly cleaner, whose work ethic, though sound, was based on rules that only she understood, has finally been replaced by someone of the Bursar's choosing – that is to say, someone cheaper.

I extended a hand. 'Good morning,' I said. 'I am Mr Straitley, the current inmate of room 59. And you?'

The new man looked slightly taken aback to be addressed by a member of staff. 'Er – I'm Winter, sir,' he said. 'Do you mind if I finish? I just thought – it's so dusty in here. I've done the floors already, but—'

His voice was more cultured than I'd expected, but hesitant, like that of a man who might have stuttered as a boy.

'Of course. Pleased to meet you, Mr Winter.'

He looked a little surprised at that. The likes of the Bursar and Bob Strange always call ancillary staff by their Christian names. But I make no such assumptions. Until he tells me otherwise, my new cleaner will be *Mr Winter*, as I shall be *Mr Straitley* to him.

'And where are you from, Mr Winter?'

'White City. Near Bank End.'

At least he's a local. That's a good sign. Not as good as Mary, who called us *her boys* and sometimes brought me slices of cake, home-made and heavy as concrete, which she left, wrapped in a napkin, in the bottom drawer of my desk, for me to find in the mornings. But better than a member of a contract crew from Sheffield or Leeds, working for the minimum wage and for half the time spent by the old team.

I finished my tea and put down the mug. 'Liquorice Allsort?'

I held up the bag. Winter chose a blue one. I selected a sandwich; pink and yellow over black. The sharing of food has always provided an elementary connection. It works with everyone – colleagues, boys; even Devine enjoys the odd austere morning cup of coffee. Of course, the likes of Dr Devine would never be seen hobnobbing with a man in a boiler suit. But in thirty-four years I have learnt that the ancillary staff – the Porter, the cleaners, the secretaries – actually run St Oswald's. This is an open secret that folk such as he and Mr Strange do not understand, being mostly obsessed with status, money, the National Curriculum and other completely irrelevant things.

'Careful, Mr Winter,' I said. 'Don't be too harsh on the dust, if you please. The dust and I are old friends. We understand each other.'

He smiled. 'I'll do my best, sir.'

By now he had finished the door-frame and moved on to the top of the bookshelves. I doubted anyone had cleaned up there since Mary's predecessor – Gloria, with the Spanish eyes. Well, at least he's thorough, I thought. But efficiency isn't everything. There ought to be room for more than that. There ought to be room for loyalty.

I gave a rather mournful sigh. Things are changing too fast aboard the dear old frigate. Johnny Harrington at the helm. Mulberry girls in the Sixth Form. Male cleaners, for gods' sakes. I settled into my chair and took out the register for this year. At least my form remains the same. That counts for something, I suppose. Though members of staff may come and go, the boys remain a constant; vibrant and unquenchable; a reminder that Life goes on.

Today has been a long day. I got home late, well after dark. The central heating hadn't come on. I must have forgotten to set the timer. I lit the living-room gas fire and made myself some cocoa. In such familiar surroundings, it seems hard to believe that anything could be amiss. But that's the danger of being in this job. That's how St Oswald's draws us in. It makes us feel safe, cocooning us with the illusion of permanence. That's why the Harry Clarke affair came as such a surprise to us all. Even Dr Devine was rocked. Even Shitter Shakeshafte. It was as if something had died, slyly and unobtrusively, and the stench of it still lingers now, like the stench of poisoned mice behind a classroom skirting-board.

Oh, but I'm getting ahead of my tale. That's what happens when you get old. You start to ramble. You lose track of time. Things that happened a long time ago suddenly seem so much closer than the things that happened yesterday. And things you thought you'd forgotten about suddenly pop into your mind, just as you're about to drop off, making sleep impossible.

Today it's a Public Information Film of the kind you saw in the old days, a film I haven't seen in years, but which I remember clearly. A sinister, hooded figure watches a group of children playing beside a flooded gravel pit, waiting for the moment when the bank gives way, or the tree-branch breaks, or the submerged, abandoned car inhales its youthful victim. A DANGER! NO SWIMMING! sign comes into view, but the children do not notice it. And now comes the voiceover; sinister, rasping out its challenge: *I am the spirit of dark and lonely water—*

Why remember that? Why now? What message from my subconscious is trying to rise to the surface? A pebble dropped into the dark and lonely water is still making ripples, twenty-four years on. And now, from the archives of memory, comes the voice of the hooded man . . .

9

Michaelmas Term, 1981

Dear Mousey,

Goldie thinks David Bowie is gay. He said so today at lunchtime, in Harry's room. Goldie's dad sometimes preaches in Church; he thinks the Homosexual Stranglehold on the Arts is what's holding Britain back.

I said: '*I* don't think he's gay.'

Poodle said: 'It's a persona. In real life, he's married and everything. Besides, it's the eighties. What do you care?' Goldie looked disgusted. But Poodle was defiant. 'I know it's a sin in the Bible,' he said. 'But so is eating shellfish.'

Harry was marking books at his desk. I was sure he was listening. His head was at an angle, you know, as if he was paying attention. And there was a look on his face. Not quite a smile, but nearly.

'What do *you* think, sir?' I said.

Harry looked up. 'About what?'

'You know. *Sin*.'

Harry smiled. For a moment I was almost sure I'd gone too far. Then he said: 'I don't believe God really cares what you eat, or what you wear, or whom you love. I think that if God made the stars, He must have a greater perspective.'

We didn't say anything more after that. But I thought about it, Mousey. What Harry meant is that God's too big to care about who you have sex with. After all, why would He care? Why does He care about anything? And then that started me thinking about My Condition, Mousey, and how much God would really care if He found out I was different—

Of course, my parents think He would. But then, my parents go to Church. They believe in all that stuff. My dad even preaches there sometimes. After Bunny and Netherton Green, they started making me go, too, to help with My Condition. But although I got better at hiding it, My Condition never changed. I guessed either God wasn't listening, or He wanted me this way. I got pretty good at pretending, though; speaking in tongues and fainting. That's what you do in *our* Church – at least, if you know what's good for you. It's even kind of fun sometimes. Like scoring at a football match, with everyone shouting and hugging you. No one hugs me, generally. I'm not very huggable.

At Netherton Green, everyone thought I was a freak and a weirdo. But this time, Mousey, it's different. St Oswald's has turned out OK for me. I even have a nickname. Didn't I tell you that, Mousey? Yes, they call me Ziggy now. Because of my favourite album. *Ziggy and the Spiders from Mars*. Nicknames are important when you're trying to be cool and fit in. And Ziggy's such a cool name. Even my dad seems to think so.

'Your chums look very sound,' he said over the dinner table last night. (*Sound* is the highest praise from Dad.) *Chum*. That's a kind of dog food. How appropriate, I thought. But I didn't say it aloud. I've learnt that with Dad, my jokes don't always go down very well.

'Yeah, they're pretty cool,' I said.

'It isn't *yeah*, it's *yes*,' said Mum. 'Or do you think you're American?'

I grinned inside. Americans are almost as bad as gays, in her world. Except for those Americans who run charismatic churches, and preach against the gays, and the blacks, and the Jews that are ruining the country.

The fact is, my two almost-friends are anything *but* sound. Goldie's a stuck-up hypocrite, and Poodle is a little freak who doodles over everything. It's compulsive, he tells me. So are his other habits, he says; his tapping, jigging and twitching. In the old days, they'd have called him possessed. Those Church folk love their demons.

Dad enjoys his demons too, being such a big churchgoer. And Poodle's mum makes puppydog eyes at the visiting preacher. It's funny, how certain preachers attract so many female fans. Our Church has plenty of those, being a charismatic church with lots of audience participation. Sometimes a girl from Mulberry House comes in to play the guitar and sing. Bright red hair and a long neck, like maybe a flamingo. One of those Churchy voices, clear, with not too much vibrato. I've seen her around St Oswald's. She's got a part in the school play. She likes to perform, in Church and on stage. I've seen the others watching her; Goldie and Poodle especially. I can't see what they see in her, though. Pretty enough, but not my type.

'If you want to invite your friends over, you can.' That was Mum, trying to be supportive of my social life. God knows, she ought to be grateful that I've even *got* any friends. She's always wanted me to have some.

'It's Bonfire Night next Thursday. There's a bonfire in the park. I thought we could go, the three of us. Then maybe back here for tea. Maybe invite their parents.'

Mum and Dad don't like Bonfire Night. They think it's a soft door to paganism. Like all that burning people alive never happened under the Church's rule. But I also knew that Mum was dying to meet my shiny new friends and their parents. And that's why we're going on Bonfire Night – Goldie, me and Poodle – while Goldie's and Poodle's parents have sherry with my mum and dad, and talk about Church and St Oswald's.

I know. It sounds revolting. But Mousey, it's all part of my plan. What Poodle calls a *persona*. With the right persona, I can hide in plain sight. I can do whatever I want as long as I keep up appearances. With the right persona, I can make them do anything – my parents, Poodle, Goldie, my teachers – make them dance like puppets.

Why? Because I can, that's why. Why did God make me this way? Why did God take Bunny? Why? Because He could. Because He's God. He made us all in His image, right? So I'm a little piece of God. And God is a killer; a joker; a thief. So how can He fail to be proud of me when I want to be just like Him?

10

Michaelmas Term, 1981

My talk with Johnny Harrington had one beneficial effect. The complaints from his father ceased forthwith, although I did not feel I had made any significant progress in getting to understand the boy.

I remember his School report word for word, handwritten on the penultimate page of his blue report book. *Harrington is an able student, well behaved and punctual.* That's Master's shorthand for Not Much to Say – for how could I articulate that sense of something wrong with him, of something strangely *missing*? Not that he'd ever done anything wrong. His name had cropped up only once or twice, in the context of misbehaviour by others (a minor riot in the class of an ineffectual member of staff; graffiti on the scarred oak panels in the School refectory), but Harrington – like his two friends – had been declared innocent of blame. A little *too* innocent, I felt; it just wasn't normal for a fourteen-year-old boy to have so few apparent vices.

However, his English Literature grade reflects his disappointing lack of commitment to the reading list. I hope that in the new term he will apply himself more diligently and raise his performance to the fine standard he has already achieved in other subjects.

Dammit, it made me nervous. It wasn't natural at all. It wasn't that I favoured troublemakers, precisely; but at least I could *understand* them. I myself was no paragon when I was a boy of fourteen; it's what has made me the Master I am, alert to all possibilities. And although there was nothing I could find to incriminate Harrington, Nutter or Spikely in any kind of misbehaviour, there was something in their aloofness that I found disquieting.

Of course, I *would* say that, wouldn't I? But even without the benefit of hindsight, that flawless rear window through which we observe the aftermath of the car crash, I'll swear there was something not quite right about the Harrington threesome. Call it intuition, perhaps. In any case, *something* was wrong. I could feel it approaching.

The latter half of the Michaelmas term brought Bonfire Night, my birthday, and, a fortnight later, the dubious gift of an early snow, which the boys received with uncontrolled glee, and the staff with less enthusiasm, knowing how disruptive snow can be to the efficient running of things.

The Old Head held an Assembly in which he delivered all kinds of threats – most of them unenforceable – to boys who indulged in snowball fights, or failed to wipe their feet on the mat when entering the School buildings. All the boys ignored him, of course. They came into Latin with wet shirts and wet feet, and left their shoes on the radiators to dry, with the result that for three days the whole of the Middle Corridor smelt of damp boys and their footwear.

Three evenings in early December were reserved for meetings with parents – to discuss form reports, exam results or any other matters for concern – but I wasn't expecting Harrington to bring up anything serious. In fact, since our talk in the locker rooms he hadn't said a word to me, except to answer questions in class, which he did with a cool condescension, as if conferring a favour.

Besides, there were other demands on my time. One boy had failed his Latin exam and needed extra tuition; another's parents were divorcing and he was taking it badly; and the girls of Mulberry House were putting on a production of *Antigone*, in which four of my fifth-form boys were also participating. Result: two of them had already fallen in love with the girl who was playing the lead, a rather attractive redhead apparently destined for greatness, which ill-timed attack of puppy love would probably cost them at least a grade.

And so you see, when Harrington came to me with alarming news, it took me entirely by surprise. First, that he should have noticed the problem before I did myself; second, that a boy of fourteen should have such unusual insight. It made me reassess the boy – and question my own instincts.

It was during Assembly on Friday, the last week in November. The boys had gone to Chapel, but I'd stayed in room 59 to go over some fourth-form papers. At eight forty-five, the sky was still dark, with a sick orange glow that boded no good.

Harrington came in, alone; fresh-pressed and looking like springtime. 'I wondered if I could have a word with you, sir.'

I put down my pen. 'Of course,' I said. 'Anything the matter?'

He seemed to consider the question. 'Perhaps.'

'Right,' I said. 'Sit down. Take your time.'

I'll admit my heart had sunk a bit. After the whole *mensa-merda* débâcle and the raft of complaints that had followed it, I was more than half expecting another account of profanity in *The Canterbury Tales*, or immoral conduct in Geography, even though, since the talk in the locker rooms, Harrington Senior's complaints had ceased as abruptly as they had begun.

The boy took a seat at a desk at the front. I've always thought room 59 had a vaguely nautical character; two double rows of wooden desks facing an elevated deck, on which I stand like a captain on the deck of his pirate ship, surveying the galley slaves below. This time I felt like a High Court judge listening to a plaintiff. Harrington's voice was as colourless as it had always been, but I thought that this time there was a tremor there – perhaps of some concealed emotion.

'It's a friend of mine,' he said. 'Sir, I think he's in trouble.'

A friend of mine. That usually means a problem of a delicate nature. I wondered why Harrington, of all people, should have chosen to come to me with such a problem, instead of to the Chaplain, the School's official counsellor in matters of the heart and soul.

'It isn't *me*,' said Harrington. 'It really *is* a friend of mine.'

Well, the boy didn't have many friends. If he wasn't talking about himself, it could only be Nutter or Spikely, the other two-thirds of the threesome. David Spikely, an average boy from an average family. Rather slow in French, perhaps; but there was nothing to suggest the boy might have a problem. And Charlie Nutter; pale, uninteresting; with patches of eczema on his hands. Never spoke a word in class. Never drew attention.

But his father was Stephen Nutter, one of our local MPs; a rubber bulldog of a man, known for his outspoken views. I'd always guessed that Nutter, MP, might have been disappointed in his rather ordinary son – some men feel the need to affirm themselves through their offspring, and

I'd imagined Nutter Senior to have had something very different in mind when he became a father. Mrs Nutter was pale and bland – rather like her son, in fact – a thin, sharp-faced woman, active in local charities, who often appeared in the *Malbry Examiner*, promoting some good cause or other. Between them, I doubted that Charlie Nutter had much of a chance to get into trouble of any kind.

'Does – your *friend* – know you're talking to me?'

Johnny Harrington shook his head. From my vantage point I could see the pencil-straight parting in his hair.

'Then what makes you think he's in trouble?' I said. 'Has he told you so?'

'No, sir.'

'Then what?'

I'll admit that the fact that he'd come to *me* made me feel strangely paternal. Perhaps I'd judged the boy too fast; after all, he was new to the School – in fact, new to most schools – and he might have had trouble settling in. For the first time, I considered the possibility that my robust approach to pastoral care might not have been the best in his case.

I said: 'While we may not see eye to eye on matters of English Literature, I hope you believe that whatever you say will be treated in confidence. I don't go running to the Head when one of my boys comes to me for help. Now, what seems to be the problem?'

For once, I thought he struggled to find the right words to express himself. 'Sir,' he began. 'I don't – I mean—'

'It's all right,' I said. 'Take your time.'

For a moment he looked away, keeping his hands very still in his lap. Then he raised his eyes to mine. 'Do you believe in possession, sir?'

PART TWO

O mihi praeteritos referat si Iuppiter annos!

(Vergil)

1

September 8th, 2005

Officially, the first day of term, when boys invade the premises. How much more efficient things would be if they did not; and yet, how dull.

'Morning, sir!' That was Allen-Jones, who always manages, even on the first morning of a new term, to look as if he has slept in his clothes. There was ink on his collar, and his tie was at half-mast. But that grin of his was unchanged; brash and curiously sweet.

'Good morning, Mr Allen-Jones. From your studious demeanour, I take it you spent the summer holidays in useful toil, meditation and contemplation of the ablative absolute.'

'Absolutely, sir,' he said, flinging his schoolbag on to his desk. Last year's *Hello Kitty* item has been replaced by one equally unsuitable; this year's offering featuring the comic-book character Wonder Woman. This is, of course, against the rules, which clearly state that schoolbags should be plain, marked only with the School crest. In the case of Allen-Jones, the School crest, in the form of a sticker, has been placed provocatively in Wonder Woman's ample cleavage. These small transgressions, I knew from experience, were entirely for effect, and, as always, I disappointingly failed to rise to the bait, but turned my attention instead to my new class register, delivered from the School office in a pristine paper folder.

I have kept last year's 3S. Now they are 4S – a move designed to reassure, to provide continuity in these changing times. I find myself slightly unsettled – of course, one knows that boys can change, but after all these years I am still surprised to see how much they *grow* over the summer holidays. Last term they were still boys; this term, they have thickened and grown like young trees, pushing and jockeying for space.

Here are my jokers, my Brodie Boys: Allen-Jones, Sutcliff and McNair. Here's Anderton-Pullitt, the odd little boy now showing the signs of the odd little man he will one day become. Here's Jackson, the schoolyard scrapper, and Pink, the class philosopher. There's Brasenose, a fat boy whose mother overfeeds him, and Niu, the Japanese boy, who defies every cultural stereotype by loving English Literature and hating Maths and Science.

There is one notable absence, of course. Colin Knight, whose name I crossed off the register in November of last year, but whose silent presence still endures, sullen as the boy himself. He alone has not thickened or grown: his face is still hairless, his voice unbroken. Not that he ever speaks to me; except sometimes in my darkest dreams. Some of the boys have had counselling following their schoolfriend's death – not that Knight had many friends, but death is always upsetting to those who consider themselves immortal.

Even now, no one sits in Knight's place – the left-hand corner desk at the back – though no one is really conscious of this, except for this old warhorse, of course, who remembers far more than is good for him.

I have a new class register now; neatly printed; unblemished. Even so, I find myself leaving a slight pause after *Jerome, B* – before going on to *Knockton, J* – a tiny, barely perceptible pause, just long enough, perhaps, for a Master to clear his throat, or for a sullen boy at the back to say – *Sir!* – in that cold, bland voice.

It occurs to me now that Johnny Harrington was the boy Colin Knight would have wanted to be; cool and self-possessed and bold; unafraid of authority. Was *that* why I disliked Colin Knight? Because somehow he reminded me of little Johnny Harrington?

'I've heard we're getting girls this year,' said Tayler, whose parents are both Governors, and who hears all the news before I do.

'Is that true?' said Allen-Jones.

'It's a merger with Mulberry House,' said McNair.

'Well, technically, not a merger,' said Anderton-Pullitt in his ponderous tone. 'Dr Harrington says it's all about consolidation of resources.'

It seems that Harrington's Crisis Team have taken a special interest in Anderton-Pullitt. Maybe because of what happened last year, when he was so nearly a casualty of the tragic events that claimed the life of Colin Knight. Or perhaps it is because this year, Anderton-Pullitt has been diagnosed as having 'special needs', which, his mother assures me, explains his eccentricities.

I'd always assumed that this was true of *all* my boys, but nowadays some are more special than others, it seems. I have already informed Mrs Anderton-Pullitt that, as long as her son continues to fulfil all *my* special requirements – such as prompt delivery of homework and full attention given in class – then I shall attempt to cater to his.

I have no great expectation of this, however. Anderton-Pullitt has been indulged far more than is good for him, and now that he has a Syndrome, I fully expect him to use it. I anticipate many meetings with Mrs Anderton-Pullitt, in which she attempts to persuade me that her son needs extra time in exams, exemption from Games (which he dislikes) and permission to ignore any homework that gets in the way of his interests. I sense a confrontation. And if the New Head has taken his side—

'So, no Mulberry girls,' said McNair.

'Not for us,' said Allen-Jones.

'As if *you'd* care,' said Pink.

He grinned. 'This class is a fruit-free zone.'

Pink gave a snort of laughter. The rest of my Brodie Boys joined in. I thought there was an edge to the sound – something not quite familiar – and I caught Allen-Jones looking at me, just for a moment, obliquely, as if to gauge the level of my interest.

'*Do* Mulberry girls count as fruit?' said McNair.

'Only if you're making a pie,' said Pink, and they were off again into a burst of that laughter that comes so easily to boys; the almost existential mirth that simply comes of being young. The feel of it; the rib-racking way it grabs you and shakes you breathless – I almost remember how that felt, in the days when I was fourteen. That feeling of something wound up tight, like a clockwork animal, springing into action somewhere within the region of the solar plexus and coming out as laughter. Nowadays that mechanism has become old and rusty. I rarely laugh aloud any more. And when I do, it sounds like the call of a lonely bird, ungainly and harsh.

What *is* it with me nowadays? I never used to be so sentimental. Perhaps it's this Harrington business, coming back to haunt me. Damn it, why did he have to come *here*? There must be a hundred 'failing schools' in need of the touch of a Super-Head. Why here? Why St Oswald's? Even allowing for the peculiar nostalgia of a man approaching middle age, his memories of the dear old place can hardly be the sweetest.

The bell rang, marking the start of the first lesson. The boys all left for their classes, some more efficiently than others. Anderton-Pullitt was the last to go, still rummaging in his desk even after most of my group (a first-form class) had already found their places.

I bit back a sharp reprimand. Anderton-Pullitt is *always* late, due to his inability to stop rearranging his schoolbooks. According to his personal file, this is an obsessive-compulsive disorder connected with his new syndrome, and must be treated with sympathy. I have my own opinions on this. But in the current climate, it's best to keep those opinions to myself. Besides, the ghosts of pupils past were whispering to me today – and to such a degree that, turning to the blackboard again, for the first time in twenty-four years, I almost wrote *merda, merdam* instead of the usual *mensa*.

The knock at the door, when it came, took me completely by surprise. As a rule, St Oswald's staff do not wander from form to form during lessons, nor does the Headmaster inflict surprise visits on his colleagues when they are attempting to teach the First Declension to twenty-four fidgety first-years.

'*Quid agis, Medice?*' I said, making a joke of my surprise.

Harrington came in, his smile like a rack of headlights. 'I hope you don't mind, Mr Straitley,' he said, 'but I'm going to be sitting in on some classes over the next few weeks. I'm just a New Boy here, you know. I have to learn the ropes, and fast!' This was addressed to my first-years, who obligingly shuffled and grinned.

Harrington found himself a seat – the left-hand corner, at the back. Knight's old place. Of course. I should have expected it. But thirty-four years of St Oswald's have given me a poker face. I managed a smile at Harrington.

'Very well, young man,' I said. 'The subject is first-year Latin. Don't think you're getting an easy ride. Let's see what *you* remember.'

2

Michaelmas Term, 1981

Dear Mousey,

Remember, remember, the Fifth of November. Gunpowder, treason and plot. Funny, how we celebrate death. Even in Church, the pictures all seem to be about some kind of torture. Do you know what they did to Guy Fawkes? He jumped off the scaffold and broke his neck, cheating the audience of their show. They hanged and quartered him anyway, and put his severed head on a spike, as if he could never be dead enough. My dad says it's barbaric. And yet, he's fine with us going to Church, seeing Jesus nailed to a cross and St Stephen all full of arrows. I mean, what's the difference? Dead is dead, and martyrdom is in the eye of the beholder. Jesus died so we might live. That sounds better than it is. Like paying for a new sofa in monthly instalments, only to find that by the time you've paid, the thing's already worn out.

I once asked Miss McDonald why people had to die. She said: 'To make room for babies who haven't been born.'

Well, Mousey, I wasn't convinced. Why did we need more babies? And if there were no more babies, then would I live forever?

Tonight was the bonfire in Malbry Park. They'd been building it since last week. By now it was a massive pile; hundreds of pallets, and firewood, and mattresses, and newspapers, and guys made of rags and old clothes stacked as tall as a building. Next to the bonfire, the fireworks were pretty uninspiring. I got as close to the fire as I could. The heart of it was bright orange and roaring like a lion. I wondered if that was what Hell was like. I got a toffee apple. Then Poodle got a bit sick with the smoke, and we had to move further away.

'What d'you want to be so close for, anyway?' said Goldie, whose face had gone red with the heat.

'I wanted to know what it felt like,' I said. 'Standing at the gates of Hell.'

Goldie gave me a funny look.

'You know, when they used to burn witches,' I said. 'They thought they were being kind to them. Getting them used to what was to come. You know, like endurance training.'

'That's sick,' Poodle said.

'I don't know. It's kind of cool.'

The thing is with Goldie and Poodle, they don't always get me. We don't really have much in common. Apart from being New Boys, of course. And apart from not having siblings. Still, it's pretty cool sometimes to have someone to talk to in Church, and sit next to in lessons, and have a laugh with occasionally. It means that I fit in at last. I don't attract attention. And *that* means there's no trouble from Dad – a welcome change from Netherton Green.

When we got home, there was parkin, and ginger biscuits, and sandwiches, and Mr and Mrs Poodle and Mr and

Mrs Goldie, all of them in their Church clothes, sitting in the lounge and discussing St Oswald's. Mr Poodle was saying how it was the best thing that had happened to his son in years, and all the others were nodding like dogs.

'Not sure about the form-master, though. He doesn't seem altogether sound.'

Sound. Oh, Mousey. That word again.

Goldie's father nodded. 'The Chaplain's a sensible chap, though,' he said. 'And of course, there's John Speight. If ever you need a sensible man to have a quiet word—'

Dad looked at me. 'Yes. John Speight's a marvel with the boys. Pity he doesn't have a Middle School form. Who are the other Middle School form-masters?'

'There's Mr Straitley, Mr Scoones, and—' *Harry*, I almost said. 'Mr Clarke.' I picked up a piece of parkin. I noticed that Poodle was looking at me kind of sideways. I smiled and went on: 'Mr Speight's cool. I wish he was *my* form-teacher.'

I could tell my dad was pleased. 'Well, we can't like everyone,' he said. 'That's what school is for. To learn how to get on with people who don't necessarily share our ideas.'

If only he knew. I gave Poodle a wink. Poodle looked uncomfortable. His eye began to twitch a bit.

'Oh, Mr Straitley's all right,' I said. 'As long as you're one of his favourites. There's a little group of them. They sit with him at lunchtimes.'

Dad frowned. 'I'm not sure I approve. I've never thought masters should fraternize with pupils.'

'Oh, *we* don't get invited,' I said. 'We're not special enough for him.'

I didn't say anything more after that, but I could see the seeds had been sown. Just a few seeds, but with luck they may grow. These are the best years of our lives. We should be having fun. Right? So far, I've not had too much fun, except when I've been with Harry. But that could change. I hope it will. And Mr Straitley had better not get in the way. Because when people get in my way, bad things sometimes happen. Mr Straitley deserves a surprise. I deserve a little fun. And, as Harry said himself: there's more to me than meets the eye.

3

Michaelmas Term, 1981

'What do you mean, *possession*?' I said, perhaps a little too sharply. 'As in nine-tenths of the law, perchance?'

He shook his head. 'No, sir.'

'Then what?'

Of course, by then I already knew that young Harrington's parents were deeply religious. They belonged to a local outfit, rather too modern for my taste, called the Church of the Omega Rose, which was housed in a modest square building down in Malbry Village. The Satanic Mr Speight was a regular visitor, as were a number of our boys. Beyond that information, I hadn't given the place too much thought.

I myself am Church of England by habit, birth and nostalgia; I go to church at Christmas because I happen to like it, and because I enjoy the hymns, but would never describe myself as *devout*. I tend to believe that certain ideas (love, charity, and the like) are worth promoting, while others (such as stoning, narrow-mindedness, demons, fasting, original sin and contempt for those who are different) are best left to wither quietly on one of the dying branches of faith. Others, I knew, did not agree. Harrington Senior was one of them.

'You mean, *demonic* possession?' I said.

Harrington nodded. 'Yes, sir.'

I had to laugh. I thought the boy looked slightly offended.

'I'm sorry,' I told him. 'Please go on. You were telling me about – your friend.'

'Well, sir. He has all the signs. Mood swings, nervous tics, bad skin, obsessed with death—'

'That's *adolescence*, Harrington. I think you'll find that's normal.'

The joke, mild as it was, failed to melt his composure. 'Sir. It *isn't* normal. He thinks about it *all the time*. He keeps saying he's going to die, and then he's going to burn in Hell and there's nothing anyone can do.'

That made me sit up a bit. Unlike the girls of Mulberry House, my boys were not generally prone to fits of excessive sensibility. Harrington didn't seem the type to indulge in morbid thoughts, but nevertheless, I told myself, this might be a cry for attention. I found myself checking his face for blemishes, but apart from a single spot on his chin, the boy seemed remarkably acne-free.

'Is – your friend – a believer?' I said.

'He used to be,' said Harrington. 'Now, I don't know what he is.'

'And do you know of any reason he might be feeling – unhappy?'

He shook his head. 'He's not *unhappy*, exactly. My father says there's something missing in him. Like a light's been turned out.'

'*He* thinks there's a problem, then?'

Harrington shrugged. 'He thinks we should pray. That's his answer to everything.'

I said: 'The idea of possession doesn't have to be literal. When you say something like: *What's got into you?* you really mean: *Is there anything wrong?* And when you say: *I'm not myself—*'

'Sir, it isn't me, sir.'

I lied. 'Of course I believe you. But if you can't tell me the name of your *friend*, or why you think he may be—'

'Possessed.'

'Quite.' I was starting to wonder now whether this might all be some kind of joke. But Harrington's agitation was real. I would have bet my life on it.

The boy gave me a sideways look. 'Sir. You don't believe, sir.'

'Do you?'

I thought he flinched at that. 'I only want to help, sir.'

I only want to help, he said. Who wouldn't have believed him then? Sincerity tempered with awkwardness – and just the right amount of concern.

'Then why not tell me the name of your friend?' I asked, just as the lesson bell went. Outside, in the corridor, came the sounds of activity. Harrington glanced at the door. For a moment, I thought I saw a shadow of something cross his face. Had he seen someone standing there? Someone he wanted to avoid?

'Look at me, Harrington,' I said.

Obediently, he turned to me. Through the frosted glass of the door, I could see boys lining up for class. Had one of them made a sign? Was a member of staff with them? There was no way of telling.

'Come on, Harrington,' I said. 'How can I do anything to help unless I know who we're discussing?'

'I thought you'd be able to find out. Now that you know what to look for, I mean. It wouldn't have to come from me. You could find out by accident.'

'By accident?' I said. I suppose I still hoped for a confession. The whole 'my friend has a problem' line was old when Noah was a boy. But something had changed, I realized. In that interval, brief as it was, Harrington had recovered his poise. Perhaps he'd seen someone through the glass; perhaps he'd simply got cold feet. But the look of vulnerability I'd thought I'd glimpsed in his face was gone; instead, the old aloofness was back, as bland and hateful as ever.

I gave it one last try. 'Are you sure that's all you can tell me?'

He nodded. 'Yes, sir. I've got to be in Maths, sir.'

I sighed. 'Adolescence is difficult. Boys can get angry and confused. That doesn't mean they're all possessed. It's just – well. Hormones. Teenage angst. What my colleague Dr Devine undoubtedly refers to as *Weltschmerz*.'

Harrington picked up his briefcase. 'Thank you. I feel better now. Sorry I took up so much of your time.'

I thought about what he'd said all day.

Possession? Demonic possession?

Of course I didn't believe him. Perhaps he didn't expect me to: Harrington was clever enough to choose his targets appropriately, and if he had really intended to sell someone an outlandish idea, he would have gone straight to Dr Burke, or better still, to St Oswald's own version of the Witchfinder General, the Satanic Mr Speight, whose interest in all things occult rivalled even the Chaplain's.

No, I concluded; Harrington had come to me for a reason. Perhaps he even *meant* for me to disregard this far-fetched hypothesis. Perhaps mine was to be the voice of good sense when everyone else was losing their head.

Which made me wonder whether *he* really believed in the nonsense, or whether this was an oblique way of trying to warn me about something entirely different. In any case, Parents' Evenings were imminent, and if Johnny Harrington – or one of his friends – was having emotional difficulties, now was the time to find out why.

A good form-master knows how to delve without seeming to question openly; he knows when to use the velvet glove and when to deploy the iron fist. He knows when to tackle a problem head-on and when to skirt it delicately; in short, a good form-master has to be part detective, part social worker, part saint. I am *not* that Master. My general pedagogic approach is based on a policy of benevolent neglect – it works in the case of most boys, but neither Harrington nor his friends seemed to respond to my methods. No, I needed someone else; someone who spoke the boy's language; someone who had the authority, but also the humanity, to cross the gulf between Master and pupil. I knew who I needed; a man who had earned the boys' liking and trust; someone who knew them better than I; someone who could advise us both.

And so, at the end of the morning, I went in search of Harry Clarke.

4

Michaelmas Term, 1971

I remember arriving in '71 as a Junior Master. Eric Scoones had been there two years. In fact, he was the reason that I'd applied for the job in the first place; Eric and I had been good friends ever since we were schoolboys. Now we were newbies together again – along with the young Dr Devine, an Alka-Seltzer of a man, fresh out of college and fizzing with energy and ambition.

So many things have changed since then; and yet, at the same time, nothing has. We still live in isolation, like goldfish in a series of tanks, moving in the same circles, term after term, year after year. Nothing much ever happens here – and when something does, it happens with the suddenness of a dropped stone falling into the water, leaving a series of ripples that all too soon smooth over.

I first encountered Harry Clarke near the end of my first half-term. St Oswald's staff do not generally fraternize with members of other departments, and Harry Clarke, although his form-room was directly above my own, was attached to a department that was famously antisocial, of which the head was Mr Fabricant, an Oxford man with an eye twitch, who in his youth had written a book on the life of the Marquis de Sade, thereby earning himself an undeserved reputation for sexual permissiveness. As a result I barely knew Harry Clarke, except as a face in the Common Room, to which he rarely came, except at Headmaster's Meetings. That day, I'd gone into room 54 – that was Dr Devine's room, the next one along the corridor from mine – to borrow a box of coloured chalks. For some reason the German Department had them all, and was stockpiling them in the back of Devine's store cupboard. Well, when I say 'borrow' – I was hoping Devine would be out. From what I already knew of him, he wasn't the philanthropic type.

Sadly, he, too, liked to arrive in School at seven thirty, and would sit at his desk, drink a single cup of black coffee (using the School china, of course) and mark books until the boys came in. That late-October morning, however, I found him with his back to me, standing on the lid of his desk, holding a garden gnome in one hand and looking both furtive and furious.

He turned, startled, as I came in. '*Straitley!*'

'Oh. Hello,' I said.

He looked at me with annoyance. Dr Devine as a young man looked much the same as he does now – the eyes a little brighter, perhaps; the nose a little more sensitive. We had disliked each other on sight, with the instinctive recognition of two antagonistic species. Everything in his form-room was the antithesis of my own: the neatness of his bookshelves; the gown that hung on a clothes hanger behind the door; the pristine blackboard, wiped with a sponge rather than a messy board-rubber; the posters of famous Germans neatly pinned to the noticeboards.

In such Teutonic surroundings, I was surprised to see the gnome. One of those painted plaster affairs, wearing a dissipated grin and what looked like an Amadeus House tie. Dr Devine climbed down from the desk and put the gnome in his briefcase.

'It isn't mine, of course,' he said. He sounded annoyed at having to explain. 'I found it there this morning.' He spoke in a sharp, percussive tone, like a talking typewriter. 'In fact, I've been finding it around every day for the past two weeks. It's someone's silly idea of a joke. And when I find out who's been *doing* it—'

I grinned. I couldn't help it.

'Well, I'm glad *you* think it's funny,' he said. 'Because clearly you have no idea how disruptive it can be, when you're trying to teach a class, to open a cupboard, or to pull out a dictionary from a shelf, or to look inside a desk drawer and see *that thing* grinning out at you. Today it was balanced above the door. It could have caused an injury.'

I bit my lip. 'Of course,' I said. 'But – couldn't you just throw it away?'

'You think I haven't tried that?' said Devine impatiently. 'Whoever it is keeps retrieving it. Last week I found it outside my door – on my *doorstep*, Straitley – holding a German sausage. Someone actually came to my *house*. This has gone beyond a joke. And when I find out who's doing it—'

I schooled my countenance to reflect nothing but solemnity. 'Quite right.' I stifled a cough. 'Er, have you discovered a motive?'

Devine looked affronted. 'A *motive*?'

My words were not idle. Since the start of that term, Devine had already put into detention fourteen boys in my form alone, as well as lodging several complaints against his neighbours along the Upper Corridor for such various crimes as playing music at lunchtime; failing to tidy his room after use; stealing his chalks; moving his plants and failing to wear a gown to morning Assembly. Dr Shakeshafte famously referred to him as 'that little shit', and the boys had already given him his current nickname of Sourgrape.

'What possible reason could there be, except the desire to disrupt?' he said.

I shook my head and returned to my room – sensing that my request for chalk would be met with a cool reception. Instead I went up to room 58, which was Harry Clarke's room, and from which the sound of music emerged dimly, from behind the door.

I knocked and went in. A rail-thin, untidy young man in round glasses and a Harris Tweed jacket was trying to fit a cardboard box under a desk that was already stacked with boxes of records, towers of books and a portable record player.

He looked up as I came in. 'You're from downstairs, aren't you?' he said.

'Straitley, Latin,' I told him.

'Harry Clarke. English Lit.' He grinned. 'For a moment I thought you were that German chap, complaining about my music again. I've been expecting him any time over the past two weeks. I was going to play him *this*—'

He grinned again and took a record from the pile on his desk. He slipped it on to the turntable and waited for the song to begin. A sunny little tune rang out. Then I glanced into the cardboard box that he'd slid under the desk, and saw a row of plaster gnomes, neatly packed in polythene, all of them identical to the one I'd seen in Devine's hand—

The record on the turntable went on playing that bright little tune. I later learned that Harry was fond of collecting novelty records. After a time I started to laugh, and Harry Clarke laughed with me.

The song was, of course, 'The Laughing Gnome'.

5

Michaelmas Term, 1981

Dear Mousey,

The end-of-term exam results are out. I've got As in History, Maths, RE, Geography, Latin and Chemistry. English was a C (boo-hoo), and French was disastrous – not because I'm bad at French, but because on the day of the exam I was feeling particularly bored. And so, instead of the essay that Mr Scoones had asked us to write (*Racontez ce que vous avez fait pendant vos vacances*), I wrote an account of a murder (*un meurtre*) that I'd committed at the weekend, and how I'd disposed of the body (*le cadavre*) by cutting it into tiny pieces (*en petits morceaux*) and leaving them in the school kitchens, where they were speedily incorporated (*rapidement incorporés*) into a batch of shepherd's pie.

Turns out Mr Scoones doesn't have that kind of sense of humour. Besides the note to my parents, which was bad enough, I've got two weeks' lunchtime detention, starting from next Monday, which means that I won't see Harry again until after the Christmas holidays. Funny, how quickly I've got used to these lunchtime sessions of Harry's.

I'll miss them, Mousey. I'll miss *him*. Stupid, pompous Mr Scoones.

Meanwhile, Poodle's up to no good. He didn't do well in his exams. I saw his Chemistry paper, all covered in those doodles that he's always drawing in class. Plus he isn't happy here. You can tell from watching him. There are patches of eczema on his fingers and up his arms, and acne on his forehead. (My dad thinks acne's a sign of self-abuse.) And he's started avoiding me before school and at lunchtimes. After school, he sneaks away before you can try and talk to him. I wonder if it was something I said – maybe that day in Harry's room. Or something preying on his mind. Something or *someone*, Mousey.

Some people are good at hiding things. Some are better at finding things out. I'm good at both, actually. Which is why, when he left school today, I followed him at a distance. I could tell straight away he wasn't going home. He lives on the far side of the park, at the top of Millionaires' Row. But I could see he was heading for the other side of the Village; Sunnybank Park, the White City estate, and all the waste land that comes after.

Poodle's very secretive. I had to be careful not to be seen. But I thought I knew where he was going, and it turned out I was right. There's a place on a piece of waste land, down behind the White City estate. There's a bit of canal there, and some grassed-over slag heaps. There's a quarry filled with brambles, then there's a bridge, then an old metal gate, and then, beyond that, there's the clay pits. This is Poodle's secret place, where he does his secret things. And the reason I know this, Mousey, is that it used to be *our* place, as well.

There must have been over a dozen pits, once. Some were up to a hundred feet deep. They used to climb down to the bottom on ropes and send up the clay in buckets. Now the pits are all flooded out, and people use the place as a dump. I've given all the flooded pits names. The biggest is the Long Pond, and people sometimes go fishing there, among the old cars and abandoned junk. It's safe enough, if you stay on the low end of the bank. The water's shallow. You can play boats. But some of the other pits are deep, and the bank gets slippery in the rain. There's one that I call the Pit Shaft. It's only a few dozen feet across. But the bank is so steep that if you fell in, you'd probably not get out again. Sometimes you see animals that have made that mistake. Drowned rats; even dogs. I stay away from the Pit Shaft now. Then there's the Crescent; the Sugar Bowl; the Three Little Injuns and the Sink. None of those are completely safe, except for the Crescent, which is mostly filled in, with just a deeper bit at one end. Elsewhere by the clay pits, there are old abandoned cars, and shopping trolleys, and carpets, and piles of wooden pallets and crates, and bundles of comics and magazines. Even ovens and fridges, too, and TV sets with the fuses blown. It's a good place if you need somewhere to hide, or to meet the kind of people that your parents might not approve of. I could tell by the way he approached that Poodle went there all the time.

I can walk pretty quietly. I managed to get right up close to Poodle before he realized I was there. I hid behind a big rock and watched as he made himself comfortable. He was sitting inside a rusted old car, reading a copy of *Fiesta*. He looked like he was expecting someone.

He jumped when he finally saw me, and tried to hide the magazine. 'Oh. It's you, Ziggy,' he said.

'Come here often, do you?'

He shrugged. I thought he looked uncomfortable. He had fixed up the old car with pieces of carpet, a mattress and some bundles of magazines to make a decent-looking den. From a distance, it just looked like another old wreck. It was pretty cool, actually.

'Don't tell my mum,' said Poodle. 'She thinks I'm over at your place.'

'That's OK,' I told him. 'My dad probably thinks I'm with you. Got any smokes?'

Poodle seemed to relax a bit. He had a packet of sherbet dabs, and some cigarettes, which we shared, sitting on the worn-out seats and watching the silent water. I'm not supposed to smoke, of course. Even though Dad does, in secret. But then again, I'm not supposed to read comic books, or listen to David Bowie, or look at pictures of ladies with their clothes off. All because of My Condition, of course. Still, it does occur to me that Dad might be just a little confused about what My Condition really is.

Poodle had left his magazine on the back seat of the old car. I don't know much about cars, except that it was a soft-top, shredded by the elements. I also saw that Poodle had been doodling on his magazine, giving the cover girl a moustache and a massive cock and balls.

Poodle noticed me noticing, and made a grab for the magazine. I managed to hang on to it, though. I opened it, and saw the same kind of drawings inside. *Oh,* I thought. *Maybe the red Flamingo girl from Church isn't his type, after all.*

Poodle went red. His acne scars looked almost white against the colour of his neck. He said: 'It's just a bit of fun. I'm not *bent,* or anything.'

'Course not. And those *other* books – the ones hidden under the car seat – those are just Enid Blyton. Right?'

Poodle looked sick. He turned away. I guess he knew there was no point in denying it. The car seat was stuffed with magazines – some of them what my dad calls *beefcake mags*, but a couple of novels, too, with titles racy enough for dear old Dad to have himself a heart attack.

'I thought you fancied that girl from Church. The one who plays guitar,' I said.

He gave a sick little smile. 'I wish. That would be so easy,' he said. 'I mean, she'd never look at me, but at least it would make me *normal*—'

'Normal's overrated,' I said.

He looked depressed. 'That's not what Dad thinks. I'm expecting the Talk any day now. The one about how self-abuse sends you blind, and spots are just God's way of telling you to take more cold showers.'

'I know that talk,' I said, and grinned. 'I've been getting it since I was nine.'

'I thought if I – you know – got rid of my *curiosity*—'

'Then it would magically go away?'

He made a face. 'It's an addiction,' he said. 'An honest-to-Jesus addiction. You let it in, just once, and – *poof*! It's part of you for ever. Don't tell my dad. Don't tell anyone. I'll kill myself if he finds out. I mean it. You'd be a murderer.'

'Of course I won't tell,' I promised him.

'Cross your heart and hope to die?'

'Cross my heart and hope to die.'

So Poodle has a Condition, too. And no, I didn't *mean* to tell. But schools are funny places. It's hard to keep a secret here. Tell one person a secret, you're apt to become notorious. I guess that's what happened at Netherton Green. Still, that's all in the past now. That was an aberration. A flare-up of My Condition, which I now have under control.

But I've been watching Poodle. I watch him in class, when he's doodling. I watch him at Break, in the schoolyard. I watch him in Church as he's looking up at Jesus, naked on the cross, and I know *just* what he's thinking. Poor Poodle, lusting for Jesus. So much easier to lust after the red Flamingo girl who plays the guitar so prettily. But God doesn't like it *easy*. God likes to make things difficult. Instead of making people *good*, he gave us the illusion of choice. Way to go, God. Nice one. That's what we get for trusting in You.

I went up to Harry's room today, to tell him about Mr Scoones and my two-week lunchtime detention. He laughed when I told him about the essay.

'A little too creative, perhaps, for the good folk of St Oswald's.'

I shrugged. 'I guess so. I'll miss you, sir.'

He laughed again. 'You mean you'll miss my record collection. Tell you what, why don't you borrow one of my LPs, just to tide you over? But don't scratch it. OK?'

I nodded. I knew how important Harry's records were to him. Even more so than his copy of *Nineteen Eighty-Four* – with his handwritten notes inside.

'What's it going to be, then?' he said.

'*Ziggy Stardust*, please, sir.'

Mr Clarke laughed at that. 'You're insatiable,' he said. 'But let's see what you think of this. I know you like the older stuff. You must be an old soul.' And then he opened his briefcase – not the box with the records in – and carefully took out an album. '*Diamond Dogs*. I think you'll like this one,' he said. 'It's very dark and dystopian. *Ziggy Stardust* meets *Nineteen Eighty-Four*. Human beings in their animal forms cavorting at the end of the world.'

I looked at the album cover. Well, I guess you know what it's like. Strange and ugly and vicious and true and beautiful all at the same time. And he had seen it and thought of me, just as he'd thought of me when he'd chosen the ugly apple.

He gave me that smile. You know the one.

'Ready for me to blow your mind?'

'Yes, sir. Yes, *Harry*,' I said.

6

Michaelmas Term, 1981

And that was how Harry and I became friends. Just like that, in room 58, with 'The Laughing Gnome' on the turntable and the late-October sunshine coming in at the window. This may not seem unusual to those outside St Oswald's, but to me it came as quite a surprise. Apart from Eric, I had no friends, merely colleagues and pupils. Not that I cared. I'd never been gregarious – even as a young man, I was happiest with my books, my wireless and my solitude.

Harry Clarke changed that. Over the weeks and months and years we saw each other every day; not just in the mornings, but after School, where we would sit in Harry's room and drink innumerable cups of tea, mark books, read the papers and talk until at last the cleaner – Gloria, with the Spanish eyes – would come to stand in the doorway, hands on shapely hips, and say: 'Don't you boys have a home to go to?'

What did we talk about? Everything. Politics; music; people; life. I learnt that he voted Labour (I supported Edward Heath); he liked *Monty Python* and *Doctor Who;* he listened to music on Radio 1 and went to hear bands play in Manchester. He hated football, liked cricket; read Kurt Vonnegut and Muriel Spark. He lived alone, in a terrace house down in Malbry Village. He'd never married; as far as I knew, his family was St Oswald's.

Sometimes we would go out for a drink with Eric – who even then was fond of a glass or two of claret – to our local, the Thirsty Scholar, still reassuringly unchanged, with its leather armchairs by the fire and battle-scarred old tables. That was where *all* the Masters went – except perhaps for Dr Devine, who either didn't drink at all, or whose dignity forbade him to be seen in the company of lesser beings – and some of my happiest memories are of that place, and the three of us, and the laughter that came so easily whenever Harry was around.

Some exceptional teachers can inspire that kind of affection. Pat Bishop was one of them; so too was Harry Clarke. Some men you trust instinctively, wholly and without question; which was why, a decade later, when Johnny Harrington came to me with his sinister tale of possession, I went at once to Harry Clarke, certain he would know what to do.

I found him that lunchtime in his room, surrounded by boys, as usual. Harry rarely went in to lunch, but spent the time in his form-room, drinking tea and listening to records.

He looked up and smiled as I came in. 'Aha! Mr Straitley! Just in time to resolve a discussion. Status Quo or Procul Harum? As a Latinist, you should know.'

'It's actually procul *harun*,' I said. 'But I know it's all Greek to you.' I turned to the little group of boys. 'Gentlemen, I hate to interrupt such profound and meaningful study, but I need a word with Mr Clarke. The status quo can be resumed at a later date.'

The boys accorded my lame joke all the hilarity it deserved. Left alone with Harry, I said: 'It's Harrington. I need your advice.'

'Oh.' Harry looked thoughtful. 'How is he?'

I shrugged. 'He came to me today with a tale about a friend, and demonic possession.'

Harry grinned. 'Possession? Doesn't surprise me. Harrington Senior's a tough nut. That happy-clappy church of his is Old Testament through and through. Fire and brimstone. Death to the queers. Women in their rightful place. Speaking in tongues; mass hysteria; casting out demons from teenagers using nothing but faith and a Gospel choir. It's a miracle Johnny's the way he is.'

'And what way is that?' I said.

He shrugged. 'I know you've had trouble recently. But Johnny isn't a bad kid. A bit uptight, perhaps, but sound. Has a good head on his shoulders, in spite of his unfortunate parentage.' Harry opened the desk drawer and brought out a tin of Quality Street. 'Here. Have one of these.'

Harry maintained that you could tell a man's character by the chocolates he chose. I took a strawberry cream; soft-centred under a bitter chocolate coating. He took a purple Brazil nut.

'So what exactly did Johnny say?'

I told him. He ate his chocolate.

'Do you think he was talking about himself?'

'Who else could it be?' I said. 'It's not as if he has dozens of friends. There's only David Spikely and—'

'Charlie Nutter,' said Harry.

'That's right. Charlie Nutter,' I said. 'Do you know anything I don't?'

Once more, Harry looked thoughtful. 'He used to come here every day,' he said. 'Now he barely says hello. I got the feeling that maybe he was going through a rough patch, but he hasn't said anything.'

'What kind of a rough patch?'

Harry shrugged. 'Some boys find it hard to come out. Especially the son of a man like Stephen Nutter, MP. Maybe he came out to Harrington. And maybe Harrington didn't know how to process the facts, except through his father's preaching. Some people find it easier to believe in demonic possession than to believe a friend might be gay.'

For a moment I wasn't quite sure what he'd said. 'What do you mean, *gay*?'

He smiled. 'Sometimes you just know,' he said. 'Sometimes it shows early. And Charlie Nutter – let's just say I always thought Charlie was different. We talked about it once or twice.'

'You think Charlie Nutter's—'

'*Gay*. You can say it aloud, you know.'

His smile robbed the words of a possible sting. And remember, this was a long time ago: the word used far less commonly – and perhaps with more respect – than today.

He smiled again at my puzzled look. 'Go on. Say it aloud. It helps. At least, it always did for me.'

Once more, for a moment I paused. 'I'm still not sure what – oh.'

Oh. This may be hard to imagine now. But things were very different then. I'd never thought of my colleagues – my friends – in any other context than that of St Oswald's. I'd never been to Harry's house, or asked him about his personal life. It was different with Eric Scoones. We'd been schoolboys together. I'd known him since we were first-year Ozzies in blazers and caps. I'd been to his birthday parties, in the little White City house he still shares with his mother. We'd fought for the same scholarships; faced our bullies together; waged imaginary wars; drawn legions of stick-men across generations of Latin books, and if it had ever occurred to me that he might be somehow – *different*, I would never have mentioned it. But Harry – I'm not proud of this, but it floored me completely.

He saw my expression. 'Really, Roy? Did it never cross your mind?'

I had to admit that it had not. 'Who else have you told about this?' I said. 'Did you tell Nutter? Or Harrington? Or anybody else on the staff?'

He shrugged. 'I don't go out of my way to mention it, if that's what you mean. But why should I lie? I've done nothing wrong—'

Of course, he was right. He'd done nothing wrong. But was he really so naïve as to think *that* would make a difference? Even nowadays, to admit to being a homosexual – especially when teaching in a boys' school – is to incur suspicion and perhaps run the risk of dismissal. Twenty-four years ago, it was worse. Gay Liberation had barely begun. Harry knew the risk all right. He just didn't seem to care.

He gave me a wry look. 'Does it make a difference?'

'No. No. Why should it?' I lied.

The truth is that of course it did. It made me feel uncomfortable. I like to think I know languages, but this was a language I barely knew – the dialect of intimacy. I didn't like Harry any the less for what he'd just admitted to me, but to know that I'd been his friend for ten years, and never even suspected—

Was I really so naïve? The thought was profoundly disturbing. I'd always thought myself rather a good judge of people. So how could I have overlooked something so fundamental – something, I now realized, so blatantly, stupidly *obvious*?

It occurred to me then that I, too, could be seen in the same light. I, too, was unmarried. I, too, spent my lunch-times with the boys. Plus, I made no secret of the fact that I enjoyed Harry's company. Could anyone – a colleague, perhaps – have ever considered that *I* might be gay? Could the *boys* have believed it? I am not proud of admitting it, but the very thought filled me with horror.

No, I am not the most liberal of men. I never had the chance to be. My parents were ordinary northern folk, the products of their generation. My upbringing was St Oswald's, via a School bursary, then a dull university, then teaching in two lesser schools before St Oswald's claimed me again. By the time I was forty-two, I was as institutionalized as my parents – both of them long-term residents at the Meadowbank old people's home, not far out of Malbry.

Perhaps for that reason I appeared older than my years to Harry, whose background was very different, and whose lack of ambition and disregard for convention made him seem much younger than I. It strikes me now that one of the reasons I'm fond of young Allen-Jones is that he reminds me a little of Harry Clarke, especially in the eyes.

Harry took another Quality Street. 'You have that look on your face,' he said. 'That *anywhere-but-here* look. It only makes a difference, you know, if you allow it to matter. We all find comfort where we can, and who's to say that one kind of love is better, or more worthy?'

Of course he was right. I took his point. But this was all too personal, too unexpected for me to digest. We Tweed Jackets don't like to talk about our innermost feelings.

It's one of the reasons I'd rather teach boys than a gaggle of Mulberry girls. Boys have a pleasing lack of depth; an emotional inarticulacy that means they talk about football; books; music; TV; computer games; but rarely matters of the heart. Of course I know they *feel* things; but, thank gods, they seldom *share*.

I said: 'It's none of my business, old man. It won't make the slightest difference.'

He smiled, a little sadly, I thought. 'Have another chocolate.'

7

September 12th, 2005

Another day of surprises as the assault upon St Oswald's goes on. The first came just as I reached the School gates, which, as of today, are flanked with a billboard as big as a barn, depicting two young Spartans in St Oswald's uniform, apparently conducting some kind of experiment involving test tubes, smoke and crème de menthe, below the giant slogan, *Progress through Tradition*.

I took a few moments to remember where I'd heard the phrase before; then I identified it as part of Harrington's opening speech. Is this what he means by 'rebranding' the School? And what kind of a slogan is *Progress through Tradition*?

There were more of the photographs inside the School – the lobby and the Porter's Lodge – all framed in light oak and depicting schoolboys engaged in a variety of exciting-looking extracurricular activities: theatre; sculpture; trampolining; training with the Army Cadets; competing in cricket and rugby. None of the boys were pupils of ours, being clean, well dressed and suspiciously lacking in skin blemishes of any kind. But it will impress the parents, of course – which, I suppose, is Harrington's plan.

Personally, I prefer the battle-scarred lines of Honours Boards along the Lower and Middle Corridors, dating back to 1885 (not the School's Foundation, of course, but when the New Building was opened), inscribed with the names of our old boys, in gold leaf, on a dark oak ground.

Over the years, some of these boards have faded in the sunlight, and the combined effects of damp and heat have caused the wood to warp and shift, breaking the varnished surfaces into a honeyed crackle glaze. This is most obvious in the boards that happen to face a window; with the result that the corridors have become chequered in light and shade, passing from gold to amber, to black, shifting like the seasons. Some of the names on the sunniest boards have faded into transparency, becoming insubstantial, legible only in sunlight. Others are almost as fresh as the day they were painted – traditionally, by a Sixth-Form boy studying calligraphy – and if you look under the frame, you'll often find the signatures of the young artists, in Latin:

J. Jordan, scripsit.

P. Jolly, scripsit.

There is something very poignant about those names; those hopeful dates; those lists of awards. Boys who were dead before I was born immortalized in gold leaf, linking us all with past glories, every name a shared triumph, every scar a story. The School stopped commissioning Honours Boards when old Shitter Shakeshafte began his reign; but if you look on the Middle Corridor, opposite the window, you can still see, in the top right-hand corner, the name of R. H. Straitley – almost entirely faded away except for the last three letters, tucked into the side of the frame, gleaming out defiantly from a wedge of shadow.

Or so it was until today. This morning, on my way into School, halfway down the Lower Corridor, I found Jimmy Watt with a stepladder, taking down the Honours Boards, scars, stories and all.

'Sorry, boss,' he told me. 'Orders from the New Head. We're going to have display boards instead. You know, for the parents.'

I was too stunned to say anything. The spaces where the boards had hung were framed with dust, revealing the paintwork of decades past: powdery patches of sky-blue; iron-grey; or that curious hospital-green. Nowadays, the plasterwork is usually painted magnolia, with the wooden panels painted in brown to hide the scars; but no one paints *under* the Honours Boards, and the result looked unspeakably sad; a row of trompe-l'oeil windows, looking on to a blind wall.

'The *parents*?' I said at last. 'What the hell have the parents got to do with it? The Honours Boards belong to St Oswald's, they're not something you can just move because some bloody interior decorator tells you they're out of style!'

Jimmy looked mournful. 'Sorry, boss.'

I took a breath. There was no point in berating Jimmy – nicknamed 'Forty-Watt' by some of my less tolerant colleagues, he's paid to do what he is told, and would never argue with a superior.

'What kind of display boards?' I said.

Jimmy seemed to brighten a little. 'Nice ones. Like in the lobby,' he said.

For a moment I imagined it. *Progress through Tradition*. The Lower Corridor stripped of its past and converted into a glossy brochure. Yes, the parents would like it. The parents like anything that makes them believe that their money is buying them something more than just teachers, classrooms, chalk and dust. St Oswald's parents are paying fees that seem to them extortionate; and value for money, in their eyes, means more than traditions going back to the sixteenth century.

It means computers; science labs; impressive new facilities. As if a good schoolmaster wasn't worth a hundred new computers. I may have said something of the sort – I may even have raised my voice – because as I was expressing myself, Thing Two, aka Ms Buckfast, came out of the office that had once belonged to Pat Bishop and fixed me with the kind of smile a nurse might give to a lunatic.

'Is there a problem?' she said.

'Yes, I think there is,' I said. 'Much as I appreciate the quaint reasoning that led to the appointment of a Rebranding Guru, if that's what you are, St Oswald's has been standing for a lot longer than either of us. I don't think its demolition counts as progress of any kind.'

That might have been a little too blunt, I told myself, a little too late.

Ms Buckfast blinked at me. 'You must be Mr Straitley,' she said.

I gave her the Straitley 3D-stare, the one that works so well on boys who overstep the mark in class.

Ms Buckfast stared back, with a little smile that totally failed to reach her eyes. A rather attractive woman – well built, and with that striking red hair – but I can't help thinking there's something far too polished about that exterior, like a Christmas bauble, shiny on the outside, but hollow and easily broken. I wondered just *how* easily.

I said: 'In which case, you'll know my motto: *Verveces tui similes pro ientaculo mihi appositi sunt.*'

The smile did not waver for a second.

So, she doesn't know Latin, I thought. Her eyes were exactly the same shade of green as the paint beneath the Honours Boards from 1913 to 1915, and their expression was just as flat.

'I'm Rebecca Buckfast,' she said. 'The Head's told me all about you.'

'Has he now?'

'Oh, yes, he has. He's one of your biggest fans, you know.'

I grimaced. Somehow I doubted that.

'He says he always expected to hear that you'd been given a senior post. Second Master, Head of Year – maybe even the Headship.'

I had to laugh. 'A Headship?' You don't ask the barnacles on the hull which direction to steer in. Not that there'll *be* any barnacles once Johnny Harrington has finished with us.

'I was never Caesar,' I said. 'At best, a reluctant Cassius.'

She smiled. Once more, her eyes stayed cold. 'In which case, I think our motto should be *Victurus te saluto.*' And at that she went back to her office, leaving me with two conclusions.

One: Rebecca Buckfast may not be as brittle as I first thought.

Two: she *does* know Latin, after all.

8

September 12th, 2005

But that was only the start, I fear, of the New Head's expansion plan. The pigeon-holes in the Quiet Room have also been removed, in preparation for the new workstations, which will be delivered some time during the week. There are rumours of staff assessments, to be carried out throughout the term by various senior colleagues. Even more disturbing, I hear that the *boys* are being asked to contribute – rating facilities, even staff, with a view to making improvements.

My Brodie Boys make much of this. 'Three out of ten for punctuality, sir,' said Sutcliff, as I came in late for this morning's Registration.

'And only five for deportment,' said Allen-Jones, with a grin.

I looked at him over my spectacles. '*Aut disce aut discede*,' I said. 'Which, roughly translated, means, if you don't have your Latin homework ready for me by lunchtime, I shall be forced to reassess your after-school activities.'

Allen-Jones, who has been known to do his Latin homework at Break, during Assembly, or sometimes on the morning bus, gave me a look of reproach. 'Wouldn't that be *punitive*, sir? Dr Blakely says that we're at a very sensitive age. I could be suffering trauma right now.'

I pretended to cuff his ear. Allen-Jones pretended to dodge. It struck me then, that if Harrington – or any of his Crisis Team – had happened to walk past my room at that moment, they would have witnessed a member of staff appearing to assault a boy. I must tread more carefully. Like the Honours Boards, I am from another time, and I am certain Harrington wants nothing more than to see me retire. I must not give him the satisfaction of finding a reason to do so.

'I've heard they're selling the School fields.'

That was Sutcliff, whose father, a local property developer, can usually be counted upon to know such things.

'They try that every year,' said McNair. 'It never works. It's the old St Oswald's burial ground that always puts them off in the end.'

'The bones of generations past,' intoned Allen-Jones lugubriously. 'Boys who failed their Latin exams, doomed to lie under the sod.'

'*You*'d know all about that,' said McNair.

Allen-Jones pretended to hit him with a copy of Vergil. I wished my own unease could be dispelled as easily. The School fields – a buffer of land that separates the main grounds of St Oswald's from the encroaching estate beyond – have been part of the School since the first, and many Headmasters have tried and failed to sell them off for development. But remembering the Bursar's comment about the sale of School assets, my heart sank. The School doesn't have many assets to sell. A strip of waste land, bordered by hedges, more or less worthless at present; but if designated as building land, it could be worth millions.

That's what Johnny Harrington sees. Development potential. He does not see the open fields where generations of Ozzies have played. He does not see the birds' nests hidden in the hawthorn hedge, or value the horse-chestnut trees with their autumn load of conkers. Instead, he sees a new housing estate; perhaps a supermarket; investment in the future, not nostalgia for the past.

And yet, those fields are part of something that he cannot understand. Fifty years ago, Eric and I played at pirates under those trees. Fifty years from now, those trees will still be standing sentinel. The Captain of our old ship is bound for dangerous new territory, and only the gods – or a mutiny – can save us from his ambition.

And the most dangerous thing about Harrington is that he does have a measure of charm; unlike the last Headmaster – who had a tendency to lurk in his office, avoiding boys and members of staff in favour of mountains of paperwork – he likes to be seen around the School, greeting boys by name and flashing that heliographic smile. As a result, 4S have awarded him their highest accolade, declaring him to be 'all right', with admiring looks at that silver car.

Yes, I'm afraid that where status symbols are concerned, my boys are as shallow as Jimmy Watt, or Danielle, the School Secretary, who views all Headmasters as legitimate prey, and whose failure to captivate a Head over the past twenty years or so has forced her to lower her sights as far as the current Third Master (though Bob Strange, a bachelor, is far too canny to fall for the charms of a member of the ancillary staff).

Not that Johnny Harrington would be eligible in any case. The grapevine tells me that the man is safely, respectably married. The couple have no children, I am told – which is, I suppose, a mercy. No one wants the responsibility of having to teach the Headmaster's son; after all, some of us barely survived teaching the Headmaster.

Damn him. *Why* does he haunt me so? At my age, I don't sleep well, even at the best of times, and all this week my nights have been troubled by unquiet dreams of Harrington. It's strange, how a distant event can be so much more immediate than something that happened this morning: a set of house keys absently placed in a Tupperware box of sliced ham on the middle shelf of the refrigerator; slippers left outside in the rain; a volume of Ovid's poetry down the back of the sofa.

No, dammit, it *isn't* old age. It's just that the past has a habit of creeping up on a person, like a child in a game of Grandmother's Footsteps, before delivering the cry of *Gotcha! You're it!* – then slyly, cruelly, running away. I've tried to relax by the usual means – by going through my class records, copying out form-lists, listening to the wireless – but nothing seems to relieve that sense of something just behind me, moving with inexorable stealth towards the spot, just between my shoulder blades, where the knife is likely to fall.

Meanwhile, the occasional Gauloise or Liquorice Allsort sustains me, as Jimmy puts up the last of those glossy new promotion boards along the Middle Corridor. Surprisingly, the Bell Tower has been granted a reprieve from the Great Rebranding – perhaps because parents don't go that far. As a result we have retained the last half-dozen Honours Boards – shabby, faded and marvellous in every way – and I have made it clear to Ms Buckfast that I will defend them with my life.

Ms Buckfast seems unimpressed with this. Apparently Ms Buckfast – Rebecca, as she prefers to be known – has been inspecting the School since the end of July, noting its many deficiencies. Paintwork; water damage; asbestos; draughty windows; worn steps. Woodworm is the official explanation of the removal of the Honours Boards, which, she assures me, are being kept in storage until such time as the School can afford to have some of them restored.

'*Some* of them?'

That PR smile. 'Well, yes. Though tradition *is* important, we feel that a more approachable image will help raise the profile of the School and make it more competitive.'

'*Competitive!* What are we, a lacrosse team?'

She raised an immaculate eyebrow. 'King Henry's School came ninth in the Independent Schools League Tables this year.'

'Ah. That.' I rarely pay attention to league tables at the best of times, but no one would have expected St Oswald's to top the charts after the kind of year we've had. As for King Henry's – our rival school – they have been looking down on us since the end of the Hundred Years War. They had a rebranding of their own ten or fifteen years ago, and now they have mixed classes, a new theatre, an Olympic-sized swimming pool *and* something called Academy Status, as well as a full-time Promotion Team to sell their services to the world. We call their staff *Henriettas*. There isn't a Tweed Jacket among them.

'Well, much as we aspire to compete,' I said, 'I also happen to believe that certain things are worth keeping. *Augustus found a city of bricks and left a city of marble*. It doesn't work the other way round.'

Sadly, my opinion seems not to be shared by the majority. Dr Devine, who, as Health & Safety Officer, has been complaining about the state of the School since he was offered the post last year, scents a potential ally. I suspect that the Buckfast combination of shiny efficiency and a pretty face may have turned his head a little. In any case, I have found him smug and unsympathetic. He makes much of the five-year age gap between us (in spite of the fact that he was appointed almost at the same time), and likes to convey the impression that he has a youthful flexibility of mind, whereas I am set irrevocably in ways that have long since been obsolete.

'Face it, things are going to change,' he told me today in the Common Room. 'And those who refuse to change with the times are doomed to fall by the wayside.'

'That's rather poetic, Devine,' I said, helping myself to tea. 'They'll be asking you to write their slogans next. *Progress through Tradition*. Or is it the other way round?'

Devine gave his percussive sniff. 'I thought you'd cut up over those Honours Boards. But face it, we've been stuck in the past. The page has turned. And I, for one, am far from ready for the scrap heap just yet.'

Rather a speech for old Devine, whose nose had gone quite pink again. I found myself feeling almost sorry for him – at sixty, he is far too old for the post of Second Master, although, with typical arrogance, he has never considered this. The Crisis Team, as well he knows, is only a temporary measure. Once Harrington has established his rule, the deputies will be sent elsewhere. Which is when old Devine believes his chance for high office will emerge – a chance that has eluded him repeatedly over the years, like a glimmer of gold at the end of a cruel, fleeting rainbow.

'If you think the New Head will give you a sniff at any kind of promotion,' I said, 'then you're just as deluded as Bob Strange. He'll be looking for a younger man, someone he can pull from the ranks and fast-track with courses and IT. Someone like your new man – what did you say his name was again?'

'Markowicz,' said Dr Devine.

The topic of the new man is rather a sore spot for Devine. Appointed by the doctor himself, he comes so well recommended that he has not seen fit to appear as yet, leaving Devine to cover for him.

'Of course, if you think that toadying will earn you a place at the Headmaster's side, feel free to get in line,' I said. 'But the fact is, you, like the rest of us, come with too much baggage.'

That was putting it bluntly indeed – more bluntly, perhaps, than kindness allowed – but I was still feeling the outrage of those Honours Boards pulled from the walls, like the stripes from the faded uniforms of soldiers deserting in battle, and the prospect of our School fields being sold to pay for new IT facilities had filled me with a newly militant spirit.

Dr Devine did not reply, but the nose was pinkly eloquent. Instead he poured a cup of tea – he still uses the School's own china, disdaining those domestic mugs that most of our staff bring from home, reflecting their personalities – rambling roses for Kitty Teague; Homer Simpson for Robbie Roach; Padre Pio for the Chaplain and Princess Diana for Eric Scoones. No, Dr Devine's tea remains steadfastly corporate, balanced on a saucer too narrow to hold a biscuit. This time, it wobbled a little, as if his hand were not quite steady.

I said: 'It's Johnny Harrington. Don't tell me you've forgotten.'

'That was twenty-four years ago,' said Devine, avoiding my eye.

'No one changes *that* much. Look at you. Look at me.'

'*I* wasn't involved,' he said.

'*Bella gerant alii.*'

Whenever my Teutonic friend approaches the moral high ground, the judicious use of a Latin phrase can usually be relied upon to bring him back into the fray.

This time he looked up sharply and snapped: 'For God's sake, Straitley, if you think that because I didn't learn Latin at school I don't understand *every single one* of your little *bons mots* by now, then you're living in a dream world. *Someone else can fight the war*. Isn't that right? Well, yes, they can. I'm not going to jeopardize *my* career for the sake of a man who, for all we know, really *did*—' He quickly bit off the rest of the phrase. 'Well. I can't sit around here all day. I have Health & Safety reports to look through.' And he made his dignified exit, rather more quickly than usual.

I took another biscuit.

'Looks like you rattled his cage all right,' said Robbie Roach from across the room. 'What was it this time? *Lebensraum*?'

'A matter of honour,' I told him.

'Really? How quaint,' said Roach, and went back to his *Daily Mirror*.

9

September 13th, 2005

You can tell as much by a boy's schoolbag as by the inside of his locker. Little Johnny Harrington's was what they called an *attaché case*, a term that has gone out of vogue since laptop computers have replaced the need to carry such things as paper files.

Twenty-four years later, Dr Harrington, MBE, still carries the same kind of case; sleek black leather; expensive and with a combination lock to keep the contents secure. An old style for the young Harrington, whose contemporaries of '81 mostly had sports bags, or battered canvas satchels bought from the School Supplies shop, and one that set him apart from the rest in yet another intangible way.

Now, of course, most of our boys carry messenger bags or backpacks emblazoned with various rock bands, comic-book characters and computer games. These are against School regulations, but like the rule on School socks, I make no attempt to enforce this. The outside appearance of bags and boys are of far less interest to me than their contents, which is why, when young Allen-Jones came to find me today just as the bell rang for Lunch Break, I ignored the Wonder Woman satchel and went straight for the crux of the problem.

'Anything wrong, Allen-Jones? You're usually first in the lunch queue.'

He gave the ghost of his usual smile. 'I just wanted a word, sir.'

'Latin or English?'

'Both, sir.'

I reached into my top desk drawer and brought out the Liquorice Allsorts. 'Allsort?'

'No, thanks.'

'Now I'm getting worried,' I said. 'No one ever turns down an Allsort except for Dr Devine, who, as we know, has issues.'

'OK.' He took a pink one. 'Let's call it preventative action.'

'I think that's very wise,' I said.

I waited for him to finish his sweet, and used the opportunity to wipe down the blackboard – upon which in my absence, some youthful, exuberant hand had scrawled the oldest phonetic joke in the Latin book: *Caesar adarat forte. Brutus adsum jam. Caesar sic in omnibus. Brutus sic intram.* The oldest, silliest jokes are the best, and that one was old before I was. But it still comes out occasionally; like a Christmas bauble brought out every year, missing a little more glitter each time, but mellow with nostalgia. I find it reassuring; a reminder, perhaps, of more innocent times.

'Now, what's on your mind?' I said.

'Well,' said Allen-Jones. 'I'm gay.'

That *wasn't* what I'd expected to hear. As a rule, boys don't talk to me about their sexual proclivities, or, indeed, about anything of what you might call an intimate nature, traditionally preferring to confide in one of the French assistants – who are generally far more approachable than Dr Burke, the School Chaplain.

'Gay?' I repeated foolishly.

I thought of what Harry Clarke had described. *That anywhere-but-here look*. I wondered if I had that look now, and how often Harry had seen it before on the faces of his friends. As if being queer could be catching, somehow, the fear of contagion eclipsing the warmth. And yet my Brodie Boys seemed just as cheery as ever. I remembered them talking the other day about the impending Mulberry girls – *this class is a fruit-free zone* – and how they'd all laughed. How I wish I'd been able to laugh like that with Harry Clarke. Instead, it was awkward for a while, after which we never spoke of it again.

Allen-Jones just looked at me. He has a very direct gaze, rather adult for such a young boy. 'It's just that I thought I should tell you, sir. In case it causes problems.'

'Problems?' I said. 'What do you mean?'

He shrugged in a rather world-weary way, more suited to my own age than his. 'Well, it's hardly what you'd call a sympathetic environment,' he said. 'I mean, much as I love the dear old place, it's more of a rugby-and-chapel place than a stage for musical theatre.'

I took a breath. 'I see,' I said. 'Well, as far as I'm concerned, unless this somehow affects your ability to do your Latin homework, I don't think we'll have a problem. In fact, unless you need my advice, I'll probably forget about it altogether.'

Allen-Jones looked a little startled, as if he'd expected resistance. 'Really?'

I helped myself to an Allsort. 'You seem surprised.'

He grinned. 'No, sir. It's just that – other people aren't always as – well.'

'What other people?'

'The Chaplain.'

I was surprised. 'You *told* him?'

'No, of course not,' said Allen-Jones.

St Oswald's – which has no official School counsellor – has always encouraged boys to go to the School Chaplain for spiritual and moral guidance, but as far as I know, few boys do this. The fact is that Dr Burke, though sound in his way, and well meaning, is most definitely one of the Old Guard. A member of staff since the sixties, unmarried and wholly devoted to his work, he has encountered, in his role as School Chaplain, such diverse aspects of adolescent behaviour as drug abuse, anorexia, glue-sniffing, depression, various mental disorders and, of course, sexual issues of all kinds, none of which he had previously encountered, and which even now fill him with disbelief. The thought that one of our boys might be a friend – or even a passing acquaintance – of Dorothy would probably leave him speechless.

The Chaplain's answer to most things is *Pull yourself together, boy,* often combined with instructions to play more outdoor sports (he was a rugby man in his youth, and still has the nose to show for it). Nowadays our boys prefer to shelter him from Life's more brutal realities and to take their problems to a different confessional; that of the Modern Languages lab, where the youthful French assistants are available, both for linguistic advice and contemporary, Gallic sympathy.

'It started last term,' said Allen-Jones. 'The Chaplain teaches me RE. And when he sets us homework, I have to go into his form-room to hand it in.'

This is common practice at St Oswald's; members of staff setting homework sometimes prefer to have it marked before they see the boys again. As Allen-Jones's story emerged, I began to understand his concern. Apparently, a fifth-form boy by the name of Rupert Gunderson has been giving him trouble since the beginning of term.

'What kind of trouble?' I said.

He shrugged. 'Every time he sees me, he hits me and calls me names. It's really very tedious, sir.' A tiny tremor in his voice indicated how close he was to tears. 'I have to go into the Chaplain's room to hand in my RE homework. And now it's Gunderson's form-room. I see him all the time. And this morning he said if I came in again, he'd – well. I'd rather not say, sir.'

'I see.'

It all made sense to me now. Of course, Dr Burke never spends more time in his form-room than he absolutely needs to. It's a Middle Corridor room, not very far from the Chapel, where he has a very nice office, in which he likes to spend his free time listening to choral music and looking after his collection of orchids.

I considered Gunderson. An undersized, aggressive boy to whom I'd once taught Latin (with little success), I wasn't surprised to hear that he had found someone younger to bully.

'I know him,' I said. 'I'll have a word. He won't trouble you any longer.'

Once more, Allen-Jones looked surprised. 'But you don't have any proof,' he said.

'I don't need proof,' I told him. 'I know Gunderson. I know you. It's really quite straightforward.'

For some reason, this didn't seem to reassure him as much as I'd hoped.

'What's wrong?' I said.

'I thought you'd need proof, sir.'

'Well, I don't.'

'I could *give* you proof.' And, keeping his back to the glass door, he lifted his shirt to show me a complex arrangement of duct tape strapped around his skinny ribs, holding in place something that looked to me like a toy walkie-talkie.

'What on *earth*?' I began.

He explained his projected scheme. Allen-Jones is a bright boy, though he sometimes over-complicates things. In this case, his solution to the Gunderson problem was characteristically elaborate. He planned to take this contraption around to Gunderson's form-room, where, he assured me, he would be duly menaced by Gunderson, and I would be able to listen in by means of a *second* receiver, connected to a recording device, which would permit Allen-Jones to take the evidence straight to the Head of Middle School, and thereby to Thing One and Thing Two, and yea, unto the Head himself—

I interrupted this fantasy. 'I don't need evidence,' I said. 'Trust me. Henceforth, at your approach, young Gunderson will melt away like the snows of yesteryear. Do you have a book to hand in?'

Allen-Jones nodded.

'Then come with me. We'll face the beast together.'

10

September 14th, 2005

I'll confess, it has been some time since I had to get angry. Over the course of thirty-four years, I've earned a reputation; and nowadays I find that I need not raise my voice more than two or three times a year, usually with a New Boy as yet unacquainted with the ropes. Still, there's no harm in beginning a term with a nice big bang, especially if there's a bully involved. I followed Allen-Jones to the Chaplain's room and lingered outside the frosted-glass door for just long enough for Gunderson to incriminate himself.

Gunderson was at his desk, holding court to a circle of friends. The Chaplain, once a rugby man, has a soft spot for sportsmen, and Gunderson, though academically weak, happens to be on the rugby team. He has grown since I taught him, acquiring a sheath of muscle. But the face remains the same; the pinched and slightly simian look, grinning with mean enjoyment.

He stood up as Allen-Jones came in. 'I thought I told you last time,' he said. 'No queers allowed in here.'

Allen-Jones walked up to the desk, looking nervous, but composed. 'Why? Do you feel threatened?' he said. 'Or is it because I don't fancy you?'

The other boys – Gunderson's friends – had stood up in solidarity. Now they stared at the younger boy as if they couldn't believe what he'd said.

'You're dead,' said Gunderson, making a lunge for Allen-Jones.

Allen-Jones dodged, only to be caught by two of Gunderson's friends. At this point, I made my entrance, just as Gunderson was about to administer the beating. The boys let go of Allen-Jones as if he were on fire.

'Exactly what is going on?'

Gunderson just stared at me. Allen-Jones made for the door as I moved in for the kill. I shan't bore you with the details of what I said to Gunderson, but it began in the percussive whisper I like to use when hypnotizing prey, and finished with a cannonade that resonated all the way down the Middle Corridor and brought boys' heads to classroom doors like razor clams to the shoreline.

That should have been the end of it. At any other time, it would have been – but Harrington's influence in the School is already becoming apparent. Whatever leads a boy to complain about some aspect of School life – be that a method of teaching Latin, a choice of set text in English or a Master's way of enforcing discipline – the rot is already spreading.

Yes, there's an atmosphere in School; something vaguely unsavoury. Not at all like last year – when a *Mole* managed to infiltrate its way inside our not-so-hallowed gates and wreak the kind of havoc that such creatures of the dark may plan – but nevertheless, I can feel it.

It seems that Gunderson has complained – to his parents, and via them, to his form-tutor – about yesterday's intervention. The result – a summons from Dr Burke – was delivered to room 59 at the end of School by a member of the Junior Choir, and I obeyed with some reluctance and a looming sense of foreboding.

I found the Chaplain in his office, lovingly misting his orchids. He has a surprising number of these, although I confess I don't see the appeal. There's something rather unwholesome about those fleshy, mottled heads; so like the pattern of freckles on the Chaplain's own head, which has been bald since I've known him. The spider plants in my form-room are more appropriate to St Oswald's; like our boys, they require virtually no attention, tolerate water but do not demand a complex delivery system, and respond more positively to neglect than to sensitive handling.

He turned towards me as I came in. 'Ah. Straitley. *Gunderson.*'

The Chaplain is a man of few words. A fact generally appreciated by the boys in Chapel – and, in his day, on the rugby pitch – but which in this case gave his words a somewhat brusque delivery.

'What about him, Chaplain?' I said.

'Parents complained to the Head,' said Burke. 'Said you humiliated the boy in front of half the Upper School. Boy's got issues, apparently. Seeing a child psychologist. HM says we need a policy to help us deal with vulnerable boys.'

'Vulnerable?' I said. 'I'll have you know that Gunderson was having a go at one of *my* boys.'

The Chaplain looked pained. 'Who, Gunderson? Surely not. Wouldn't hurt a fly, you know.'

I took a moment to convey what I thought of Gunderson, his hurt feelings, his psychologist and his parents. Then I explained about Allen-Jones.

The Chaplain looked vaguely bewildered, and said: 'The boy told you that? Said he was queer?'

I admitted that he had.

The Chaplain raised his eyebrows. 'Funny thing to tell a chap. No wonder Gunderson was upset. But that's not what I called you for. Fact is, I've had a communication.' He held out a piece of paper. 'Thought you ought to know, Roy. This part was addressed to you.'

I knew at once. Don't ask me how; perhaps because he'd called me Roy. All the same, I went through the motions of expressing surprise and concern; even though I was swimming through a cold and lightless tunnel of dread. The worst of it was, I'd expected it – known of it – for twenty years, sensed it hanging over me like the sword of Damocles. And how appropriate that it should come *right now*, with Johnny Harrington back on the scene, with his black sack of memories.

I took the piece of paper. A single sheet of cheap blue bond, of the kind they sell in prisons and long-term mental institutions. No date; no address; closely written in blunt grey pencil, in Harry's unmistakable hand – slanting, almost feminine, with an academic flourish that was worthy of a better, nobler instrument:

Dear Roy,

It's been a while since I wrote to you, but really, nothing much happens here, and I'd rather hear about life in St Oswald's than bore you with tales of the everyday. People have been generally good, and have kept me in touch with developments. Eric wrote to me once or twice, and the Chaplain, and 'SS'. I heard he died soon afterwards. A pity. He was a good man. Certain men seem to project something of immortality.

But no one really escapes in the end. Not from the past, not from ourselves, and especially not from St Oswald's. Which is why I write to you now, after a silence I hope you'll forgive, but dying is a dull enough business, even for the interested party, without having to inflict the tedium on to others. Suffice it to say that I'm comfortable – at least as much as I can expect. One institution isn't very much different from another, although here, of course, they have better soap, and rather more flexible visiting hours.

I thought of getting in touch again, once I was free to do so. I'm still not sure why I didn't; except that, after what happened last year, I didn't want St Oswald's to suffer further embarrassment. An old friend is caring for me now, and will be with me at the end. So instead of writing, which tires me, I have made my Will, of which, as you'll see, I have asked Dr Burke to be the executor.

There isn't much to execute. I don't have much, although I have left you and Eric a couple of keepsakes, which I hope you'll accept in memory of our friendship. I've left the rest to the School, of course. My funeral is paid for. I've always despised those who left the arrangements to others. I've asked Dr Burke if he can hold the service in the Chapel. As for my ashes, just scatter them somewhere in the School grounds.

Ubi bene, ibi patria. (I think that's what you used to say.) And thank you for staying in touch, Roy, when so many others slipped away.

Ad astra per aspera,
Harry

I read the letter twice. How very like him it sounded. I could almost hear his voice; warm and somehow woody, like a good old piano. Gods, how I've missed Harry Clarke;

his humour, his friendship, his decency. *Ad astra*. To the stars. If only I believed it.

I turned to the Chaplain. 'When did he die?'

'Last month. In an old people's home. They've already had the cremation.'

Of course. A man of seventy, childless, unmarried, living off the state – of course. Why waste time with ceremony? Why even bother telling his friends?

'But what about the service?' I said. 'The service in the School Chapel?'

The Chaplain looked slightly uncomfortable. 'Not a good idea, Roy.'

'Who says?' I demanded.

'Who do you think?'

The Head, of course.

'And maybe he's right,' the Chaplain went on. 'No one remembers Harry Clarke, and maybe that's the way it should stay. Water under the bridge, and all that. Forward, not back.'

'*Progress through Tradition?*' I said, so angry now that I could see little flecks of brilliance dancing between us, like fireflies. The invisible finger that still sometimes jabs its warning into the caesura between my third and fourth waistcoat-button applied a note of pressure.

'Don't be like that, Roy,' the Chaplain said. 'You know it wouldn't make sense. Don't want the papers all over us, not after the year we've had. Not when things are looking up.'

'And – *are* they looking up?' I said.

'Nowhere left to look down at, Roy,' he said, turning back to his orchids. 'Face it, we're in crisis. That's why we've got a Crisis Head. This Head fails, the School goes down. We're all in it together.'

11

September 14th, 2005

I made my way home through Malbry Park. I've always liked that place. It's safe; its changes are always predictable. The leaves are already autumnal now; a sparrow-like scatter of small boys were throwing sticks at a horse-chestnut tree, without much success. The tree is old, and takes its time; the conkers not quite ready. In a week or two, however, they will be plump and glossy.

I used to like conkers as a boy; of course, in those days there was no Devine to tell us all how reckless we were. In those days our pockets were full of them – strikers and chippers and smashers – and our combats were gladiatorial all around the Lower Quad, with the heroes carried in state on the shoulders of the adoring crowd, while the vanquished slunk off, unnoticed, unmourned, to rejoin the proletariat.

I thought about Harry, dying alone to spare his friends the tedium. And I thought about the last time we'd met, and felt a pang that it should have been so many years ago.

What happened to the three of us? What happened to our friendship? It's hard to think back to those days now, not because my memory fails but because I remember too clearly. That's the price we pay, of course, for having survived St Oswald's so long. Current events blur and recede, while the past becomes clear and pitiless. Passing the Thirsty Scholar, I stopped for a modest libation, and found the place full of strangers, laughing and talking and living their lives.

A brandy, I think. For Harry Clarke. And another for myself.

I don't suppose I shall sleep tonight. As if I didn't have enough on my mind, with the Honours Boards, and the pigeon-holes, and Gunderson, for whom I shall draft a letter – a sharply worded letter, I think, pointing out the fact that when parents are incapable of curbing their son's bullying tendencies, we of the Old Guard are forced to invoke the time-honoured rule – *in loco parentis.* What happens in School should stay in School. Isn't that what they pay us for?

And as for the Head – whose toxic interference in every aspect of School life has become far too disturbing to be dispelled by a *podex* joke, a Liquorice Allsort or a Gauloise – I find myself, for the first time, considering our erstwhile *Mole* with something approaching sympathy. The interloper within our walls knew how to bring down a citadel with nothing but guile and a handful of stones – and tonight, as I drink my brandy, I wonder where that *Mole* is now. Gone to ground? In prison? Dead? Watching our decline from afar?

This Head fails, the School goes down.

At least, the Chaplain thinks so. But Caesar was killed to *save* Rome from his monstrous ambition. And now, for the first time, I think I can see why a loyal son of St Oswald's might contemplate that treachery, and I wondered if, in *our* Senate, there might perhaps be a Brutus to Johnny Harrington's Caesar.

12

Michaelmas Term, 1981

Dear Mousey,

It's been a week since Poodle confessed to me about his Condition. Since then, he hasn't been looking too good. People have started to notice. In Poodle's case, it didn't take long for those telltale signs to reveal themselves. Besides, he has a history. And history always repeats itself.

No, not like *my* history. Something from his junior school, involving a local boy from the estate. Nothing much, just show-and-tell. But Poodle's mother went crazy. Not so much because her boy was doing the dirty round the back of the bike sheds, but because of the *other* boy; a boy who wasn't One of Us. That's why his little secret could never stay a secret for long. And now this thing with the magazines and the hidey-hole by the clay pits, which everyone knows is a meeting place for perverts and drunks and scum of all kinds, as well as boys from Abbey Road, the technical school on the estate, which has bars on the windows and pebble-dashed mobile classrooms all around the central building, like calves around a concrete cow.

That's why they sent Poodle to Middle School instead of starting St Oswald's. They thought that the healing presence of girls would cure whatever was wrong with him. And of course they prayed – well, *everyone* prayed – so that when the trouble died down at last (or Poodle learnt to control himself), he could make a fresh start as a Seventh Term Boy, all neat and clean and virginal.

That was the idea, at least. But now, with the start of Advent, it's open season on demons. We've had some new faces in Church recently, with lots of visiting speakers. Mr Speight is one of them. He's very big on demons. He gave a talk on Dungeons & Dragons, that American role-playing game, and how it preys on the weak-minded and encourages boys to use magic and to conjure Satan in their hearts. Then there was the speaker who was cured of homosexual thoughts by fasting and electricity; a woman whose son was lured away from her by the gay community; and this Sunday, a preacher from one of our sister churches in America, who brought a ton of leaflets directing parents how to deal with sons who might be having gay thoughts, and who wore yellow cowboy boots and a T-shirt that said KICK OUT THE SIN, LET JESUS IN!

That was a good one, actually. We got chocolate brownies. And all the time, Poodle was looking at me, like *I* was the one who had done something wrong. Which is unfair, don't you think? It's not *my* fault he has gay thoughts. I'm not the one who should feel guilty.

Afterwards he came up to me. We were having brownies and squash. Goldie was talking to Mr Speight in the little chapel. 'You told, didn't you?' he said, making sure no one else heard.

'No I didn't,' I said (it was true).

'So how come everyone's suddenly talking about it?' He glared at me. 'Coincidence?'

I shook my head. 'Don't be paranoid. No one's mentioned you – *yet*.'

Poodle pulled a face. 'They will. My mum's been going through my things. My dad's been asking questions. It's not like they're subtle, or anything.'

'So? You just deny it.' I didn't see why he needed to *tell*. He could have lied, even to me. But Poodle isn't like that. He always ends up confessing things. So far, he hasn't spoken out about his Condition to anyone else. But his complexion speaks for itself, as does his greasy hair and the fact that for the past few lunchtimes he's been hiding out in the library and not eating anything—

He says it's a stomach bug. I know it's not. It's a cancer, eating away at him. And he hates himself. The more he talks about it, the more you realize that. He thinks his Condition is something that he can put aside, not think about, not deal with. He thinks he deserves to be punished, and so he pinches and slaps himself. I've seen him doing it, when he thinks that nobody's looking. And the other day in Games, there was a row of sticking plasters up his arm. Well, Mousey, you know what *that* means.

'I think I can help,' I told him.

He looked at me with hopeful-dog eyes.

'But only if you *want* to be cured,' I said. 'I mean it. This is serious.'

Poodle nodded eagerly.

'Plus you can't tell *anyone*. Not your parents, or Straitley—'

'I'd never talk to Straitley, Zig.'

'All right,' I said. 'We'll give it a try. Meet at the clay pits this afternoon. Four o'clock. Tell Goldie to come. And tell him not to tell anyone.'

* * *

By four o'clock it was nearly dark. I'd been there for almost an hour. That's how long it takes, realistically, for the rats to start to come out. There are rats by the clay pits. There's always something to scavenge. Leftover sandwiches. Dead things. Stuff that people have dumped there. I'd brought some bait. Not cheese, though. That only works for cartoon mice. Rats like meat. I brought dog food. Dog food always worked before.

The trap was simple. I made it myself. Chicken wire on a frame, with a door that slides open and shut. You put the food inside. You loop a piece of fishing-line through the top of the door. You pull the door up, using the fishing-line. You practise pulling the door up, then letting it drop. You do it a few times, to get it right. Rats are pretty clever. If you miss, they'll never come back. Then you run your piece of line somewhere quiet and out of the way. Like an old abandoned car. Then you wait for Ratty.

Ratty must have been hungry today. I got him in twenty minutes. Of course, rats get hungry in winter. Or maybe I've just had practice. Anyway, there he was in the cage, a young rat, brown, with long whiskers, sniffing anxiously at the food. You could tell he wanted to eat it. But he was worried about the cage, and the fact that the door was shut. I went to have a look at him. He looked back at me nervously. I could see him wringing his paws. Yes, I thought. He'd do nicely.

At four o'clock Goldie arrived, with Poodle trailing after him. I'd been sitting in Poodle's den, wrapped in my duffel coat to keep warm. I'd brought my Bible and found the right place. I'd left the cage, with Ratty inside, at the back of the old car. When Poodle saw it, his eyes went round.

'What's that?'

'What do you think?'

In his cage, Ratty was still wringing his paws and sniffing at the wire.

Goldie came closer. 'Why've you got a rat?' he said.

I said: 'I'll tell you later. First of all, Poodle's got something to say.'

Poodle looked at me. 'What?' he said.

'I promised I wouldn't tell,' I said. 'But for us to help you, you have to come clean. It's like what Mr Clarke says. All you need is courage.'

Poodle's eyes went even rounder. He shook his head.

'Come on,' I said. 'You want to be cured, don't you?'

'Ziggy, you're crazy,' said Poodle. 'How's a rat going to cure me?'

I opened my Bible and read from it. '*And they came over to the other side of the sea, into the country of the Gadarenes. And when he was come out of the ship, immediately there met him out of the tombs a man with an unclean spirit.*'

'You've got to be joking,' said Poodle.

I went on. '*And always, night and day, he was in the mountains, and in the tombs, crying, and cutting himself with stones.*'

'It isn't like that,' said Poodle.

I looked at the flooded clay pits, the broken-down cars, the dead TVs and the hills of junk. 'Isn't this the wilderness?' I said. 'Isn't this the mountains and the tombs?'

Poodle didn't say anything. I told him, 'Go on. Roll up your sleeves.'

He shook his head. I grabbed his arm. Pushed up the sleeve of his parka. There they were again, like I'd seen, the ladder of pink sticking plasters going up his wrist and arm all the way to the elbow.

I shrugged and looked at Goldie. 'Well?'

Goldie looked uncertain.

'Look, it's in the Bible,' I said. '*The wages of sin is death.* Right?'

Goldie nodded. Poodle, too.

'And being queer is a sin. Right?'

Poodle made a strangled sound.

'That's why we need a sacrifice. To wash the sin away,' I said. 'It's all in the Bible. The blood of the Lamb. He gave his life, that we might live.'

I ended up doing most of the work. Goldie said the words, though; I wasn't going to let him off without even a speaking part. Poodle cried a bit when I made him put his hand in the cage, but as I explained, we needed him to make contact. And Goldie was always a talker; just like his preacher father, in fact: and once I'd explained what was needed, he managed to come up with the goods.

'This man has been infected with the demon of homosexuality. Get thee hence, foul demon; enter into the soul of this rat and leave Thy humble servant alone.'

By then, Poodle was crying a lot. I guessed it must be the demons. Or maybe it was just relief; the relief of sharing the burden; of having someone take it away. I know what that feels like, Mousey. Don't you? It's good to confess to *someone*, even if they're already dead. *Especially* if they're already dead – that way, no one gets to tell tales.

Then I drowned the rat in its cage.

Well, it worked for the Gadarene.

PART THREE

Qui desiderat pacem, praeparet bellum.
(Vegetius)

1

September 15th, 2005

A term at St Oswald's, like a good book, takes some time to reach full velocity. Like the Juggernaut, it rolls; slowly at first, but inexorably over the days and weeks of the year, usually reaching cruising speed at around the third week of the Michaelmas term, when the terrain starts to get rocky.

I suspect that this term, that moment has arrived sooner than usual. Already, the New Head has introduced certain elements that may prove most disruptive to me – not least, the arrival yesterday of the first of my Mulberry girls.

I am fortunate, I suppose. I have only a handful of girls, all of them Sixth-Form students. They arrived in room 59 just before the beginning of Period 2, accompanied by Miss Lambert, the Headmistress of Mulberry House, and a strong scent of something both musky and sugary, like civet cats in a sweet shop.

Providentially, I was free during Period 1 that day. I dread to think of the disruptive effect on a class of Middle School boys of the arrival of a phalanx of Mulberry girls – out of uniform, of course (their Sixth Form doesn't have one), and exhibiting all the sartorial subtlety of an evening in Bangkok. Miss Lambert herself – a blonde, by choice – was wearing a shocking-pink tweed ensemble with a very short skirt and very high heels, plus an Aztec abundance of jewellery.

'Girls, this is Roy Straitley,' she said, as if introducing some interesting museum exhibit, previously encountered only in books.

Then, turning to me, she said: 'I thought I'd introduce the girls myself. They're *such* fun, aren't you, girls? This is Frankie, Helena, Chanelle, Angelina, Paris and Ben. Ben's real name is Benedicta, but she'd rather be called Ben, wouldn't you, dear?' She gave me a smile, half-lipstick, half-teeth. '*All* my girls use given names as soon as they enter the Sixth Form. It gives them a sense of community. And they call me Jo, don't you, girls?'

The girls acquiesced, with varying degrees of enthusiasm. Miss Lambert sets the house style among the girls of Mulberry House. A Mulberry girl, as she often says, is confident; ambitious; up-to-date and popular. From what I could see, they were also rather on the flashy side, long-legged and short-skirted, with the exception of the one she'd called Ben, a small-featured, vaguely mousey girl, who looked embarrassed to be there.

'Now I'll leave you in Roy's capable hands,' announced Miss Lambert to the girls. 'The rest of the class should be here before long. Now remember what I said. *Know your place*. Which is, of course, at the top of the class, looking down at all those boys.'

At which she made her exit, amid sycophantic laughter from the girls (except for the one she'd called Ben, whom I was rather beginning to like), leaving me to explain to them that while I occupy the Bell Tower, I shall remain

Mr Straitley, regardless of how forbidding that seems to girls who call their Headmistress *Jo*.

The rest of the lesson, I'm afraid, was spent in trying to reconcile my own methodology (tried and tested over thirty-four years at St Oswald's) with that of girls who, since their first year at Mulberry House, have been trained to believe that Latin is *fun*, and should include as little actual work (such as grammar, prose translation or literature) as possible. The three boys in my Lower Sixth who have opted for Latin this year were rendered speechless by the fact that the Mulberry girls had spent most of last year watching films, rather than learning the language. I myself have grave doubts as to the historical authenticity of such cinematic treats as *Gladiator*, but apparently the mistress hitherto responsible for teaching Classics at Mulberry House is in fact a history specialist – with the result that Classics became Classical Studies, a combination subject in the form of coursework modules, chosen by the girls themselves.

Most of them seem to have chosen some aspect of Roman fashion, with the exception of the girl Benedicta, who – rather defiantly, it seems – decided to study Cicero.

In other news, Devine's new man, Markowicz, has finally arrived. A Suit, as I'd expected. Apparently he wasn't here at the very beginning of term because he was teaching some kind of course on new methods of using IT in Languages. A sandy individual with eyes of a curious, grapey green, he wears the same silk ties as Devine, drinks from the School china like Devine and speaks the same language as Devine – that is, the dialect of bureaucracy, customer satisfaction and general smugness.

Devine is delighted, of course. It's like having a bonsai version of himself.

'I thought it was supposed to be bad luck to meet your *Doppelgänger*,' I said.

'You mean young Markowicz?' He smiled. 'I think he'll shape up perfectly.' He glanced through the frosted glass of the door right opposite his office, where Markowicz happened to be teaching a class of first-years. I'm not sure what was happening in there, but whatever it was, it was noisy. I said as much to Dr Devine, who just smiled again in that supercilious way and said:

'Yes, a refreshingly modern approach. I wouldn't expect *you* to know anything about *that*, Straitley.'

'*Stercus accidit*, Devine,' I said, without much enthusiasm. Since Devine revealed his secret knowledge of my saltier Latin phrases, insulting him has become less amusing.

I retreated to room 59, that bastion of civilization. Even so, I could still hear Markowicz and his German class, apparently re-enacting the rise and fall of the Third Reich.

I took a Liquorice Allsort and tried not to care about the noise. Discipline within the German Department falls to Devine to enforce. Whatever the provocation, I knew that I could not intervene, not without breaching etiquette. Still, if the new man can't handle a first-form German class without having to resort to glove puppets and juggling, just think what he'll be like with my 4S.

As for the two new additions to the French staff – only time will tell, I suspect. Miss Smiley, a wispy blonde, seems to have only Lower School boys, which accounts for her nursery manner in class – I've heard her bleating through the wall. Miss Malone is more of a foghorn, better suited to cutting through the riotous Friday afternoons, but I'm beginning to suspect that she may be all noise and no substance. In any case, the Foghorn was ringing out all today from various parts of the Upper Corridor, and by the end of School she seemed all too eager to leave the premises. The fact is that, although our boys are generally sound, they are also unusually spirited. Their values – such as they are – instilled by many years of rebelling against the management, are more on the lines of questioning authority than submitting to the yoke. This is why St Oswald's boys go on to achieve so many diverse and impressive things, but to teachers like the Foghorn they do present a challenge. From this afternoon's performance, I suspect that my 4S have found themselves a new toy.

As for Johnny Harrington—

I never liked him as a boy, and as an adult, even less. But I never imagined that even he could be as callous as to deny Harry Clarke his dying wish – to rest in peace in the place he'd loved most—

The Chaplain had warned me to let it go. To rake up that old business again would only harm St Oswald's. I knew that, of course. I knew he was right. And yet I couldn't take his advice. I couldn't let Harrington win again. Harry deserved better than that. And so, at the end of School today, I went to see the Headmaster.

I found his office door shut, in spite of his having promised us that it would always be open. Danielle, who forms the first line of defence between the Headmaster and the outside world, looked at me with sympathy.

'He's in there with Dr Markowicz,' she said, consulting her diary. 'Could you see Dr Blakely instead? He's free after School on Thursday.'

I informed her in cogent terms that I had no desire to deal with Thing One.

'In that case, he could do Friday Break,' said Danielle. 'Unless it's really urgent—'

'It *is*.'

We finally agreed that the Head might see me tomorrow morning. 'He comes in *very* early,' she said. 'If you could get here at seven fifteen—'

'Seven fifteen? He must *sleep* here.'

Danielle gave me the kind of smile she reserves for boys who have missed their bus, lost their lunch money or skinned their knees in the playground.

'I know,' she said. 'He's *wonderful*.'

Oh, gods. Not you, too. But I refrained from comment; knowing from past experience that to argue with a School Secretary is as futile as it is dangerous. Instead I went to the Quiet Room to calm my nerves with a cup of tea.

I found Eric at one of the Head's new workstations, glumly trying to access his e-mails at the computer.

'Bloody Harrington,' I said, filling my mug with tea from the urn. 'Who does he think he is, eh? *My door's always open.* Yes, as long as you're here to complain about some poor sap doing his job, but when it comes to a dying man's last wish—'

Eric looked up from the screen. 'You've heard about old Harry, then?'

'Yes. And if Harrington—'

He made a hushing gesture. 'Please, Straitley. Not so loud.'

'What? You're taking *his* side?'

He looked vaguely distressed. 'Look, Straitley, it isn't that. I just think maybe the Chaplain's right. What good can come of digging things up? Especially now, after all this time.'

'Harry deserves better than this. We owe him that memorial.'

'Now you're just being stubborn,' he said, still keeping his voice low. 'I know how you felt about Harry. But all that was such a long time ago, and we still have a job to do. *In medio stat virtus* – no? *Virtue takes the middle ground*. There's no point in sticking your neck out, now. Not for ancient history.'

I should have known. I *do* know – Eric is no hero. When we were boys, he was always the one who liked to play the percentages; who knew when to fight and when to run, while I always stayed, whatever the odds, whatever the size of the enemy. It has made me the Master I am today – that all-or-nothing mentality, that teaches boys not to mess with Straitley because he's crazy and *never gives up* – while Eric, for all his gruffness, has a tenderness inside, a weakness all too evident to boys trained to go for the jugular.

Still, I'd hoped for more loyalty – to Harry, and St Oswald's. I'd hoped that, this time, Eric might have chosen courage over self-interest. I poured another mug of tea and took it back to my form-room, once more feeling the imperious digit of my incipient heart condition moving along my ribcage, as if selecting the best place to strike. I tried not to take it personally, but – and not for the first time – Eric had disappointed me.

I found the new cleaner in room 59, watering my spider plants. He looked up as I opened the door.

'I hope you don't mind, Mr Straitley,' he said. 'But I noticed your plants needed watering.'

'You'll only get them used to it. Before we know it they'll be going on strike, demanding more sunlight and a better grade of compost.'

Winter shrugged. 'I don't mind. I'm already looking after the Chaplain's orchids.'

'He trusts you with his *orchids*?' I said. 'You must be some kind of a hypnotist. No one touches those orchids. They're like the children he never had.'

Winter smiled. 'I know,' he said. 'But those orchids and I are old friends. The Chaplain gave one to my ma when she left St Oswald's.' He went on to explain: 'Ma was one of the cleaners here. She used to bring me with her, sometimes, when I was a little boy.'

I looked at him more closely. Brown hair; blue eyes. Late thirties, at a guess. A face that could easily pass unseen, and yet he'd looked oddly familiar. Given he lives in White City, I'd thought that maybe I had seen him around. But if he'd come here as a boy, thirty years ago, give or take—

I said: 'I *do* remember you. You're Gloria's boy.'

'That's right,' he said.

Gloria Winter, she must have been. I remember her rather well. In those days, the cleaners were all women, and we called them by their Christian names – not from any sense of superiority, but simply because it gave us the illusion of female companionship.

I told you I remember distant events far more clearly than recent ones: I reached into my pocket for my Liquorice Allsorts, having forgotten that I'd slipped them into my desk drawer; and yet her face came back to me with remarkable clarity. A rather attractive woman, if a little hard-featured, with crow-black hair and those Spanish eyes. And now I think I remember him too, a solemn boy of seven or eight, who would sit and watch from the stairs while his mother walked the polishing-machine up and down the parquet floors of the Middle Corridor.

He looked at me now – with amusement, I thought, perhaps remembering Straitley as was, in the days of my empire.

'How is Gloria?' I said.

'Oh, Ma died a long time ago.'

'I'm very sorry to hear that,' I said.

He shrugged and emptied the waste-basket into a black bin-liner. 'You never think it'll happen,' he said. 'You think they'll live for ever.'

I nodded. He was right, of course. I'd learnt the same lesson when I was his age. I remembered my own parents, side by side in the Meadowbank home, like the world's oldest pair of Babes in the Wood. I said: 'Certain people seem to project something of immortality.'

He looked surprised at that. He said: 'Yes, that's right. Exactly right.'

Quite an unusual young man, I thought, as I left him to his work. Not like a regular cleaner at all, though it still remains to be seen if he will prove as efficient as Mary. But Gloria's boy is no stranger here. He knows these walls and corridors. Unlike Johnny Harrington, who after less than a year at St Oswald's when he was a boy of fourteen, thinks he's an Old Centurion.

I walked back home through the park again. I like the way it clears my head. The wind had brought down the horse-chestnuts: broken shells lay on the ground, with the occasional fat brown nut rolling out as I kicked through the leaves. I couldn't resist picking one up and slipping it into my coat pocket. Talismanic, it will remain there until the gloss has faded.

Once more, I considered Harrington. Has he ever deigned to pick up a handful of conkers from the ground? Did any of those three boys? The three of them were always so clean; so impeccably virtuous. Or at least, I thought they were. Later events made me question that. Of course, young Harrington wasn't the cause of that sorry business. But he was *there*. It began with him. And now he's the one releasing the ghosts, like a child with a magic lamp that, instead of casting light, releases nothing but darkness . . .

2

Michaelmas Term, 1981

My conversation with Harry Clarke did little to solve the mystery of Johnny Harrington's troubled 'friend'. Charlie Nutter was absent that week, apparently with some kind of stomach bug, which meant that neither Harry nor I had the chance to talk to him. Harrington, whatever his motives in confiding in me, was once more his uncommunicative self, and Spikely, as always, annoyingly slow in spite of his intellectual's brow – rather like my own Anderton-Pullitt, in fact; middle-aged before his time, and given to odd little habits, but showing no visible sign of distress, or concern for his absent schoolmate.

I did see him once after Chapel, though, outside the Chaplain's office. This was traditionally where boys went to discuss their problems, although there was usually more sympathy to be had from the School Secretary than from the ingenuous Dr Burke. I contemplated asking Spikely whether he, too, had a friend who might be possessed, but thought better of it when the Chaplain himself emerged from his inner sanctum, carrying a stack of rugby shirts and looking, as always, slightly harassed.

'Straitley!' The Chaplain has always had a somewhat peremptory manner.

'Chaplain,' I said politely.

Dr Burke and I were not quite friends, he being more on the side of rugby and cold showers, while I preferred the comforts of Liquorice Allsorts, Catullus and the odd Gauloise. But I liked to think we got along, even though, to him, I suppose I represented the worst elements of Roman civilization.

The Chaplain gave me a meaningful look. 'A word in my office, Straitley,' he said.

I followed him into his sanctum, lined with rugby-team photographs and predatory with orchids. There was a teapot on the desk, from which he helped himself to a cup of his *special formula* – the Chaplain famously believed that caffeine was harmful to body and soul, and instead swore by an undrinkable blend of something that looked like grass clippings.

'Been hearing about your form,' he said. 'Seems they're a bit of a handful.'

I shrugged. *A bit of a handful* covers every Middle School form I've ever taught. But that year, there were no characters in my form; no exuberant pranksters. Only that feeling of something sly, just below the surface.

'Has anyone complained?' I said. 'And if so, why complain to you? Why not go to the form-master?'

The Chaplain cleared his throat. I could see he was uncomfortable. 'Delicate nature,' he said at last. 'Didn't want it getting out.'

'Ah.' That meant self-abuse, perhaps, or some other sexual problem. The Chaplain, though priding himself on being friendly and approachable, was peculiarly sensitive to what he called *problems of a delicate nature,* and took them very much to heart – another reason for the boys to avoid confiding in him.

'Fact is,' said the Chaplain, 'one of your boys seems to think that a member of staff – a member of St Oswald's staff—' He paused to drink his herbal brew, looking increasingly flustered. 'I mean, it's probably nothing. But the boy seems to think he's promoting a – *homosexual agenda.*'

Well, there was only one member of staff who might fit that description. And the pupil— 'Let me guess. Johnny Harrington, perchance?'

'He came to me in *confidence,*' said the Chaplain admonishingly. 'Of course I wouldn't reveal the name. But if there's a Master involved in – well, *that* kind of activity' – he shrugged – 'I'd have to inform the Head. And, of course, the Chairman of Governors. Can't have a Master corrupting the boys. Letting down the School, and all that.'

'Chaplain,' I said firmly. 'I'm afraid you've been the victim of a practical joke. A couple of boys in this year's 3S specialize in making complaints. You're not the first to be taken in, but in future, if you could refer the boy in question back to me, we could save time and embarrassment.'

I thought the Chaplain looked relieved. 'You think it's a hoax?'

I nodded.

'Yes, I mean – I thought it was odd. I mean, respected member of staff—' He sighed. 'Nothing in it at all, then?'

I thought of Harry; his innocence; his genuine belief that telling the truth was always the best solution. Then

I thought of Harrington, and Spikely, the tattletale. I've always hated tattletales.

I squared my shoulders and looked the Chaplain firmly in the eye.

'Nothing in it at all,' I said.

3

Michaelmas Term, 1981

I thought of talking to Spikely, but decided against it. I had no doubt that it was he who had made the complaint against Harry. I was equally convinced that Harrington had set him up to it: and bearing in mind the amount of time that the three boys spent in Harry's room, and knowing Harry as I did, I was sure that if Charlie Nutter was having doubts about his own sexuality, Harry would have given him any reassurance he could.

Harrington, with his narrow views, would hardly have been expected to approve. Spikely, I guessed, was easily led. And from that to the two boys lodging a complaint against Harry with the Chaplain – a complaint that, without my intervention, the Chaplain would have duly passed on to the Head, and to the Governors—

Yes, I misled him deliberately. I don't regret that, even though it caused me some trouble later. What I regret was not seeing the signs. But my mind was taken up with other things; and once the crisis was over, Harrington and his two friends faded once more into the background.

It had been a busy few weeks. Over the second half of the Michaelmas term, I'd been engaged in a number of domestic affairs, including some Sixth-Form Latin coaching, the impending arrival of twenty French Exchange students from La Baule, with all the disruption that would entail, another untimely fall of snow and that School production of *Antigone*, which, aside from having claimed the souls of two of my brightest fifth-formers, also meant that Harry was taken up with rehearsals every lunchtime and every night till the end of term.

Then there were the rabbits. A rather nasty incident involving a half-dozen rabbits in a run at the back of the School and cared for by members of my form as part of a science project – all of them found dead one day by the boy assigned to feed them.

At first I assumed that a fox had got in. But there were no marks on the rabbits, which were discovered neatly laid out side by side in their little pen, damp, but otherwise intact. Rumours of black magic instantly ran through the Middle School. The boy, a susceptible youngster by the name of Newman, was very upset by the whole thing, and was duly offered counselling by the Chaplain *and* the Satanic Mr Speight, the combined influence of which froze him into a rigid pillar of misery – rather like a rabbit himself, caught in two sets of headlights.

This isn't to say that I *forgot* about Charlie Nutter, or Harry Clarke; but they were not my only concerns, and besides, I only had Harrington's word (and Harry's, of course) that anything was wrong at all. Given his son's lacklustre results, I expected to see Stephen Nutter, MP, at one of our end-of-term Parents' Evenings, at which point I thought perhaps I might broach the subject of Charlie's unease – no, *not* his sexuality, which I'd decided was none of my business unless it affected his Latin verbs, but maybe his general state of mind. In any case, I wasn't looking forward to it. Meanwhile, Harrington's parents were due to see me about their son's progress, and after the poor start to the term, I was eager to make as good an impression as possible.

They came on a Wednesday evening – the first of three devoted to meetings. In those days, we held these in our form-rooms, at intervals of ten minutes each. Some had allocated times between the hours of six and nine, others just turned up on the night. A row of chairs outside the door enabled the parents to wait their turn. An almost foolproof system, made near-impossible to predict by the fact that St Oswald's parents, like their sons, are often late for meetings; often rude and badly organized; and anyway, are quite incapable of keeping to their allocated ten-minute slot. As a result, these evenings rarely finished before ten thirty, after which we were all exhausted and in no condition to teach the next day.

I'd taken a break in the Common Room, rather than go home for dinner. The kitchens always sent a tray of refreshments for those who preferred to stay in School, and many of the staff availed themselves of the opportunity. On this occasion, I'd barely started my first sandwich when Dr Devine came into the room, looking pressed and efficient. He gave me a look that seemed to take in every detail of my person, from the crumbs on my tie to the chalk marks on my gown – his own, of course, was immaculate; I suspected he'd actually *ironed* it – and said: 'When you've finished, Straitley, there are parents waiting to see you.'

When you've finished, Straitley. As if a ham and cheese sandwich – and maybe a scone, followed by coffee and a leisurely Gauloise – were some kind of orgiastic feast, which maybe, to Devine, it was.

'They're *two hours early*,' I pointed out.

Devine just gave me one of his looks. It was a look that conveyed in a glance everything that was wrong with me: my unruly hair – more of it then, of course, and distressingly curly; my lackadaisical posture; my tweed jacket, which was durable, if not exactly glamorous; even the smell of chalk dust and smoke that seemed a part of my essential being – all of it marked and judged lacking by Dr Devine, the self-appointed arbiter of everything.

I cursed Devine in Latin and went back to room 59, where I found the Harringtons, sitting outside and dressed for church; she in a beige fur-collared coat and a modest string of pearls, he in the kind of charcoal suit that manages to convey both affluence and self-restraint. I shook their hands and invited them in (much as folklore dictates we should invite a vampire before he can feed).

Mrs Harrington sat down. Dr Harrington (MA, Oxon) remained standing, which meant that I was obliged to perch uncomfortably on the teacher's desk, neither seated nor standing. Not a good position for a Junior Master trying to project a confident sense of authority. Nowadays, his son relies on just the same kind of tactics.

A moment for Harrington Senior. It was the first time I'd seen him. A tall man with dark-blond hair and a striking resemblance to his son. Long, elegant, brain-surgeon's hands; an obstinate line between his eyes. Five years older than I was, at most; and yet I found myself stumbling through my words of welcome like an ill-prepared schoolboy.

'Mr Straitley,' said Harrington Senior, cutting short the pleasantries. 'Perhaps, as Johnny's form-master, you could give us some insight as to our son's lack of progress over the term.'

That took me rather by surprise. Most parents do not initiate discussion on Parents' Evenings. In fact, most parents do not expect to hear specific concerns from members of staff, but only attend in order to feel (however wrongly) that they are taking an active part in their son's education. The truth is that most parents are best kept as far away from their sons' education as possible, while the professionals deal with the day-to-day business of teaching. Parents' Evenings are simply a means of reassuring parents that they are doing all they can, and ensuring that they do not feel the need to visit the School again. There are exceptions – boys who actually *need* the School to involve their parents; but for the most part, parents are the least helpful port of call for a Master trying to do his job.

The thing is, no parent can possibly have the objectivity of a Master. No parent really believes, deep down, that their son could be a liar; a bully; a cheat; a thief – or worse still, just an average boy, unexceptional in every way. Masters know the truth, of course. Few boys are exceptional. All boys are lazy. All boys lie. And parents, however progressive or realistic in theory, have a ridiculous blind spot where their particular boy is concerned, making them unreliable at best, and at worst, a downright liability.

'Lack of progress?' I said. 'I don't think that's entirely—'

'With respect, Mr Straitley. You've known my son for less than a term. I have known him for fourteen years. And I know when he is not working to his full capacity.'

I gave an inward sigh. Oh, gods. An *educator*. Some parents are not content to let a mere Master teach their son. They have to teach him by proxy, poking a thumb into every pie, making themselves unbearable, proffering opinions on all subjects, from PE to School dinners. I suppose I should have expected this; the fact that the parents had home-schooled the boy should have warned me that they were not yet ready to relinquish control over their son's education.

'Johnny's very bright,' I said. 'Well above the class average. Top marks in Latin. Top marks in Maths. He can't be top in everything.'

Mrs Harrington waved aside her son's achievements in Latin and Maths.

'We're quite aware of how bright he is,' she told me. 'But, as you already know, he's finding it hard to fit in here. He isn't used to being in such a large school environment, and, of course, he's extremely sensitive.'

Sensitive. Now there's a word that strikes unease into a Master's heart. Parents and psychologists use it when combating instances of inappropriate behaviour, where it acts as a get-out-of-jail-free card whenever the boy in question feels the need to assert his personality.

'But Johnny *has* been to school before,' I said. 'Two years in a junior school. Did he have the same problems there?'

I saw Mrs Harrington's face twitch. 'That place wasn't good for him,' she said. 'Too many negative influences. That's why we sent him here, Mr Straitley. A good, traditional boys' school. We thought that would make things easier.'

'What kind of negative influences do you mean?' I was curious. The file I had on young Harrington from his previous school contained nothing untoward. Certainly, nothing to suggest that he had left under a cloud, or that any kind of incident was connected with his departure.

Mrs Harrington twitched again. Her husband put a hand on hers. She dropped her gaze immediately.

'We feel that most schools in this country try to sexualize children far too early,' said Dr Harrington. 'We'd rather see our son brought up with unambiguous moral values, rather than being led to believe that immorality is a *choice,* or that foul language, or references to sodomy or fornication are acceptable because they occur in so-called "literature" rather than the real world.'

I gave another inward sigh. 'I see. This is about Johnny's English exam.'

Dr Harrington nodded. 'In part. When a boy is given trash to read, he becomes lazy and indolent. Before long, he starts to believe that learning doesn't matter, or that hard work can be faked, or that his elders can be mocked—'

I sensed the approach of a sermon. 'I'm afraid the School curriculum can't be altered just for one boy. I'm sure Johnny's faith is strong enough to withstand a bit of Chaucer.'

'It isn't just a question of faith,' said Dr Harrington crisply. 'It's a question of innocence. Our son is an innocent. It's your job to see that he stays that way. As for the curriculum, we've arranged for Johnny to be moved out of Mr Fabricant's group. We think a sound teacher and a different reading list would solve most of his problems.'

'Well,' I said. 'Perhaps it would. But don't you think—'

'We've taken advice from Mr Speight, who happens to be a member of our church. He fully supports our decision. In fact, he believes that it should be up to the parents to decide which books are suitable for their sons to study. And I, for one, don't think that Mr Fabricant, with his predilection for French pornography, is fit to choose the syllabus.'

French pornography? 'You mean his book on the Marquis de Sade.'

'Absolutely. And I mean to speak to the Headmaster about this. Parents have a right to know if a pervert is teaching their sons.'

'I wouldn't call Mr Fabricant a *pervert*,' I protested.

'Then what exactly *would* you call a man who makes a celebration of filth, and writes books encouraging young people to treat it as literature?'

I steered the discussion back to less difficult waters. Of course, Johnny Harrington's parents had a right to their beliefs, but as far as education is concerned, I've always believed that religion, like politics, is something best left at the School gates.

'English aside, how does Johnny feel about the way he's settling in? It's sometimes hard for a seventh-term boy to make friends as quickly as the rest. But he does have a couple of good friends. Charlie Nutter, for instance—'

'That's not a connection we're keen to encourage,' interrupted Dr Harrington.

'Really? Why?'

There was a pause. They looked at each other.

'Charlie Nutter is a troubled young man,' said Mrs Harrington at last. 'Much as we sympathize, we don't think Johnny should be spending too much time with him. He has—'

'Demons?' I suggested, and smiled.

'Quite,' said Mrs Harrington.

4

September 16th, 2005

Ira furor brevis est. Rage is a brief insanity. My anger over the Head's refusal to allow Harry's memorial service had not cooled overnight, but it had become a little more cautious. Thus this morning I arrived at Harrington's office at seven fifteen, to find him already in there, pouring a cup of coffee from the espresso machine in the corner and looking fresh and guileless.

Some men do not change very much from the teenage boy they used to be. Harrington has grown, of course, but the essentials remain the same. The smooth, blond hair; good skin; the suit that might have come from a fashion magazine. I caught the briefest glimpse of his unguarded expression before the politician's smile appeared, stretching over his features like a cartoon mask.

'Mr Straitley! Please, come in.'

That was disingenuous. His deliberate use of my surname – inviting me to ask him to call me Roy, or seem churlish in not doing so – the smug, proprietary way in which he gestured towards the chair positioned in front of the Headmaster's desk – the blotter still scarred by repeated explosions from Shitter Shakeshafte's torpedo pen – oh, he was a politician all right; smarter than most politicians, double-dipped in a toxic brew of arrogance and sanctity.

'I'm sorry you had to come in so early,' he said. 'There are so many things to do. Good thing I need so little sleep.'

He poured me a cup of coffee in the Head's own china. 'I'd be lost without my espressos,' he said. 'Beats the staff-room brew any day.'

He waited for me to take it. Finally, I did. It would have been foolish not to; but the thought that he had manipulated me, even in such a small way as to accept an unsolicited cup of coffee, was enough to make my heart notch up, and the invisible finger prodded me admonishingly.

I sat in the chair in front of the desk. 'You should call me Roy,' I said. 'Don't tell me I intimidate you, after all these years.'

He smiled. 'Is anyone ever *really* at ease calling an old schoolmaster by his Christian name? But I was never shy of you. I always respected you very much.'

Really. How utterly warming, I thought.

'That's why I wanted to see you today, even though I know what you want, and *you* know why I can't give it to you.'

I sipped my espresso. It was too strong, and would have me running to the bathroom all morning. At my age, these things matter; besides my legs are not as spry as they were twenty-four years ago. A bathroom visit takes planning and time.

I wondered who had warned him. The Chaplain? Devine? Ms Buckfast? Or maybe even Eric, still trying to curry favour with a management that has long since ceased to think of him as management material?

'I had no idea I was so predictable,' I said. 'Or indeed, so prescient.'

He smiled again. 'Oh, Roy,' he said. 'You can't imagine how sorry I am. But at this stage, to hold any kind of memorial for Harry Clarke, or even to mention that business in connection with the School, would mean the worst kind of publicity. All schools have their scandals, of course, but the nature of the Clarke affair makes it all the more urgent for us to keep the story away from the press. It's not a personal grievance, you know. It's for the good of St Oswald's.'

For the good of St Oswald's. I suppose he thought that would move me. After all, St Oswald's has been my life. I am as firmly attached to the place as the gargoyles on the Chapel roof, and, like the gargoyles, I am trained to divert the foul water of scandal away from our saints and effigies.

'There was no *proof*,' I told him. 'The boy was obviously disturbed.'

Harrington looked at me closely and with unsettling sympathy. 'Roy, I'm getting the sense that somehow you hold yourself to blame.'

'I don't blame myself,' I said, rather more sharply than I'd intended. The invisible finger prodded and sought the soft spot under my breastbone. 'I don't blame anyone but—'

You. I almost said it aloud. *You. You're the one I've always blamed. You, with your little attaché case, and your pair of sycophants. As if God cares who a man loves, just as long as he* can *love—*

Harrington was still looking at me. 'It was a very difficult time,' he said, with that look of compassion. 'What happened that year marked us all. Did you ever have any counselling? I did, and it helped me. I know you're not a man of faith, but Survivors helped me enormously.'

I said: 'I don't need counselling.'

'But you *are* concerned about closure.'

Closure. What a loathsome word, with its transatlantic affectation of sympathy and psychobabble. No, I am not concerned about closure, you hypocrite, but about *justice*. What happened to Harry was *unjust*: and as we grow old, and our memories blur and shift and recede with time, *injustice* is the one that stays most poignant, most persistent. Injustice outlives a broken limb; the death of a parent; a heart attack. Injustice is the tiny shard of something broken in the soul that can never be mended.

'Well, if it helps,' said Harrington, 'the Chaplain gave me this for you.'

And from under his desk, he brought out a cardboard box – one of those boxes that used to contain half a dozen reams of paper – before the days of the paper-free office and the ubiquitous e-mail. It was sealed with parcel tape, and felt surprisingly light in my hands. I'd expected something heavier.

'You know what it is?' said Harrington.

I nodded. 'Yes. I think I know.'

'Well, it's all yours,' said Harrington. 'I hope it gives you peace of mind. And – speaking of which – Rupert Gunderson.'

'*Gunderson?*' I'd been so lost in the past that I'd almost forgotten him. 'Listen, the boy's a bully. I dealt with the situation. And it's hardly my fault if the parents think—'

Harrington looked pained. 'Roy, please. There's more to this than meets the eye. Gunderson has some serious emotional problems. In fact, Marcus Blakely's been looking into his case.'

I made the Old Head's favourite sound. *Oof*. From what I'd seen so far of Dr Blakely, the boys would run circles around him.

'I'll thank Dr Blakely to leave it to me where any of *my* boys are concerned.'

He sighed. 'I appreciate your feelings, Roy, but it looks as if, in this case, young Allen-Jones may be mostly to blame.'

'What, for being bullied?'

He shook his head. 'I think we should both leave this to Marcus. It's what he's best at, and besides, you and I both know how easy it is to let a personal preference get in the way of the facts of a case. Marcus is new. He doesn't have any – preconceptions.'

Preconceptions? Personal preference? Was he accusing me of favouritism?

Ira furor brevis est. If I'd had the chance to reply, I might have ended my career. And maybe Harrington knew that, because when Danielle came in with the news that the Chairman of Governors was on the phone and needed a word, I saw a look come over his face – just for a second, but it was there: the look of a cat disturbed with its prey – and I wondered if he'd been trying to make me rise to the bait, to push me into an argument that could only end in my resignation—

Then the look was gone; in its place, a wry smile and a shrug.

'Sorry, Roy. Have to go. We'll talk about this another time.' He indicated the cardboard box. 'Don't forget your legacy.'

I left the office, box in hand. Danielle was back at the front desk. I like Danielle; in spite of her big hair and hoop earrings and unquenchable enthusiasm for television reality shows, her instincts are generally good. I was certain that, at another time, she would have fielded the call from the Chairman of Governors and left the Head and Yours Truly to finish their conversation. I owed her something, I told myself.

She shot me a sympathetic smile. 'Everything all right?'

I shrugged. 'All the better for seeing you. You must have come in very early.'

I thought she coloured a little. 'Well, the Head starts early,' she said. 'And, of course, I work flexible hours.'

'He doesn't deserve you,' I told her, making it sound like a joke.

She laughed. '*None* of you deserve me,' she said. 'Now how about a cup of tea?'

It was a long, long day today. Domestic matters; marking books; an altercation between two boys. I was on duty all lunchtime, opposite Devine in the yard, and then I was teaching all afternoon. I didn't have the chance to open Harry's box until I got home; at which point I was almost reluctant to look inside.

I left it on the hall table as I went to make myself a snack: I hadn't had time for lunch, and so had been forced to compensate by eating biscuits between lessons – against my doctor's advice, but how does he expect me to plan sensible meals when there's always so much to be done?

I poured myself a glass of wine and made myself a Welsh rarebit. Wholegrain mustard and cheddar cheese on a fat brown doorstep of granary bread. Here again, the upstart who calls himself my doctor would have had more than a few things to say, but how can you take the advice of a boy who, only a few years ago, was incapable of distinguishing a present from a past participle?

I poured myself another glass. A man has to unwind somehow. I finished the rarebit and opened the box, still feeling vaguely apprehensive.

Is this all it comes to? Is *this* a man's life? A plastic urn of the plainest kind, the lid secured with masking tape. Some photographs in an envelope; some newspaper clippings; a vinyl record. Some letters, bound with a rubber band. Old St Oswald's diaries – over a dozen of them, the kind in which Harry used to write his classroom notes. An assortment of smaller objects that must have meant something to him once – a watch; a ring; a paperweight; a medal; cufflinks; a penknife. The flotsam and jetsam of a life – and then, a parcel, tied with string, and carefully labelled with the words:

To Roy Straitley:

Use it well.

I took the parcel out of the box. Narrow at one end, thicker at the other, it seemed about the same shape as a wine bottle, though weighing rather less. I poured myself another drink. I tore off the wrapping paper. And then I took out the object and put it on the mantelpiece next to my clock and the plastic urn and the photographs of my parents. It looks a little strange there – perhaps a little sinister. Still, no one is likely to see it – at least, not until I put it to use.

Then I raised my glass again, and I made a promise to Harry. It wasn't the kind of promise you break, even though no one was listening. Then I reached back inside the box and took out the record he'd left me, and put it on my turntable and played David Bowie's 'The Laughing Gnome'.

And then, all alone, in my empty house at eight o'clock in the evening, I finally began to laugh. I'm not the kind of man who tends to laugh aloud much nowadays, but tonight I did, and heartily; and I drank a toast to Harry Clarke, that joker, that innocent, that friend, who, in spite of everything, had never lost heart, or given up hope, or ever stopped looking at the stars.

5

Michaelmas Term, 1981

Dear Mousey,

Those rabbits were a mistake. They attracted too much attention. But what can I say? I was having fun. Besides, catching rats takes time. We needed something meatier.

At first I thought Ratty had done the trick. But Goldie and I could both see that Poodle still wasn't cured. In fact, he seemed to be getting worse. The magazines. The nightmares. The scars. We needed a better solution. Besides, I had my own problems. The rabbits helped with that, too. Poodle cried, but Goldie – well, he's almost as good as you, Mousey, when it comes to the dirty. *And* he's good at saying the words, just like his dad and Mr Speight.

Of course, he believes in all that stuff. Angels and demons and Heaven and Hell. Plus, like his dad and Mr Speight, he thinks being queer is a mortal sin. *I* think they make too big a deal. I mean, it's hardly life and death. But that's what he's like, Mousey. Shiny and clean on the outside, but crawling inside with nasty thoughts. Well, can't blame him for *that*, I guess. Sometimes I look at myself in the mirror and I wonder why they don't see what I am. Most people are pretty stupid, though. I guess you just have to expect that.

Poodle was sick again afterwards. We made him wash his mouth out, before he took the rabbits back. Then we waited and hoped for the best. But even though he was sick for days, we could tell he wasn't cured. He's staying away from school now. I think it's because he's avoiding me. Well, that won't work. We can't stop now. We'll finish what we started.

I know. You're wondering why I'm doing this. Poodle's my friend (well, almost). And you and I know that I don't have a particular problem with being queer. The thing is, I can't help myself. I think it must be the drama. Poking the wasps' nest with a stick until they fly out like lottery balls. Who will they sting? Not me, for sure. No one knows about me at Church. No one knows about me at school. Except for Poodle and Goldie, of course, and they're not going to talk. Not now. Both of them are in this too deep. There's no way they're telling anyone.

Meanwhile, back in school, Harry's directing the School Play. *Antigone,* by Sophocles. (Last year was *The Frogs*. I guess that's what happens when the Head of School is also the Head of Classics.) Anyway, what it means is that Harry's busy most lunchtimes; supervising rehearsals and helping with the production. Not that it matters. Thanks to horrible Mr Scoones, I'm spending my lunchtimes practising French essay techniques. Mr Scoones sits by, eating his lunch, listening to old French songs on his portable cassette player. People like Edith Piaf and Jacques Brel. Sometimes he puts on a French film. He seems to think it's a great treat for me, which makes it all even worse. Mr Scoones is the kind of teacher who gives out detentions when he's in a rage, and doesn't dare go back on them. So now, he's being really friendly, as if I'd *chosen* to be with him, instead of being with Harry.

Harry's lent me some more books, though; a book of poems called *Crow*, and a big book of prints by Escher. There are notes in both of them. It's nice. It keeps me in touch with him. And of course, there's *Diamond Dogs*, hidden behind my bookcase. I have to keep it hidden, because if my parents found it, they might guess about Harry and me. But I hardly see him now, except sometimes in the mornings, or when he's on duty in the yard, or on the Upper Corridor. He always smiles when he sees me. I think perhaps he misses me, too.

Everyone else is excited about the stupid school play. Mostly because Mulberry girls are in it. One of them is Becky Price, the red Flamingo girl from Church. Goldie told me that. (I think he's got a crush on her.) Not that I care about the play, or the red Flamingo girl. But the end of term's coming up. One more week till the Christmas break. Not that I care much for Christmas, either. Bad TV, and fruitcake, and presents that well-meaning relatives think will appeal to a boy of fourteen. But at least I'll be free of Mr Scoones. For a couple of weeks, anyway.

I'll really miss seeing Harry, though. But I can come to his house, he says. He's got a lot of stuff at home. Rare discs, concert programmes. Books. Lyric sheets and posters. He says I can pop round any time. I can borrow whatever I like. I can always tell my folks I'm going for extra English tuition. They'd believe that. I know they would. And I already know where he lives. It's a terraced house in White City, not too far from the clay pits. He has a whole room full of records and books; red curtains and a red rug. From the street his house looks like a Chinese lantern, all lit up.

I can't stop thinking about it. And him. We're so alike, Harry and me. I know he's older, and everything. But he's not like the rest of them. We talk to each other like equals. Even when we don't talk, we communicate without words. Sometimes, I think that when I escape I could get a house in White City. Somewhere close to Harry's house. I could see him every day. Maybe then we could be more than just master and pupil.

Don't be disgusting, Mousey. Of course there's nothing like *that* going on. There's more to life than sex, you know – although you wouldn't believe it here. Goldie's obsessed with it, in spite of his holy attitudes. He's always thinking about Mulberry girls, or trying to see up their skirts on the bus. But sex is just a distraction. Harry's above that kind of thing. Harry's an intellectual. Harry values the spiritual over the mere physical. That's why, when I go to see him, I won't tell Goldie or Poodle. I'll go alone, and we'll talk about music, and writing, and art, and death, and drink tea in the living room; and maybe, if I'm feeling brave, I'll tell him about Bunny, and you, and even about My Condition.

All you need is courage, he said.

Yes, I'm sure he'll understand.

6

Michaelmas Term, 1981

Nutter's parents didn't keep their Parents' Evening appointment. Instead, there came a note the next day, saying that Charlie was ill with 'flu and asking his teachers to send work, to be completed during the Christmas break. I sent a number of Latin past papers and some Vergil, plus some Ted Hughes from Mr Fabricant and some German prose from Dr Devine. There was also a large amount of reading from the Satanic Mr Speight. It looked as if Nutter's Christmas was going to be a busy one.

The last week of term progressed more or less as normal. *Antigone* proved a great success, especially among some of the more susceptible of my fifth-form pupils. The red-haired temptress from Mulberry House who had caused such devastation took her final curtain-call and left, much to my unspoken relief. The pupils from La Baule came and went in a haze of illicit Gitanes. And Harrington and Spikely were quiet, polite and respectful – except that sometimes I thought they looked at me with a hint of anxiety, as if they were waiting for something that I had not yet delivered.

As for Harry – I'll admit I still felt embarrassed by what he had confessed to me, and by what the Chaplain had said. I didn't exactly *avoid* him – we were both very busy that term – but neither did I go out of my way to seek him out. No more cups of tea at Break; no drinks at the Thirsty Scholar. Instead, I dealt with wet lunchtimes and Christmas card deliveries, and bullies and smokers and homework evaders and Dr Devine's repeated complaints about his disappearing supplies. Eric, too, seemed distant – although I'd said nothing to him of what Harry had said. He'd never really warmed to Harry in the way that I had, and he could sometimes be puritanical about the strangest of things. Perhaps he was slightly jealous of the way Harry and I had become friends. But Eric was subject to changes of mood – one day cheery and talkative, the next day curiously withdrawn – and so I gave little thought to his silence.

I suppose that even if I had known what was going on, I wouldn't have known how to intervene. At least, that's what I tell myself now. But sometimes, I still think about what *might* have happened, and I feel that absurd sting of guilt, just as I do when I hear the news that a boy I once taught has died – which happens more often now, of course, although I never get used to it – that feeling that *I should have been there*; I should have been looking out for my friend.

Tonight, in my dark and lonely house, I returned to Harry's box. Over a pasty and a beer, I opened one of his blue School diaries; read until I strained my eyes. There was nothing much to see: scribbled reminders; lesson notes; drawings; a few lines of poetry – his own, or another's, I could not say.

I dreamt that I was old. And you – you were beside me
Forever young – in your hand, a cup of stars.

And now I could hear his voice again; strong against the press of years. I'll get through all the diaries eventually, but it will be slow reading. Harry's writing is small and cramped, sometimes interspersed with little caricatures; boys, or sometimes Masters. Sometimes a line of writing straggles vertically up the page, like a climber on a rock-face; or circles erratically, like a string of wagons round a campfire.

My eyes are not as strong as they were; after a while, my vision rebels. Still, I am certain that there is something in these notes for me to discover. Harry would not have left me them otherwise. He knew I would read them diligently; every note; every scribbled line. And so I shall. I will find what he left for me. All I need is a little time.

7

Michaelmas Term, 1981

It was a cheerless end-of-term: dark, wet and stressful. A number of the boys fell ill with a kind of intestinal 'flu, as did Eric, whose classes I was obliged to cover in his absence. Newman, still upset about the rabbits, took to crying in the Middle School toilets, from which defeatist behaviour neither the Chaplain's manly exhortations nor the Satanic Mr Speight's more sinister whisperings managed to dissuade him. After two weeks' absence, Charlie Nutter had not returned, and when the final School bell rang, the boys all scattered like sparrows over the newly fallen snow, in search of roast dinners and mince pies and presents by the fireside.

I don't enjoy Christmas very much. It's a miserable time of year for people like me, who live alone, and even in those days, when I was young and my parents were still living, I felt the burden of the year's end heavy on my shoulders. Now, in some ways, it's easier. I have my books; my radio. I go to church or not, as I choose. I have no family commitments. My Christmas decorations are limited to a sparse length of tinsel on the mantelpiece, a log, and a few greetings cards on the window ledge.

But in those days, it was different. I spent Christmas at the Meadowbank old folks' home, where my parents were residents. My mother was deep in dementia, and barely responded to anyone – except for the woman who came in once a month with a collection of small, docile animals – rabbits, cats, guinea pigs – which they would encourage the old folk to pet, believing it to be therapeutic. My father had Parkinson's disease, and could no longer care for himself, or for her, which meant that they both lived in care: one able-bodied, but out of reach; the other proud and still rational in a body that was falling apart.

We were never very close. I was a late child, born of a couple old enough to have been my grandparents. Of course I was fond of them, in my way; but there were no football games in the park for us, no youthful adventures. Both were greying by the time I could walk, and my most vivid childhood memories were of the three of us on Blackpool beach, both of them wrapped in blankets, braving the cold and rain for my sake, while I climbed and ran and built my sandcastles alone, and my mother drank sweet tea from a flask and my father read the paper.

Now, they still had the blankets, but my father no longer read. That Christmas, which was to be his last, he seemed to have given up the fight, and barely even spoke to me when I arrived on Christmas Day, bearing boxes of biscuits (the only presents I was sure they would both appreciate). My mother, by contrast, was having what passed as a good day: sitting up straight, like a child at Sunday School, wearing a silver paper crown and stroking a fat brown rabbit.

There was sliced turkey on cold plates, and roast potatoes, and mince pies, and party games, and weak orange squash served in tin jugs and beakers of coloured metal. We had the exact same beakers in the refectory at St Oswald's, and it was strange to see them there now, in the hands of the old folk; those papery, misshapen hands that spoke more eloquently than voices could of age, and the fear of the darkness.

'Nice bunny,' my mother said, stroking the rabbit's glossy fur. 'We used to make rabbit pie, you know. Our little boy likes rabbit pie. Would you like to hold him?'

'No, thank you, Mother.'

I'm not a fan of pets, as a rule. And that rabbit made me think of Newman and those St Oswald's rabbits, all found dead in their open pen as the boy came to feed them with lettuce and carrot-tops . . .

'It was a fox. Poor boy,' she said.

I looked at her, startled. 'What did you say?' I hadn't mentioned Newman to her, or the dead rabbits.

'That's what we told him. It was a fox. But it was wartime. We had to make do. I told him a fox must have got it.' She gave her sweet and singular smile. 'He loved the pie. He told me so.'

'Mother?'

Memory's a funny thing. I seem to remember more about my early childhood nowadays than I remember of yesterday. That little house where I was born; the square of dirt in the backyard; the rabbit hutch, with its biscuity smell. At that point I'd long forgotten that I'd ever had a pet; but now the memory returned with shutterclick clarity—

'Poor little boy. He cried and cried. Don't you tell him now, will you?'

'No, Mother. No, I won't.'

'Here. You can cuddle this one instead.'

'No, Mother. You keep him.'

It was the last time I heard my mother say anything that made close to sense; after my father died, she stopped responding, even to the animals. But that Christmas she was bright; beaming in her silver crown; fussing over the rabbit. And there I was, between them like Alice at the Mad Hatter's tea party; pouring more squash; wearing a crown; cutting up my father's turkey slice into tiny pieces.

I tell you all this so you'll understand why my mind was elsewhere. Why I'd forgotten Nutter; why Harry Clarke was so far from my thoughts. Eric had invited me to his house for Boxing Day, but I decided against it, and spent the day alone instead, listening to the wireless and watching the snow turn to sleet outside. *Kill me, please,* I told myself. *Kill me if I ever get old.*

And then it began. Out of the blue, from that strange and sinister twilight that falls between Christmas and the New Year. In the Mayan calendar, the five days that came at the end of the solar cycle were 'nameless days', during which demons walked, and the portals between the living world and the world of the dead were left ajar. I am not superstitious, but the time between Christmas and the New Year has always felt the same to me; a limbo; the fag-end of the year; a time when nothing good can happen. Suicide rates go up; road traffic accidents multiply; the season of goodwill degenerates into a series of fist fights, break-ups, quarrels and burglaries. The local newspapers try to balance this with heart-warming stories of comfort and joy, but these are only the fires we light against the coming of the dark. Under the tinsel, under the snow, something bitter and bleak endures.

A squib in the paper. A child's pet – a Christmas gift – vanished from a garden shed: a reward was being offered for the return of a brown-and-white rabbit. Three days later, another piece reported two more attacks, one in a henhouse in Red City, the other, the theft of a guinea pig from a garage on Abbey Road. Urban foxes, or maybe a dog, suggested the *Malbry Examiner* – although there was no explanation of how a dog could have opened the door of a henhouse, then closed it after stealing the hens. I remembered Newman's rabbits, dead and damp in their dry pens, and felt a little uneasy. That's why I don't keep pets, I thought. They make you feel so vulnerable.

And then, the day before New Year's Eve, came the news that a boy had disappeared. Not in the local press this time, but in *The Times*, and on TV, on *Nationwide* and the nine o'clock news. At four fifteen or thereabouts, a teenage boy had disappeared on his way home from White City, barely half a mile away.

No one had seen anything suspicious. No one knew where the boy might have gone. Last seen at a corner shop, where Mill Lane turns into Parkside Road, he'd stopped to buy a bottle of squash, and then had apparently disappeared from the face of the planet—

The boy was Charlie Nutter. And he had last been seen less than a hundred yards away from Harry's house on Parkside Road, just over from the clay pits.

Part Four

Fama volat.
(Vergil)

1

December 1981

So that was Christmas, Mousey. Old films; Queen's Speech; dinner in front of the TV. It's OK, unless you're used to a higher level of excitement. And then there's the way you have to pretend that you're having a brilliant time; opening presents; reading cards; pretending they're just what you wanted. The new bike on the front porch that you have to pretend is *such* a surprise. The money from your grandparents in a re-used envelope, with a card that looks as if it came from a second-hand shop in the fifties. And then there's the turkey, dried to a crisp, and the pudding, and the mince pies; and the carol service in the Church, with the red-haired Mulberry girl wearing a long white nightgown and singing 'Little Donkey'.

I've not seen Poodle or Goldie much. Poodle's had some trouble at home. Doesn't surprise me, really. He never could keep a secret. Anyway, his Condition now seems to be public knowledge, thanks to his mother. Seems she found some of Poodle's drawings, hidden inside a schoolbook. It didn't take long to get him to confess, and then it was just a matter of time.

Poodle's mother took the lead, with the Church's help, of course. A group of regular preachers, including Goldie's dad, Mr Speight and some visitors from another Church, got together, had some talks, and finally staged a Group Event. I didn't join in. I could have done, but I'd been through something similar after what happened at Netherton Green, and I didn't want reminding. I still remember what it was like: standing in front of everyone; the shouting; the chorusing; the noise; the way the preacher spoke to me, as if I wasn't really there, but somewhere else, and floating. And then there was the baptism, in a font of water. Not so much a baptism as a *drowning*, I thought at the time; a means of getting those demons out. But the water was cold; and his hand on my head was pushing me under the surface; and the noise of the congregation was a giant clatter and baffle and roar, and I couldn't breathe, and I thought I would die—

'Why didn't he go to the Chaplain?' said my dad to Poodle's mum.

As if Dr Burke would have known what to do. A useless jellyfish of a man, who couldn't spot a *real* problem if it were happening right under his nose. I didn't say that to Dad, of course. But honestly, the idea of going to the Chaplain for any kind of personal advice is just too hilarious for words. He'd probably just tell you to run a few laps, take a shower, and pray.

Poor Poodle. Goldie says he's been ill. Stomach 'flu, or something. But Goldie has other things on his mind. Or rather, one thing. Becky Price, the red-haired Flamingo girl from Church. Turns out she's a goer – at least as far as third base – and Goldie's completely obsessed, both with her and with all the nasty thoughts that generally come with the package.

'Just don't tell my dad,' he said. 'He's nuts about chastity. If he finds out about me and Beck, he'll go crazy. He's done it before.'

Turns out Goldie's dad once caught him playing with himself in bed, or something, and came to the conclusion that he'd been corrupted by the other kids at his school. I can't say I'm surprised, actually. It's what I would have expected of him.

Goldie grinned. 'You would, though,' he said. 'Given a chance, wouldn't you?'

I shrugged. No, Mousey, I don't think I would. Personally, I think I'm immune to that kind of temptation. But Goldie's spending all his time with Becky down by the clay pits. They use the back of Poodle's old car. They've got a mattress in there, and rugs, and sometimes they light a fire outside, in a metal dustbin. I don't think Poodle knows about that. He's more or less grounded till term starts. Now, with everything at Church, it won't be long before he cracks. What will he do then? Who knows? And isn't that all part of the fun?

2

September 19th, 2005

I did not sleep well last night. As a result, this morning is tiled with the gritty light of insomnia. This happens more often than not nowadays, especially when I indulge. And it does not help that Dr Devine is a whirlwind of nervous energy; organizing litter patrol, reporting potential Health & Safety risks and bonding with his new protégé, Markowicz, whose term so far – at least from the number of times I have had to cover his classes – seems to have been almost entirely taken up by meetings, conferences and courses.

In Devine's book (and the Head's, it seems) this makes Markowicz a Promising Young Man, destined for the greatness of a full-time administrative post, rather than actually teaching boys. A dull old business, this teaching of boys, to which such sticklers as Eric and I have devoted our whole careers, but which Markowicz will escape within three years, as one of the Heads of the future.

As for Devine, I believe he sees himself as Dr Blakely's potential successor, once the Crisis Team has completed the salvaging of St Oswald's. Like Bob Strange, he still expects the new, streamlined St Oswald's to find a special place for him in reward for his years of service. The likelier outcome, I believe, is that he will be encouraged to take premature retirement to make way for a younger, cheaper man, knocked off like the rest of the barnacles while the likes of Markowicz rise to take the helm of the ship. He may speak highly of courses, but he himself avoids them, preferring to work at the chalk-face (although he would never admit to this), and I suspect that Markowicz's all-too-frequent absences will soon begin to gall him. Devine believes in departmental self- sufficiency, which means that when a colleague is absent, the other members will cover for him. And Devine has too much pride to ask the League of Nations to fill the shoes of his absent protégé, besides which, as Head of House and Health & Safety Officer, he has by far the most free time of anyone in the department. This means that, in effect, Devine teaches *two* timetables every time Markowicz goes on a course. As a result, I thought he looked tired as he came into the Common Room for his morning coffee.

'Overdoing things, Devine? You're looking a little worse for wear.'

He sniffed. 'Never better, thank you.'

'How's young Markowicz?' I asked. 'Shaping up, is he?'

Again, that sharp, percussive sniff. I don't think he knows he's doing it. 'Very nicely, thank you,' he said. 'Give him a term, he'll be right at home.'

'Well, he's certainly got *you* where he wants you,' I said. 'How many days has he been in School? Is he even house-trained yet?'

'That's ridiculous,' said Devine. 'I'll have you know that Markowicz has been fast-tracked for success. We're very lucky to have him here.'

I sensed a note of depression, and smiled. 'Of course we are. What is it this time? Assertiveness training? Computer skills?'

'Visual aids.'

'Marvellous.'

Gerry Grachvogel, the well-meaning ass whom Markowicz has now replaced, was a firm believer in visual aids – and was even rumoured to use glove puppets with the younger classes, a tactic which had earned him the nickname *Kermit* from my Brodie Boys. I wonder whether Markowicz will ever earn himself a nickname, or whether he will be one of those staff members – like Thing One and Thing Two – that the boys barely recognize when they meet them in the corridor. I suspect the latter.

'Come on, Devine,' I said. 'I can practically hear your teeth gnashing. Glove puppets and flashcards?'

'Not at all,' said Dr Devine. 'Educational computer games to aid in language acquisition. Given the current trend for using IT in the classroom, Markowicz – and *I* – felt it would be useful to investigate the new software available. Now if you don't mind—' He gathered his papers under his arm and picked up his briefcase. 'I have to go. Registration in five minutes.'

First lesson was Sixth-Form Latin with my boys and the Mulberry girls, to which the Headmistress, Miss Lambert, had chosen to invite herself, ostensibly to check on the girls, but in actual fact to check on me.

Call-me-Jo installed herself right at the back of the classroom, legs crossed almost high enough to reveal her stocking-tops under the sky-blue tweed skirt.

I could tell that the boys found this alarming, as did the girl Benedicta, the only one of the Mulberry girls who seems to have any kind of sense. The rest of the girls clearly adore their stylish Headmistress, and there was a great deal of giggling during our translation of a passage from *Aeneid* IX, mostly instigated by the Headmistress herself, who believes that learning should be 'fun', and that 'fun' entails a great deal of giggling. At this rate my boys will be out of control by Christmas, and the whole curriculum will be *raptus regaliter* – as Allen-Jones puts it, or 'royally screwed'.

I'll admit I was a little short with the woman, especially when she asked the class whether 'romance had blossomed yet' between any of my boys and her girls. Damn the woman to Hades and back. She's like a Jane Austen character. Next she'll be picking out muslin and asking the vicar for afternoon tea.

The girl Benedicta gave me a look of sympathy as the class filed out. 'Sorry, sir,' she mouthed at me almost inaudibly as she left.

I watched her go, intrigued and concerned. That girl is far too sensible. Mulberry House will spit her out like a cat with a furball. The other girls are trouble enough, with their hair-flicking antics, their eye for the boys and their interminable giggling, but if ever *real* trouble raises its head, I'm guessing Ben will be behind it. This feeling is exacerbated by the fact that she seems to be getting friendly with Allen-Jones, of all people. I've seen them together, and although fourth-year boys are not allowed into the Sixth-Form Common Room, she sometimes comes into the fourth-year room (sixth-formers can go anywhere), where she can often be seen chatting to my Brodie Boys, in defiance of the convention that states that boys and girls do not mingle, and that different year groups exist in a state of mutual antagonism. Still, my boys are unusual, and rather more fun than her peers, I suspect. Their friendship is a small ray of light in Harrington's growing darkness.

The rest of the day was difficult, fraught as it was with potential for war. Eric is still avoiding me, following our recent fracas. Miss Malone – aka the Foghorn – was absent, which meant that I had to cover for her. According to Kitty Teague, she suffers from depression. I sympathize, of course – but St Oswald's is not for the sensitive, and I suspect that the Foghorn may commandeer many more of my free afternoons, now that the honeymoon is over.

Meanwhile, Bob Strange has teamed up with Ms Buckfast on a plan to improve security. Henceforth, all visitors to the School will have to wear a name tag, and sign a special register. There is also talk of police checks for all ancillary staff, with the likelihood that staff members, too, will be subject to the same scrutiny. Bob Strange has been dreaming of this ever since he became Third Master, and his adoration of Ms Buckfast has now reached such a level of sycophancy that he leaves a trail of slime behind him whenever he is with her.

As if that wasn't enough, Devine has discovered that there are mice in the Bell Tower. Contrary to my live-and-let-live approach, which has served me well over thirty-odd years, he has therefore decided – on Health & Safety grounds, of course – to purge the whole Upper Corridor of its rodent population. A sensible man would understand the limits of his authority, but Devine is not a sensible man, especially when he is competing with a promising upstart like Markowicz.

Markowicz has a rodent-free room, so Devine must have one too, regardless of the fact that Devine's room is in a part of the building dating back to the eighteenth century and filled with eccentric conduits, blocked-up chimneys and hollow walls, which make infestation by rats, mice, cockroaches and other assorted vermin not only probable, but downright inevitable.

'You see, Roy, *this* is the reason we don't eat in our form-rooms,' he said as he delivered the news to me this lunchtime in room 59, his sensitive nose twitching with ill-concealed complacency. Of course, with impeccable timing, he'd caught me in the act of dispatching a furtive ham-and-cheese sandwich between Registration and afternoon school, and the look on his face suggested that he considered this kind of depravity to be the source of all our ills.

'One sandwich,' I said, brushing the crumbs into the inkwell on my desk.

'Food attracts vermin,' said Dr Devine. 'We'll have to put down poison bait.'

There was no point in trying to argue with him that the stench of dead mice inside the walls is far worse than the presence of living ones. Dr Devine was adamant: the mice must go. I resigned myself. When Devine gets the bit between his teeth, nothing short of physical violence will wrest it from him. I furtively transferred the bag of Liquorice Allsorts from my desk to the pocket of my tweed jacket. That's where it will have to stay, at least for the foreseeable future.

I finished the afternoon's classes with a renewed sense of *Weltschmerz* (it's no coincidence, I feel, that Devine's adopted language throws up so many of these melancholy concepts, unknown to the more civilized Romans). My fourth-form was listless and uninspired; even my Brodie Boys did not display much of their usual joie-de-vivre. Allen-Jones had a torn shirt and looked even more unkempt than usual; Tayler had a hacking cough. Thanks to Dr Blakely, Anderton-Pullitt's 'special needs' have evolved to include a dispensation from Latin altogether, while he concentrates on what he prefers – generally Maths and Science. I do not *miss* him, precisely, but when a disinclination to learn becomes a reason to stop doing so, the floodgates of Chaos are opened. I've tried to explain this to Dr Blakely, but Dr Blakely is adamant. Anderton-Pullitt's condition, he says, needs a specialist approach. Apparently a forty-odd-year career of dealing with boys does not meet this requirement.

And so, during the last lesson of the day, feeling less than lustrous, I gave the boys a translation from Vergil to do in test conditions, while I rested my eyes behind a copy of the *Telegraph*. I was still resting them at five o'clock, when a sound of clanking buckets roused me from my somnolence, and I opened my eyes to discover that the fourth-formers were all gone, and that it was getting dark.

Winter was at the classroom door, carrying his bucket and mop. 'I'm sorry,' he said. 'I thought you'd gone home.'

'It's all right. I was just – resting my eyes.' I sat up, adjusted my waistcoat and tried to look alert.

Winter gave me a curious look. 'Long day?'

'Long? Only about thirty years.'

I stood up too quickly. The room began to spin, and I had to steady myself by putting a hand on my desk. The air smelt of disinfectant and boys, and there was chalk on the desk-top. Which is just as it should be, I thought: how can a man call himself a schoolmaster if he doesn't have chalk under his fingernails, fire in his belly and a pounding head at the end of the day?

'*Homines, dum docent, discunt.*'

'A man – learns – as he teaches?' ventured Winter cautiously.

'That's right,' I told him. 'Seneca.'

I have to admit, I was surprised. It's not every day you come across a cleaner who knows Latin. But Winter is a far cry from Jimmy Watt, the Porter. For a start, he is intelligent – I can tell that from his voice and by the way he expresses himself. And he *sees* things – my fatigue, my anger with the management – that even my colleagues do not see.

'But who teaches the teachers?' he said.

Certainly not men like Markowicz, I thought, or administrators like Thing One and Thing Two: stuck all day in their offices, going on courses every week, drinking their coffee from the Headmaster's cups and having as little to do with boys as possible.

'Who, indeed?' I said.

He smiled. His smile is curiously endearing, although there is something odd there, too. He reminds me of a boy I once taught, a quiet, self-possessed young man called Joseph Apple, who, ten years after leaving St Oswald's, raped and stabbed a girl of sixteen, before lapsing into a fugue state from which he never recovered. I'm not sure why my cleaner should remind me of that troubled young man, but there's something in his eyes that seems to look into the shadows. Or maybe I'm just imagining it. After all, I have shadows of my own.

'I hope I'm not speaking out of turn.' His voice was slightly hesitant, and once again I wondered whether he'd stuttered as a boy. 'But I know how you feel about the Honours Boards being taken down, and I thought perhaps you ought to know.'

'Know what?'

'They're stacked up outside the Porter's Lodge. I think they're going to get rid of them.' Once more, Winter looked awkward. 'I don't think I'm supposed to know. But a hundred and fifty Honours Boards take up a lot of storage space. And I heard the Head talking to Jimmy Watt—'

I stood up. 'What did you hear?'

He shrugged. 'I got the impression he meant to sell them to a building merchant. You know, those people who reclaim things from condemned buildings and churches? There's quite a market for old school memorabilia. They use them for theme pubs and things like that.'

'*Theme pubs?*'

'I'm sorry,' he said. 'I don't know what I expected you to be able to do about it.'

I frowned at him. 'Why do you care? You were never a pupil here. *Were* you?' I suppose I was remembering last year's *Mole*, whose initial devotion to St Oswald's had turned into an obsessive desire for revenge.

Winter shook his head. 'I suppose I'm just sentimental. Those boards belong to St Oswald's. They don't belong in a theme pub.'

'I couldn't agree more,' I said. Then I had a brainwave. 'Do you have a car?'

'Yes.'

'Then – shall we call it – fifty quid?'

His eyes lit. 'That sounds reasonable.'

And that was how Roy Hubert Straitley became a felon. I, who had never even failed to bring back a library book on time, did knowingly and without remorse initiate the theft of a hundred and fifty Honours Boards, removed from the back of the Porter's Lodge in batches of a dozen or so, and transported in Winter's car to the basement of my house in Dog Lane, while I treated the Porter, Jimmy Watt, to a few rounds of drinks at the Scholar by means of a diversion.

I'd thought it would be difficult. In fact, it turns out that committing a crime is surprisingly easy. My accomplice did all the heavy work of stacking and unstacking the boards; I paid for Jimmy's drinks (and two of Bethan's ploughman's lunches), and then I paid off Winter in cash and returned to Dog Lane for cocoa and a slice of pie, feeling at the same time victorious and a little uncomfortable.

Yes, I have crossed a line. Strangely, I feel no different. In fact, I feel better than I have felt since the first day of term, when Johnny Harrington arrived to steal our past and our peace of mind. Those Honours Boards were not his to sell. I stole them from a criminal. And if the necessity arises, I shall steal *all* of St Oswald's, board by board, stone by stone, rather than let the upstart win.

The cocoa was pleasantly warming. I drank it in front of the living- room fire, reading Harry's journals and looking up from time to time at the object which had been his last gift to me, still sitting on my mantelpiece. Then I played his record again, and remembered the look on Devine's face as he told me about the garden gnome that had haunted him throughout that term, popping up unexpectedly in his locker, on his desk, behind the wheel of his car, even outside his front door at midnight on a Saturday—

That gnome. Poor, hapless Dr Devine. He had tried every means of exorcism. First he tried throwing the figure away. When that didn't work, he threw it out of his Bell Tower window (in defiance of all Health & Safety) to smash on to the cobbles far below. But Harry Clarke had access to an unlimited number of duplicates, because the moment one gnome was purged, another emerged to take its place; an army of leering minions, their single weapon ridicule.

Dr Devine's annoyance grew – along with his discomfort – as gnome after gnome popped its impudent head out from stock cupboard and locker room; from briefcase, bookshelves and flower beds, sometimes wearing a House tie, sometimes bearing a label – *Peripatetic Gnomad, Gnomic Utterance* or simply *Human G-gnome*.

I suspect that there was something about the relentlessness of the assault that made my colleague uneasy. He'd never had much of a sense of humour, and he mistrusted anything he saw as proof of irrationality. Men of Devine's ilk pride themselves on their common sense; they do not recognize the joys of the absurd and the meaningless. Devine disliked Harry Clarke because he saw him as a bad influence, encouraging boys to waste their time discussing pop music instead of Prep; studying Edward Lear in class instead of William Wordsworth; wearing elbow patches on his tweed jackets and failing to don his academic gown for Assemblies. In Devine's book, this made Harry Clarke a sloppy, unprofessional teacher. In mine, he was an original; refreshingly unconventional; blessed with ideas and values that were decades ahead of his time.

Harry called boys by their first names at a time when no one else did this; which, far from undermining discipline, seemed actually to enhance it. Harry believed individuals ought to be treated as such, and made an effort to know as much about the boys in his care as he could. Worse still, Harry encouraged those boys to see *him* as a human being; even inviting them to his house at weekends and after School. The reason Harry's Laughing Gnome had remained an ongoing joke for so long was that every boy in Harry's form was privy to it and part of the plan. That's twenty-nine boys, each with a gnome, each one with instructions of military precision on when and where to position it next for maximum disruptive effect.

Yes, it was ridiculous. Yes, it was juvenile. But when, on the last day of Michaelmas term, Devine came into his form to find twenty-nine gnomes sitting on desks in front of twenty-nine grinning boys, the mad surge of laughter that ensued was enough to lift the lid off the sky and allow the blaze of the sun to shine through.

I heard it from my form-room; the Old Head from his office; and Harry Clarke, in the Bell Tower, gave his boyish, open grin. It had been a cold, dark term. But just then, for a moment, all the world was in sunlight.

Once more I looked up at the mantelpiece. Harry's last gift to me grinned back, the paint a little faded now, but the gleeful expression unchanged.

Use it well, says Harry's note. I mean to do him justice.

3

December 1981

Dear Mousey,

So what with the fuss about Poodle, I've had to put some of my plans on hold. Most of that's due to my parents, who, on learning of his Condition, wanted to know *exactly* how close I was to Poodle, and what kind of things he'd said to me.

Now they keep trying to introduce me to nice girls from Church (nice girls from Church, like Becky Price), in case being queer could be catching. I wish they'd stop. It's embarrassing. What happened to Platonic love? Why does it always have to be about *sex*?

And then there are the little talks: talks about friends, and girls, and school, and if anything's ever happened to me at school that made me feel uncomfortable. I thought about saying: *My teacher's queer. He likes to put his hand on my leg and touch me through my trousers.* That would make them both sit up. They might even believe me. They'd certainly take it to the Head, and to the Board of Governors, and even maybe to the police. But then they'd take me out of school, and I'd never see Harry again.

I've thought about Harry a lot this week. I've ridden my new bike past his house. Once or twice, I've even stopped to have a look in at the windows. Harry has curtains, like everyone else, but they don't quite meet in the middle. If you stand by the window, you can see inside. Harry's got a Christmas tree all covered with stars and glass baubles. A proper one, not a tinsel job like my parents always have. And he has candles burning there; and a holly wreath on the door; and everything looks warm and safe, all lined with books and records.

Yes, it looks *safe* in Harry's house. Safe, and warm, and welcoming. The kind of place where you can go to talk about anything at all, and someone's there to listen. I'd already been there so many times, always meaning to knock at his door. But somehow I'd always chickened out. I guess it's a big step, Mousey.

Today I went back, on my bike. This time, I was planning to knock. I'd brought Harry's present with me – a special edition of Pink Floyd's *The Wall* – and his Christmas card, of course. I knew they'd be late, but that was OK. At least he'd have them before New Year. And I'd get to see his face as he read the card, and maybe then, I'd tell him—

It was cold. There was snow on the ground. I was wearing my duffel coat. Even so, I was freezing, and I could see my breath in the air like the ghosts of the people I'd been. I left my bike by Harry's front gate and looked through that gap in the curtains. The fire was lit in the front room. I could see a pot of tea on a stool next to the fireplace. Two cups.

I wondered who was there with him. He hasn't got any family. He's never mentioned a girlfriend. Perhaps a colleague from work, I thought – perhaps Mr Straitley, or even Scoones. I know they're friends. I don't know why. They don't have a thing in common. Then the kitchen door opened, and two people came into the living room. One was Harry. The other was skinny, and curly-haired—

Oh, Mousey. It was *Poodle*.

For a moment I could hardly breathe. *Poodle*? What was *he* doing there? It wasn't that I was jealous – not then – but simply astonished.

Poodle?

Poodle isn't special, I thought. Poodle isn't supposed to be here. And yet he was, in a V-necked jumper with a snowflake on the front, talking to Harry as if he had every right in the world. And then he turned towards the light from the starry Christmas tree, and there was a great big smile on his face, a smile I'd never seen before. It was like Harry had given him the best Christmas present of his life. And then he *kissed* him, Mousey. That little queer kissed Harry.

When I was still at Netherton Green, there was a book: *The Pied Piper*. It was the story of a man with a magical gift for making people follow him. After saving the town of Hamelin from rats, when the greedy Mayor wouldn't pay him his wage, he started to play a tune on his pipes and all the children followed him. They followed him right out of the town, and into the side of a mountain, where they vanished forever – except for one little lame boy, who couldn't keep up and was left behind. Well, that's what I felt like, Mousey; like the one that was left behind. And though I was angry at Poodle – oh, angry enough to do *anything* – I also felt angry with Mr Clarke, who had played me his music, and led me a dance, for whom I'd made such sacrifices – but who, in the end, had left me behind, because I wasn't special enough.

I watched for another few minutes or so. I wasn't going to knock at the door. I guess I thought Harry would push him away, maybe simply throw him out. But Harry didn't do that. Instead he let Poodle hold him, but keeping his own arms by his sides, and then, very gently, he stepped away, and poured them both a cup of tea from the brown pot by the fire.

Mousey, I didn't know what to do. Wasn't Poodle meant to be ill? Had he been avoiding me? And what had he said to Harry? Had he mentioned the rabbits? The rats? The games down at the clay pits?

The clay pits. The thought of them made me feel calmer, somehow. Perhaps it's because I associate them with getting rid of bad feelings. Poodle was still drinking his tea, looking stupidly happy. I couldn't just march in there, so I did the next best thing. He'd stolen from me, Mousey. The moment I'd been waiting for; the look on Harry's face as he opened his present; the perfect day we would have had if stupid Poodle hadn't been there – *that's* what he'd stolen, Mousey. All I could do was pay him back. And I knew right then what to do.

So I rode my bike down to the clay pits. I found Poodle's den in the rusted-out car. And for thirty minutes or so, I went about building a bonfire. First, I took out Poodle's books and ripped out all the pages. I stuffed his magazines inside the back of the car with some bits of wood and added some stacks of old comics. Then I used one of his cigarettes to set it alight, like a longship at a Viking funeral.

It didn't take long to start burning. But I wanted something more. Something bigger, to match the fire already burning in my heart. So I dragged some pallets across from the far side of the dump and made a wooden cage, in which I stuffed some cardboard, paper, rags – anything at all that would burn. Then I went around the dump, collecting empty cans of paint, petrol, turpentine, solvents, aerosols – things that would help the fire to take (and maybe explode like fireworks). Pretty soon it was getting hot; but I went on feeding it until it really was a funeral pyre, sending a column of thick black smoke high into the winter sky.

Maybe it was the fumes, or the heat, but I think I zoned out a bit, Mousey. And next thing I knew, I wasn't alone. Another boy was standing there. He was about my age, I guess. Maybe a little bit older. A boy from the estate, in a brightly coloured nylon jacket, like the Sunnybankers wear. You'd never see a St Oswald's boy wearing that kind of jacket, or a balaclava, or carrying a sports bag instead of a leather satchel. I knew then that he wasn't *One of Our Sort*, but that was OK. I'm not, either.

'All right?' said the boy.

His face was small and pinched, like a rat's. He was quite a bit smaller than me. But he looked scrappy – like a rat – with greasy hair and beady eyes and a little wisp of something on his top lip that might have been the beginning of a moustache. He took out a tin of tobacco and rolled a skinny cigarette.

'Here. Have one of mine,' I said, handing him one from Poodle's stash.

Ratboy took one and put it behind his ear. Then he took another one and lit it from a match, cupping the flame in his bony hands, his face bright red in the firelight.

'That your bonfire?' Ratboy said.

I nodded.

'Wicked,' said Ratboy. 'What's your name?'

'Ziggy.'

'Mine's Lee. That your bike?' I'd left it propped up against a rock down by the side of the Long Pond. I nodded. 'Wicked,' said Ratboy.

We didn't talk much after that. Just stood and smoked and watched Poodle's stash go up in flames. Estate boys don't talk much, as a rule. They play football, eat chips, smoke roll-ups. They say, *All right*? instead of *Hello*, or sometimes they just nod, or spit. There's a whole language of spitting, there on the Sunnybank estate. It's got its own grammar, and everything.

And then, a few minutes later, Poodle came ambling along. He stopped ambling when he saw the smoke, though, arriving in a hurry. I saw him coming up the path below the ridge between the Long Pond and the Pit Shaft, and went to meet him, taking a route between the junked cars and rocks and ancient fridges. I didn't want him to see me talking to Ratboy.

I dodged around the back of a rock and came out behind him.

'What happened?' he said.

I jerked my head to where Ratboy was standing, up on the ridge, fifty yards away. He looked bigger from where we were. The bonfire made him look dangerous.

'Who is it?' said Poodle.

'Dunno. A Sunnybanker.'

Poodle isn't very good with Sunnybankers. He's the kind of boy they like to wait for in the park, and bully for his lunch money. Up on the ridge, Ratboy didn't look back, just kept on looking into the flames. The air smelt of burning rubber, and smoke, tobacco, charred paper and secrets.

Poodle looked on helplessly. Of course he thought Ratboy had burnt his stash. I wished there'd been more for me to burn. I wished it could have been Poodle's *house*. I wished it could have been Poodle.

'You were at Mr Clarke's,' I said.

Poodle looked at me, surprised. 'He told me I could come any time. He's helping me with my problem.'

'Since *when*?'

That anger again. Since when did Poodle call the shots? Has he not learnt anything? I started to think that he might be in need of another lesson. He cried like a baby when we did the rabbits, but that was ages ago.

And yes: perhaps I needed it, too. It's not my fault; my Condition means that sometimes I just do these things. And sometimes, yes; I go too far. But if God made me, which my dad and everyone else at Church seem to think – then I guess it's God's fault I'm this way. You can take it up with Him.

Poodle was looking at Ratboy again. 'Bastard Sunnybanker.'

'We need to teach him a lesson,' I said.

I was looking at Ratboy too, but I was thinking of Poodle.

Poodle looked at me doubtfully. 'How?'

I explained what we would do. The Pit Shaft wasn't far away. If we could get him to come to the edge, to look into the water—

'It'll be all right,' I said. 'We'll pull him out – eventually.'

Poodle looked uncertain. 'No way. Ziggy, he'll kill us. He's crazy.'

'No,' I said. 'He'll be soaking wet. Anyway, it's two to one. He'll know that he can't mess with us, and he'll never come here again.'

Poodle bit his finger. 'You'll stay with me? You promise?' he said.

'Course I will. I promise.'

'OK.'

Still keeping his eyes on Ratboy, he started to move towards the pit. Ratboy didn't turn round. The sound of the bonfire was still too loud.

'Stand by the edge. Right there,' I said. 'Then we'll call him over.'

'What are we going to say?'

I shrugged. 'Say you saw a body in there. Pretend you can see it floating.'

Poodle shivered.

'Come on,' I said. 'Look as if you've spotted it. Just a little further—'

And that was what happened, Mousey. I honestly didn't mean it to happen that way. Well, of course I *meant* it, but not the way it turned out. That was an accident. Not my fault. The best-laid plans of mice and men—

Which brings us back to you, Mousey.

4

September 20th, 2005

How do criminals manage their guilt? I arrived at St Oswald's today fully expecting to find the police waiting for me in the Bell Tower, ready to accuse me of the theft of the Middle Corridor Honours Boards. In fact, after a fitful night's sleep, I had become so convinced of this that I had already prepared a short speech, to be delivered on the occasion of my arrest.

Not that I felt guilty, no. But I was convinced that my countenance would reveal my crime, and so I was slightly taken aback to find not the police but Devine at my door, looking annoyed, and carrying a brightly coloured garden gnome.

'Straitley, a word,' he said.

A few of my boys had already arrived and were reading, or talking among themselves. My Brodie Boys, Allen-Jones, Sutcliff, Tayler and McNair, were exuberantly discussing the weekend's exploits, which seemed to have involved a great deal of song, and the wearing of several shades of sparkly nail varnish, the remnants of which still endured.

'*Do* boys wear nail polish nowadays?' I said when Allen-Jones pointed it out. My lackadaisical attitude to breaches of uniform protocol usually suits the boys perfectly, but in this case they were aiming to shock, which was precisely why I'd ignored them.

'The *girls* wear varnish,' said McNair. 'If they can, then we can too. Otherwise it's gender discrimination.'

'Alas, the rules of the outside world have yet to make an impact here. If I were you, I'd take it off,' I advised, without looking up from the pile of books I was marking.

It was at this point that Devine arrived, holding the gnome and looking as dangerous as a man *can* look whilst holding a garden gnome. I have to admit, my mind had been so fixed on those Honours Boards that I'd almost forgotten Harry's gift, and how I had deployed it . . .

I stepped out into the corridor. 'How can I help you, Devine?' I enquired.

'*This*,' he said in a damning tone, 'was on my porch on Sunday morning.'

'Gnome, sweet gnome,' I quipped – rather ill-advisedly, because Devine's nose went alarmingly pink.

'Well, of course I'm assuming that *you* put it there.'

'Oh, really?' I said. 'And do you have any reason for this, or is it simply a question of *Conlige suspectos semper habitos*?'

Dr Devine gave a kind of hiss. 'There *are* no usual suspects,' he said. 'Only you, Straitley, would find this amusing. Besides,' he went on, 'I hear Harry Clarke left you some of his effects.'

I nodded. 'You heard correctly.'

For a moment Devine peered at me through narrowed eyes. 'The Chaplain also tells me you've been talking about a memorial.'

Once more I nodded.

He gave a sigh. 'That isn't going to happen,' he said. 'You, of all people, should understand why.'

I said: 'He should be remembered.'

'He *is* remembered,' said Devine. 'Isn't that the problem?' He handed me the garden gnome. 'Let the past be the past,' he said, in a rather gentler tone. 'I know how you felt about Harry Clarke.'

'No, I don't think you do,' I said. 'And I know you weren't exactly friends. But Harry was part of St Oswald's, just as much as you or I. Whatever else you thought of him, he still deserves a memorial.'

Devine shrugged. 'It can't be done. Not under the current Head. Or indeed, under *any* Head—'

I looked at him. 'It isn't *right*. You know that as well as I do.'

'I *don't*! And even if I did—' He stopped. That legendary self-control was on the verge of breaking. I am not fooled by his chilly façade. I know Dr Devine as well as anybody knows him. He is driven by ambition, not love. The gods of progress have claimed him, of course, but his heart is as sound as the Bell Tower. When that business erupted last year, I saw his confidence falter. I know how close he came that term to breaking down completely. We all have our comforts, our touchstones. Mine is tradition – the Honours Boards, the photographs, the scent of books and chalk dust. His are somewhat different: Health & Safety; e-mail; Information Technology. He thinks that if he stays abreast of all the current developments, then he will never have to grow old, retire or claim his pension.

Though it annoys me, I understand. Both of us share the unspoken fear of a life beyond St Oswald's; a life without the discipline of lesson bells or timetables; no Quiet Room; no marking; no Prep; no weekends or holidays. St Oswald's

Masters do not live long past retirement. Captivity sustains us; too much freedom eats us alive. Devine has no more love for Johnny Harrington than I, and yet he will follow him to the grave, not from loyalty, but fear.

I said: 'I think you'll change your mind once you've given the matter some thought. And beware the Ides of Markowicz. I've heard the omens are terrible.'

And, tucking the garden gnome under my arm, I went back into room 59, to my little empire, my Brodie Boys and the comfortable scent of chalk, old books, damp socks, wood polish and mice.

I kept the gnome in my briefcase. Devine hasn't heard the last of this. Harry left that gnome to me with the instruction to *use it well*. Though, short of bludgeoning him to death with it, just *how* I can bring down Harrington with nothing but ire and a garden gnome, I have no idea for the present. Maybe time will tell. But I will see it done – for my friend; for St Oswald's; for myself. Even perhaps for Devine – and for Eric, who has tried his best to forget what happened all those years ago.

Poor Eric. I'm fond of him, and yet I sometimes wish he were stronger. Loyalty was never his strong suit, neither to me nor to Harry. And when we were boys at St Oswald's, always getting into scrapes, it was always Scoones who broke under interrogation; who gave up his friends to save himself; who claimed not to have been there.

He's still avoiding me, by the way. He greets me, but he won't meet my eye. As if that old story could hurt him now, or do any damage to his career. I considered hiding the garden gnome in his classroom, under the desk. That would bring the message home. But, as it happened, there was no chance today to deploy my secret weapon. There are other games in play; games that I do not control.

This morning's Assembly, led by the Head, was on the subject of bullying. Not an unwelcome topic, of course; although I thought he looked at me rather too often for comfort. Dr Blakely was at his right hand, Ms Buckfast at his left. Together, they formed an unholy triptych that made my very entrails writhe.

'Bullying, like so many other kinds of antisocial behaviour,' he said, 'basically comes from a lack of faith. Faith in God, faith in oneself, faith in other people. That lack of faith creates a void, which we try to fill in all kinds of ways, including addictive behaviour. And bullying *is* an addiction,' he said, earnestly addressing the boys. 'It makes you feel good in the short term by giving you a sense of control, but actually, *it* controls *you*. It changes who you are inside.'

There was more of this in the same vein (I told you he was an orator), and the boys all listened attentively. Young Harrington is not just a Suit. He is becoming a Snake-Charmer – open, articulate, plausible – projecting, if not actual warmth, then at least the illusion of caring. Don't the boys realize this is an act?

I looked at the faces of my form. Anderton-Pullitt, nodding his head as if his salvation depended on it; Brasenose (often the victim of bullying himself) looked almost in tears. In the row opposite, I saw Rupert Gunderson, watching with the rapt attention of a recent convert. Only my Brodie Boys seemed immune to his oratory: Sutcliff jiggling his foot; McNair staring blankly into space; Allen-Jones with his arms crossed, mouth set in a wry quirk that was not quite a smile.

The Chaplain took over after that, with a droning passage from St Luke. The charm was broken; the usual chorus of furtive coughs and rustling ensued. Devine snapped at two of his boys, who had started whispering. Normality had been resumed.

After Assembly, Allen-Jones came to see me, looking grim.

'Sir, it's Rupert Gunderson. He's made a counter-complaint to the Head. He says he's sorry he hit me, but that I made him uncomfortable, which *he* says is a kind of bullying. And now the Headmaster's saying that *I'm* the evil influence, and that challenging Gunderson about his homophobia counts as victimization. He's asking *me* to go for counselling. I'm seeing Dr Blakely today.'

That explains the Assembly, I thought. 'Ye gods. He can't be serious.'

Allen-Jones gave me a look that was both knowing and world-weary.

'That Assembly was all about me,' he said. 'All that stuff about lack of faith and antisocial behaviour. He's making this all about me, sir. He said I was going through a *rebellious phase*. He said I needed to show tolerance to the beliefs of others.'

I gave an inward sigh. 'All right. Let me deal with this,' I said.

I could see the boy was upset, but on the other hand, Allen-Jones has always had a tendency to over-dramatize. I went to see the Headmaster as soon as my timetable allowed; I found him in his office, with Dr Blakely and the Chaplain.

'Ah, Roy. Just the man,' he said. 'We were discussing policy.'

'I'm sorry to intrude,' I said. 'But could I have a quick word?'

Harrington beamed. 'Of course,' he said. 'In fact, I'm very glad you're here. This concerns you, after all. Please, take a seat.'

I remained standing. The Chaplain gave me a suspicious look. Dr Blakely gave the kind of smile a doctor gives a patient just before announcing that he has only months to live.

'I didn't come for a meeting,' I said. 'I'd like a word with you alone.'

Harrington smiled. 'Of course you do. But let's just put that on hold for a while. I've been talking to Marcus here' – at this, Dr Blakely gave a canine nod – 'about our Bullying Policy. We think it's important for boys and staff to be aware of bullying. In fact, we've drawn up a document outlining the School's aims.'

How typical of him, I thought, to assume we needed a document. In the old days, common sense was all a Master needed – that, and the guts to tackle the boys directly, in the classroom, and not from behind a document drawn up in an office.

'The thing is, Roy,' went on the Head, 'bullying can take many forms. Many bullies are not even aware that their behaviour is affecting others. It isn't always physical. It can be psychological, which in many ways is even more damaging. We feel that *anything* that makes a boy feel uncomfortable – be it hitting, name-calling or just imposing one's beliefs on others – counts as a form of bullying, and we need to combat this at all levels, including members of staff.'

'I'm not sure I understand,' I said.

Harrington gave his PR smile. 'What I mean, Roy, is that if we want to eliminate bullying among the boys, we have to examine our own methods. To be shouted at and humiliated – in public or in private – can be a traumatic experience for a young adolescent. These methods *may* have been valid – once. But things have moved on. Our customers expect us to be sensitive to all needs.'

Damn the man, I thought. Was he accusing *me*, now?

'I don't think we always appreciate the impact we have on these young minds.' That was Dr Blakely, finally finding the courage to speak. With his lashless, fishy eyes, he looked like a trout in the headlights. 'The psychological scarring caused by public shaming can be immense. As a survivor myself, I feel we have a long way to go here. We're instigating a programme to discover the extent of the problem, after which we can start to address it.'

For a moment I was confused. *A survivor?* Had Dr Blakely been involved in some kind of terrible childhood accident? Or did he mean a survivor of Life?

'We're *all* survivors here,' I said. 'So are my boys. I insist on it. In fact, a great deal of my teaching methodology is based on the assumption that, however much they may long for death, I expect them to survive the term, and preferably score well in Latin, although—'

'Colin Knight didn't survive,' said Blakely in his colourless voice.

I stopped mid-sentence. Damn the man. Carried away by my oratory, I'd forgotten Colin Knight. 'That was different,' I said at last. 'Damn it, the boy was *murdered*.'

'There's no proof of that,' he said. 'All we know is that the boy was unhappy, that he was bullied, that he disappeared from School and was never seen again. All we know is that the School failed to spot the signs of abuse. All we know is that a boy – a lonely, desperate, *vulnerable* boy – felt that there was so little support for him here at St Oswald's that he had to run away. It happens, Mr Straitley. Even here, it happens. And I know this isn't the first time—'

Charlie Nutter. Damn his eyes. The man knows my vulnerabilities.

Harrington gave a tiny smile. 'I know you're *fond* of Allen-Jones—'

'That has nothing to do with it. The boy came to *me* with a complaint. I did what any form-master would do.' I was starting to feel under siege.

Harrington sighed. 'I'm sure you did what you thought was best.' Patronizing little *stercus*. 'But Marcus's role in Survivors means that he sees this kind of thing every day. He's had experience in many schools, and spoken to many survivors.'

That word again. As if School were like a plane crash, with certificates at the end saying: *I survived St Oswald's*! Come to think of it, Dr Blakely would probably approve of that. He strikes me as the kind of man who likes to put stars on wall-charts and hands out lollipops after class. Not that he does any teaching; no. He's far too busy *having experiences*.

'I hope we can count on you,' he said. 'I really think a different approach would help resolve the conflict here.'

I took a deep breath of the pine-freshened air. I could see what was happening. Rupert Gunderson; the Honours Boards; the refusal to host Harry Clarke's memorial; and now Allen-Jones and Survivors – all had been part of the same campaign. I felt as Socrates must have felt when his colleagues conspired against him. Next, it would be the hemlock bowl – or as men of Harrington's ilk prefer to call it, voluntary retirement.

'Well?' said the Headmaster.

For a moment, I considered it. To simply let go, like Socrates – to drink the hemlock and be damned. Apparently it's an easy death; a creeping numbness, then sleep. No more conflict; no more pain; a legacy unblemished. *They* had all of the twenty-first century on their side: computers; committees; paperwork. And as for political correctness, they ran the asylum.

What did *I* have to fight them with? A school cleaner and a garden gnome. If it hadn't been so sad, it would have been hilarious. Better perhaps to accept defeat than death by a thousand paper-cuts—

Then there came a knock at the door. Danielle came in with a tea-tray. Once more, I was saved by Danielle, with her gold earrings as big as satellite dishes; her hair dyed in improbable stripes; her smile as sweet as springtime. Her entrance broke the tension that had built up without my realizing it; the snake-charmer's spell was broken and I suddenly knew what I had to do.

No, I won't drink the hemlock, I thought. If they want me out, then they can fight me all the way to the gates. This is *my* School, not theirs, and I will not go willingly. *Progress through Tradition* may be Harrington's new slogan, but St Oswald's motto remains *Audere, augere, auferre*. To dare, to strive, to conquer. And that is what I shall strive to do, in defiance of all opposition.

I smiled at the Head. 'Headmaster,' I said. 'St Oswald's has *all* of my loyalty. Whatever I can do, I will, *in service of St Oswald's*.'

And on that I summoned my dignity and went back to my room in the Bell Tower, that last survivor of the fleet, while all around, the cannons roared and the rising tide of iron-grey Suits lashed at the beleaguered decks.

5

December 1981

Mousey was my bestest friend. (Mousey, you were my *only* friend.) We were both in Miss McDonald's form at Netherton Green, and we did most things together. Mousey had a Condition, too – not like mine. It had a special name. I don't remember it now, though. He was in the Slow Readers at school, but actually he could read just fine.

I liked Miss McDonald. I liked her a lot. She went to our Church, and sometimes, if we were good, she would play the guitar during Storytime. She used to wear a blue Indian-print dress with little bells stitched on the hem, and though she was old – twenty-five, at least – she was totally gorgeous. I was the classroom monitor. I wore a badge and everything. I used to bring the chalks from out of the stock cupboard every day, and sometimes I used to stand on a chair and wipe the board clean with the board-rubber. I also watered the plants, collected books, stuck gold stars on the star chart and looked after the class hamster.

Miss McDonald called me her 'special little helper'. Mousey helped too, but only because I let him. Mousey was from the White City estate. He had two brothers, but no dad. My dad didn't like him, because his mum didn't go to Church, and because she was a cleaner. But Mousey was OK. We used to go to the graveyard down by old St Mary's Church, and lie down on gravestones and play dead.

In the days before God took my brother, I'd never thought about death. Perhaps I was too young to get my head around that kind of thing. Or perhaps I was in that state of grace that Mr Speight keeps talking about. Of course my parents had mentioned it. They told me that you went to sleep, and then you woke up in Heaven. And for a while, I believed them. The way I believed in Santa Claus, and babies coming from cabbages. Grown-ups lie to kids all the time. The Tooth Fairy; the Virgin Birth; how the red stuff doesn't sting and how the ice-cream van only plays music when they've run out of ice-cream. Kids are pretty stupid like that. They'll believe almost anything.

And then, Bunny died, and suddenly, I was an only child again. Nothing else seemed to have changed. I still went to school; there was still TV, with *Play School* and *Scooby Doo* and *Looney Tunes* and *Doctor Who*. The sun still rose in the mornings. Bedtime was still at the same time. Everything went on as before, except that Bunny wasn't there. His toys were still in his toy-box. His cot with its patchwork coverlet was still there, forever empty. It's not that I cared about him much. But the thought that he could just be *gone*, while his toys and his cot were still around—

And it hit me. *Death is forever*. A hole in the ground. A headstone. People walking around on the grass above you, while you're down there in the earth. Kids watching TV; playing football; doing their homework; growing up. Except that Bunny would never grow up. Bunny was gone forever. And if Bunny could die, then anyone could. Mum.

Dad. Miss McDonald. Me. Unless I believed in Heaven, of course. And all that, forever, unless I *believed*.

And that was it, Mousey. I *didn't* believe. I knew about Jesus, and Heaven, and Hell. I believed in them all, in the same way I believed in Santa and the Easter Bunny. But I believed in Death more. God was small. Death was huge. I used to lie in bed at night, trying to imagine it. All that *forever*, just waiting for me—

I told myself that I had at least sixty years before I really needed to think about it, but somehow sixty didn't seem long, compared to all that eternity. I used to lie awake at night, paralysed by the numbers. Nothing – no one – could help me. Mum and Dad were too busy with arrangements, then too busy with praying and support groups to care much about what I was doing. I remember the long, whistling silences around the table at mealtimes; the way my mother looked at me; the whispers from the people at Church.

If I'd been the one who died, I thought, would my brother have understood? Or would I have just been a photograph in someone's photo album, like Grandma and Grandpa, who died before I was even born, and who I always remembered in black and white, like an old film? I'd always known that people died. But the thought that *I* would, too – Mousey, I thought I'd go crazy. And then, you taught me to play The Game, and everything changed for both of us.

Now I was friends with Mousey at school, but I wasn't supposed to play with him. Dad was very strict about that. White City boys were a different class. They didn't even go to Church. Mousey came to our house just once, when I was new at Netherton Green. We played trains in my bedroom. Mum made oatmeal biscuits. Dad looked in a couple of times, I guess to see if Mousey was 'sound'. And then, when Mousey had gone, they explained that Mousey wasn't Our Kind of Boy, and that I wasn't to invite him any more. Maybe it was because he'd eaten all the biscuits. Anyway, I never did invite him back to play at my house, but Mousey liked the old churchyard, and so I'd go there to meet him, and we'd lie down on a gravestone and play at being dead, which was basically just lying there, seeing who could keep his eyes shut for longest.

And then, one day, after Bunny died, Mousey taught me another game. He called it *Mousey, Mousey*, and it's why I gave him his nickname. But it was a top-secret game, that no one else could know about. Except maybe his fat brother, Piggy, who sometimes came to look after him, but who wouldn't tell anyone, because he was scared of their ma finding out.

The game was pretty simple. We played it down by the clay pits. That was where you got the mouse. You needed a mouse to play the game, and there were lots in the clay pits. You get an empty milk bottle (those little ones from school work well). You put some food in the bottom; a sweet, or maybe a broken biscuit. You stick the bottle half in the ground but at a tilt, so the mouse can climb in, but it can't get out again. Come back a bit later, or the next day, and – boom. You can have fun with the mouse.

We played on Saturday mornings, when Mousey's mum often liked to lie in, and my mum and dad went to their support group. Mousey would bait the traps the night before, and by morning they were always full. We used the largest of the pits, the one we called the Long Pond, and we dropped the bottles in, one by one, and watched to see what the mice would do.

Mostly, they died almost straight away. That was fun, but it didn't last. So Mousey and I began to think up ways to make the game last longer. We used to make little boats from wood and float them in the Long Pond, or sometimes the shallow Crescent, or the three small pits that Mousey and I called the Little Injuns, but never the Pit Shaft, with its steep banks, which was much too dangerous.

Anyway, we'd launch the boat, and then we'd put the mouse on board. The mouse was always the captain, and then we'd bomb the boat with stones, or set it on fire with newspaper, or make giant waves with a piece of board and watch it pitch and rock until it sank. Sometimes the mouse tried to swim back. Then we'd just catch it and start again. Sometimes the mouse just stayed there, twitching a bit, but not moving. That was never as much fun. I preferred the lively ones.

After a while, our games began to get a bit more ambitious. We'd catch a dozen mice at a time, and float them away, like Noah's Ark. Sometimes the mice used to pray to God to save them from the rising flood. God never answered. But that was OK. After all, *we* were God.

Sometimes Piggy came along. He was meant to look after Mousey when his mother was asleep. He was a bit older than Mousey, but he wasn't anything like him. He was fat and stupid, and he was afraid of everything. He used to cry like a little girl when Mousey made him watch what we did. Sometimes he cried so hard that he could barely breathe, and his heart beat so fast that we thought it might burst. It was lots of fun, actually. Even better than the mice. It was like we'd taken all my fear and made it go into someone else. There's a story like that in the Bible, you know. Jesus and the Gadarene. Jesus came across a man possessed by a whole load of demons. And he made the demons leave the man and go into a herd of swine. Then, Jesus made the herd of swine jump off a cliff into the sea, where they all drowned, and the man was saved. It's a pretty cool story, actually. And it's in the Bible, so it must be true.

And then, something awful happened. It was after the Christmas holidays. Bunny had been dead for a year. And Miss McDonald came into school with a ring on her finger, and said that from now on, we had to call her Mrs Lumb. She'd got married over Christmas, to another teacher at Netherton Green. She showed us the pictures and everything. We all got a bit of wedding cake. Everyone was excited. Except for me and Mousey, that is. Mousey because he rarely got excited about anything, except for the games in the clay pits. Me, because something important had changed, and I didn't even know what it was.

It took me a while to figure it out. My mum and dad weren't what you'd call super-big on the facts of life. I mean, I knew the important stuff, like touching yourself makes you go blind, and even *kissing* can send you to Hell, but stuff that married people do – that was still a mystery. I knew it must be disgusting, though. All the words for it were swears. Even *thinking* about it was a sin, and learning about it at school was wrong, which was why I wasn't allowed to be in sex education classes. No, sex was like toxic waste, only to be handled by specialists. So the thought of Miss McDonald (I refused to call her Mrs Lumb) actually *having sex* with Mr Lumb, the Games teacher – who everyone called *Lumbo* because of his big muscles and tiny little elephant eyes – was just too revolting to imagine. And yet I kept imagining it. There were all kinds of things at the clay pits; all sorts of rubbish that people had dumped; piles of newspapers and magazines. Some of them were called *Knave*, and *Penthouse*, and *Playboy*. Those were sex magazines, I knew. I wasn't supposed to look at them. But I couldn't help it sometimes. I wanted to know. And Mousey, of course, knew everything. His brothers had already told him the lot.

Frankly, it was disgusting. I knew people had to make sacrifices, but honestly, this was too much. Between Mousey and those magazines, I soon knew more than I wanted to. And the worst of it was that, once those pictures were in my head, I just couldn't stop seeing them – except that instead of the women in the magazines, I kept seeing Miss McDonald, and instead of the men, all I saw was Mr Lumb.

I had to do something about it. But I was a kid, not nine years old. What could I do? I waited. I talked about it with Mousey. Mousey didn't seem to care as much. But then, Mousey didn't go to Church. He didn't know about demons and stuff. He didn't even know about the sin of self-abuse. And so I watched Miss McDonald and her horrible husband coming to work together. I saw them talking in the yard when she was on supervision duty. When she was still Miss McDonald, I used to go and talk with her as she drank her coffee. Now, she talked with Mr Lumb instead, and laughed, and sometimes slapped his arm, and I was no longer her special friend.

It wasn't fair. I still helped out; I still cleaned the blackboard and watered the plants. But Miss McDonald wasn't the same. She didn't talk to me as much as she had before she was married; she went home straight away after school, in Mr Lumb's horrible car. She even stopped wearing those Indian cotton dresses. And once, when I called her Miss McDonald in class, she actually *snapped* at me and said: '*You know that's not my name any more!*' It wasn't like her. Not like her at all. And now I knew what it was at last; that horrible man had got into her, infecting her with the demon of sex.

Yes, I know. I was naïve. But all I really knew about sex was what I'd seen in those magazines, and what I'd heard from sermons in Church. And I thought about the possessed man, whom Jesus cured by sending his demons into the swine, then herding them off a cliff. And I thought about those games with the mice. And then I thought about Piggy, and how he used to wheeze and cry when we drowned the mice. And the more I thought about it, the more sense it seemed to make. I needed to get Miss McDonald's demons to leave, and go into something else, and then all I had to do was drown them, just like Jesus did.

And so I tried to think of a plan. Failing Miss McDonald herself, I needed something that belonged to her. I decided on her silk scarf, which used to hang on the clothes peg at the back of our classroom. One day, after school, I stole the scarf and took it away and hid it by the clay pits. It still smelt of her perfume, a mixture of incense and coconut. Now, all I needed was the swine.

Mousey was in on the plan from the start. Because he didn't go to Church, he never really understood how the thing was supposed to work. But that was OK. He went along. As long as he was drowning things, I don't think he minded.

We started with mice, as usual. I'd collected about a dozen of them. How many swine make up a herd? I hoped a dozen was enough. Anyway, we took out the scarf. It still smelt of Miss McDonald. I wrapped it around my shoulders, and then I performed the exorcism. Obviously I didn't know the right words for an exorcism, but I thought if you said *thee* and *thou*, like the preacher does in Church, the demons would get the picture. Then we herded the mice off the cliff (it was only a small cliff, only a clay embankment into one of the pits, but it must have looked bigger to the mice) and waited for the charm to work.

It was great. It should have worked. But the next day, the Headmaster, whose name was Mr Rushworth, called me to his office. Miss McDonald was there, too, looking very serious.

'I've received a very serious report,' Mr Rushworth told me. 'Do you know what that might be?'

I shook my head.

Miss McDonald gave me a sad look. 'If only you tell the truth,' she said, 'then everything will be all right. Now listen. This is important. Did you take my scarf last night?'

Once more, I shook my head. I know it was lying, and lying was wrong, but I could hardly admit that I'd stolen her scarf for a mouse exorcism. Besides, I figured that demons were a much bigger sin than lying, or even stealing; so God would be bound to forgive me as long as, next time, I got it right.

Mr Rushworth stood up. 'I think you're lying, boy,' he said. His face was always very red, and now it was nearly purple. 'You were seen taking Mrs Lumb's scarf from the peg in the form-room. Now, for the last time, tell the truth. *Why did you steal it?*'

Once again, I shook my head. It felt like a betrayal, but Miss McDonald couldn't know what I'd sacrificed for her. Turns out the scarf was a Hermès – which meant it was something expensive and rare, and not just an ordinary scarf like Mum used to wear over her curlers.

And so I got the cane: three strokes on the back of my hand for the theft; three more for the lying. It hurt, but not half as much as the look on Miss McDonald's face when she took off my special helper's badge and pinned it on Mousey's jumper instead.

You see, Mousey had told on me. Mr Lumb had seen him walking with me to the clay pits, and he had told him everything: the scarf; the mice; the ritual. Not the *reason*, thankfully – I don't think he understood it himself – but he'd told them enough to condemn me. Apart from the cane, which was bad enough, I lost all my form privileges: the badge, the plants, the board-rubber. I also had to pay for the scarf out of my own pocket money. And Miss McDonald's demons stayed in Miss McDonald; I could see them in her eyes whenever she happened to look at me.

After that, Mousey was class monitor, and I didn't talk to him any more. He'd let me down; they'd *both* let me down – and instead of going to the clay pits on Sunday mornings, I had to go to Sunday School with my dad, who was horrified at what Mr Rushworth had told him. Not so much about the mice, or even about Miss McDonald's scarf, but the fact that I'd been playing out in such a notorious spot, and with boys of a Different Class.

I tried to explain about the demons, but Dad was too angry to listen. And so the horrid school term wore on, and people started to call me names like *poncey* and *spazzer* and *poofter*. I didn't know what those things meant. But I knew who was responsible; and during the weeks that followed, I racked my brains to think of a plan that would help me get back at Mousey.

6

September 26th, 2005

A blustery day at St Oswald's today, tearing the paper leaves from the trees. Wind, almost as much as snow, is the schoolmaster's enemy, making boys excitable; tugging at blazers; pulling off caps; sending papers flying. Perhaps it's the ozone in the air, but boys are disruptive on windy days, and today St Oswald's was riddled with little pockets of turbulence. The Foghorn's mournful cry rang out for most of the morning, and even Devine – still irked, perhaps, by his experience with the gnome – sent a boy out to stand in the corridor, sheepishly, awaiting the dreaded one-to-one. Kitty Teague was looking harassed, following a series of incidents. At present, the Head of Department's job consists of cover and administrative work – not a great use of Kitty's time, as I'm sure she is aware. But between Miss Malone's spiritual malaise, and Dr Markowicz's frequent incursions into the world of Visual Aids, *someone* has to hold the fort. Thus: Kitty's classes have been left in the hands of the wispy Miss Smiley, with predictable results.

Only Bob Strange seems happy. His smile, rarely seen in happier days, illuminates the Lower Corridor, where he has taken to lurking, clipboard in hand, outside Ms Buckfast's office. Doubtless he feels that proximity to the seat of power will give him a better chance when it comes to taking back his fiefdom when the Crisis Deputies leave.

However, it was my own Brodie Boys who caused the most disruption today – or rather, they were the catalyst for what happened afterwards. You wouldn't think a bit of paint – even in such enticing shades as Sexy Cerise, Victoria Plum and Spangly Watermelon Surprise – could affect the discipline of an entire year-group, but according to Markowicz, it represents the thin end of a dangerous wedge that could culminate in anarchy.

I refer, of course, to the nail varnish still adorning the finger-ends of Tayler, McNair, Sutcliff and Allen-Jones. My personal policy is to ignore such trivia as untucked shirts, subversive socks and similar *accoutrements*, designed to draw attention away from the *really* important things, like Latin translation, irregular verbs and keeping the classroom litter-free. Indeed, I've always found that where teenage rebellion fails to shock, it quickly loses its appeal – but the idiot Markowicz, in spite of having attended more courses than a normal human being can stand, is apparently unaware of the most elementary rules of teenage psychology.

As ill-luck would have it, this lunchtime my boys were in the Middle School Common Room with the girl Benedicta while Markowicz was on duty there. If I hadn't already judged the man, his method of dealing out discipline would have already marked him in my mind as one of life's hopeless cases – a Jackass, according to my Rough Guide to the Common Room – a man who believes that anything can be achieved simply by braying loudly enough, and who invariably comes down hardest on the most harmless of miscreants, in the hope that the *real* toughs will be fooled into obedience.

This was why my Brodie Boys, conversing with their usual level of exuberance, were immediately singled out by Markowicz, who took offence, first to their high spirits and then to the nail polish, and who, after a slight altercation of the kind no member of staff should ever allow in a public forum, found themselves summoned into the presence of Dr Blakely, aka Thing One. The girl Benedicta tried to object, and was duly sent to Ms Buckfast, who seems to have had the common sense not to make a fuss. However, as a result of this, Sutcliff and McNair were late to afternoon classes, and Allen-Jones never reappeared. When I made enquiries (via Bob Strange) I was told that the boy had been suspended, following a 'serious breach of discipline', details of which could be found in an e-mail sent by Dr Blakely and copied to the Head of Year.

As soon as I was free, I went to Dr Blakely's office to complain. I found him with Markowicz and the Head, which did nothing to allay my disquiet.

'Ah, Mr Straitley,' said Dr Blakely. 'I'm glad you popped in. Your boy Allen-Jones—'

I sat down in his armchair. Pat Bishop's armchair, to be exact; moulded to his proportions. The new man will never enjoy it: he is too straight, too angular. He has an ergonomic chair to match his shiny new workstation, and a series of abstract prints on his wall replace Pat Bishop's photographs of rugby players and sporting heroes throughout St Oswald's history.

'My boy, Allen-Jones,' I repeated. 'Rumour has it you've sent him home. How considerate of you to step in on my behalf, without taking the time to consult me.'

Dr Blakely recoiled a little. 'I sent you an e-mail,' he began.

Briefly but pungently, I expressed what I thought of his e-mail. 'We have a pastoral system,' I said. 'The form-master is the first port of call. And if one of my boys misbehaves – which, in this case, I question – then I expect to be informed in person, not by a programme on a machine.'

Markowicz gave me a look. Close up, his resemblance to Devine is not as marked as I'd previously thought. Devine, for all his faults, remains a Suit, not a Jackass.

'The boys were wearing nail varnish,' he said. 'I asked them to take it off. They refused. After that I had no choice but to refer them to Dr Blakely.'

I shook my head, pained by his ignorance. 'And what did you expect?' I said. 'You allowed a group of fourth-form boys to draw you into a ridiculous – and public – confrontation. It's the classic beginner's mistake. Trainees do it all the time.'

The Head gave an admonishing cough. 'I think there's more to it than that,' he said. 'I'm looking into the incident. Besides, as you already know, I believe there's something unwholesome about Allen-Jones's influence over the boys in your form. Perhaps this needs a different approach. After what happened with Gunderson—'

'Gunderson's a bully,' I said.

'That's not what the Chaplain says.' He smiled, and once again I saw a glimpse of that troubling, dangerous charm. 'Listen, Roy, I'm sorry,' he said. 'I shall be looking into this myself, and I promise I'll keep you informed throughout. In person, not by e-mail.'

Oh yes, he *sounded* reasonable. But all my instincts told me that I was being sidelined, manoeuvred, cajoled into acquiescence. Little Johnny Harrington was always used to getting his way, and he still knows how to manipulate people into doing exactly what he wants. I can understand his trying to get back at me – a Master he'd never liked as a boy, and who will never accept him. But what does he want with Allen-Jones, a bright, articulate student – perhaps a little impertinent, but certainly no troublemaker? What does Harrington think to achieve by targeting my Brodie Boys?

It annoyed me – perhaps more than it should. Or perhaps I was still feeling nervous about the theft of those Honours Boards. At the end of afternoon school I marked some books, had my tea in the Common Room, then went in search of Winter, my partner-in-crime of the other night, hoping for reassurance.

But Winter was talking to Jimmy Watt outside the School boiler house, where Jimmy spent most of his time in cold weather. I wondered what they were talking about. Jimmy must have noticed the theft of the Honours Boards by now. Did he suspect my accomplice? Or did he suspect *me*?

Jimmy is no detective, but I feared that the disappearance of the Honours Boards on the same day I'd asked him to the pub might have given him pause for thought. After all, I am not in the habit of fraternizing much with the ancillary staff. The idea that Jimmy might already be questioning Winter about me doubled my anxiety.

I decided to play it cool, and left by the rear of the building.

Jimmy saw me and lifted a hand. 'Good day, boss?'

'Nothing that a pint won't cure. How about the Scholar again?'

Jimmy honked laughter. 'Sounds good, boss. But I got my jobs to do.'

I shook my head with feigned regret. 'Then I must drink alone,' I said, and left him, feeling reassured. Jimmy is a simple soul, not given to pretence. If he'd been suspicious, I would have seen it in his face. For the present, at least, my crime has gone unnoticed. And yet I can feel them closing in; the army of Suits and their General. I may not have much time left. Was I wrong to refuse the hemlock bowl? Perhaps. But it's not in my nature. I will fight them to the death, and if I fail, so be it. Better to fall by the wayside than never to start the journey.

Perhaps I'll have that drink after all. After the day I've had, I think a nice, relaxing pint might be just what the doctor ordered. (Well, not *my* doctor, naturally – who in spite of a C in Latin and a less-than-promising boyhood has grown up to embody all the more sickening virtues, as well as managing to maintain a happy marriage: moderation in drink, regular exercise and, most sickening of all, a strict vegetarian diet.) But, having survived today (so far), a couple of pints and a ploughman's are hardly likely to kill me. Once more unto the Scholar, then, to drown my sorrows in light ale. And who knows, maybe a crafty Gauloise to seal my deal with the Devil . . .

7

December 1981

There's something about a betrayal of trust. Something that really preys on you. What Mousey did to me – what *you* did to me, Mousey – changed my view of the world for good, just as Poodle did that day – the day I saw him kiss Mr Clarke. Of course I was only a kid back then. I had no idea what was happening. I only knew that my best friend had ratted me out to Mr Rushworth, that now everyone hated me, even Miss McDonald, who now thought I was a liar.

It was worse than that, though. Something else had got into me. It must have done, because suddenly the bad thoughts were back, and this time, it seemed, they wouldn't stop. One of them was about Sin, and Miss McDonald and Mr Lumb. The other was *the Wages* of Sin, and what really happens when you die. And then there were the games with the mice – but now they didn't seem like games. Now they seemed like something more, and I was starting to *need* them.

I began to go to the clay pits alone, in the mornings, and after school. There wasn't time for pirate games, or toy

Noah's Arks, or bombings. But I was growing out of that. All I liked was the drowning. I'd bait a few milk bottles every night, and in the mornings I'd harvest them. Most days I'd catch one or two. More, if I was lucky. I'd put them in the little cage I'd made from string and chicken wire, and I'd lower them from the top of the bank into the Pit Shaft, the deepest of all the clay pits. Sometimes, the mice were Mr Lumb. Sometimes, Mr Rushworth. Sometimes, Miss McDonald. But, whoever else they were, Mousey, they were always you.

It had been a whole term since the thing with Miss McDonald's scarf. The clay pits were green and flowering, and there were ducks on the water. Pretty, except for the burnt-out cars, and of course the litter. Spring was in the air at last; wild garlic grew in the hollows. And, with the spring, there were lots of mice. Mice are rapid breeders. Rats, too. The females can get pregnant every three weeks, with litters of a dozen or more. That means a lot of sex, I guess. That's why we call them *vermin*.

Meanwhile, at school, Miss McDonald announced that she was leaving at Easter. No one told us why, but I knew. It was because she was pregnant. All that sin had finally made a life inside her. They call it a miracle, Mousey. But the truth is, it's disgusting. On TV it's different; a nice clean baby, wrapped in a sheet. But really, it's disgusting. Did you know that mice and rats actually *eat their babies*? They do it when they get upset. They eat their babies, Mousey.

That's when the nightmares started again. I'd started to have them when Bunny died. Nightmares about drowning, and nobody coming to save me. Sometimes I used to wake up in the night and realize I'd wet the bed. Of course I knew Miss McDonald wouldn't eat her baby. But

I sometimes imagined her giving birth, and that too gave me nightmares. I tried to keep those bad thoughts away by staging mass drownings of rats and mice. But the bad thoughts kept coming back. Thoughts, and dreams, and terrors. I started to feel it was all my fault. That the demons I'd given birth to were coming back to eat *me*.

And then, without warning, Mousey turned up one sunny day at the clay pits. I was sitting by the Pit Shaft, looking into the water, when I heard him come up behind me. He'd never been all that talkative, so I wasn't expecting an apology or anything. Still, I thought there might have been some reference to what had happened between us. Instead, he just came to sit on the bank beside me, looked into the Pit Shaft and said: 'I know where we can get a dog.'

I mean, *a dog*. It was tempting. 'What kind of dog?'

'A Jack Russell,' he said.

'Whose is it?'

He shrugged. 'A stray, I guess. It doesn't have a collar.'

By then, I was thinking hard. Not about killing a dog, though. Those demons were talking to me again, and this time, I was listening.

I said: 'How soon could you bring it here?'

He thought about it for a while, and then said: 'I could bring it tomorrow. It comes to me. I've been feeding it.'

I pretended to hesitate. 'I dunno.'

Mousey waited patiently. He must have known I'd come round. But why had he come to find me? I thought. Was this his way of making amends?

Finally, I nodded and said: 'Tomorrow morning, before school. Bring the dog. Don't tell anyone.'

I hardly slept at all that night. I was too excited. I went over my plan again and again, imagining every scenario. I knew I had to get it right. I knew I'd only have one chance. And I knew that if it worked, then all my demons – a legion of them – would vanish for good in the clay pits.

My plan was pretty simple. Miss McDonald had told us in school about the danger of playing near water. You could fall in, she told us. Even if you could swim, you might not be able to get up the bank. There are things under the water; old cars; fridges; traps. A kid could get his foot caught. It could happen tomorrow. And we'd all seen that Public Information Film, both at school and on TV. *I am the spirit of dark and lonely water; ready to trap the unwary, the show-off, the fool.* When I first saw it, it gave me nightmares. But after the clay pits, I realized that I *was* the Spirit of Dark Water. My victims – the mice – were all part of my plan. And now, I had another plan. I was going to get Mousey.

I got up early the next day. I had some preparations to make. I told my parents I'd promised to get to school early to water the plants, and then I ran to the clay pits and waited there for Mousey. At eight o'clock sharp he arrived, with a dog trotting at his heels. It didn't look much like a Jack Russell to me, more like a kind of mongrel, but it seemed happy enough to be there, eating biscuits from Mousey's hand. Dogs are pretty stupid, I thought. Still, so are most people.

Mousey came up to me with the dog. 'How are you going to do it?' he said.

'We'll throw him in the Pit Shaft. The bank's too steep for him to get out. He'll swim around a bit, I guess, but in the end he'll drown. It'll be like—' I racked my brains for a good analogy. 'It'll be like the *Titanic*,' I said.

'The what?' said Mousey.

'Never mind. Did you bring enough biscuits?'

Mousey nodded.

'All right. Bring him here. Right up to the edge of the pit. I'll tell you when.'

Mousey went right up to the edge of the flooded Pit Shaft. The water was so deep it was black. The bank was like an overhang; not too high, seen from above, but I guessed that even for a boy, it might be very hard to get out once you'd fallen in.

'Bit closer,' I told him again, and Mousey bent down to call the dog, pulling out a handful of biscuits from his pocket.

All I had to do was push. That had been the plan, at least. But Mousey was stronger than I'd thought. I tried to lunge forward, to push him in, but he must have guessed somehow. He grabbed hold of my hair and pushed back, yelling and swearing like a mad thing. The dog got excited and started to bark. Then it bit me on the leg.

I told you I didn't like dogs. Well, that's one of the reasons why. If that stupid mongrel hadn't got in the way of things, I might have managed to keep hold of Mousey and push him in. But the stupid dog got in the way, and started to bite at my trouser leg, so that when Mousey started to fall, I went with him, and Mousey screamed – not just a little muffled scream, but a huge and terrified scream – and we both fell, with a giant splash, into the freezing water.

I remember hitting the water; how cold it was, and how dirty, with a film of oil on the surface and that stink of mud and rotting things. I went under – not a long way, just a foot or two, I guess, trying not to think about traps beneath the surface; rusty cars and shopping trolleys, and fridges with their jaws half open, like giant clams in adventure books about pearl-diving in the South Seas.

Of course I could swim. We all could. We used to go down to the local baths and jump in in our pyjamas. So I could swim pretty well, but the bank was slimy. I reached it in moments, but, try as I might, I couldn't get enough of a grip. Next to me, Mousey was panicking; scrabbling against the clay; crying and screaming and sobbing. I thought that if I tried to stand on his shoulders, I could maybe climb out, but before I could try out my theory, I heard the sound of footsteps, and a face looked down over the bank at me.

'Oh, my God. Oh, my God.'

It was Piggy, Mousey's fat brother. He must have been hiding away somewhere, not wanting to see what we'd do to the dog. I thought at the time that it was a bad sign that he'd invoked God that way. Of course I didn't seriously think that, given a choice, God would favour Mousey's pig brother over me, but you never know with God.

For a second he stared at us both, hair in his eyes and mouth open. Mousey screamed. The dog barked. It was like a nightmare.

Finally, Piggy managed to break his paralysis and move. 'Ma's going to *kill* me for this,' he wailed, and reached out to haul Mousey out of the pit. He looked completely terrified. Tears were running down his face, but he managed to grab hold of Mousey's hand and pull him up the banking.

Mousey was screaming all the time. *'He pushed me! He pushed me!'* But I was screaming too, of course, and the dog was barking like crazy. I guess it was pretty funny, but I didn't think so at the time. At the time, I was thinking: *Is this what Bunny felt that day?* – and: *So much for those sixty years.*

Finally, Mousey was back on dry land. I shouted for him to help me. But he and Piggy just stared at me from the top of the bank; Mousey wet through and shivering; Piggy shivering nearly as hard; just staring at me in silence, as if they were waiting for something. Now that I saw them so close together. I could tell they were brothers. They had the same blue eyes, the same mousey hair, the same *look* – except that Mousey was thin, of course. *This is the wrong way round,* I thought. *The swine should be in the water, not me.*

It was the dog that saved me. Someone walking his own dog heard it and came to investigate. He found me still in the water, and Piggy having a choking fit, with Mousey trying to shut up the dog by feeding it biscuit after biscuit. I know. It sounds quite funny now. Even so, I might have died. I might have drowned, like Bunny.

Both of us left Netherton Green after that; Mousey, to Abbey Road Juniors. My mum and dad tried to teach me at home, at least until they were sure of me. I never saw Mousey again. Of course, I denied his story that I'd pushed him in, and although his brother supported his tale, the waters had been muddied enough for me to escape retribution. The school made a few enquiries, but by then I was already gone. I don't suppose there was much point after that. I think my dad guessed something, though. In any case, I got to see a whole lot of specialists; people from different churches who decided that I was susceptible, and that My Condition (yes, *that* was what they were calling it now) needed careful monitoring.

And that is how, eventually, I ended up at St Oswald's, which has actually turned out to have quite a few compensations. At least until Poodle messed it all up. Talking about me behind my back. Taking my place with Mr Clarke. Just like that business at Netherton Green.

Just like you, Mousey.

8

September 26th, 2005

The Thirsty Scholar public house has been a traditional annexe of St Oswald's for over half a century, providing Games teachers with a lunchtime pint and Sixth-Form boys with a place in which to meet their Mulberry counterparts. We have an unwritten rule whereby if they take their ties off, we, the staff, do not know them, or ask if they have turned eighteen. The boys return the compliment. Of course, to a St Oswald's boy, the thought of a Master letting his hair down – of indulging in a couple of pints and maybe a pasty and a Gauloise; of buying a few groceries at the local corner shop, or, still less conceivable, of socializing with the opposite sex – is a freakish occurrence akin to two-headed dogs and plagues of locusts from the sky. My boys, for all their affection, secretly imagine me spending my nights at St Oswald's; sleeping at my desk, perhaps, or hanging behind the stock-cupboard door, next to my discarded gown.

Of course, we are all of us prone to these assumptions. We prefer our people to stay in context. Perhaps that was why Harry Clarke's revelation came as such a surprise to me – not the idea of his homosexuality, but of *any* sexuality. And perhaps that's why, when I went in today, I was so surprised to see the Headmaster alone at the bar, smoking a cigarette and drinking something on the rocks.

The end of his silk tie stuck out from the top pocket of his suit – it seems that Johnny Harrington still believes in the talismanic removal of the necktie to confer invisibility – and he was already slightly drunk. Not enough to fall over, but there was an absent look on his face, an unusual vagueness in the way he moved his hands, which strongly suggested the man had imbibed. Which was strange, as I'd always believed that, like my own GP, Johnny Harrington *didn't* drink spirits, or smoke cigarettes, or indulge in anything stronger than a glass of wine with his evening meal.

I found a seat by the window, where I hoped to go unseen, and ordered a pint and a ploughman's from Bethan, the young woman who serves at the bar. I wasn't *spying*, precisely – but something told me that Harrington wouldn't be happy to see me, and besides, I was very curious to know just what he was doing there, drinking alone in a village pub, when he had a wife at home—

I suppose I was thinking along the lines of an illicit liaison. I don't have much experience in these things, but Shitter Shakeshafte was well known for his dalliances with a string of School Secretaries, and I'd already noticed that Danielle was slightly starry-eyed about the new boss. I suppose he's not unattractive – at least not to people like Danielle. But that Shakeshafte, bad-tempered and pachydermic as he was, should find such a degree of romantic success speaks volumes for the aphrodisiac effect of high office, and Harrington, with his youthful face, smooth hair and easy charm, is the kind of man any woman might find passably attractive.

So much for my speculation. Harrington had come in alone. The girl Bethan told me as much, when she came to deliver my pint and my ploughman's. I am not what you might call a regular at the Scholar, but people tend to remember me. In fact, I believe that Bethan (who runs the Pink Zebra during the day, a small café at the edge of the Village) goes out of her way to spoil me with larger-than-regulation servings of cheddar with my crusty cob. I rather like Bethan, in spite of the black star tattoos that spiral tribally up her arms, and the row of studs in her eyebrow. *Not* a look I admire, as such, but she has a glow.

I sat in the Scholar for over an hour, watching Johnny Harrington. During that time he ordered two more doubles on the rocks, and ate a packet of peanuts. He did not speak to anyone, except for Bethan at the bar, and later on his mobile phone. Then, he left in a hurry, without even finishing his drink.

I would have liked to follow him. But he would have seen me. Instead I watched from the window as, rather than heading for the car park – where that silver BMW gleamed under a lamp-post – he set off at an angry pace towards the trees of Malbry Park, where he was soon lost from view. I had no way of knowing for sure where the man was heading. But the path he'd taken led across the park towards the big houses of Millionaires' Row. Was that where Harrington's caller lived? Or was I chasing moonbeams?

Of course I had no answers to any of these questions. But I could tell one thing, at least: that under the remaining veneer of charm and sophistication, under the fog of alcohol, little Johnny Harrington – the perfect politician, a man as sleek as a bag of weasels – was in the throes of a rage that he could barely control. I wondered what could have provoked it. He'd always seemed so coolly immune to normal human weakness—

And then the thought occurred to me that perhaps the thing that I'd been hoping for ever since that first Briefing had just been handed to me on a plate – a weapon to use against him. Do I *need* a weapon? The fact that I reacted so quickly to the idea suggests that perhaps I do. I tried it on for size, like an unexpected new hat, and found that it rather suited me. Who would have known it? That Straitley, of all people – the rock of St Oswald's; the loyal arm, the stone and mortar of the School – should have looked inside himself and found an assassin looking out?

An assassin. How melodramatic. And yet, how curiously apt. What was it the Chaplain said? *This Head fails, the School goes down*. That, of course, must not happen. But last year, a solitary *Mole* demonstrated with what ease a stone can bring down a giant. And St Oswald's has weathered storms before. The old ship is a survivor. Harrington and his posse are nothing but suited privateers, stripping her of everything that might still be of value.

A little thing. That's all it was. But I'd thought the man impregnable. Now he has shown his underside, and for the first time this term, there is hope. Shakespeare's Caesar said it best: *The fault, dear Brutus, is not in our stars, but in ourselves, that we are underlings.*

Well, it's never too late to change. The underling has seen the light. Harrington and I are at war, and I mean to bring him down. And if St Oswald's goes down with him? But that won't happen. The Chaplain is wrong. The old frigate has survived too many storms to be wrecked by a cabin boy.

She will survive. *I* will survive. *Ad astra per aspera.*

9

September 27th, 2005

My form was rather subdued today. Allen-Jones is still suspended in the wake of the nail-varnish incident, and the chemistry of the whole group is different without him. His influence, though not what you'd call *disruptive*, is certainly tangible, and in his absence, the rest of my Brodie Boys were unusually silent. Sutcliff and McNair are on report, which means that for every lesson they have to produce a card that the relevant Master has to sign, with space for comments on appearance, behaviour and punctuality. No boy likes being on report, but today I thought I sensed something more; a silent resentment in their eyes, as if they felt I had let them down.

Something has to be done, and fast. But Harrington is untouchable; hedged about by his deputies, he has no obvious weaknesses; his prejudices kept well under wraps. Except for that anger. But what good is that? And how can I use it against him?

Know thine enemy. But how? It occurred to me that, with the right skills, one might hack into his computer; find incriminating notes – love letters to his secretary, falsified accounts, pamphlets preaching hatred – that would lead to his disgrace and removal. But the computer is not my friend. I spent twenty minutes after School at my new work-station, and barely managed to turn it on. No, I needed a younger man. Someone technologically adept.

And so, after School, I went to find Winter, my erstwhile partner-in-crime. I found him outside, by the bins, and by the time I'd explained my difficulties, he was laughing so hard he could barely speak.

'The computer doesn't think for itself,' he said at last. 'It's only as smart as you are. Unless you know just how to look, you're like a budgie with a mirror, bashing your head against the glass.'

Not a complimentary assessment of my technical know-how, but all the same, quite an accurate one. I'm beginning to wonder how Gloria's boy ended up being a cleaner at all.

'Do *you* know about computers?' I said.

He smiled. 'What do you need to know?'

I told him. 'Of course, I'll pay for your time. Consider it research,' I said.

'Research?' said Winter. 'I'll do it for free. Consider it a favour.'

I wonder what I have begun. Roy Straitley, the subversive. You'd as soon expect the gargoyles on the Chapel roof to rebel, as to think that I would do *anything* that might harm St Oswald's. But the New Head is a parasite. The Honours Boards; the old ways; our relationship with the boys; everything is being siphoned away, to be replaced by mixed classes; Suits; computer stations; e-mail; paper-free offices; Abuse Gurus – things that may look good on paper, but that never touch the heart of the place, because St Oswald's has always run, not on paper, but on blood, sweat, chalk dust, work and most of all on *loyalty* – loyalty to the boys, the School, and most of all, to each other—

I may be playing the role of Canute, trying vainly to hold back the tide. But nevertheless, I have to believe that I can save St Oswald's. Any weapon is fair game – a garden gnome; a computer. For years I have resisted change in the hope that it may pass me by. Now I must be the agent of change, uncomfortable as that may be. I find myself thinking back to that old joke of Harrington's: *How many St Oswald's Masters does it take to change a lightbulb*? Perhaps the question should really be: *How many lightbulbs will it take to expose Johnny Harrington's infamy*?

All schools have their skeletons. St Oswald's is no exception. Most of the time, we try our best to keep them in the closet. But this time, the only recourse we have is to throw open *all* the closets, light as many bulbs as we can and catch the vermin as it comes out.

Winter agreed to call round later this evening, after work. He told me he'd look up Harrington, using my staff workstation. I wasn't entirely convinced that the internet was the means of snaring Harrington, but Winter has a way with technology, and I cannot afford to overlook anything that may be useful. To whom was Harrington speaking last night on his flashy mobile phone? And where did he go afterwards?

Winter arrived at seven o'clock, by which time it was already dark. I forget how fast the nights draw in at this time of year; how much earlier autumn starts than it always used to. My partner-in-crime was carrying a blue folder containing a number of printed sheets.

'You found all that *today*?' I said.

Winter shrugged. 'It isn't much. The New Head's online profile is very clean. He doesn't use social networking sites – at least, not under his own name. He doesn't have a MySpace, or a blog. He doesn't use Friends Reunited, although he is mentioned there once or twice. He sometimes buys books on Amazon, but never leaves a review. As for Google—'

I stopped him there, and explained that he'd lost me at 'online'.

He grinned at that. 'Sorry. I'll start again.'

Half an hour later I was, if not fluent, then at least vaguely conversant in the language of the internet. Winter is, of course, a native speaker. He tells me he spends hours online every night, 'posting' and 'blogging' and so on.

'But what does it achieve?' I said, genuinely mystified.

He shrugged. 'It's a community. People online interact in much the same way they do in any other community, except that they get to choose who they meet and who they interact with. In real life, you might never meet the handful of compatible people who share your specific interests. Online, you can find them in seconds. You can engage. You can be someone else. You can pretend, for an hour or two, that you're not stuck here in Malbry.'

How interesting. I had no idea. I wonder if Winter has any friends outside of his virtual community. I suspect his social skills may be lacking; or maybe he simply prefers to be 'someone else', as he puts it.

'Where would you rather be?' I said.

Winter gave a wry smile. 'I sometimes think of Hawaii,' he said. 'Did you know the Hawaiian archipelago is the longest island chain in the world?'

I shook my head. I've been to France a couple of times (mostly on Eric's insistence) to help out with School trips, but otherwise, St Oswald's has been my life's adventure, remaining as exotic now as it was on the first day.

'Planning a holiday?' I said.

I thought Winter looked wistful. 'Maybe someday. Not right now. The flights are pretty expensive.'

'Maybe you'll win the Lottery.'

'Maybe one day I'll get to play.'

I looked at the file. It contained all we had on little Johnny Harrington. A sparse, if spotless record of online purchases (mostly books); membership of a golf club; donations to several charities, including Survivors and Save the Children; a stay-at-home wife called Elizabeth, prominent in local good works, who likes to buy cashmere sweaters and who lists her calories online. Both his parents are alive and living in the Cotswolds. He has no siblings, and as far as we know, no remaining ties with Malbry.

'Is that all you found?' I asked.

Winter opened the blue file. 'No, sir. I also found this.' He passed me a printed facsimile of the *Malbry Examiner*.

Well, you know the page, I suppose. It's the page everyone remembers; with Harry in *that* photograph. Not the most flattering picture, taken on a Sports Day in September '81, with Harry in shorts and a running singlet, each of his arms flung around a boy. One of those boys was Harrington, impeccable even after his run, the parting in his hair as straight as if the Romans had built it, and even after all this time, I felt a stab of irrational rage at the boy; his loathsome smoothness. The other boy at Harry's side was a third-year boy from Harry's form called Tencel or Tessel, whom I'd never taught. Standing apart from the little group was Charlie Nutter, looking away as if at something beyond the frame. And in the background was David Spikely, whose asthma excluded him from Games, grinning at the camera. I wondered how he'd managed to get into the picture at all. He certainly hadn't run the race. Maybe he'd come to watch his friends. Probably the photographer hadn't even noticed him.

Winter looked at me curiously. 'You must have been aware of this,' he said. 'Why didn't you tell me?'

I sighed. 'I meant to tell you,' I said. My heart was still pounding alarmingly. The invisible finger, having poked, moved on. 'But not tonight, if you don't mind. It's rather a difficult story to tell, and I think we both need time to prepare.'

He nodded. 'Another time, then, sir.'

'Thank you, Mr Winter.'

When Winter had left, I poured myself a glass of wine and made myself a Welsh rarebit, and read one of Harry's old diaries. Nothing much there; except for a note about Eric Scoones, who was in charge of the French film club, showing *La Cage aux Folles*, and a sketch of Dr Devine as a drill sergeant, sharp nose twitching fretfully, watching a phalanx of schoolboys running laps around the Quad. From his mouth came a speech bubble, containing the words *Quick, March!* Beneath it, the legend: *Metro-gnome*.

My eyesight was protesting by then. Or maybe it was the smoke from the fire. And so I put the book away and thought about my partner-in-crime, alone in his dead mother's house, his face illuminated in blue from the glow of the computer screen, talking with his invisible friends. It seems a very lonely way for a man of his age to live. And yet he seems to enjoy it. Of course, he may feel the same about me. But I have St Oswald's. For now, at least – and for ever, I hope—

Thank gods, I have St Oswald's.

Part Five

Veritas nunquam perit.
(Seneca)

1

January 1982

It was the morning of New Year's Day when the police arrived at my door. Two officers, both men, both with the look of officials with an unpleasant task to perform.

'Roy Straitley?'

'*Mea culpa*,' I said.

Perhaps not the happiest choice of words. But I had been expecting them. I was Nutter's form-master. And it had been a couple of days now since the boy's disappearance. Two officers, one old, one young, both with the same appraising eyes – they might almost have been father and son. I invited them in, but they would not sit down, remaining in the hallway, like door-to-door salesmen with nothing to sell.

I told them what I knew, which wasn't much; that the boy had been away from School during the last two weeks of term; that I had been making enquiries.

The elder of the two men, a man in his fifties called Stackhouse, said: 'Why's that?'

I explained that one of Nutter's friends had expressed concern.

'Concern about what?'

I shook my head. 'He just thought Nutter wasn't himself.'

'And what do you think he meant by that?'

I thought back to my interview with little Johnny Harrington. 'I'm really not sure,' I said at last. 'Something about not going to church, and seeming preoccupied.'

Stackhouse wrote something in his notebook. 'And did you speak to Charlie Nutter about this?'

'No,' I said.

'Why not?'

I thought he sounded unduly sharp. But then, I thought, the British police were trained in the art of suspicion. It was their job to question and probe, and their close proximity to the baser elements of the community meant that trust and goodwill were not likely to feature high on their list of priorities. The only real contact with the police I'd had in my professional life was when Sergeant Rose, the liaison officer, came in once a term to take Assembly.

Sergeant Rose was twinkly-eyed, friendly and nearing retirement. His role was to establish links with St Oswald's and the community, and try to recruit as many of our less academic boys as possible. He was also a consummate actor, and on the few occasions when we'd needed one of our boys to receive a salutary shock, he had dropped his cloak of affability to reveal the gimlet-eyed lawman beneath. I liked Sergeant Rose, but did not believe for a moment that his act was anything other than a clever PR strategy. Stackhouse and his partner, Noakes, were not from the PR branch of the force, and their eyes were frankly hostile in their flat, expressionless faces – much like those of boys in my class forced to study Vergil against their inclination.

'Won't you sit down and have tea?' I said.

Stackhouse shook his head. 'No thanks. Lots to do this morning. You were telling us why you didn't speak to Charlie Nutter when you had the chance.'

I started to explain about the end of term, and absences, and School reports, and commitments. Stackhouse wrote it down in his book. Noakes just nodded occasionally, as if he rather sympathized. I realized later that the nod was merely a meaningless tic, indicative neither of understanding nor approval.

'Did anyone else speak to the boy?' he said. 'A colleague, maybe?'

'I think Harry Clarke may have had a word. He knows him better than I do.'

Stackhouse and Noakes exchanged glances. 'Thank you, Mr Straitley,' said Noakes. 'You've been extremely helpful.'

That made me feel slightly uneasy. I didn't feel I'd told them much. But I had seen the face of the older man as soon as I'd mentioned Harry's name, and the way his eyes had lit.

'Is there news of Charlie?' I said. 'Does anyone know where he might have gone?'

Stackhouse's face was expressionless. 'I'm afraid I can't discuss that,' he said. 'I shan't disturb you any longer.'

Even then, I think I sensed that something bad was happening. The days between Christmas and the New Year had always seemed dark and ominous; but now, with my father growing increasingly ill and one of my boys missing from home, the darkness had grown like a shadow. But one boy's disappearance was far from being headline news. A bombing by Welsh nationalists; mass disruption from the snow; the imminent threat of a miners' strike – all took precedence over one missing boy. Nutter appeared on Page

4, where, in the absence of real news, speculation was all we had. A number of theories had been voiced, including the possibility that this might be a kidnapping, designed to put pressure on Nutter, MP, whose outspoken views – on Northern Ireland, for instance – might have attracted attention. But Nutter was neither interesting, nor photogenic, nor young enough to win readers' hearts, and so, for the first few days, at least, other things took centre stage.

One was my father's condition. The other was Eric, who'd been facing troubles of his own, and whose mother (with whom he lived) was already beginning to show the first signs of dementia. Eric was devoted to his mother, and, knowing I'd experienced something similar with my own parents, had taken to calling on me at home for reassurance and advice. Not that I had much to give; but over that Christmas he called at my house every couple of days or so. He called by again on New Year's Eve – the day after Nutter disappeared – looking, as always, slightly harassed.

Eric knew Charlie Nutter, of course, although he'd never taught him, and the boy's disappearance had obviously upset him more than I would have expected. We talked about it for some time, speculating fruitlessly on why the boy might have run away – neither of us dared believe that Charlie Nutter might be dead – until I happened to mention my conversation with Harry on the subject of Nutter's sexuality.

'Did you tell the police?' Eric said.

I shook my head. 'Is it relevant?'

Eric shrugged. 'You hear stories,' he said.

'What kind of stories?'

'I don't know. Perverts, preying on young boys.' He lit a Gauloise. He'd recently taken up smoking, mostly, I thought, to calm his nerves. Eric could be sensitive about the most unlikely things, and his mother's illness, the end of term, and Nutter's disappearance all seemed to have added to the strain.

He said: 'Have you spoken to Harry yet?'

'No,' I said. 'Do you think I should?'

Eric shook his head. 'No. I think you should keep well away. Because if that boy turns up dead, they're going to be asking questions.'

'That's ridiculous,' I said. 'Why? You think because Harry's gay—'

Eric gave me an odd look – scornful, and yet somehow envious. 'You always were an idiot, Straits,' he said, using my nickname for the first time in over twenty years. 'You never could help jumping in with both feet, when you should have run like the wind.'

Later, I wondered what he'd meant. Was he accusing Harry? Was he, like the Chaplain, afraid that Harry might corrupt the boys?

I sometimes wondered what might have happened if I'd gone to see Harry that night. Could I have warned him, somehow? Or would that just have made things worse? Of course, there's no way of knowing now. Hindsight is a cruel gift, always arriving much too late. And so, when Eric had gone, I did what I always did at that time of year: I started to prepare for the new term. Class lists; lesson plans; Sixth-Form essays to be marked. I did not *forget* Charlie Nutter – but I muted him, like a radio, while other things took precedence.

And then, on the third of January, came the call I'd been dreading. My father had been taken ill. Pneumonia, the doctors said; but I knew better. He'd given up. I'd known in my heart that it was the end as soon as I'd seen him at Christmas, and part of me was as relieved as the other part was guilty. I went at once to Meadowbank, where I waited with him for twenty-four hours. Typically, he chose to die during the fifteen-minute break I'd taken to pick up some supplies – a toothbrush, a packet of Gauloises, a sandwich, the local paper – so that when I returned, it was over, and he was already cooling.

How very like my father, I thought. How like him to withdraw from even that small, final contact. Throughout his life, I could not remember him touching me, except to shake hands. And now he was gone, I couldn't find the grief that I was meant to feel: only a sense of deep fatigue and a headache that refused to shift.

I couldn't face going home straight away. I ate my sandwich (tomato and cheese), although I'd lost my appetite. I drank a cup of Meadowbank tea – which always tasted mysteriously of fish – and read the paper I'd just bought. And that was how I came to learn that a body had been found in one of the White City clay pits – the body of a young boy yet to be identified . . .

2

January 1982

I don't want to discuss that now. Have some decorum, Mousey. New Year is a Fresh Start, filled with Resolutions. Number One: no more clay pits: no more hanging around playing games. This year is an Important Year, so my father tells me. I'll be fifteen. I need to Shape Up. Number Two: no more moping around Mr Clarke's room at lunchtimes. He's just a teacher, not a friend. He doesn't know shit about me. Number Three: Get a Girlfriend. Get my parents off my back.

I'm also going to tear three pages out of my St Oswald's diary. That's because this is a Fresh Start, and we're going to forget about that. Instead, I will think about New Year; ride my new bike around the estate; do some homework from Straitley, who seems to think that Latin should play a role in every part of my life; then maybe a trip to the pictures (*Excalibur*), with Goldie and his girlfriend necking on the back row and me in front with the popcorn, pretending not to notice.

Nothing very different from any other holiday; bad TV and leftovers; New Year's Eve and pantomime; thank-you notes; snow turning to slush all along the pavements. Nothing special, except for *one* thing, which you and I will not discuss.

No, I haven't seen Poodle. I've already told that to the police. It's not like we're *close* or anything, and Christmas is a family time. I'm sure he's OK, though. That's what I said. He's always been a bit nervous. And he's been under pressure, too, especially from Mr Straitley, who doesn't seem to like him much, and picks on him all the time at school. That's what I told the policeman who came to talk to my parents. He wrote it all down in his notebook. He seemed very attentive. I mentioned Mr Clarke, too. I said he and Mr Straitley were friends. He asked me if Mr Straitley ever made me uncomfortable. I told him yes, he did. (It was true.) I think he's been over to Goldie's, too. And to Mr Speight's house. But I don't think Goldie will say much. I know he won't mention the clay pits. He's been too busy this Christmas trying to get inside Becky Price's knickers, and he knows that if he opens his mouth, I'll tell his dad, and he'll give him hell.

As for Harry – *Mr Clarke*—

Mousey, that's all over now. Poodle's gone and spoilt everything. I can never go to his house; or talk to him in his form-room; or even give him his present. It's over, just like Netherton Green. I may as well get used to it. I don't need to tell *you* what happened, of course. That's something I'll *never* forget. But it makes me feel like something died. I mean, something apart from the obvious. And the worst of it is, I can't even tell – not even you, Mousey.

I kept the copy of *The Wall* I was going to give Mr Clarke. I've hidden it away, along with the list of albums I'm going to buy. Except I probably *won't* buy them now. I don't know if I'll ever dare. Not because it makes me feel bad to remember, but actually, quite the opposite. I know I *ought* to be feeling bad. But Mousey, I feel so alive. More alive than I've ever been; like I'm immortal, or something. For the first time since I can remember, I'm not afraid of dying. I can see everything clearly now. My Condition; my future. Everything is shiny and new, like a fresh fall of Christmas snow. When it snows, you can forget what's hidden under the surface. Even the clay pits are beautiful under a nice fresh fall of snow. The old cars are wearing crisp white hoods; even the dogshit on the ground is erased. When the sun shines, it's like everything is covered in powdered diamonds. The surface of the Pit Shaft is dotted with small islands. And the dark and lonely water is under a layer of silver lace, like a zombie bride beneath her rotted, mouldy wedding veil.

Resolution Number Four: stop thinking about it, Mousey. Let the memory stay buried under that layer of virgin snow. There's no point hanging on to it, except that it makes me feel so good, and maybe that's the problem. Some things just feel too good to stop. Drugs, I suppose. And the Sin of the Flesh – at least, if Goldie is to be believed. Maybe I'll even stop writing things down. Give it up altogether. Stamp down on the temptation like stamping down on new-fallen snow. Except that we'll still know it's there, whatever the surface may look like. We all know I'm not *really* pure. Just as we know that the snow will melt. Just as we know My Condition won't change. And just as we know Resolutions – like some people, Mousey – are really just there to be broken.

3

January 1982

Those clay pits were notorious. Ringed with chain-link fences and peppered with NO TRESPASSERS signs, they had been a traditional place for boys to misbehave since Eric and I, in caps and St Oswald's blazers, had used it as our combat-ground, more years ago than seems possible. What they really were, of course, was *dark and lonely water*: a series of abandoned pits not quite large enough to count as quarries, now mostly flooded and commonly used as a tipping ground for household waste and junk of all kinds.

Any boy from St Oswald's would have been wary of that place. Charlie Nutter certainly was. Thanks to that old TV campaign, shown to all our feeder schools, Charlie Nutter knew the risks of dark and lonely water. And he'd been missing for nearly a week before they searched the clay pits. Everything else had already been tried. A sign saying PRAY FOR CHARLIE had been put up by the church. Flowers and candles had been left by well-wishers at St Oswald's gates. Mr Speight and the Chaplain had organized a vigil and

Stephen Nutter, MP, had appealed to the public on *Look North*.

The response had been eager, though fruitless. Sightings of Charlie had been reported in Manchester, Sheffield and even Hull, but none of these turned out to be anything more than false alarms. Malbry and St Oswald's began to prepare themselves for the worst. The media, too, now upped their game as the national press picked up the story. That pallid, twitching, colourless boy had become gilded by tragedy. The boys who had ignored him at School made tearful declarations of friendship. Even the *Malbry Examiner* (never a friend to St Oswald's) described the missing boy as *popular*, which, as everyone knows, is only a step away from *the tragic loss of a young life*.

No one wanted to believe that the boy was dead, of course. But what else could have happened to him? Nutter was a quiet boy, shy to the point of sullenness. His pastimes were quiet; his friends were few. He never misbehaved at School. His family was affluent. He had whatever he wanted. For Christmas, his father had bought him a BMX bicycle. Why would he have run away?

Besides, it was winter. In July, boys can run away from home and live like outlaws in the woods, but at Christmas 1981 it snowed. No boy would have survived sleeping rough, and a number of sinister theories were beginning to gain popularity – theories ventured by Mr Speight, a firm believer in sacrifice rings, black magic and Satanic covens, whose *actual* knowledge of the occult was mostly taken from the novels of Dennis Wheatley.

And so, when a body was retrieved from one of the flooded clay pits, the reaction within the community was of sorrow, rather than surprise. And when the news came that the Nutter family had failed to identify the body, the general consensus was that the grief-stricken parents had been too deep in denial to face the truth. The *Examiner* ran the story the next day, flanked with a picture of Charlie – which made what happened later all the more remarkable.

What happened was, they found him. *Where* and *when* remained unclear. The papers seemed to suggest that it was on the fourth of January, but the time of day was unknown. Some said the boy had been found in a house somewhere in White City. Some said he'd come home of his own accord; some, that he had resisted. But whatever the truth of it, Nutter was safe. It was our Christmas miracle.

Back from the Dead! the headlines exclaimed; and for twenty-four hours, the excitement of finding the Nutter boy safe and sound was almost enough to make us forget that a boy – an as yet *unidentified* boy – had been pulled out of the clay pits. That boy, too, had been someone's son. That boy, too, had lost his life. It wasn't that we didn't care about the unnamed boy in the pit; but when all was said and done – that boy wasn't one of ours.

As for Charlie Nutter, I went to see him as soon as I could. Not straight away – remember, I had a funeral to arrange – but a couple of days after his return. I think I felt responsible, as if there were something I could have done to prevent what happened. Not that I *knew* what had happened, of course: the grapevine was stubbornly silent on the subject of Charlie's return, which meant that his homecoming had been tinged with a kind of awkwardness, a sigh of relief tempered by the vague dissatisfaction of a community preparing itself for the worst, only to find that its energies could have been better spent elsewhere.

Now, over a week from the day Charlie Nutter had disappeared, no one seemed to know where he had been, or what he had done during that time. The parents had made a statement, saying that Charlie was in good health and expressing their joy at his return. That was all anyone knew, and, much to the chagrin of the *Malbry Examiner*, neither Charlie nor his parents were prepared to divulge anything more. But I was the boy's form-tutor. I felt obscurely responsible. And so I went to see him at home, to offer what help and support I could.

The Nutters lived on Millionaires' Row, the nicest street in Malbry. Big stone houses with metal gates and walls to keep the trespassers out, with nicely mown lawns and flower beds and broad gravel paths under the trees. One of my colleagues lived there – an Art Master, now long since retired, working on a book in one of those gracious old houses. The Nutters' house was especially large, especially well kept, with electronic gates and a set of cameras surveying the drive. I supposed that Nutter, like all MPs, had to be suspicious. The troubles in Northern Ireland had spread since the hunger strikes at the Maze, and might one day spread even to Malbry. It had briefly occurred to me, too, that Charlie might have been kidnapped; that his parents had paid the ransom and that this was the cause of their reticence.

But a kidnapping, in Malbry? It seemed barely conceivable. Malbry is one of those places where nothing really happens. Even now, in the Village, people still leave their doors unlocked – although it is very different down in White City, where the pebble-dashed houses are often fitted with grilles to safeguard the windows. White City is less than a mile from the Village, and yet it is a world apart. Even the pubs are different; and the takeaways are all fish-and-chip shops, rather than places like the Pink Zebra, which sells salads and ethnic food. White City boys (and girls, of course) go to school in Sunnybank Park, the concrete abomination on the Abbey Road estate, and wear expressions of cocky disdain to hide their essential self-loathing. They also push their fish-and-chip wrappers into my hedge at the end of Dog Lane, as if doing so absolves them of the responsibility of disposing of their litter. And yet, the Sunnybankers, too, have parents who would grieve for them. Who *was* that boy in the clay pits? I thought. Was there someone still waiting for him?

Mrs Nutter answered the door. I remembered her as a thin, elegant woman. Now she looked almost skeletal. She was wearing a long, flowing thing with some kind of looping, swirling pattern; she looked like a child dressed in a bedspread. Mrs Harrington was with her, holding a cup of coffee.

'Mr Straitley! What a surprise!'

From her face, I wasn't sure whether the surprise was good or not. I touched my hat. I'd taken to wearing one in the winter; it was unfashionable, but very practical in the snow, and besides, it gave me something to do when I was dealing with women.

'Mrs Nutter. Good morning. I just came to see if Charlie needed anything. Books, class notes, anything. We've all been very anxious.'

She gave a brittle smile. 'Thank you. Charlie's resting, but he's well. I'll tell him you called. I'm sure he'll be glad. I'd ask you in for coffee, but—' She gave an abstract little wave that took in Mrs Harrington, the drawing room beyond the hall, the shapeless garment she was wearing – A kaftan? A housecoat? – while at the same time conveying the impossibility of receiving guests.

Mrs Harrington looked at me. Her eyes were like her son's, a brown so dark that it might have been black. 'We were praying,' she told me. Prayer, that get-out-of-jail-free card for every social embarrassment.

'Of course,' I said. 'I won't intrude. I just wanted to make sure that Charlie was all right. If there's anything I can do to help – if there's been any trouble at School—'

'No, there's nothing, thank you,' said Mrs Nutter. I noticed that her hands were like her son's, red with patches of eczema. She lingered in the doorway, waiting for me to leave.

I said: 'It's just that if there's something at School – bullying, or anything else . . .'

'No.' Her voice was thin and sharp. 'Thank you, Mr Straitley. But none of this has anything to do with St Oswald's. Charlie's a little highly strung. He's been under the weather. My husband's work, the pressures, you know—' She let the sentence trail off.

I nodded. 'Of course. I do understand.' And then I touched my hat again and went back down the long drive.

I turned once, and thought I saw a face at one of the upstairs windows, blurry with condensation. I think it might have been Charlie, although I could not be certain.

If so, it was the last time I was to see him for seven years.

4

December 1981

Drowning is quiet, Mousey. A man who can struggle can also breathe. A man – or in this case, a boy – who can scream is not running short of air. St Oswald's has a swimming pool, which pupils visit once a week.

But Ratboy was a Sunnybanker. Sunnybankers don't have a pool. Ratboy could paddle a bit, but that was it. And it was cold; the Pit Shaft glazed with a film of ice. Not enough to slow his fall; but enough to make sure that his struggle was brief. They say all your life passes before your eyes at the moment of drowning. Ratboy's life can't have been much. A couple of gulps, and he was gone. Still, what a feeling, Mousey. This must be what God feels like *all the time*.

I didn't push him, Mousey. But I was the one who pushed Poodle. Wound him up like a clockwork toy, and watched him do the rest. It was fun. Like pouring my demons into someone else and watching them run off a cliff. But the water was too cold, I guess, and Ratboy went under too fast. It doesn't take long, in cold weather. It's called the Instinctive

Diving Response. Ratboy dived. And Poodle – well. Poodle went a bit crazy.

First he started to shake and cry, just like with the rabbits. Then he sat down and couldn't get up; all he could do was shiver. I took him to the burnt-out car (I was feeling cold as well), and waited till he could talk again. It took a while. I watched the fire, which by now had died to orange and black, with the leaves of Poodle's beefcake books curled up and red round the edges. I found a couple of cigarettes lying on the ground, and lit one each for Poodle and me. Poodle dropped his. I picked it up.

He said: 'We'll have to tell the police.'

I finished my cigarette. I said: 'Really? You'll tell them you pushed him?'

Poodle looked at me like a dog about to be put down. 'Ziggy, what else can we do?'

I shrugged. 'I know what *I'll* do,' I said. 'I'm going home to watch TV. It's *The Two Ronnies* on tonight. I'm going to watch TV, and eat leftovers, and maybe read a book, and – oh, probably *not* say I was with you today when *you* pushed that Sunnybanker.' I flicked the cigarette end away into what was left of the fire.

Poodle looked at me with big eyes. 'You wouldn't.'

'Oh, grow up,' I said. 'Imagine what would happen if you actually told the police. Everyone would know about you. There'd have to be a trial. You'd get expelled from school, at least. It would be on your record for life. You'd never get into uni, or even get a proper job. You might have to go to a special school, maybe even Borstal. And even if they all *believed* that it had been an accident, what would your parents say? Your dad? What about the papers? What's *that* going to look like, an MP with a killer son?'

Poodle began to cry again. 'You can't. We've *got* to tell,' he said.

'No, we don't. And neither do you. You don't want to say a single word. Because if you do, I'll deny it. And that'll make it even worse.'

He looked at me in misery. 'I can't.'

'You can,' I told him. 'Listen to me. It's not like you *meant* him to die, is it? It's not like you *knew* he couldn't swim. It was just an accident. Accidents happen all the time. He could have been standing there alone, and the bank could have given way under his feet. Or he could have slipped on the ice, or fallen when he reached in to pick something up out of the water. *Anything* could have happened to him. Anything at all.'

Poodle was watching me, glassy-eyed.

'Think about it, Poodle,' I said. 'Telling people won't bring him back. That would only cause trouble – for us, and for our families. You know what Sunnybankers are like. They all hate St Oswald's. He's probably got friends who'd tell the police we planned to get him from the start. They'd never believe what really happened. So even if the police let you off, the Sunnybankers would get you.'

That made him twitch a bit. I smiled and passed him half a cigarette.

'Look, the worst is over,' I said. 'All you have to do is go home. Have your dinner, watch TV, forget this ever happened. You can do that, can't you?'

Poodle didn't answer. He just wiped his face with the back of his hand, turned and walked away from me. The last I saw of him, Mousey, he was heading down towards White City, looking like a dog with no tail. And that was how it ended that day. Not even with a whimper.

* * *

Dad's already talking about sending me to another school. Perhaps he'll wait till the end of the year, but then again, perhaps he won't. He has a way of looking at me, when he thinks I'm watching TV. And I'm nearly certain that Mum's been looking through my things again. She'd never say, of course. But there's something about the way she goes through my books and papers, straightening loose edges that have been carefully left crooked. She may even have glanced at my St Oswald's diary, which is why I'm going to hide these pages where no one will ever find them.

The thing about my parents is that they don't *really* want to know. They'd rather live in ignorance, believing they've done all they could. Bring it into the open, and *everything* begins to stink. My parents; the Church; Goldie's dad; Mr and Mrs Poodle. That's why they won't say anything. Especially not at school, or to me. Instead, they'll pray, and light candles, and hold fund-raising coffee mornings, and shake their heads, and wonder why Poodle ran away.

We know, Mousey. Don't we? But we're never going to tell. Some things are too secret even to whisper to the reeds. That's why I tore these pages out. I *was* going to burn them. But now I have a better idea. I'm making a time capsule. I'm going to leave some things inside – you know, to mark the occasion. The card I wrote to Mr Clarke. The pages from my diary. That copy of Pink Floyd's *The Wall*. My list of special albums. I'm putting it all in a box. Then I'm wrapping it in plastic. Then I'm going to bury it, somewhere safe, by the clay pits.

After that, well, who knows? Maybe I'll forget where it is. Maybe I'll get on with my life, and take exams, and leave home, and get a job, and maybe one day get married, have kids, maybe even a cat or a dog. Sometimes I think about those things. Sometimes, it even seems possible to put aside my memories, to wrap them in layers of plastic, to bury them deep, where no one will look; where no one will *think* of looking.

Goodbye, Mr Clarke. Goodbye, clay pits. Goodbye, happy memories. Maybe I'll be back for you, one day, when it's safe to look. Till then, I'm putting childish things aside. Look after them for me, Mousey.

5

January 1982

I buried my father on January 6th, a Wednesday, in the morning. My mother was there, in a grey dress and two overcoats. She told me, very earnestly, that there was a thief at the Meadowbank home; that someone had been stealing her clothes.

'The only way to stop them,' she said, 'is to wear *everything all the time*.' She lowered her voice and smiled at me confidingly. 'I'm wearing three pairs of tights,' she said. 'And look—' She showed me her pockets, which, I saw, were bulging with socks. 'Let's see those fuckers steal from me now,' she said, again with that childish, confiding smile. (My mother had once been a woman whose loathing of profanity had banned even the word 'damn' from our house. It was this, and not the fact that she seemed to have no idea of *whose* funeral we were attending, that finally brought it home to me that she and my father were equally gone.)

I put my arm around her. Under the thickness of the wool she felt like an armful of birds. She said: 'Perhaps we'll have rabbit tonight. You know how much you like it.'

I nodded and said: 'That would be nice.'

I never saw her as lucid again.

The dead boy from the gravel pit was finally identified. He was a boy from Sunnybank Park, an undersized fifteen-year-old with the unpromising name of Lee Bagshot. He too made the *Malbry Examiner* – not the front page, but the third, next to the news of a series of burglaries in Pog Hill and a drunken driver in Huddersfield. I vaguely remember his photograph: the mullet; the V-necked pullover; the pinched and grinning little face.

Lee Bagshot was the son of Marie Bagshot (30), a shopgirl from White City, and John 'Lefty' Sykes (32), a self-employed plumber from Barnsley. Lee Bagshot spent his time between his mother's house and his grandparents', and due to a confusion over whose turn it was, his absence between December 30th and January 4th had gone unnoticed on both sides.

There were no tearful eulogies for Lee Bagshot; no vigils; no claims that he had ever been promising or popular. The mother appeared on *Nationwide*, pleading, a little shrilly perhaps, for the clay pits to be filled in. She was not a powerful advocate. She had bleached hair and too much make-up and seemed to be wearing every piece of jewellery she possessed. And yet there was something in her eyes that Nutter, MP, had never shown, not even at the height of the search for his son. At the time, I thought it was confusion, or guilt, or maybe just the excitement of being on TV. Now I think perhaps it was grief – the kind of grief that is hard and dry-eyed and belongs with those pebble-dashed houses with their bleak little squares of lawn and the steel shutters on the windows to make sure the stones don't crack the glass.

'He were allus going down to them pits,' she kept saying, as if it excused the fact that for nearly a week she had partied, and gone out with her friends, and smoked, and drunk beer, and slept with several different men, and twice gone to the beauty shop without even knowing her son was dead, without even asking herself where he was—

'I telled 'im,' she said. 'I kept tellin' 'im. But he were a lad, they dun't listen.'

He wasn't the only one, it seemed. Nobody listened to Marie. If Mrs Nutter had spoken out – elegant Mrs Nutter, with her round vowels and her place on the governing bodies of the choral society and the Women's Institute – then things might have been different. As it was, the clay pits stayed as they were for seven more years, after which the council had them filled in, and grassed over the place where they'd been to make a park that nobody used, except for youngsters up to no good. Lee Bagshot's case was quickly closed. The coroner ruled it an accident, and life went on as usual.

Well, not *quite* as usual. The fact was that we'd had a shock. One of our own had disappeared, and so far, the grapevine had failed us. But one of the things about a school is that nothing stays secret for ever. Knowledge filters through in the end, searching out the weak links, following the path of least resistance. And our particular weak link was the Chaplain of St Oswald's; a man whose goodwill was never in doubt, but whose ability to keep a secret, even when given in confidence, was very far from reliable.

St Oswald's Chaplain has never been what you'd call a firebrand. Even twenty-four years ago, Dr Burke was more of a liberal than anything else, although this may have been because he never really believed in the world outside St Oswald's. Devine, a Methodist who disapproves of the Chaplain's High Church leanings, has been known to call him 'that old Papist', which is slightly unfair, given that he and Devine have only a few years between them. Nor is the Chaplain a Catholic, although his penchant for incense and candles might seem a little too florid for a plain old School Chaplain.

But this is perhaps what made Harry Clarke come to him with his secret; that comforting sense of authority; that whiff of the confessional. Harry *had* been a Catholic, once – he still took comfort in the Church, even though she had proved to be a rather judgemental parent. And the Chaplain kept his mouth shut for fully two weeks before he slipped – after which the news had spread all around St Oswald's. Not only was Harry Clarke a practising homosexual, but for the few weeks preceding the Christmas break, he had befriended Nutter, talking to him, lending him books, even inviting him to his house. And that was where the boy had been found, a week after his disappearance . . .

6

January 1982

Harry told me the story himself. Of course I heard it later, in court, but by then it had bloated and festered, poisoned by time and circumstance. What Harry told me was simple: a single sequence of events, as yet untainted by the press. I had no reason to think it anything other than the truth: whatever else he may have been, Harry Clarke wasn't a liar.

He'd come home late on New Year's Eve to discover there'd been a break-in. A pane in his back door had been smashed, though there were no signs of a burglary. However, on entering the house, he found someone on the sofa: it was Charlie Nutter, asleep and bundled in a parka.

'Why didn't you phone the boy's parents?' It was the obvious question.

'I knew there was trouble at home,' Harry said. 'I didn't want to wake him.'

'What kind of trouble?'

Harry shrugged. Then he took from his pocket a folded pamphlet, cheaply printed on pink A4 paper. 'Go on, take a look,' he said, and handed me the pamphlet. The title read: *HOMOSEXUAL, HELLBOUND*.

I still remember it, twenty-four years on; that nasty little pamphlet. Most of its kind are ridiculous; badly written, badly spelt; filled with inappropriate capitalizations. This one was not: the style was good; the grammar flawless; the argument clear and almost reasonable.

Homosexuality is an addiction, it said, *born of doubt and a lack of faith. Into that emotional void, demons sink their ethereal claws, drawing the victim into a descending spiral of abhorrent behaviour, including rape, bestiality, incest – all abominations listed in the Bible. The only way to avoid damnation is to face up to these demons, to ask for forgiveness and cast them out. Otherwise, there can be no hope. The Bible is very clear on this. To refuse God's help is to repudiate God: damnation will surely follow.*

'It was in Charlie's pocket,' he said. 'The latest of a series of charming little booklets, warning against the dangers of masturbation, sodomy and any number of other things, from Dungeons & Dragons to rock music.' His tone was light, but I could see that, underneath, he was angry. 'Charlie had told me a few things,' he said, 'but I didn't know the half of it. They'd been trying to *cure* him, as if there were a cure for being gay. And by the time he came to me, he was already half convinced that he was possessed.'

'Possessed? As in by demons?' I said. 'People really *believe* in that stuff? I mean, people other than Mr Speight—'

'Oh, yes, Roy. They believe in them. Speight is far from being alone. And when the minister in charge is none other than Dr Harrington, then they see demons everywhere, including in a troubled teenager trying to come to terms with being gay.'

So *this* was what young Harrington had been trying to tell me, I thought. It all made perfect sense now. The boy's divided loyalties; his natural concern for his friend; his fear of speaking out in church; and Charlie Nutter's impulse to reach out to the one adult he could really trust.

Now, little by little, the story emerged. By no means a complete account – for a start, Charlie Nutter never revealed where he had been for those twenty-four hours *before* arriving at Harry's house – but enough to ensure Harry's silence. The boy was ill and feverish from sleeping rough the previous night, and not all he said made very much sense. But one thing was certain: he was afraid. He spoke of committing suicide; begged Harry not to tell anyone where he was; described himself as unclean and scrubbed his hands until they bled, but was so incoherent when it came to explanations that Harry was left with nothing but fragments of a story; all of which led to the Church of the Omega Rose as the source of his misery.

The Church of the Omega Rose. Till then, I'd never given the place much thought – in fact, as I discovered later, I'd been walking past it for years without even knowing it was there. A nice Edwardian house on the street that Malbry folk call *Millionaires' Row*, with nothing but a small brass plaque to indicate its purpose. Mr Speight spoke of sing-alongs, visiting preachers, friends' meetings, fundraisers and families' support groups. But according to Charlie Nutter, it was a place of darkness and dread, where public confessions, 'cleansings', speaking in tongues and ecstatic laying-on of hands were a weekly occurrence, and where a boy in doubt about his sexual identity was told that his soul was in danger.

'You can't be serious,' I said. 'These people are *educators*, for gods' sakes.'

Harry gave a weary smile. 'A lot of people believe it, Roy. The Church of the Omega Rose takes a very literal view on Scripture. Leviticus, chapter 18, verse 22: *Thou shalt not lie with mankind, as with womankind: it is abomination.* That's what that poor kid was taught to believe, and worse: that his perfectly normal feelings were caused by demons of sexual impurity that could enter him through his own self-doubt. On the other hand,' he went on, 'there are some sharp words in the Gospels about teachers whose version of pastoral care leads to damaging their charges. *Better for them that a millstone be tied around their necks and they be cast into the depths of the sea.* But I'm guessing Dr Harrington, Mr Speight and the rest of them aren't quite as interested in those verses.'

'I had no idea you knew so much about the Bible,' I said.

'I was brought up a Catholic,' said Harry. 'I suppose I still am, in my way, although there are plenty of things I no longer believe. I don't believe in the Devil. There are plenty of humans to do his work. And the God I believe in doesn't care *who* you love, or *how* you love, but simply that you *do* love. That's what I told Charlie Nutter when he came to me with this.'

It should have been me. I knew that at once. The fact that it wasn't spoke volumes about me as a schoolmaster. I blamed myself then, as I do now, that my attention had been elsewhere; that my mistrust of Harrington had caused me to turn a blind eye to a pupil in distress. That's what hurts most, even now. Even after what happened, I knew. It should have been me, not Harry.

By New Year's Day, Harry went on, the news of Charlie Nutter's disappearance had broken. Malbry was about to become the centre of a national investigation. Charlie had developed a bad cough, which needed antibiotics. Harry's position was untenable. He needed someone to arbitrate. He knew that the longer Charlie stayed away from his family, the more damage would be done. And so he finally went to a man he felt he could trust to deal with the matter in confidence. A man with a strong moral outlook and the welfare of his pupils at heart. That man was Dr Burke, of course – the Chaplain of St Oswald's.

7

January 1982

The Chaplain told me the story, in his little office. Even then, it was filled with orchids – pink and yellow, purple and white – heads bowed like penitents in the cool blue shadows.

'Fellow phoned me at home,' he said, in a slightly tremulous voice. 'Said he needed to talk to me. Told me the Nutter lad was there. Bit of a surprise, that.'

I imagine Harry felt that the Chaplain, used to confidences, would know what to do about Charlie. And so he told him everything: Nutter's problems at home; the situation at the church; Dr Harrington; Mr Speight; the leaflets; the ritual cleansings. Dr Burke was deeply shocked; first that the boy had run away, next, that a Master of the School had encouraged his behaviour. Result: the Chaplain went straight to the Head, and Shitter Shakeshafte, always pragmatic, called the parents straight away.

That was a bad time for everyone. Harry was furious at what he saw as a basic betrayal of trust; the Head was furious because of the threat of a scandal at St Oswald's; the

Chaplain was equally furious because of Harry's reaction; the Satanic Mr Speight was furious because Nutter's story had brought his church into disrepute; and Stephen Nutter, MP, was furious because, having paid good money for Charlie's education, he hadn't expected to deal with a lot of unnecessary parental problems.

Shakeshafte was unapologetic, however. For the sake of St Oswald's, he said, it was best not to get any further involved. And, to do him justice, although he said some harsh things to Harry in private – and some equally harsh things to me, for lying to the Chaplain; for failing to investigate Harrington's story and, most of all, for having known something he himself had not – he stood by both of us throughout.

Shitter Shakeshafte was old-school. He believed above all in protecting his staff. I doubt if later Headmasters would have been so loyal. Certainly, Johnny Harrington would not hesitate to throw a colleague to the wolves. But Shakeshafte just ordered Harry Clarke to lie low for a couple of weeks, and to take a little time off School, until the crisis was over.

Oh, there was some unpleasantness, mostly from the family. But Nutter, MP, was as reluctant as Shakeshafte to involve the police. Nutter, MP, had a reputation to protect, and when it became more than clear that any mud flung at St Oswald's would also damage him and his son, he soon became co-operative. The Church of the Omega Rose had already denied involvement. Harrington Senior made a statement, describing Charlie Nutter as a 'troubled young man', but declined to comment on any therapies the church had offered to cure him of homosexual thoughts. When challenged by the *Malbry Examiner* about rumours of demon exorcisms within his congregation, he said:

'I'm aware that some churches encourage belief in the literal existence of demons. But we prefer to take the psychological view. We encourage our worshippers to look inside themselves for the truth. The days of the Inquisition are gone. We are a progressive ministry.'

And so the scandal was contained, barring the inevitable rumours. Nutter, MP, and his entourage left Malbry early in '82, citing the pressures of government as the reason for their departure. Charlie never came back to School, although they paid his fees in full. The story grew old; the rumours died. Little by little, St Oswald's returned to a kind of normality.

We lost two dozen boys that year, and the next year's intake was not good, but that was to be expected. Ballast in the wake of the storm; the old ship sailed on, regardless of the time-bomb waiting to explode below decks . . .

8

October 3rd, 2005

And here comes old October again; like a snake with its tail in its mouth. Time speeds up as you get older, of course, and what seemed to cycle at leisurely speed now races at lethal velocity towards a dark horizon. The horse-chestnut tree in my garden is laden with fat, shiny conkers, and I pretend not to notice when the Sunnybankers jump over the wall to collect them. It's nice to know that Health & Safety hasn't yet reached Sunnybank Park.

At St Oswald's, conkers are banned, courtesy of Dr Devine, as are many other things: throwing snowballs; running too fast; climbing the trees in the Lower Quad. Even more disturbing than this is his current obsession with name tags, which, he claims, if worn by staff and visitors to St Oswald's, will ensure that intruders in the School are swiftly apprehended.

'What kind of intruders?' I wanted to know. (This was in the Common Room, after the Headmaster's Briefing.)

Devine gave me one of his looks. 'Anyone could wander in,' he said. 'Look what happened to President Reagan.'

'Oh, please. Johnny Harrington hardly qualifies as an assassination risk. Besides, if a shooter *did* wander in, how would his wearing a visitor's badge stop him from running amok?'

'Well, according to Markowicz—'

Markowicz. I should have known.

'I'm not wearing a badge,' I said. 'If thirty-four years at the dear old place hasn't made me recognizable enough, then I doubt whether a badge will make any difference. I shall prowl the corridors in shadow, incognito. I shall strike fear in the hearts of the weak. Boys will look at me and say: *Who was that man of mystery?*'

Devine sniffed. 'Now you're being ridiculous.'

'No, *you're* ridiculous, Devine. You always were, but this is beyond farcical. And frankly, watching you try to compete with a man half your age makes me queasy.'

He looked indignant. '*Compete?*' he said. 'Straitley, I have nothing to prove.'

Of course, he's deluded, poor Devine. The man has no sense of proportion. His feelings of inadequacy towards the younger Markowicz have completely addled what little common sense he had. The genocide of the Bell Tower mice; the removal of the Honours Boards; the crackdown on litter; the endless Health & Safety reports, and now, visitors' badges for staff—

'Oh, please,' I told him. 'You're *this* far from matching outfits.' I held out my index finger and thumb about a millimetre apart.

Devine's nose went slightly pink, but he maintained his dignity. 'I know you're under stress,' he said. 'But there's really no need to be puerile. Some of us have a purpose, Roy. Some of us are not stuck in the past. Some of us still have ambitions beyond the playing of silly practical jokes.'

'This is no joke, it's a tragedy,' I said, and walked out of the Common Room, only to meet Eric Scoones coming in with a garden gnome under his arm.

'Did *you* put this in my locker?' he said.

I've known Eric sixty years, of course, which means that I know every wrinkle and crease. I know when he is lying, when he is feeling insecure and, most of all, when he is feeling guilty. And guilt was in his face then – as well it might be, given the circumstances. A joke, but all the same, I suspect it gave old Eric a nasty shock, much of the kind that Billy Bones received from Blind Pew at the Admiral Benbow.

I assumed a Sphinx-like expression.

'Don't pretend it wasn't, Straits. I *know* it was you. And I'm not amused.'

I turned and gave him my most quizzical stare, the one I reserve for first-form boys trying to persuade me that Rover has eaten their Latin book, or that they are allergic to Prep. 'Why would I put a garden gnome in your locker, Eric?' I said.

He stepped back into the corridor and pulled the Common Room door closed. 'Because you're vindictive, that's why,' he said, sounding almost plaintive now. 'Because you'll never let me forget that awful business with Harry Clarke. Do you think it was easy for *me*?'

'Easier than for Harry,' I said.

'Harry was an idiot.' The plaintive expression hardened. 'Fraternizing with the boys – what did he *think* would happen, eh? Everyone knows you don't bring boys home. Especially not when you're – *you know*.' His voice, already low, now dropped to a baleful hiss. 'No one sane runs that kind of risk. We all know what it leads to. Who knows what really happened? But no schoolmaster worth his salt would have put himself in the firing line.'

The invisible finger plucked at my ribs. I felt myself getting angry. 'So you're just fine with what happened, then? You think Harry deserved it?'

Eric took on a stubborn look. 'That's not what I'm saying. I just think that you should let it go, that's all. I mean, Harry's gone now. It's over. There's no point in the both of us being tarred by association.'

'No chance of that with *you*, eh?' My voice was sharp, and Eric flinched. Of course, he knew what I meant by that; he'd left St Oswald's for eight years, right after the Nutter affair, to teach at King Henry's Grammar School, where he'd tried for promotion several times without success, before at last admitting defeat and coming home to St Oswald's.

The fact is that King Henry's School is Oxbridge to the battlements, and Scoones, with his degree from Leeds, was neither polished, nor subtle, nor young enough, nor impressive enough to hope for anything more than a Junior Master's post and the chance to run the French Exchange. Most days we make a joke of this, but Eric's defection still rankles; especially for what it meant to Harry, when the time came for his friends to rally round.

Eric handed me the gnome, which seemed to have been laughing throughout. 'I'm guessing this is yours,' he said. 'I never want to see it again.' Then, without another word, he went on his way to the Bell Tower, slouching a little, as if still burdened with something too heavy to carry upright.

I went back to my form-room feeling unexpectedly depressed. I put the gnome on my bookcase, where it continued to laugh at me throughout the day. Sixth-Form Ovid came and went, without the girl Benedicta, who seemed to be missing this morning; then fourth-form Latin, and then on to lunch, where my Brodie Boys seemed distant, almost secretive, and then a long afternoon that dragged on like the tail of a particularly slow and bedraggled bird – a pheasant, perhaps – as the day grew darker and wetter. Devine, too, came and went, with Jimmy, bringing traps to poison the mice. During my free period, Markowicz allowed his class to make so much noise that I could barely concentrate enough to read the paper.

By the end of School I was feeling tired and discouraged. I looked at the gnome, still watching me with an air of jaunty dissipation, and felt ridiculous. Eric was right, I told myself. I'm wasting my time. And for what? That business is over. Harrington is untouchable. So far, Winter's 'research' has given me nothing I do not know. And as for shaming Devine or Eric into joining my campaign – how could I ever have thought that would work?

The girl Benedicta was waiting for me outside the Common Room after School.

'Sorry I wasn't in Latin today,' she said. 'I was in the Library.'

'Really?' I was curious. St Oswald's Library is hardly the obvious place for truancy. 'Is there a problem?' I asked.

'Yes.' The girl was nothing if not forthright. 'It's Allen-Jones,' she told me. 'He's being bullied for being gay.'

I felt the old heart sink a little. 'Rupert Gunderson again?'

She gave me a look designed to convey the full extent of my incompetence. '*He* isn't the problem,' she said. 'It's the Head; Dr Blakely; the Chaplain; pretty much all of the Games staff – basically, St Oswald's, sir. It's a toxic environment.'

'I see,' I said. 'What happened?'

'They've been making him talk to the Chaplain,' said Ben. 'Telling him he *isn't* gay, but that he's reacting inappropriately to undue influence, or something. As if you could *choose* to be gay or not. As if it's a fad, like Pokémon.'

'Excuse me?' I said.

'Oh, never mind.' The girl Benedicta waved aside my pitiful ignorance and went on: 'The point is, sir, that they're talking as if being gay's his *choice*, or even his fault. Like they caught him smoking, or taking drugs. Like it's a *phase*. It isn't fair. You have to stop it, sir.'

I nodded. Yes, of course I must. But it isn't as simple as she appears to think. Her trust in me is commendable, but I am a single old King on the chessboard, surrounded by Queens and Bishops.

'I'll do what I can,' I promised her. Then, as a sudden thought crossed my mind: 'You're taking this very much to heart. Is it – I mean—?'

She looked at me with a mixture of annoyance and amusement. It struck me that in ten years' time, she would make a natural schoolmistress; a trainee Dragon of a calibre to which Miss Smiley and Miss Malone could only ever dream to aspire.

'Well, of *course* I am,' she said. 'Can't you tell?'

I admitted that I hadn't had a great deal of exposure.

'Will it make a difference?' she said.

'Not in the least,' I told her. It struck me that, from having lived in (almost) total ignorance of the world of what she and Allen-Jones would undoubtedly term the 'sexually diverse', I was now apparently surrounded by them.

'I'll do what I can,' I told her.

She looked relieved. 'Thank you, sir.'

Of course, she is still young enough to have confidence in her elders. But frankly, I found my heart sinking as I considered what to do. A King, alone, has little power. He relies on the other pieces to act, dictating strategy from afar. But what pieces do I have? Only Winter; a single pawn, who may perhaps one day graduate to something a little more weighty.

I tried Dr Burke. But the Chaplain was vague, even beyond his usual level of vagueness, speaking of 'changing policies' as he misted his orchids, while refusing to meet my eye. I suspect the Head has got to him. But what is Harrington trying to do? I do not think for a moment that this is just about Allen-Jones. He is merely one of the pawns. I am the primary target. And though I cannot see the shape of the trap that the Head is preparing, I know it's just a matter of time before it finally closes on me . . .

9

October 7th, 2005

Today, the theft of the Honours Boards was finally announced in the Common Room. I was conscious of Devine watching me as Dr Blakely made the announcement, calling it a 'despicable crime', and urging us to be vigilant in our search for the culprit. His implication was that someone in School must have been privy to the theft, possibly a pupil, and that the boards would probably turn up in a local lumber yard or garage sale. Alternatively, opined Dr Blakely, the theft may have been intended as a prank of some kind – here I felt Eric's eyes on me – in which case, it was likely that they would turn up sooner, rather than later.

Sooner, rather than later, repeated Dr Blakely, with a sinister emphasis, and once more I felt Eric's eyes shift – oh, so briefly – towards me. Devine said nothing – in fact, Devine might have been stone – and I found myself feeling grateful for my colleague's Teutonic composure. Eric could never keep a secret, not even when we were boys, and if I give him the tiniest hint, my crime will be public property before you can say *Carpe diem*. I see that I'm going to have to be very careful around Eric, at least until the Honours Boards are safely hidden somewhere else. It shouldn't be too difficult. That garden gnome still rankles, and he barely says a word to me.

After morning Break, I was called into the Headmaster's office. Thing One and Thing Two were both there, as was the Chaplain. Thing One – Dr Blakely – was looking rather smug, I thought, and the Chaplain slightly put out, which I thought boded ill for me. Ms Buckfast was sitting by the window, in a linen dress that managed to be at the same time demure and obscurely provocative, her red hair caught into a loose bun. My immediate thought was: *This is it: they've found me out.* But if so, why was the Chaplain there?

'Roy,' said the Head. 'We've had a complaint.'

For a moment I was back there, in Shitter Shakeshafte's office, the smell of old leather and cheese as strong as if it were only yesterday. It was a surreal feeling, that of being flung backwards in Time, to find myself as an old man summoned before the boy who was.

'Let me guess. Rupert Gunderson.'

'Almost,' said Harrington. His expression was serious, and yet I could see him smiling. 'Rupert Gunderson's girlfriend. Her name is Chanelle Goodman. I believe you're teaching her Latin group.'

I was taken slightly aback. Then I remembered the Goodman girl, one of my Sixth Form from Mulberry House. A clone of her Headmistress, trailing clouds of hairspray, with a tendency to sit at the back and giggle at the rude words. I remember wondering why she had chosen to study Latin, as she seemed to have so little interest in either the language or literature. But why would she have made a complaint? And about whom?

'Apparently, you've been studying Vergil's *Aeneid* IX,' said the Head. 'More specifically, the tale of Nisus and Euryalus.'

I was puzzled. 'And?' I said.

'The girl claims that you, Mr Straitley, were using the text as a manifesto for what I believe the ancient Greeks referred to as *Paiderastia;* a distasteful cultural phenomenon in which young men – minors, I believe – were known to indulge in erotic relationships with older men. Quite an inappropriate topic for a Latin lesson, I would have thought.'

I was completely dumbfounded. 'Is that what she told you?' I said. 'I mean, I may have touched upon the subject – this is Classics, Headmaster – but that's hardly the same thing as *using the text as a manifesto—*'

The Head gave me a sympathetic look. 'I know, Roy. But this is 2005. We have a responsibility. We have to be very careful about the kinds of message we give out. And after that business with Allen-Jones—'

'Being beaten up is a *business* now? Are you saying I encouraged him?'

'I'm not saying anything,' said the Head. 'But boys, as you know, are susceptible to all kinds of influence. If, consciously or otherwise, a respected Master allows, or even seems to approve, a practice that society has deemed reprehensible . . .'

'Now wait a minute, Headmaster,' I said. I could feel the invisible finger pressing against my sternum. Beneath it, I was all rage. 'If any allegation has been made against me by Miss Goodman – with or without the collusion of her *boyfriend* – I think I'm entitled to hear it, and to have representation.'

The words sounded odd coming from my throat. In all my years of teaching, I've never asked for Union help. Partly because Dr Devine happens to be my Union representative, but mostly because I've felt able to deal with my problems myself. Of course, in the old days I could always rely on the Head to support me (in public, at least). Now I strongly suspect that the Head is cheering on the lynch mob.

Harrington smiled. 'Do you think so? Well, perhaps it's for the best. I'll ask Danielle to arrange a time for all of us to meet again. Until then—' That smile again. 'Chanelle's parents have asked that she be withdrawn from Latin lessons until the matter is correctly resolved. She's a very sensitive, spiritual girl, and easily triggered.'

'*Triggered?*' I said.

Dr Blakely intervened. 'Some references tend to upset her. Apparently both she and Rupert Gunderson find your championing of – certain sexual practices – distasteful and upsetting.'

I snapped: 'Well, *I* find Gunderson's bullying of one of my boys equally distasteful. From what I hear, Allen-Jones—'

Dr Blakely smiled. 'I think that may be a discussion we have to keep for another day. For the moment, let's reconvene – let's say as soon as possible, John?'

Harrington nodded. 'I'll make a date.'

And at those words, a Century of duty and teaching were dismissed – by an upstart in a shiny suit and his pair of lackeys. The Chaplain had the grace to look awkward, and tried to catch me as I went out, but I was far too angry (and beneath that, too afraid) to deliver more than a curt *Goodbye*. I went through the business of today like an automaton; smiling; talking to the boys; taking tea in the Common Room. But there was a bleakness inside me.

This is how it begins, I thought. Just as it did twenty years ago, a Juggernaut fuelled by rumours and spite, crushing good men beneath its wheels. Just as it did with all of us. Just as it did with Harry Clarke.

10

October 14th, 2005

The golden lion of autumn is unusually subdued this year. Head tucked quietly over his paws, like a bronze statue over a grave. The dead walk in October; and not just on All Hallows' Eve. Even the boys are oddly subdued. They sense the coming of winter. I sense it too, deep in my bones, just as I knew instinctively, when Colin Knight went missing last year, that I would never see him again—

Colin Knight. That wretched boy. I thought perhaps I'd put him to rest. But as Hallowe'en approaches, I find myself remembering the dead. Colin Knight. Harry Clarke. Even Lee Bagshot – although he was not one of ours – perhaps even *because* of that.

With the passing of time, I find that the concept of *belonging* becomes less and less easy to believe in. I once belonged to St Oswald's. I was a part of it, heart and soul. Now I am in the shadows, contemplating the darkness. Harry, too: now, even in death, he is a pariah. Our sense of belonging is nothing more than bright reflections on water; on a sunny day, we can see the sky; the clouds; each other. But dark water lies in waiting for the unwary; for us all. Dark water doesn't discriminate.

My hearing with the New Head has been confirmed for next Monday. I already know what it will bring. The presence of my Union representative (Dr Devine in person) suggests that I shall receive a written warning, pending further enquiries. Ms Buckfast is already collecting ammunition – she thinks I don't know about this, but I do. The trace of her scent between lessons betrays her visits to room 59; besides which, my Brodie Boys see everything, and report to me accordingly.

This was why I was unsurprised, returning to room 59 after my usual cup of tea after School in the Common Room, to find La Buckfast herself at my desk, reading a book of Latin verse.

'You're looking a little tired,' she said.

'Really? I've never been better.'

Ms Buckfast put down the Latin book. 'I was hoping we might have a chat.'

I did not reply immediately, but instead went to my desk drawer and found a bag of Liquorice Allsorts. I offered her one. She took a pink coconut ice. Funny. I hadn't thought of her until then as a pink person.

'So, what is it today?' I said. 'Boys not co-operating? Some complaint about irregular verbs? School mash not lumpy enough? Or just another pep talk on the inevitability of Progress?'

La Buckfast smiled. It occurred to me once again that Ms Buckfast reminds me of our erstwhile Miss Dare. Beneath all that professional veneer, there's something else in hiding.

'Benedicta Wild,' she said.

'Ben, to her friends.' My heart sank. 'You're not telling me *she's* made a complaint, are you?'

That smile again. 'No, Roy, she hasn't. But the Headmistress, Miss Lambert, feels she's spending rather too much time with you and – what do you call them? Your Brodie Boys?'

'I work in my room at lunchtimes,' I said. 'Boys – and anyone else – are free to stay and socialize, if they please. As for *Call-me-Jo*, I thought she was only too happy to see her girls fraternizing with our boys.'

'It really depends on which boys,' said Ms Buckfast. 'Benedicta's – *circumstances* mean that a friendship with Allen-Jones may not be the kind Mulberry House wants to encourage. She's going through a rebellious phase, and—'

'You mean a *homosexual* phase?'

'Roy, please,' said Ms Buckfast. 'I think you ought to step away.'

There's something about her tone of voice when she uses my Christian name. A kind of soothing, coaxing note, as if addressing an old horse. I found myself bristling at the sound, and the invisible digit that always lurks, ready to prod at my breastbone, gave an angry little twitch.

'You're being ridiculous,' I said. 'We're here to teach the pupils, not to determine their sexual orientation. It seems to me that *Call-me-Jo* and Harrington are far too interested in things that are not remotely their business. I'll deal with my pupils in my way, as I've always dealt with them, which means that unless their predilections affect their Latin homework, I shall ignore them completely. And I'll thank you and the other Suits not to interfere.'

That would have worked against Dr Blakely. Ye gods, it was my Bell Tower voice, the one that reduces boys to pulp. But La Buckfast held my gaze.

'I'm sorry you think of it that way,' she said. 'But this isn't a suggestion. You're a fine form-master, Roy, but I think you have a blind spot regarding certain members of your form. Nowadays, it's considered unwise for a teacher to spend quite so much time with the boys. After all, isn't that the mistake made by your friend, Harry Clarke?'

'Who told you that? Was it Harrington?'

La Buckfast shook her head.

'John's at a seminar today. But you'll see him on Monday, of course.' She smiled, and once more I saw a gleam of that feline, disconcerting charm. 'Believe it or not, Roy, I sympathize,' she said, and touched my shoulder. 'Perhaps you ought to take a break. You're really looking quite unwell.'

The old Straitley might have protested. But I was feeling a little tired. *Do* I spend too much time with my boys? In Harry's day, to spend time with boys was a natural, even a good thing to do. How quickly things change. There were School trips; field days; informal chats over tea and cake. To be a St Oswald's Master was to be available at all times; to be at the same time a teacher; social worker; detective; confessor; father; sometimes, even a friend. At least, Harry Clarke was all those things. Others, like myself and Eric, settled for a lesser role. But even we had our share of that. In my case, it's my Brodie Boys – Allen-Jones, Sutcliff, Tayler, McNair. Where would I be without them? Where would they be without *me*?

'I'll take it under advisement,' I said.

She smiled. 'I think it'll do you good. Take the weekend off. Clear your head. Get a bit of perspective.'

Perspective. Is that what I lack? In the old days, we ran on instinct. But now, we have guidelines to follow, for our safety and that of the boys. Between them, Bob Strange and Dr Devine have removed the peril from teaching.

Never speak to a boy alone. Always keep the door ajar. No physical contact with boys, not even to offer comfort (or, as Eric would have preferred, to clip them around the ear). No fraternizing at the pub, as generations of Games teachers were wont to do in Harry's day. No impromptu trips, or at least, not without risk assessments, consent forms, dietary sheets and a mass of assorted paperwork designed to predict (and likely, prevent) any possible diversion from the humdrum. And yet, as any Master knows who *doesn't* spend his time staring at a computer, teaching is the essence of risk, the home of the unpredictable. There is no risk assessment for Life. And Life is what we are teaching.

I walked home through the park again, hearing the sounds of night in the trees. The cold air smelt of woodsmoke; the leaves were wet beneath my feet. I'd almost reached the end of the park, where Millionaires' Row turns on to Westgate. A little group of teenage boys in hooded sweatshirts and knitted hats were standing under the lamp-post near the swing-set in the children's playground, looking up to no good. Of course, that's how teenage boys *always* look whenever adults are around. It's a kind of default setting, comprised partly of guilt and partly of resentment. But sullenness breeds more of the same, and I have always made a point of treating teenagers the same way I would treat any adult. My boys tend to appreciate it, and although I could see that this little group was made up of Sunnybankers, I assumed that they would too.

I smiled and said: 'Good evening.'

The boys said nothing, but stared at me. One of them, a freckled boy with long hair under his knitted cap and a cigarette stub between his fingers, smirked and said something under his breath. The other boys sniggered unpleasantly.

The freckled boy said: '*Pervert.*'

I felt a trickle of unease, all the more galling for the fact that I was on my own ground, less than three hundred yards from home. But boys are like house-cats, gentle by day, unpredictable by night. A schoolmaster, on the other hand, is always a schoolmaster; at home; in town; in the post office queue; in the park in the evening. Boys do not really believe, deep down, that Masters have a life outside St Oswald's. They secretly imagine us hanging like bats, upside-down in our stockrooms, emerging only to mark books, to collect detention slips or to hatch inscrutably evil schemes to bring about the downfall of the young.

I summoned my best schoolmaster's voice and levelled my sternest gaze on the boy. 'I *beg* your pardon?'

The freckled boy sniggered again. He looked about fourteen; half-grown, with nicotine stains on his fingers. 'Fucking pervert, chatting up lads.' He gave me a look like that of a dog unsure of whether to bite or run. Alone, he probably would have run; but the presence of the other boys gave him a kind of bravado.

'Give us a tenner and I'll not report you,' he told me, his grin broadening.

'Give him twenty and he'll suck you off,' chimed in one of the other boys. 'Assuming you can still get it up.'

For a moment, I stared at them. Yes, I'll admit it, I was shocked. Not so much by the language – after all, St Oswald's boys can swear as roundly as the best of them – but by the hard and cynical look in those teenagers' faces. Some of it was a joke, I knew; but beneath was a stratum of knowledge. Boys may be children during the day, but at night they can become predators. And in a world that turns on fear, suspicion and entitlement, they have learnt to manipulate those levers that make adults afraid.

Afraid of *what*? They were only boys. I work with boys almost every day. And yet, boys have an instinct for fear; they sense it as a shark scents blood. I've seen it happen often enough at St Oswald's – at St Oswald's and elsewhere. Teaching is a game of bluff, in which the smallest weakness shown can mean the end of authority. And everyone has a weakness. Mine was a word. Just a word, but a word that can tear a schoolmaster apart.

Pervert. There's a dangerous word. Of all the accusations that could be made against a Master, that's the one that does not need the slightest shred of evidence. Sticks and stones may break my bones, but words – *that* word – can obliterate every part of a man's life; every good deed; every kindness; as if the man had never lived.

I tried to summon my schoolmaster's voice, but for once there was nothing. No sarcasm; no anger; no joke; not even a Latin epithet. I'm ashamed to say that I actually *ran* – head down, as if against the wind – hearing their laughter behind me and with the invisible finger pressing against my breastbone with a dreadful persistence.

A thirty-second run is as long as I manage nowadays. Even so, it was enough to take me out of their orbit. I slowed to a shamble behind a row of laurels and finally reached the gates of the park, my heart now beating uncomfortably fast, and bent over like a runner at the end of a long race.

I must cut down on the Gauloises, I thought. And maybe the cheese, and the claret. I remember a time when I could have run from St Oswald's to the clay pits without so much as breaking sweat; but that was a long time ago. The clay pits are gone, and so is that boy, whom Eric called 'Straits' because he was constantly falling foul of the authorities.

Well, I'd rather not fall foul of them now, especially not for chatting up boys in the park on a Friday night. I went back to my house on Dog Lane with a fluttering sense of doom, almost expecting to find those boys waiting for me with the police.

I know. It was ridiculous. But as I opened my garden gate to see the shadow of a man in blue standing by my little porch, I felt all the air in my lungs rush out. The only coherent thought in my mind was once again: *Just like Harry Clarke.*

11

October 1988

Seven years had passed since the Nutter affair. That's twenty St Oswald's terms: cut grass; rainy lunchtimes; cups of tea in the Common Room and stacks of books in the Quiet Room; School plays and small dramas; Open Days; Parents' Evenings; sporadic invasions of Mulberry girls and sleepy Friday afternoons. St Oswald's is its own world; what happens in the world outside is of far less significance. In the world outside our gates, Margaret Thatcher was at the helm; but inside, we had Shitter Shakeshafte, and a kind of stable anarchy.

Nutter had left Malbry in early '82, giving no further explanation for his disappearance. That Easter, Harrington also left, following a series of increasingly urgent letters from Dr Harrington Senior, demanding to know whether there was any truth in the rumour that his son's English teacher, Harry Clarke, was a homosexual.

I told you, Shitter Shakeshafte was no liberal. On the other hand, like all the old guard, he believed in St Oswald's above all else. Whatever the complaint, he would *always* take the side of a staff member against a parent (albeit for the privilege of being the one to wield the axe as soon as the battle was over). He duly informed Dr Harrington that Mr Clarke was an English Master of exceptional ability, and that how he conducted his private life had no bearing on his work, and that furthermore, if Dr Harrington preferred to send his son to another school, then he should do so without delay, or lose a term's fees in lieu of notice. Then, in the privacy of his cheese-fetid office with the leather-studded double doors, he gave Harry Clarke such a rocket that all the Lower Corridor overheard him; warning Harry to keep his Gay Lib to himself, and threatening him with the most baroque of consequences if there was another complaint.

There wasn't. Johnny Harrington left, and life went on as normal. For a time, there were whispers among the boys. Spikely also left mid-term, with no word of explanation from his parents. But staff at St Oswald's rarely leave. We tend to go the distance. Chained to the same oar, we find our comfort in each other. Harry and I remained good friends, though some colleagues removed themselves. Devine was one of them; Eric, too; so was Satanic Mr Speight. But School scandals come and go, and all but the most judgemental eventually got used to the fact that one of our number would never look at a Mulberry girl with interest.

As for Harry, as far as I knew, he never *had* a relationship. Like myself, he was chained to the oar, and St Oswald's demanded our loyalty. But he and I stayed friends, in spite of our many differences, and together we watched the passage of years, steady and, at the same time, so fast that we could barely grasp how those twenty terms had managed to slide so unobtrusively past us.

I was forty-eight. Forty-eight is the age at which we close up the shutters behind the house and watch the shadows lengthen. It is an age of uncertainty, of crow's-feet and grey hairs and fast-expanding waistlines. It is the age at which past mistakes return to claim their pound of flesh, and at which we begin to see our parents' faces instead of our own in the bathroom mirror.

But things were different in those days. Nowadays, fifty is young. Then, I was already *Old Quaz* to most of the boys in the Middle School. Harry Clarke, at fifty-three, was still younger than we were, somehow; maybe because of that smile of his. Still as popular with the boys; still with that sense of the absurd. He still wore those tweed jackets with the elbow-patches; still listened to his records at Break and wore his hair a little too long – hair that was going rather grey, but not enough to make him old.

Over the years, Harry had become a living part of the Bell Tower, just as I had. We sometimes used to joke about what would happen when we died; whether we would be buried *in situ,* or mortared into the parapet with the other gargoyles. But we didn't believe it. We were still young enough to believe that death would make an exception for us; that somehow, the sun would never set, but would shine on us for ever—

And then, in the autumn of '88, Harry was arrested.

The first any of us knew of it was when the police turned up at School, demanding to search his classroom. Harry hadn't come in that morning, which was already unusual. In all his years at St Oswald's, I don't think he'd ever been absent more than a couple of days. The officers – one senior, one not – were another version of Stackhouse and Noakes, the pair who had come to see me at home when Charlie Nutter disappeared.

'Excuse me, what is this about?' I asked, when I saw them leaving his room with an armful of cardboard boxes.

The Stackhouse prototype shrugged. 'Just following up an enquiry,' he said.

'What kind of an enquiry?' I said.

Behind me, the boys of 3S craned their necks to see the show. Harry's class had vacated the room, under the supervision of the young Pat Bishop – not yet Second Master, but already a jolly good Head of Year. He'd lined them up in the corridor, underneath the Honours Boards, and they watched the proceedings round-eyed, some looking uncomfortable (as boys often do when faced with the possibility of trouble); some grinning and whispering behind their grubby schoolboy palms.

'What *kind* of an enquiry?' I repeated, louder this time. 'Has there been a break-in?'

Along the Upper Corridor, I could see Devine watching me through the glass door of his classroom. Eric, too, was watching; his round face bland with anxiety. The younger officer walked past me without answering the question; I looked into the box in his arms and saw books, records, photographs – as well as the fabled garden gnome, which had migrated to Harry's desk, to be brought out on the special occasions when Dr Devine was teaching there.

'Those things belong to Harry Clarke,' I said, with increasing discomfort.

Bishop gave me a warning look, as if to say: *Not now, Roy*. And although it took till that afternoon for the grapevine to bring us the story, I knew right then what had happened. Instinct, maybe; or maybe the fear of something rising from the depths. The rumour mill had been working ever since the police arrived; but it was only the next day that the Head gave us the news: that Harry Clarke was under arrest following a complaint from a boy.

'*What* boy?' I demanded.

'Not a current pupil,' he said. After which he closed his office door and warned us not to disturb him: while outside, in the Common Room, the rumours flew like swarming wasps.

None of us believed it at first. *Not a current pupil?* What did that mean, anyway? It had to be some kind of mistake. Harry was devoted to his pupils. I said as much to Eric, indignantly, over tea from the Common Room urn.

But Eric was less outspoken. After nearly a decade of trying for promotion, he had become very sensitive to anything that might damage him. He never talked about politics; never discussed School policy; never mentioned his private life unless he was completely sure which side of the fence to alight on. And now, a colleague was under arrest – and I could already see him trying to shift his position.

'Well, there *was* that Nutter thing,' he said.

'What have you heard?'

'Nothing. But after what happened, I always thought that maybe there was something more to that business than we were told at the time.'

'Ridiculous,' I told him. 'This is a storm in a teacup.'

But as the news filtered down to us – as always, from the boys themselves – it became clear that, whatever it was, the affair was not something that would simply blow away. Over the next few days we learnt that Harry had been questioned, following an accusation of sexual assault on a boy. The police had opened a helpline, urging pupils to contact them with any information. Harry's house had been searched, and evidence had been removed, and a young man had been staying there – a young man not unconnected with the investigation. Finally, we heard the news: Harry had been formally charged.

There was still no information on the alleged victim. No one at St Oswald's knew, not even Jeffreys, the son of the Chairman of Governors, whose intimate knowledge of everything behind the scenes at St Oswald's made him a valuable asset to any Master. As it happened, he was in Harry's form – and in my Middle School Latin class.

'What kind of evidence?' I said.

Jeffreys shrugged. 'Books and photographs and stuff.'

'And who's making these allegations?'

The boy shook his head. 'No one in School. An ex-pupil.'

But who? The School declined to comment, although speculation ran rife. Could we have misjudged one of our own? What kind of evidence could the police possibly have uncovered? More importantly, who was the boy behind these allegations?

Some boys leave School like rats leaving the hold of a sinking ship. Some leave like kings; some leave in tears; some waving their shirts like victory flags. And some boys lodge in the throat like a bone, almost forgotten, but still a source of barely perceived discomfort.

Harrington. It had to be. I could feel it in my gut. Harrington, who had first come to me with his tale of possession; Harrington, whose complacency in the face of any sort of criticism made him completely immune to self-doubt; Harrington, whose church believed that homosexuality was a demon. And now that those demons were flying again, who else could be responsible?

And so, when Jeffreys told me the name of the boy who had accused Harry Clarke, it hit me like a physical blow. Not Harrington. Not Nutter, though Nutter had his part to play. But the third and least remarkable of that little trio: Nutter and Harrington's lacklustre friend – the tattletale, David Spikely.

Part Six

Aegri somnia.
(Horace)

1

Michaelmas Term, 2005

Dear Mousey,

How time flies. It must be twenty-four years since I last kept a diary. I still remember it clearly; my old St Oswald's Prep diary; blue, with the school motto – *audere, augere, auferre* – in gold letters on the front. They say they're the best days of your life. In my case, I think maybe they were.

No, don't laugh. I mean it. I was young and healthy. I had my whole life ahead of me. I wasn't exactly *happy* then; but at least I felt *alive*. Nowadays everything seems dead and dull in comparison. Everyone has moved forward, but me. Harry's dead; my father's dead; even you're dead, Mousey.

Funny, I thought you'd survive me. I saw it in the papers, you know. *Family Dispute Leads to Tragedy*. They flattered you more than you deserved. They always do that for the dead. You were a *promising young man*; clever, handsome and popular. No one knew what you were really like. No one but me, Mousey – and maybe that fat brother of yours who knew more than he was telling. Still, it seems right for you to be dead. I might as well have died myself. Some days, I still feel like that; a drowned man, in dark water.

As for my friends at St Oswald's – well. Harrington's Headmaster now. Imagine that. Goldie, running St Oswald's. Charlie Nutter – Poodle, as was – never quite recovered. He's spent most of his adult life in one institution or another. I'm glad. The little queer had no right to think that he could get away like that. From his parents, from the Church, from St Oswald's, even from *me*. What right had he to be happy? What right did he have to move on?

After leaving St Oswald's in January '82, he spent six months in a Church-run retreat somewhere down in Oxfordshire, then the rest of his schooldays in a place somewhere in Wales – a nice school, with nice *girls*, to take his mind off Harry Clarke. For a while he did pretty well; behaved himself; played the game. I watched him all the time, from afar. Turns out I'm good at watching. They say you discover your passion before you hit your teens: if so, I'd already discovered it at seven years old, down in the clay pits with Mousey.

Of course, not everyone gets to spend their life following their passion. Perhaps that's why I've ended up here, back in dull old Malbry. The clay pits are gone, landfilled, link-fenced; but somehow the spirit of them lives on. Kids from Sunnybank Park still go to smoke their roll-up cigarettes; some of them climb the fence at night. What are they looking for in there? Nowadays, it's decent enough, if not entirely wholesome. Gone are the fridges crawling with mould; the rocks; the cars half-buried in the soil, their fins chopping the surface like sharks'. Now it's just a grassy space, perhaps too bleak to be called a park, with a few little trees and a memorial bench that no one ever sits on.

Perhaps they sense how haunted it is; and not just by Lee Bagshot. The living make better ghosts than the dead. I know; I've been one for twenty-four years.

After I came back to Malbry, I went looking for my time capsule, with the album, the Christmas card, and the pages torn from out of my diary. I knew exactly where it was, buried under a big rock between the Pit Shaft and the Long Pond. Except that when I went looking, neither the Pit Shaft nor the Long Pond were recognizable any more, the big rock had gone into landfill, and the time capsule was lost. I'm rather disappointed: I would have liked to read those pages again, to see how much I've really changed. Perhaps I haven't changed at all. I look into my mirror at night and see a fourteen-year-old boy, wrinkled before his time, with disappointment in his eyes. But the real David Spikely is somewhere else; a demon that cannot be exorcized.

Harry Clarke stayed in his post for seven years after the scandal. I stayed on for a month or two, although, for obvious reasons, I stopped spending lunchtimes in his room. Goldie and I were both under strict instructions about that, and Mr Speight and the Chaplain both kept us under discreet supervision. It was very frustrating. I wanted to know what (if anything) Poodle had said about me. But Harry never mentioned anything, and because he wasn't my English teacher, I didn't see him much at all. Just once or twice in the corridor, at which times he spoke to me just as he spoke to everyone else. I left Malbry in '82; went to a school in Manchester. My grades were fair, but my health was poor. I developed alopecia. I lost my hair and eyebrows. My eyebrows came back eventually, but my hair did not; by sixteen I was totally bald, and looked like a man of forty.

Obviously, this had an effect on my self-esteem, not to mention my love life, which was hardly healthy anyway. I went back to killing things to make myself feel better. Rats; mice; a neighbour's cat and, finally, a mongrel dog belonging to a family friend, after which my parents intervened, appealed to the Church, consulted a variety of therapists and took me to a prayer sanctuary in Philadelphia, where I saw a faith healer, who totally failed to cure both my baldness *and* My Condition, but from whom I managed to catch a sexually transmitted disease which led to my immediate removal, both from the sanctuary and from my school, where my grades had slipped so badly that there was by then no hope of recovery.

You see how it happens, Mousey. See how those school years cling on to you. The best days of our lives, they say, and yet I was dragging them around like a dog with a stone round its neck. I'd tried so hard to forget, you know. I'd torn out the diary pages. But even so, the memories kept coming back – the smell of chalk dust, and cut grass, and wood; the sleepy sound of the classroom clock; the feel of his hand on my leg, on my head; the way he'd whisper in my ear—

Good boy. Good boy.

By then, I was in a bad way. I lived with my parents for four more years, rarely leaving my bedroom. My mother brought my meals to my room; my father, improving literature, and occasional exhortations to *pull myself together.* The dreams of escape receded. University was no longer a possibility. I settled into a routine of TV, reading and apathy. I put on weight; at my heaviest, I weighed over three hundred pounds. I knew I'd lost *something,* and yet I was unaware of what it was.

Perhaps if I'd had my diary, I might have put the whole thing to rest. But I'd torn out the relevant pages – besides, that wasn't the worst of it. The worst of it I never wrote down. I never put it into words.

Words give shape to things, Mousey. Words bring the monsters into the light. But *this* monster stayed hidden, like something rotten and mouldy at the back of a cupboard, growing less recognizable as time passed, only perceptible in dreams. And so I forgot it, Mousey. I forgot the monster.

And then, in the summer of '88, Charlie Nutter came back into my life. Just turned up at my parents' house one day, looking tanned and nicely groomed and very different from the nervous Poodle he'd once been. Gone were the little mannerisms; gone were the patches of eczema that had once straggled up his skinny arms. Now he had just turned twenty-one, and had collected his English degree from Durham University. He'd had some years of therapy, both in and out of the Church, but now he was independent, glowing with a new confidence.

He didn't comment on how much I'd changed, but I could tell he was shaken. He said he'd been visiting Malbry; staying with a friend, with whom he planned to go on holiday to Italy. It took him all of five minutes to admit that this friend was Harry Clarke; five more to admit their relationship. Poodle never could keep his mouth shut; and besides, he was happy. He was past the age of consent. His friendship with Harry was legal now; and university was his escape from his parents, and from his former life.

Turns out that he and Harry had had quite a correspondence over the years. Poodle told me everything: how he had written to Harry from school; how Harry had told him to bide his time; how Harry had said it would only be four years before he could leave home for good; how Harry had saved his sanity.

'It took me a long time to realize,' he said, 'that God loves me just the way I am. God isn't responsible for prejudice and hatred. God made me gay, and He loves me.'

I'd never heard him talk so much. I listened, but inside me, I could feel a little red ball of anger. *God made me gay, and He loves me*. What rubbish. God made you gay for the same reason that He puts temptation in your path and then fakes surprise when you fall for it.

I made a sympathetic sound. 'I presume this is Harry's philosophy.'

He nodded. 'Harry helped me so much. He made me understand that I don't have to be the person my parents wanted me to be. I don't have to share their views, or feel guilty because I'm different. For the first time in my life, I'm free.'

Poodle babbled on happily, oblivious in every way. People in love are so boring; supremely unaware of the fact that they have become the dullest, most self-obsessed person on the planet. And I pretended to listen, and nodded in all the right places, as he explained his philosophy, which was mostly Harry's philosophy. But inside I was all rage, the ball of anger in my gut moving towards nuclear fission.

Free? What right did he have to be free? What right did he have to escape his guilt? Anybody listening might have found it hard to believe that he, not I, was the murderer. And yet, Harry Clarke had chosen to help *him*, to redeem *him*. It wasn't fair. He'd chosen *me* first. Why had he abandoned me?

The fleeting scent of chalk dust; cut grass; oiled wood. The sound of clattering footsteps. Music playing;

something light. The echo of distant voices against a polished parquet floor. The feel of his hand on my shoulder, pushing me down towards the desk. Then, the sound of his voice. *Good boy*; like something you might say to a dog.

That's the thing about memory, Mousey. Sometimes the smallest thing triggers it. And this time, ironically, Poodle was the trigger: Poodle, flushed with happiness, Poodle saved; redeemed by Love.

And then an idea came to me. I thought about it as Poodle went on. It was nicely simple; neat, with square-edged hospital corners. It would, at the same time, validate my suffering and mess up Poodle's disgusting little dream of happiness. It could be done, I realized. There was a way I could escape the pit into which I had fallen. Of course, I'd need a sacrifice – God hates those unbalanced accounts – but if what I had glimpsed was right, then it might mean my salvation, and more – my return from the wilderness.

2

October 14th, 2005

Just like Harry Clarke, I thought, as I saw the figure in blue at my door. It was not a rational thought; but nevertheless, it gripped me like an icy hand on the back of the neck. I considered just turning and running away. But to where? This was home. There was nowhere else. Unlike Eric, who likes his little trips to Paris, or Dr Devine, whose wife has made of him quite the globetrotter, I don't even have a passport any more. These fantasies belonged to a world long dead. And so I took a shaky breath and stepped forward into the porch-light, and saw, not a uniformed officer, but Winter, dressed in jeans and a blue hooded parka. There was a folder under his arm.

Relief made me weak, then angry. 'What the hell are you doing here?' I'd rediscovered my Bell Tower voice, designed to cut through concrete.

'I didn't mean to alarm you,' he said. 'I heard you had some trouble today.'

'*Vae!* The St Oswald's grapevine,' I said. 'Listen, won't you come inside? I, for one, am in need of a drink.'

'Thank you, sir.'

I unlocked the door. I was feeling better by then. Those boys in the park had rattled me, but I was over the shock. Arriving in the living room, I found the decanter of brandy and poured myself a decent glug. 'One for you?'

He nodded. 'Thanks.' He sat down and sipped his drink.

'Listen,' I said. 'I'm sorry.'

He looked surprised. 'Sorry for what?'

'We should have talked about Harry,' I said. 'I should have told you everything. But I suppose I thought I owed it to Harry to keep the details to myself, especially after what happened. But Harry's gone, and St Oswald's – well, St Oswald's badly needs a friend.'

Winter put down his brandy glass and handed me the folder. 'I'm guessing you've seen most of this,' he said. 'But it looks to me like St Oswald's has a funny way of treating its friends.'

I opened the folder. Inside, there were some dozen or so sheets of paper – reproductions of newspaper clippings from the time; drawings from the trial; pictures of Harry, looking confused, and of Nutter, lost and distraught. There were even pictures of me, looking unkempt and defiant.

OLD BOYS' CLUB, said the headline. *DID THIS MAN COVER FOR CLARKE?* Then there were pictures of Harrington, not a hair or a crease out of place. Then, almost an afterthought, right at the bottom, was Spikely.

Looking back at those pictures now, I see why the press were so quick to believe him. Something had happened to Spikely. Something dreadful and lasting. The grinning little boy had grown into a bloated, pale young man who might have been thirty, or thirty-five, instead of barely twenty-one. His hair, always fine, was almost gone; his face was like uncooked pastry. And his eyes were smoky;

wild; staring at some distant point on a lost horizon. What happened, on that island of time, half forgotten in the mists? What hidden rage and resentment could have transformed that bland little boy into an avenger?

David Spikely, the tattletale. No one remembered him clearly. A boy who'd stayed less than a year in the School; undistinguished in every way; an average student, with average grades and a less-than-average personality. No misdemeanours; no incidents; no detentions; no House Points. He *had* been close to Harry, though – in fact, he was the reason we had originally coined the acronym SLF – *Special Little Friend* – to describe the soulful, adoring way the boy lay in wait for Harry at Break or, more often, at lunchtime, bringing him a cup of tea when he was on duty; watering his plants and tidying his classroom.

It wasn't really surprising. Harry had many followers. Most schoolmasters, even the least prepossessing, have the occasional SLF, but Harry had had an army of them, trained to collect his books, deliver mail, pick up litter on the Upper Corridor and report on the outrages of the ever-critical Dr Devine. He never showed any favouritism, although he *had* his favourites. Spikely was not among them, however. In fact, I remembered Harry telling me, in that humorous way he had, how David Spikely had followed him all around St Oswald's like the Laughing Gnome in the song, grinning beatifically.

And now, here he was, seven years later, making accusations of a kind that no one wanted to believe, but few dared question *too* aggressively. Guilt by association can kill a Master's career as fast as in a court of law, and some – Eric Scoones, for example – had been quick to take precautions. The rest of the School went into shock: a shock that manifested itself at first through contempt and laughter.

We shouldn't have laughed. Young Spikely was totally in earnest. Harry was removed from School, pending investigation. We were all instructed, on pain of dismissal, to have no contact at all with him. A telephone helpline was set up by the police, encouraging pupils to speak up about their experiences at School, and St Oswald's was swamped by the press, demanding to know more details about a case that promised everything a tabloid reader could hope for.

The *Malbry Examiner*, which for historical and social reasons has always hated St Oswald's, made much of the accusations. It was Harry's and St Oswald's bad luck that Malbry was still reeling from a previous case, a drama enacted a few years before, in which a little local girl had died in tragic circumstances. Of course, the Emily White affair was barely connected with the School, but even a loose connection was enough for the *Examiner* to deploy its most poisonous language.

SCHOOL FOR SCANDAL! the headline read. *St OSWALD'S GRAMMAR SCHOOL'S SECRET HOMOSEXUAL CURRICULUM!*

Harry, besieged by journalists, battened down the hatches, but his home was vandalized, and as the case gathered momentum, he had to move to a hostel for his own protection. I fared rather better. In spite of my friendship with Harry; in spite of the fact that the Chaplain revealed that I had denied that Harry was gay; in spite of the fact that Nutter had been in *my* form, and that people (including the editor of the *Examiner*) found it hard to imagine how a member of St Oswald's staff could have worked alongside a predator and not had the slightest suspicion of what was really going on.

At best, I suppose, it made me naïve. At worst, it made me a suspect. And yet, beyond a few predictable poison-pen letters and graffiti on the wall by my house, I managed to escape virtually unscathed from the dreadful business – more so, perhaps, than I deserved.

Meanwhile, St Oswald's did what St Oswald's has done for five hundred years. It carried on with business – in forty-minute segments, with emphasis on clean shirts, House ties, Assemblies, Parents' Evenings, neat lawns and no running in corridors. We wrapped our everyday routine around us like a blanket, secure in the knowledge that nothing would change, that life would go on as always. Even the Harry Clarke affair would turn out to be no more than a storm in a teacup, we told ourselves, while outside our windows the gathering clouds were heavy with foreboding.

As the weeks and months went by, we became increasingly sure of ourselves. The case seemed to be at a standstill. No one had responded to the appeal by the police, or even phoned the helpline. We heard nothing at all about Spikely, or the exact nature of his claims. No one expected the case to go any further than a magistrate.

And then, after Christmas, we heard the news. Harry was going on trial. The *Malbry Examiner* went into throes of unbridled joy. The evidence gathered over six months, it seemed, pointed to something more serious than mere sexual misconduct. Along with the charges of assault, my friend had been charged with murder.

3

Michaelmas Term, 2005

Dear Mousey,

The first thing I did when Charlie left was to ask to speak to a therapist. My parents were surprised, but pleased (I'd refused therapy for over a year); and when I then asked to go to Church, their happiness was touching. I talked to the pastor who had come in to speak to the congregation, and then I joined a prayer group. Over the next few weeks or so, I became a regular. I found the courage to confess a few things (in fact, I quite enjoyed it). I talked about my feelings. I wrote down my dreams in a notebook. And most of all, I *remembered.*

Oh, just little things at first. But memories are like dominoes, laid out in rows, ready to fall. And once the process had started, I was remembering things that I'd almost forgotten I knew. My therapist got excited, and urged me to go deeper. Her name was Liz McRae, and she reminded me a bit of Miss McDonald. She was blonde, and pretty, and sweet, and very sympathetic. She told me I'd been damaged, that it wasn't my fault I'd turned out this way; that if

I could identify the source of the pain, then I could put it behind me.

The thing about pain, Mousey, is that we build *over* it. We bury it, we mourn it, we copy it in marble. And it becomes a monument, carved with weeping angels, inscribed with words in Latin, bearing so little resemblance to the thing we put into the ground that even the memory of it fades, to be replaced by the memories of polished stone; stained glass; the bitter scent of lilies.

It started in his form-room. I used to go there at lunchtimes. He used to sit at his own desk, marking, or listening to music. One day, we were alone. He came and stood right next to me. And then he put his hand on my leg, and left it there for a long time. I didn't know what to do. He was a teacher. I trusted him. And so I didn't do anything. I just sat there and waited. And because it felt weird, I didn't say anything, either. Instead I just sat there, pretending nothing was happening, and closed my eyes, and drifted, and listened to the music.

That was a mistake, of course. Now, we had a secret. And when it happened again, then again, I found it even harder to say anything. After all, he'd done it before. And *he* didn't seem to think it was weird, which made me think I might be to blame. And anyway, what harm had we done? And how could I even describe it?

And so I never said a word. Not even to you, Mousey. That's why I never wrote it down in my St Oswald's diary, because that would have given the monster a shape. That would have made it real to me. I think perhaps I was wondering if it meant I *looked* different; if somehow he could tell that I wasn't like other boys. I used to look at myself in the mirror, and try to see what he could see. But there was nothing. No special sign. No sign we had a secret. And when he pushed me on to the desk, with his hand on the back of my head, and whispered to me: *Good boy* – I did what I'd always done, and turned my mind to other things: to Ziggy and his left-handed guitar; to *Crow*, and *Nineteen Eighty-Four*; and the clay pits, and *Diamond Dogs*.

This is where those memories start to become fragmented. It's not that I don't *remember* – how could I forget that? The smell of him, the sound of him, there in the chalky darkness. The way I had to close my eyes so hard that when I opened them, all I could see for a moment or two was a brown, swirling nothingness.

Memory isn't a camera. It's an anthill, a thing of layers, built around a central core. And inside the core, there are sleeping things. Things that change, and sting, and fly. Things that come out of the walls at night, and crawl all over everything.

But now, at last, after seven years of misery and self-hatred, I was finally starting to see. Those things I did, when I was a boy – those terrible things – they weren't my fault. Poodle, the rabbits, Ratboy and all – they were all part of my trauma. I wasn't *possessed*. I wasn't *bad*. Those things were a Coping Mechanism, brought on by My Condition, and if I'd felt aggressive, confused – even weirdly exhilarated – who could really blame me? That was just part of what I'd been through. Symptoms of an inner disease.

I tried very hard to remember it now. I searched my soul. I prayed a lot. Miss McRae taught me how admitting weakness can also be strong, and said how proud she was of me. That was nice; it had been a long time since anyone had been proud of me. It made me show off a bit, perhaps, and by the time I saw where it was leading, I couldn't have stopped it if I'd tried. Not that I really wanted to. I was rather enjoying it all. My victimhood was a novelty; the sympathy made me feel special. The other boys from my year at St Oswald's were going to university; driving cars; getting girls. The other boys had had their names painted on to the Honours Boards. Where were *my* honours? Where was my name? Why was I the only one to be left behind?

It had been nearly seven years since the death of Lee Bagshot. People had mostly forgotten him, except for his mother, I suppose. The death of an estate boy is never as widely reported as the death of a little girl. We'd already seen that in Malbry with the death of Emily White – flowers and teddy bears on the streets, prayer groups, charities, letters to the local MP. The Emily White affair lasted months. Lee Bagshot was gone in a week or so. Of course, there'd been nothing to link his death to violence of any kind. It was a tragic accident, that people blamed on the Council for not putting up enough warning signs and barbed wire round the clay pits. But when I started to recall what had happened seven years ago, the case of Lee Bagshot suddenly seemed to acquire a new distinction. And then, at last, when the trial began—

People are very suspicious, you know; always so quick to believe the worst. I'd only revealed to Miss McRae that I'd been abused by a member of staff. *She* was the one who'd assumed who it was; she was the one who brought it all out. And of course, St Oswald's has always been a windmill for boys to tilt at. At her request, I told the police. Everything but the man's name. That I couldn't – *wouldn't* – say. That one I left to someone else. Someone more charismatic.

I never *really* believed we'd win. Perhaps that was the problem. But stories are like weeds; they grow. You can never stop them. And the story that was meant to blow Poodle out of the water became something more sinister. A boy had disappeared for a week in December of '81. Another boy had drowned in the pits. That death had been ruled accidental, but now, with these new allegations of corruption at St Oswald's, the Malbry authorities saw their chance to link one with the other. The *Malbry Examiner*, never a friend of what it sees as a privileged institution (and never mind those scholarship boys from dirt-poor backgrounds, whose fees were paid by the St Oswald's Trust), had always loved to publish the worst. Now its pages were awash with rumour and hysteria. The Nutter affair was brought out again, with a whole lot of new theories. And when my tale was made public – they started making connections.

Had Charlie Nutter been lured away during Christmas of '81? Had Harry Clarke corrupted him? Was Harry Clarke the member of staff who had traumatized me so badly that I could not even say his name?

Miss McRae was supportive throughout. She searched my personal history. She sought out my old schoolfriends. One of them was Poodle, who violently denied the suggestion that he had been abused as a boy. Yes, he and Harry had had a relationship. But it had never been sexual – at least, not until Poodle was twenty-one, and legal. Poodle's parents denied this, of course. Poodle had been brainwashed. And when I told them the story of what I'd seen that Christmas, through the window of Harry's house—

Mr Clarke was a *charismatic teacher*, said the *Malbry Examiner*. Like many sexual predators, he was outgoing and popular. Was he charismatic enough for even his victims to deny that he had abused them? Could this reluctance to speak out be some kind of Stockholm Syndrome? Or was there a more sinister truth lurking behind that old story? And, yet more enticingly, could the death of Lee Bagshot now be linked to a suspected paedophile?

All right, Mousey. It got out of hand. That was Poodle's fault, not mine. But Poodle was being difficult. For a start, he denied that he and Harry had had a relationship while Poodle was still at school. He admitted to having been troubled, but blamed it all on his parents. He also blamed *me*, Mousey – talked about the clay pits, the burnt-out car, even the rabbits. He told them he'd been afraid of me – that both he and Goldie had been afraid – and that they had gone along with the games in order to humour me.

It wasn't very plausible. I didn't look like the kind of boy who could make other people afraid of me. Goldie looked like a leader, with his Cambridge-boy physique. Even Poodle looked fitter and healthier than I did. But I looked like a victim; bloated, hairless and pitiful, as if what had happened seven years before were a cancer eating away at me. But Poodle wouldn't leave it alone. He was besotted with Harry Clarke. He phoned my home repeatedly, trying to make me confirm his tale. He wrote me crazy letters, threatening to expose me. And so I did the only thing I could. I dropped the bomb I was holding before Poodle could use it against me. That way, if he told the police about the death of Lee Bagshot, it would look like a made-up story, fabricated to shift the blame away from Harry on to me.

Recovered memory therapy is such a useful tool, Mousey. Miss McRae was a strong believer in its healing powers. Thanks to her, I remembered how I'd seen Lee Bagshot in the clay pits. I was even able to describe the boy's clothes on the day he disappeared. I remembered conversations; dragged out scraps of memory; hinted and hesitated, confided and confessed, until at last there was enough for the police to build a case.

It took a while. Miss McRae helped; and Mr Speight; and my parents. I feigned reluctance at first; then, allowed them to persuade me. I felt like the kid at a party, politely refusing the last slice of cake. I let them woo me.

Well, if you insist—

All that was just bait, of course. I know a bit about bait, you know. Of course, there was no actual proof that Harry had ever *known* Lee Bagshot. But Harry's house was half a mile from where Lee's body had been found, and, now that he was in the dock for acts of gross indecency, it seemed almost poetic that he should be a murderer, too.

The evidence was pretty thin. And I never *said* it was him. But I had seen Lee at the clay pits, and I told them – reluctantly, under oath – of how the boy had boasted to me that he knew of a bloke in the Village who would pay for sex with sweets, marijuana and alcohol. Lee had described Harry to me, as I described him to the court. And when Harry denied all knowledge of ever meeting Lee Bagshot, the people in the courtroom booed like at a pantomime.

Poodle tried to defend him, of course. But by then, no one believed him. The son of a politician; privileged and wealthy; and on top of that, a little queer – he just wasn't the kind of person juries find appealing. He never spoke above a whisper, and often had to be asked to repeat himself. He never made eye contact. His tics and twitches had returned, making him tremble and stammer. With the help of his parents, who described him as *a troubled young man;* the Chaplain of St Oswald's, in whom I had once confided, and to whom Harry had already confessed his version of the story; the Head of St Oswald's, who came across, as always, as a bully; and all the staff of St Oswald's who came out *en masse* as character witnesses for the accused, Poodle ended up doing more harm than good as far as Harry was concerned.

Oh, I remember them, Mousey. All lined up like senators in their academic gowns and with their Oxbridge accents. There was Straitley, more like a toothless lion than ever, saying over and over again how Harry just *couldn't* have done those things; then Mr Bishop, the Head of Year, with his rugby-school physique; then the Head, like a Juggernaut, addressing the crowd the way he spoke to his boys in Assembly.

I noticed Mr Scoones wasn't there, even though he'd been Harry's friend; nor was Dr Devine, whose room was so close to Harry's. But standing in front of a jury of ordinary folk from the estate, who had always mistrusted *the posh school,* those witnesses all came across as shifty, smirking and arrogant. You could tell that most of them weren't taking the business seriously. Straitley, with rumpled suit and his Latin that the jury didn't understand; trying to explain that you can't hide secrets in a school, that if there'd been something going on, he would have *known* it, somehow. The Chaplain, looking confused; Mr Fabricant, with his book on the Marquis de Sade, saying boys weren't to be trusted and looking like a vampire.

Then Mrs Bagshot came to plead for justice for her dead son, triggering a battle between the Shifty-but-Rich and the Honest-but-Poor, fought on the pages of tabloids all across the country. St Oswald's was portrayed nationwide as a hotbed of privilege and vice. Mrs Bagshot wasn't ideal, but her grief was genuine. And everyone loves an underdog. I played the part to perfection.

But Johnny Harrington was the star. I could understand why, of course. He was handsome; articulate; spoke of his deep faith in God; blamed himself for not having seen what was happening to his friends; remembered how Poodle and Ziggy had always seemed so secretive;

played down his own involvement with the rats and the rabbits, but said how he'd always suspected *something* sinister was afoot. He, too, had seen the signs. He, too, had suspected something amiss. He cited Mr Fabricant's book; Straitley's Latin profanities; quietly painted a picture in which *all* of St Oswald's was riddled with vice and corruption, an Old Boys' club that preyed on the young; a place in which no questions were asked, and where colleagues would cover for even the vilest of abuse. Then he told the jury how he had come to Mr Straitley for advice after the thing with Poodle and me, and how Mr Straitley had laughed at him.

And the jury swallowed everything. Johnny's sincerity; his remorse; the fact that his northern accent had not quite vanished (at least for the trial); his portrayal of himself as the boy who'd never fitted in. Everything was perfect. He never faltered, even under the most aggressive cross-examination, but always kept eye contact and spoke quietly, but firmly. Charlie Nutter and I came across as crazy; damaged; uncertain. But Johnny Harrington came across as sincere, as well as totally sane. Of *course* people believed him. Johnny believed the story himself. He couldn't have done a better job if I'd actually coached him.

After that, Harry didn't have much of a chance. He denied all knowledge of my abuse; denied having known Lee Bagshot; denied offering boys money for sex; denied sleeping with Charlie Nutter until the boy had turned twenty-one. But none of that swayed the jury, all of them comfortable northern folk who found it hard to believe that a deviant like Harry might have any kind of moral code. Most of them thought that buggery should be illegal anyway, and mistrusted Charlie Nutter, with his ridiculous name, and his twitch, and his wealth, and his father with his seat in the House of Commons and his look of pompous outrage.

And Harry would not accuse me. That, and not his words, was what hurt. His damn superiority. His refusal to engage when his lawyer tried to destroy me. He stood behind his screen, looking old, and all he said when questioned was:

'David was a special case. I should have seen he needed help. I'm sorry. I should have helped him.'

I knew what he meant, of course. But that was enough to condemn him. The rest of his words were forgotten, as the headlines did their worst.

I'M SORRY! screamed the tabloids. The rest printed watered-down versions. *PERVERT TEACHER BREAKS DOWN IN COURT. HIDING IN PLAIN SIGHT! HOMO-SEXUAL ENGLISH TEACHER MAY HAVE ABUSED HIS CHARGES FOR YEARS!* And the most damning headline of all, flanked with a picture of Harry: *DID THIS MAN KILL LEE BAGSHOT?*

That, and not my testimony, was what turned the tide that day – not that it needed much turning. Malbry still remembered the sorry death of Emily White, and although the cases weren't the same, there were enough parallels to give the press some ammunition.

Troubled Boy Speaks Out, they said. *Thousand-Pound-a-Term School Was a Hotbed of Vice,* they said. And, faced with a chance to get even for generations of social supremacy, the jury voted with their hearts, and Harry was sentenced to twenty years.

Sometimes you need a sacrifice in order to stamp out evil. The Bible is full of reminders of this. Abraham and Isaac; the Gadarene swine; the story of the scapegoat. In this case, it was Lee Bagshot, who went to his death so that others might live purer, better, happier lives. And although

Harry Clarke didn't kill him, as such, I now understood, after seven years, that he'd died in part *because* of Harry, which made Harry almost as guilty as if he'd done the deed himself.

Under the rule of reasonable doubt, they should have gone for an acquittal. But they didn't. Is that my fault? Call it the work of Providence.

4

October 14th, 2005

Some stories enter the public eye like splinters. The Moors Murders. The Yorkshire Ripper. Malbry's Emily White affair. And to see Harry Clarke in such company – yes, it hurt. It still does. Sixteen years later, it's still surprisingly hard for me to look at those old headlines, those photographs. So many people have had their say over the Harry Clarke affair. So many bits of graffiti scrubbed off lavatory walls; so many casual references in newspapers and magazines. There was even a book, you know, by a man called Jeffrey Stuarts – a hack journalist, specializing in character assassination – in which it was suggested that Harry's victims were more numerous than anyone suspected, and which attempted to link him – and, by association, St Oswald's – with a number of disappearances. No one protested openly, even though Harry was on a School trip to France at the time of at least one of these. None of Harry's ex- colleagues – including Eric, including myself – were brave enough to stand up for him. And why? Because an unstable young man had made a vague accusation, abetted by his therapist;

his church; his parents; a prominent MP – and supported by Johnny Harrington, the boy who kept on coming back.

Everything begins with *him*. From that first visit to the Headmaster's office; from that first complaint; from the church; from that first mention of the word *possession*, back in '81. You might still wonder why I blame Harrington over Spikely. Perhaps because Spikely *was* disturbed; everything about his testimony pointed to his delusional state. But Harrington was presentable; boyish; confident; even charming. He gave his testimony in much the same way as he had spoken to me that day when talking about his troubled friend; with an air of polite sincerity. And when that Sports Day photo emerged, with Harrington looking so neatly pressed, and Harry, sweaty and grinning, the papers had a field day, and Harrington (forever fourteen in the eyes of the public) became a perpetual poster-child; the final nail in poor Harry's coffin.

Without his confirmation of David Spikely's story, there would have been no reason to give Spikely any credence. It would have been Harry's word against – at best – the fractured and inconclusive account of a pupil who hadn't named him directly, who clearly had mental issues and who had spent less than a year at the School. Without Johnny Harrington's corroboration, there would have been no inquiry; no search; no link to the death of Lee Bagshot – a tenuous link at best, and based on nothing but circumstance. In short, the case would have been thrown out of court. Harry would never have been condemned.

In retrospect, we were *all* to blame. It was all so ridiculous. Harry's arrest; his suspension from School; then, ten months later, a trial that none of us expected to see. And even when the trial began, we were still complacent. In all St Oswald's history, no one had ever struck out as hard against the body of the School. No one expected Harry to lose. No one believed that a jury, faced with so little evidence, would reach a guilty verdict.

We were wrong. History has a habit of awarding the victories to small boys armed with slingshots. St Oswald's was the giant; powerful, untouchable. The boys were Spikely and Harrington – and the ghost of Lee Bagshot, of course. Gilded by Time and circumstance, the gawky little rat-faced boy with the outdated mullet, grinning at the camera as if he has all the time in the world, had become an icon of everything that was tragic and doomed. Belatedly, the clay pits were marked for urban renewal; flowers were left at the scene of the crime; money was sent to the family. The tragedy had become something else; the symbol of a class war. And the jury – all from Sunnybank Park, Pog Hill, Abbeydale and the estates, consisting of the unemployed; housewives; old-age pensioners – were ready to believe the worst; as easily swayed by Mrs Bagshot's tears as by Spikely's tale of suffering.

And so Harry was sent to serve his time at Her Majesty's pleasure. We corresponded for a while, but I soon ran out of things to say. Eric had left St Oswald's to work at King Henry's, our rival school; the Old Head had retired at last, and I had a department to run. Time just got away from me. I know how terrible that sounds; but St Oswald's is a heartless old frigate. If a man falls overboard, the ship cannot afford to wait. The sailor sinks or swims alone.

I tried to explain this to Winter, as I worked methodically through his blue file. It was getting late by then. The fire had died down to a glow. The bottle of brandy I'd opened looked dangerously close to the dregs. Well, I'd needed *something* to give myself the courage to speak. Winter was still on his first glass, looking polite and attentive. Gloria, with the Spanish eyes, had raised an excellent listener.

The last item in the folder was printed on pink paper. It took me a moment to recognize it – the font was slightly different, the paper more expensive, but the text was almost identical to that little pamphlet: *HOMOSEXUAL, HELLBOUND* – printed and distributed by the Church of the Omega Rose.

'Where did you get this?' I asked him.

He indicated the logo on the back of the pamphlet. A stylized S, made to look like two mirrored figures, linking hands, with this year's date printed underneath. I knew that logo. I'd seen it before, on collecting tins and posters.

'Survivors.' The organization to which Dr Blakely, aka Thing One, aka the Abuse Guru, has links. Until now I'd only thought of him as another cut-out soldier, to go with Johnny Harrington's growing fortress of paperwork. But to see that little pamphlet again, published by Survivors—

'What does it mean?' I asked Winter.

'I've been looking into Survivors,' he said. 'It was formed in '88, soon after Harry Clarke's arrest. Initially a phone helpline, staffed by a handful of volunteers. It was called—'

'Survivors Speak Out.' I remembered it vaguely now: its public face had been Liz McRae, David Spikely's therapist. During the trial, she had been called as an expert witness. A young thing, I remembered now; surely no older than twenty-five, with a sensible honey-brown bob and a crowd-pleasing earnestness. It was she who had instigated the initial investigation, alerting the social services following a series of conversations with her charge, during which he had mentioned a member of St Oswald's staff, and certain unsavoury events. The fact that Spikely had never actually *named* Harry as his abuser was seized upon by Harry's counsel, but Miss McRae had kept her calm, pointing out that survivors of traumatic events were often unable to speak out, or even to articulate apparently trivial details relating to the experience.

'Survivors.' That was where I'd first heard the word spoken in that context. And here, once again, was a link to the Church of the Omega Rose, the organization that had victimized Nutter, brainwashed Spikely and encouraged Johnny Harrington to speak out against Harry. Now I looked at it again, I realized why the style of that nasty little pamphlet now seemed so oddly familiar: I'd heard it just the other day, in the Headmaster's Assembly—

'Harrington wrote it? *Harrington?*'

Winter nodded. 'It looks that way. And certainly, he was always around. After the trial, the helpline expanded, shortened its name to Survivors. Liz McRae stayed active for several more years as a counsellor, specializing in recovered memory. In 1993 she was awarded an MBE for her charity work. She married in 1991, and is no longer an active part of the group. She has no children, in spite of having had several courses of fertility treatment, and now runs a support group for childless couples in Harrogate. Friends Reunited confirms all this. Her name is Elizabeth Harrington.'

5

Michaelmas Term, 2005

Dear Mousey,

After the trial was over I spent some more time in therapy, coming to terms with my issues and going over conquered ground. It was fun; I got to talk as if I really mattered. I wasn't a failure any more. I was a brave survivor, who had dared speak out in court against his ex-abuser. For a while, it was almost exhilarating. But it didn't last for long. The feeling of triumph faded. I found myself back where I'd started; the little lame boy on the mountainside, listening for echoes.

Nowadays I rarely feel, and just as rarely dream. Perhaps it's because I'm older. Perhaps everyone has a limited capacity for strong feelings, which I exhausted in childhood. Now there's nothing left but that relentless internal counter, that says: *Thirty-two more years to go. Less, if you get cancer*. Cancer's what killed Harry Clarke. That, and what happened with Poodle.

For a while, I drifted. I suppose I was missing the limelight. I did a couple of interviews, sold my story to the *Mail*, and then looked around for something else. By then I had passed the point at which killing a dog or a rabbit would help. The thrill of pushing Poodle that time had receded into the past. Even the much greater thrill of pushing Goldie had faded.

Survivors saved my sanity. With the help of Miss McRae, the little helpline grew and grew. Survivors, it seemed, wanted to talk, and there were lots of them around. Miss McRae kept on with my therapy, and from time to time, I would come to talk at one of her meetings. Goldie sometimes came along. He'd stayed in touch with Miss McRae throughout the trial and afterwards, and she was the one who got him involved, first as a part of his therapy, then as a counsellor in his own right.

By then, Johnny was already training to be a teacher. His connection with the Church meant that he was in touch with motivational speakers from all around the world. And he was good; much better than I was. People liked and trusted him. Gradually, his influence took hold. What had been a small weekly discussion group evolved into a national resource. We had a free helpline, staffed by volunteers; we became a registered charity. Johnny wrote a series of motivational pamphlets (he'd already written some for the Church), and even published a little book called *The Survivor's Gospel*. All of this served his career, of course. Even as a teacher trainee, he was fast-tracked for success. Now, as a Head, he organizes visits to schools to talk to staff and pupils on how to spot potential abuse, what counts as abuse in the first place, and recently, online grooming.

In 1991, he got married – to Miss McRae, of all people. That was disappointing; I have to admit it rankled a bit. Plus, I think she and Johnny may have discussed me behind my back. Perhaps she told him some of the things that *I* had told her in confidence. Rather unethical, I would have thought – not that it matters to *their* kind. They were always a different breed, even when they tried to be friends. And now they'd got what they needed from me, it was back to the scrap heap for Spikely, and up, up the ladder for Harrington.

Do I sound bitter, Mousey? I don't mean to sound bitter. Objectively, I'm a success. I have done important things. To avoid unwelcome attention, I've changed my name. I delegate. I moved back to Malbry in '99, the year my mother remarried. Perhaps I needed to go back home. But it's a far cry from the home I knew, that little house in the Village. Instead, I have a very nice house near the top end of Millionaires' Row. I am respected; even feared. I have regained my healthy physique. Even my hair has grown back now. Why then do I still feel so unfulfilled, so tragically dead inside?

I thought that writing a diary again, after so many years, might help with that. And it seems very natural, Mousey, to write my diary to you. Not that I think you're still around, or anything like that, of course. But things have come full circle again. Once more the dice are rolling. And this time, it seems as if Fate may have given me the chance to settle another old score . . .

6

October 28th, 2005

A disciplinary hearing is never a very pleasant affair. This one featured Kitty Teague, as my Head of Department; Thing One and Thing Two; Dr Devine; and, of course, the New Head in all his pomp and sanctimony.

I shan't bore you with what was said. Suffice it to say that, as of then, I am on report. For the next few weeks or so, someone will shadow my classes, watching out for any irregularities. This is for my protection, says Harrington, with a little smile. The parents of Chanelle Goodman have made a serious complaint. In order to address it (and hopefully, dismiss the charge), we henceforth need to know exactly what goes on in room 59; what kind of comments, if any, are made, and how to address any problems, real or perceived, on either side.

In short, I have a Special Little Friend to accompany me wherever I go. *Two* Special Little Friends, in fact: Ms Buckfast and Dr Blakely now take it in turns to shadow me, much as Harry's Laughing Gnome shadowed the narrator of that jaunty little song. Once more, I suspect that Harrington is trying to put pressure on me to drink the hemlock. He'll have to do better than that if he means to dislodge this old barnacle from the deck. Still, it's going to be hard to keep a sunny disposition.

Ten days have passed since the hearing. Meanwhile, Kitty Teague is being disappointingly correct. She has made no comment so far on the Allen-Jones/Gunderson affair, but goes over the departmental paperwork every day with Thing One (or Thing Two, whichever of them happens to be on duty at the time). So far, however, I have given them no further cause for complaint. My teaching of *Aeneid* IX proceeds as efficiently as usual. My lessons are marvels of blandness. My Brodie Boys have noticed this, but their efforts to liven up the show have been met with a stony reception.

La Buckfast watches developments with a look of distant irony, like a Vestal Virgin at a Bacchanalia, while Dr Blakely adopts the look of a rabbit in the headlamps, as if afraid that I will involve him in any form of *teaching*; a prospect that clearly fills him with dread. Next door, in Dr Devine's room, Markowicz is present, if not entirely functional. The department is eerily silent, but for the occasional cry of the Foghorn from the Middle Corridor. Even the mice have gone to ground. Of course I know it cannot last. This is the calm before the storm.

Today it was Ms Buckfast's turn to perform the honours. I introduced her to my form as a *Special Visitor*; which works all right with the younger boys, but cuts no ice with the likes of Sutcliff, Allen-Jones and McNair.

'Are you taking trainees, sir?' asked McNair at lunchtime. 'It's just that we couldn't help noticing the elephant at the back of the room.'

I raised a quelling eyebrow. 'Ms Buckfast has expressed a desire to improve her Latin,' I said. 'And, though not *petite*, by any means, Ms Buckfast is hardly an elephant.'

Allen-Jones, still on report himself, gave me a long and measuring look.

'How's Rupert Gunderson?'

Allen-Jones shrugged. 'I'm keeping away.'

'Probably for the best,' I said. 'But if he moves in, please tell me.'

Lunch was a fairly quiet affair. A sandwich in my room, while the boys listened to music on a small transistor radio, brought in covertly by Allen-Jones and concealed inside one of the school desks on the back row of the form-room. Devine came in twice to complain; once about the music, the second time because of the number of boys eating in the form-room, against School regulations and, more specifically, creating a risk of attracting vermin.

"*Raus, Maus*,' said Allen-Jones, as Dr Devine made his exit.

Devine turned round sharply. Allen-Jones looked innocent – at least as innocent as a boy can look with half a sandwich in his mouth. Devine left, with a face like a sucked lemon.

'Just another day in *Mauschwitz*,' said Tayler. My Brodie Boys all burst out laughing. Behind the glass door, Devine paused for a moment, then walked on, with the air of a man deploying almost unbearable self-control.

The afternoon was wearisome, with Ms Buckfast in residence. On several occasions I had to bite my tongue to avoid a pithy Latin phrase – I now suspect La Buckfast knows enough Latin to disapprove. As a result, I'm afraid the lessons may not have been quite as entertaining as they might have been. Silent reading, then a spelling test, and then some silent translation. La Buckfast seemed unmoved, however – I was rather hoping that she would get bored and leave early, but no. Ms Buckfast has staying power.

Throughout the whole afternoon she watched and listened attentively, occasionally taking notes, or walking about the form-room, checking the boys' grammar. I have to say she was thorough. And she didn't yawn once. I'm starting to think she may be a worthy adversary, after all.

At the end of the day she came to my desk, smiled at me and said: 'Thank you, Roy. That was most enjoyable.'

Given that we had spent most of the afternoon in silence, I rather doubted that, but there was a look in her eye that suggested she was far from dissatisfied.

She lingered at the window, looking out into the Quad. Then she looked at me curiously.

'You don't remember, do you, Roy?'

I gave her a look. 'Is there something special that I *ought* to remember?'

She smiled. 'Well no, of course, there's no reason you should. But I was once a Mulberry girl. We even spoke a couple of times. I got the impression – even then – that you didn't approve of girls in the School.'

'A Mulberry girl?' I tried to recall why I would have spoken to her. Then it came back to me: probably because of the colour of her hair. Of course, she'd been rather more slender then, with the leggy, self-confident strut that seems to be the main attribute of the Mulberry girl abroad.

'You played the lead role in *Antigone*,' I said.

La Buckfast smiled. 'That's right,' she said.

'I recall I lost several boys to that particular production. Still, it happened every time we allowed our boys to tread the boards. Some of them never recovered. But I'm sure I would have remembered your name, if not your face.'

'I married,' she said. 'It didn't last long.'

'Oh,' I said. 'And your maiden name—?'

'Becky Price,' she told me.

Becky Price. I see it now. La Buckfast has thickened a little, but something should have alerted me.

'Did you know Harrington back then?'

'Yes. We dated for a while.' Once more, that Mona Lisa smile. 'You've been wondering, haven't you?' said La Buckfast. 'Wondering if there's something between us. There isn't, you know. John's far too clever to jeopardize his reputation.' She sat on the desk and crossed her legs. I heard the hiss of nylons. 'You know, I respect you enormously.'

'I find that sentence often precedes something less than palatable.'

She laughed. It even sounded sincere, until you looked at those eyes.

'Oh, Roy. You're such a character. But you must see you'll never win. Better to step out gracefully than to see your career overshadowed by the kind of thing that's bound to come out if you stay on at St Oswald's.'

'You mean, you think I should retire?'

'Yes, and as soon as possible. Ill-health should give you sufficient grounds, or maybe a family crisis.'

'You haven't done your research,' I said. 'St Oswald's is my family.'

She shrugged. 'We'd give you full support. Full pay until the end of the year. That, on top of your pension, should leave you more than comfortable.'

I started to feel angry at that. 'You think this is about money?' I said.

'No, of course not,' said Ms Buckfast. 'It's always been about the School. You see, Roy, I *have* done my research.

And I know that change is your enemy. But St Oswald's *is* changing. From being a second-rate grammar school, riddled with outdated traditions, we're going to make it into the finest independent school in the north. We'll have the best facilities; the best, most highly qualified staff. Boys and girls, working alongside each other in the best possible environment. But for that, we need to change certain things. We need to move on. We need our *people* to move on.'

'And you think I can't?'

'I know you *won't*.' She shook her head. 'Look, Roy. This isn't personal. I rather *like* your little eccentricities. But it's time to go. You know it is. You're no match for us, and I'd rather see you retire gracefully than leave under a cloud.'

'I don't mean to leave at all,' I said. 'I mean to die at my post, and be mortared into the brickwork, along with the other gargoyles.'

She sighed. 'That isn't an option, Roy. Health & Safety would never allow it.'

She has a sense of humour, I thought. What a pity her eyes are so cold.

'We rather thought we might not need to have this talk,' said La Buckfast. 'But since you're being so stubborn—'

'Who's this *we*?' I interrupted. 'Have you and Johnny Harrington merged as one, like Hermaphroditus and Salmacis? Or is it the pronoun of the New Order? Let me tell you, Ms Buckfast, we can have as many of these little talks as you like. You can sit in on as many of my lessons as you like, and observe as many dictations and silent prose translations as you can stomach, but you will not force me to retire; nor will you convince me that principle should ever give in to progress.'

That smile again. It occurred to me once more how much she reminds me of the intrepid Miss Dare.

'Principle?' she repeated. 'Roy, this is *all about principles*. Listen, we've discussed this. We think that you may be getting too close to a group of boys in your form. Especially young Allen-Jones. We think he's a toxic influence.'

I made the Old Head's favourite sound. 'There are *several* of those around,' I said. 'But Allen-Jones isn't one of them. I mean, what is he supposed to have done?'

That smile again. 'Oh, Roy,' she said. 'You're so protective of your boys. I do respect that, really I do. But after the Rupert Gunderson thing—'

I said, in a few choice Latin words, what I thought of Gunderson.

The smile did not waver. La Buckfast said: 'Yes, well. The fact of the matter is, Allen-Jones may be facing expulsion.'

I sprang to my feet. My lower back creaked alarmingly.

'No,' I said. 'That isn't fair.'

It occurred to me that my choice of words made me sound more like a schoolboy than an Old Centurion of St Oswald's, but the events of the past few weeks have made me feel like a schoolboy in my own department. It isn't a pleasant feeling, and for once I can't blame Dr Devine.

'It isn't about fairness,' she said. 'It's about avoiding disruption. Your boy Allen-Jones doesn't fit in here. He's a disruptive influence. Just look at Benedicta Wild. We're trying to rebuild St Oswald's, Roy, and that means getting rid of those things that stand in the way of progress. It may have been all right once for St Oswald's to be eccentric, old-fashioned and full of character. But now, it needs to run properly, and it won't if the machinery is full of old parts that just don't fit.'

'Old *farts*, you mean.'

'I wouldn't have put it that way myself.'

'But that's what you mean,' I told her. 'That's why you've been shadowing me, studying my methods. I'm an old part that doesn't fit. And I'm a bad influence on the boys.'

If I'd thought to disarm her with my candour, I was wrong. She simply smiled again and said: 'Oh, Roy. You're so funny. And I've genuinely enjoyed our little classroom sessions. But it's time to bring this to an end before it gets ugly – for you, and for your pupils. Don't you agree?'

I took a deep breath. 'Are you asking me to leave?'

'Not to leave, Roy, but to *retire*,' said La Buckfast gently. 'You've given such loyal service. But now you're a thorn in the Headmaster's side – no, don't deny it. You know it's true. Everything he's tried to do, you've tried to undermine it. The Mulberry girls; Benedicta Wild; that silly garden gnome; plus banging on to all and sundry about Harry Clarke – and then, of course, there's the Honours Boards—'

I looked at her. 'You know about that?'

'Of course,' said La Buckfast. 'We've known all along. Do you think anyone's on your side? Do you believe *any* secret can be kept for long in a place like St Oswald's?'

It must have been Winter, I realized. Only he knew about the Honours Boards. Winter, whose intervention had seemed so wonderfully well timed; whose knowledge of the internet had seemed so providential. Could this have been a set-up? A trap? Was I their target from the first?

I felt the old, familiar stab of the invisible finger, and sat down heavily on my chair. What a fool I'd been, I thought. What else did La Buckfast know? What had she told Johnny Harrington?

La Buckfast patted my shoulder. 'I think you've been over-doing it, Roy,' she said. 'You're looking tired and not very well. Why don't I get you a coffee from the Headmaster's office?'

I shook my head. 'The hemlock bowl.'

'Nothing so dramatic, Roy. Retirement. By the end of this term. You could claim ill-health, perhaps; no mention of anything untoward; no scandal, no unpleasantness. You'll have a nice pension, a holiday, even a leaving party. And maybe Allen-Jones and those other disciples of yours will get another chance to settle down properly at St Oswald's, instead of following you over the cliff. Are you sure you won't have a coffee? It's good. It's the Headmaster's personal blend.'

I shook my head. 'I don't think I like the Headmaster's blend. Dishonesty with cowardice always turns the stomach.'

She gave me a look of reproach. 'Oh, Roy. *All men make mistakes, but a good man yields when he knows his course is wrong, and repairs the evil. The only crime is pride.*'

I raised an eyebrow. '*Antigone*?'

'I was always good at remembering lines.'

I walked home through the park again. Bonfire Night is approaching fast. Stacks of wooden pallets, boxes of papers, old clothes and loosely bundled firewood are already piling up in the allocated spot. Soon, there will be children, making effigies of teachers, dancing around the pyre and singing old songs and nursery rhymes, and playing games that the likes of Devine and Bob Strange consider offensive and obsolete – and yet, how these things endure. Bonfires lit against the dark; the yearly sacrifice to the gods.

There were three boys by the bonfire. Sunnybankers, by their clothes. I remembered those boys from the other night, smoking by the swing-set. How those boys had looked at me. How easily and confidently they had called me *pervert*. How easily these things slip away – regard, respect, authority – in the face of that talismanic word.

These were not the same boys. I could see their faces now; rosy-cheeked and bright-eyed. One of them raised a hand and waved as he saw me hurry past. This time, however, I did not respond.

7

October 28th, 2005

Arriving home, I poured a drink and started to make a shepherd's pie. I often eat when I am upset, and Ms Buckfast's words had upset me. Not least because of Winter, in whom, I now realize, I have placed an unreasonable amount of trust.

Why should he have wanted to help? Why had I been so sure of him? Because he'd once reminded me of one of my pupils from long ago? Looking back at my actions, I see that I should have known he was hiding something. His secretive manner, his awkwardness; his inability to meet my eye. All signs of the man's guilt – signs that I had failed to see. Now La Buckfast and Harrington have me over a barrel; their ultimatum is very clear. *Leave, or face the consequences*. Consequences which will affect both me and, more importantly, my boys. What a fool I've been, I thought. What a sentimental fool.

I turned on the radio, found the news. The broadcaster was talking about the death of Ronnie Barker. Another light blown out, I thought. Another dead Centurion. A bottle of stout stood close to hand, from which I added a generous splash to the mincemeat and onions in the pan. The rest served to sustain the cook. I opened another bottle. I was about to dispose of the evidence when the phone rang. It was Kitty Teague.

I should have known. La Buckfast must have suggested that she give me a call – I've always had rather a soft spot for Kitty, and I suppose she knew it. Anyway, I could tell from her voice that I was in for a lecture; I've known Kitty for long enough to know when she wants to placate me. There's a particular cadence to her voice on such occasions, I imagine not unlike that of a snake-charmer, or a veterinarian as he prepares to administer the fatal dose to a sick dog. It works quite well with the boys, too; certainly I rarely hear the sound of raised voices from Kitty's room.

'Roy. It's Kitty. Are you all right? I thought I'd just check how you were doing.'

'That's very thoughtful of you,' I said. 'But I've had enough of that kind of thing from Harrington and his minions. Do you know La Buckfast sat through *every one* of my classes today? And all that because Our Gracious Leader's afraid of upsetting the customers.'

Kitty made a soothing sound. 'I know. But there's been a complaint, Roy. We can't just ignore a complaint.'

'Why not? It only encourages them.'

She laughed, but without much warmth. 'Listen, Roy. I know it must be hard to see a boy you once taught sitting in the big chair. But really, you ought to give John a chance.'

John? She calls him John now?

'You don't understand,' I told her.

'Oh but I do,' she said earnestly. 'I know you've found it hard to adjust.' That placating voice again. I hadn't realized how often she uses it to soothe and disarm, just as the knife is about to fall. 'That's really why I'm phoning,

Roy. Perhaps you should seriously think about taking your retirement. Obviously, with no loss of pay, or any implication that you've done anything improper.'

'Et tu, Kitty?' I said.

'Roy, it isn't like that.'

I laughed. 'Oh, isn't it?' I said. 'Remember, I've been here before. I know when someone's gunning for me. The Old Head, at least, was loyal. This one just sees St Oswald's as a stepping-stone to something better. Strip out the Honours Boards, sweep out the chaff, sell off the old playing fields, introduce some newfangled schemes to raise the profile of the School, then move on to something else. Of course, by then it will be too late to undo all the damage. Still, what's a career at St Oswald's worth, next to a shiny new workstation?'

Now Kitty sounded upset. 'Roy, I'm on your side,' she said. 'It's just that I have a job to do.'

'Then stop wasting time over me,' I said. 'I'm really not worth the investment.'

I know – I was rather abrupt with her. I don't suppose it's Kitty's fault. But being the Head of Department has changed certain things between us. She is now officially my superior in the School – Kitty Teague, whom I first met when she was still a teacher trainee. It rankles – I would be a fool not to admit it to myself – and yet, what really hurts is the fact that she believes so sincerely that Harrington is doing what's best – for me, and for St Oswald's.

I was about to go back to my shepherd's pie, when there came a knock at the door. It was Dr Devine, looking grim. I ushered him into the parlour, but he declined to take off his coat.

'No, I'm not going to stay,' he said. 'It's just to see how you're doing, and—' His eyes went to the mantelpiece, where Harry's gnome was standing. 'I see you found a home for your gnome,' he said, in a chilly kind of voice.

I wondered if he'd made a joke, and if so, whether he was all right, but I decided not to ask. I wouldn't say Devine is my *friend* – but I have known him a long time, and he has one virtue: integrity. I don't always share his beliefs, but they *are* sincere and deeply held, if sometimes a little unfortunate. And he is loyal, in his way. I knew he wouldn't betray me.

'I'm sorry about what happened,' he said. 'Funny kind of business. The Union's behind you all the way.' He shuffled his feet for a moment. 'Fact is, it's irregular,' he went on. 'This Gunderson thing shouldn't have gone to the Head at all. It was, if anything, a departmental matter.'

His eye fell on a thick stack of Honours Boards propped up against the near wall, covered in a dust-sheet but nevertheless unmistakable. Winter had taken some of them down into the cellar, but a hundred and fifty Honours Boards take up even more space than I'd thought. Besides, the cellar is rather damp, and the Honours Boards deserve better.

'Taking up art?' said Devine.

'Burglary,' I told him. 'A hundred and fifty Honours Boards that Harrington was planning to sell – to furnish theme pubs and the like.'

That shocked him, as I knew it would.

'Don't believe it? Report me,' I said.

Devine gave me a quelling look. 'You really *are* trying for martyrdom, aren't you, Straitley?' he said in his most superior voice. 'I'm really just here to tell you that the Union will back you if it comes to any kind of a dispute. It's clear to me that the Gunderson boy set this thing up with his girlfriend to try and settle a score with you. The Old Head wouldn't have given a story like this the time of day.'

I shrugged. 'Long live the King,' I said. 'He's had me in his sights from the start. I suppose I ought to be grateful. I get to choose my final farewell. The hemlock bowl, or the razor blade. Socrates, or Seneca.'

Devine gave an irritated kind of sigh. 'Always so dramatic,' he said. 'I don't know why I bother. Look, Straitley,' he went on. 'I've heard a rumour that Harrington's been in touch with Survivors.'

'Really?' I said, listlessly.

'Of course, he's one of the founders, and Blakely's one of its shining lights. But he thinks that after what happened last year, it might be a good idea to offer some of the boys trauma counselling. And now, with this ridiculous Mulberry girl thing, he thinks there might be what he calls a *toxic learning environment*—'

'I suppose he means the mice,' I said.

'He does *not* mean the mice,' snapped Devine. 'He means the School. Our department. Blakely's been delving into our files; the Harry Clarke affair; Fabricant's book on the Marquis de Sade; even that ridiculous thing with you illustrating the First Declension with *merda* instead of *mensa*.'

I was impressed. 'You knew about that?'

'Of course I did. Everyone did. The thing is, it was a harmless joke. But now if they're going to scrutinize every joke, every chance remark for signs of *subliminal messages*—' He looked at the gnome on the mantelpiece. 'It's bad enough Markowicz badgering me every time he's been on a course. It's bad enough having to waste my time obsessing about mouse traps, and name tags, and writing out departmental policy documents on things that any half-decent Master would already *know* how to deal with—'

He paused, and I could see he looked tense. The nose, always an indicator of high emotion, twitched alarmingly.

'But Sourgrape – I mean, Dr Devine – I thought you *worshipped* Markowicz. I thought that angel voices sang, and bluebirds flew wherever he went. I thought he was exactly what the department needed; a new broom, a breath of fresh air.'

Devine made a percussive noise at the back of his throat. '*Hck!* That may have been – *premature.*' He glanced at the garden gnome again, then said, with irritation: 'I have to say, Straitley, I would have thought you could at least ask me to sit down. I've been on my feet *all day*—'

'I thought you didn't want to stay,' I began, as he handed me his coat.

'And a cup of tea would be nice. Earl Grey, if you have it.'

In all my years, I'd never seen Devine looking so jumpy. I gestured him to a place by the fire and poured him a glass of brandy. He took the glass without comment, and sniffed.

'I've been approached,' he said at last. 'Regarding my early retirement.'

Ah. The point emerges. '*Tempus fugit, non autem memoria,*' I said, lighting a Gauloise.

'*Tempus* be damned,' said Devine. 'I'm only sixty. I'm in my prime!' He took a rather fraught sip of his brandy. 'They've spoken to Eric Scoones as well. Apparently, the department needs to be downsized. *Downsized!* With Markowicz absent half the time, and that Malone woman having hysterics everywhere—' He drank some more brandy. 'He's got to go.'

'Who? Markowicz?'

'No, Straitley. The *Head*.'

I looked at the man with renewed respect. I had no idea old Devine was such a revolutionary. And for the first time in thirty-four years, I found myself in total agreement with him.

I said: 'The thought *had* crossed my mind. But the man's untouchable.'

Devine looked morose. 'I know. He's perfect. Even my wife thinks so.' He had the grace to look abashed. 'Invited us over for drinks one day. She hasn't stopped talking about it since.'

'I see.' I tried not to smile. Mrs Devine is a lady of firm and frank opinions, one of which is a long-held desire to see Devine take early retirement, and accompany her on a world cruise before they're too old to enjoy it. From what I know of Devine, a world cruise is more or less the definition of *L'enfer, c'est les autres*. He sees retirement looming with all the unbridled joy of the captain of the *Titanic* first catching sight of the iceberg.

'In any case, Roy,' he said, downing the last of the brandy, 'it goes without saying I'm on your side. What can I do?'

I have to say, I didn't know. But the thought that Devine could take my side – *Devine*, of all people—

'It's too late,' I told him. 'I've tried. And anyway, my Brodie Boys—' I told him about Allen-Jones, and La Buckfast's ultimatum.

Devine's nose went a telltale pink. 'So you're giving up?' he said.

'I can't see an alternative. If I don't, they'll expel Allen-Jones, and maybe the other boys as well.'

Dr Devine gave a sniff. 'So much for your anti-establishment stance. You talk about rebellion, but the moment it comes to a fight, you fold. Typical Classics response.'

He stood up, rather shakily, and took his coat from the peg by the door.

'Thank you for the brandy,' he said. 'But I prefer the kind of courage that *doesn't* come from a bottle.'

He left, with something approaching a flounce. At a different time, I might have found some comedy in the situation. Devine, taking my side against the higher management. The Suit lying down with the Tweed Jacket. *O tempora! O mores!*

I don't suppose I shall sleep tonight. Harry's box has been calling me. I've already spent an hour or two sorting out his photographs, the newspaper clippings he'd kept, the old copies of the School Magazine – including a review of *Antigone*, showing Ms Buckfast as a young girl, leggy in sandals and a sheet, smiling at the camera—

I think I'd been expecting some kind of epiphany. A fifth-act *dénouement* that would simultaneously unravel the mystery, expose the villain, reveal the plot and vindicate the hero, all in one neat manoeuvre. Instead, there's nothing but fragments; memories of times gone by; snapshots; clippings; notebooks; scraps; the litter of a human life. Oh, Harry. I'd always assumed that you left me the box for a *purpose*. I'd expected the contents to lead me to some kind of revelation. But now, picking through those forgotten things – a button; a ring; a notebook filled with class notes from another school – I realize that you left them to me, not because they were important, but because you didn't have anyone else.

I wonder, when my time comes, to whom will I leave *my* possessions? The clock I had from my parents' house that sits upon my mantelpiece; my modest library of books; my wireless; my photographs? Will someone take them in, or will my house be cleared by a dealer, the contents sold off at a series of flea markets and jumble sales, or worse: to be dumped in some desolate spot like the old clay pits of yesteryear, the photographs washed white in the rain, the books gnawed by rats, my School gown falling into rags by the dark and lonely water.

I know. I'm getting maudlin. But sometimes, the futility of everything falls in on me. What have I really achieved in life? Who would really remember me if I died tomorrow? I have no family, no friends. Only my pupils and colleagues. Outside of St Oswald's, I am nothing but an old house awaiting clearance. Whether I fight back or not, tomorrow, or next week, or next month, Harrington will make his move to sweep me from the chessboard. I cannot stand against him for long. He has all the artillery. He has youth on his side; youth and influence and guile. Who am I? Just an old man, so far behind the times that even a cleaner knows more about the rules of this strange and scornful new world.

Another glass of claret, I think. And maybe a slice of fruit cake, with a piece of Wensleydale. My doctor wouldn't like it, but if I'm going to stay up all night, I'll need the extra energy. From the mantelpiece, Harry's gnome watches me with a knowing eye. Beside him, the Bowie record in its paper envelope. I'm not really a fan, of course. But tonight, that cheery little tune seems to be the only link to a fast-disappearing reality. I put it on the turntable, heard the hiss and scratch of years. Then the helium voices, suspended in music like insects in tar. It's a ridiculous little tune. And yet, somehow, it comforts me. When I play it, Harry Clarke seems somehow less forgotten, less dead. I close my eyes for a moment, not feeling anywhere near to sleep. And the next thing I know, it's morning, and I'm sitting stiffly in my chair beside the record player, with a dead fire in the grate and the dead sound of the needle jumping on the turntable – *tick, tick, tick* – like a clock counting down the seconds . . .

Part Seven

Alea iacta est.
(Caesar)

1

November 1st, 2005

Headmaster, and Chairman of the Governors,
It is with the greatest regret that I find myself obliged to hand in my notice as Classics Master of St Oswald's. Ill-health—

No. Not ill-health. Doctor's orders. Not my old GP, of course, but a far more dangerous quack. Dr Harrington, MBE, whose toxic form of medicine might once have suited a Plague Doctor mask.

On the advice of the doctor, I have come to believe that it is no longer possible for me to discharge my duties adequately. As a result—

That sounds very stiff. On the other hand, I *feel* very stiff; compressed into a jacket of words, when I want to run and shout.

As a result—

As a result, I took a small nip of brandy to warm my chilled bones this morning, which made the Bursar look at me in an odd way in the Common Room. I wondered why he didn't make some kind of hilarious comment – the Bursar loves his comments – then, when I went to the bathroom and saw myself in the mirror, I realized why he'd kept silent.

I looked terrible. Not in my usual unkempt way, with chalk dust on my suit lapels and my hair in scarecrow spikes. Today I am almost colourless, and old – as old as damnation. Usually, when I look at myself in the mirror, I see a boy of about fourteen, with eyes that crackle with mischief in a face that has suffered some kind of a collapse – but a boy of fourteen nevertheless, wearing a very convincing mask.

Today, I look like my father in the days before he died. I know I shaved, but half my face seems to have escaped the blitz. There was a brown stain – tea, I think – on the collar of my shirt. I pulled on my gown to conceal the fact that my suit was less than spotless, but now I looked like an assemblage of black litter-bags, held together with frayed string.

'Penny for the guy, sir?' chirped Allen-Jones as I entered my room. Then he saw my face, and I saw the same expression I had seen on the face of the Bursar.

'*What* was that, Allen-Jones?'

'We're collecting money for Bonfire Night, sir.'

Good try, Allen-Jones. That was a dig at my crumpled gown. Still, the boy recovered well, and to do the other boys justice, no one laughed at the little joke. That made me feel uncomfortable. When my boys stop laughing, it means that something serious is afoot.

I skipped Assembly. I wanted to finish my resignation letter. I put down my old green Parker pen and waited for the ink to dry. I suppose the Head would have preferred an e-mail. But a letter, written in midnight ink, seems much more appropriate. I will hand it in personally, at the end of the day. I want to see his face when I do. I want to see the bastard's eyes.

At least that's what I was thinking as I sealed the letter and filed it away. But today, as it happens, Harrington is out of School on some kind of a course. Ms Buckfast said as much when she came to watch my third-year class; but I will not give her the letter. To do her justice, she did not ask, nor did she ask if I had made my decision. She is far too clever to do that; besides, she knows the answer. She is so sure of her victory that she vanished halfway through my morning's lessons and did not return for the rest of the day, leaving me with my Brodie Boys, and a grammar lesson that I might have enjoyed if not for the sword of banishment suspended above me. As it was, I was mostly silent, and the boys were silent, too, while outside, the fog pressed down like a lid, and the crows on the roof of the Bell Tower gathered like judges, with murder in mind.

At lunchtime, Allen-Jones came in with Sutcliff, McNair and the girl Ben. They often spend lunchtimes together, but this time the girl Benedicta came straight to my desk, at which I was moodily contemplating a passage from Catullus.

'Sir, we've heard a rumour. We've heard you might be retiring.'

'Who says?'

She gave me an impatient look. 'Does it matter? Is it true?'

Of course. *Call-me-Jo* is very close to Harrington and his minions. And she already shares so much with her girls – I imagine that's where the leak has sprung. I attempted to prevaricate.

'Retiring? I like to think of myself as a rather outgoing person.'

'So it *is* true,' said Ben. 'Why? Because of Rupert Gunderson?'

I'll admit, I hadn't expected her to jump to the truth so easily. 'Listen, Benedicta—'

'Don't,' she interrupted. 'You're the only one we can trust. If you go, sir, there'll be no one left on our side. You *can't* leave. You just can't.'

I struggled with the impulse to tell her the truth. 'It's difficult. There are many factors here to which you may not be privy.'

I sounded unconvincing. The girl Benedicta was not convinced. 'I wish you'd answer the question, sir.'

I sighed. 'There are things I can't tell you. But, being the intelligent young person you are, I'm sure you can hazard a guess.'

Behind her, I could see Allen-Jones listening to every word. He and the rest of my Brodie Boys are far too sharp to be taken in. A partial truth, then – after that, they must make of it what they will.

'Suffice it to say, it's not my choice. *Obesa cantavit*, and all that.'

'Sir?'

'That's enough. I have marking to do.'

2

November 3rd, 2005

Headmaster, and Chairman of the Governors,

It is with the greatest regret that I find myself obliged to hand in my notice as Classics Master of St Oswald's. I thought, having survived so many changes throughout my thirty-odd years in the place, that I could withstand another assault from the twenty-first century. It would appear that I was wrong.

I belong to a time when loyalty was paramount. Loyalty to the boys, to the staff – but most of all, to the Headmaster, the Captain of St Oswald's – was what kept our creaky old frigate afloat. And now I find myself in a place where I cannot bring myself to feel or pretend loyalty to a man I believe to be the enemy of everything I once held dear. I must therefore, et cetera—

At the end of the afternoon, I went to my room to clear my desk, and found a washed-out blonde woman listlessly vacuuming the floor. She gave her name as Cynthia, and announced that she was the new cleaner.

'What about Mr Winter?' I asked.

The blonde woman shrugged. 'Dunno,' she said. 'All I know's I'm supposed to do this room.'

'But what about Mr Winter?' I said. 'Are you going to be here permanently?'

The woman pulled a face. 'I dunno. All I know's I got this job. Till I can find summat better.'

'So – Winter's gone for good?' I said.

Cynthia shrugged. 'I guess so.'

'Do you happen to know why?'

Her bovine expression seemed to reflect the level of her indifference. 'Dunno,' she said. 'But he's gone all right. Now if you don't mind, I got jobs to do.'

The new cleaner returned to her jobs, which seemed to consist of little more than emptying bins and spraying polish into the air. I gathered up my books and prepared to leave; but the thought of going home was more than I could face straight away.

The Scholar, perhaps? Too crowded, I thought. And Bethan, with the stars up her arms, has taken to looking at me in a way not far removed from compassion; as if my age and loneliness have become a *sound* that only she can hear, but that announces me from afar. Much as I appreciate the larger portions she serves me, that look of compassion is troubling, and I do not welcome it.

Equally troubling was the fact that Winter has left St Oswald's. Why would he leave so suddenly? Surely, he cannot have been dismissed. His betrayal of me to Ms Buckfast should ensure *some* level of appreciation. Unless, of course, my assumption was wrong, and the man had been sacked for my crime. But who else could have known about the Honours Boards? It was puzzling. So very puzzling, in fact, that instead of going straight home, as I'd planned, I went out in search of Winter.

I left Malbry Park from the east side, on the far side of Millionaires' Row, and headed across the Parkside estate and into the little warren of streets that marked the boundary between Malbry Village and White City. Winter's house was on one of those streets, just off the Abbey Road estate. I didn't remember the house number, but at least I knew his car.

I found the little blue Peugeot outside a modest, pebble-dashed house. A neat little house, with a square of lawn and a well-clipped privet hedge. There was a light on upstairs – Winter's bedroom, I assumed. Downstairs, the curtains were open, and I could see a row of china ornaments – dogs, I think – on the window ledge. That surprised me a little – I didn't imagine Winter as the kind of man to like china dogs. Perhaps they'd belonged to his mother, I thought, and he hadn't had the courage to give them away. I remembered what he'd said to me. *You think they'll live for ever.* I'll admit, it had touched me a little: had given us some common ground.

I rang the doorbell. I heard it chime faintly somewhere inside the house. Then I heard the click of high heels and thought – a little late, perhaps – that I might be interrupting something. That light upstairs in the bedroom. And now the sound of a woman's tread—

I'll admit it. I panicked. It had never occurred to me that Winter might have a lady companion, and the thought of having to explain my visit to some woman in a négligée (my mind gave me the image of Mrs Nutter, in her silk kaftan with the psychedelic print) filled me with embarrassment. I sprang away from the door and hid on the far side of the hedge, making sure to close the gate. It was a trick Eric and I had played many times during our boyhood, and I felt myself trying to suppress an inappropriate grin as the door swung open, and a light came on, allowing me a glimpse through the hedge of a small, wiry woman about my own age; dyed black hair; pink housedress; fluffy high-heeled mules and hands that were gnarled with knuckle-duster rings—

For a moment I wondered if I'd knocked at the door of the wrong house. Then she spoke, quite sharply, and I recognized her voice.

'Who's there?'

It was Gloria. Even through the hedge I knew – something about the way she stood, staring out into the night with a mixture of doubt and suspicion. I could – I *should* – have spoken up. But Winter had told me she was dead, yet here she was, not *quite* unchanged (I told you, Gloria Winter had been quite the pin-up, back in the day), but there was no mistaking that voice, and those eyes, that seemed to cut through the darkness—

She lingered a moment longer. Behind the hedge, I did not stir. That's a novice's mistake – to lose one's nerve and break cover – but I am a veteran of the game, and even though my back ached, and my right leg was cramping, I stayed completely immobile in the shadow of the hedge, a privet of generous leafiness, hoping that a car wouldn't choose that precise moment to drive by and illuminate me from behind . . .

From inside the house I heard Winter's voice. 'Ma? Who is it?'

'Kids,' she said. Her voice is the same as always; slightly husky from smoking. 'Gone now – lucky for them.' The threat in those words was palpable. For a moment I was nine again, crouching behind the neighbour's fence with a pocket full of firecrackers. 'Trick-or-treaters,' Gloria said, raising her voice to address the night. 'Come round again and *I'll* give you a treat. Right up the arse.'

Then, she stepped inside again, closing the door. The light went out. And I stayed there, behind the hedge, for another five minutes or so, just to make sure she wasn't still there, watching from the shadows, behind that row of china dogs that stared relentlessly into the night.

3

November 3rd, 2005

I'd already reached the end of Dog Lane when I heard a sound behind me. I turned. It was Winter; in blue jeans and a hooded sweatshirt, looking as guilty as I felt. He must have run from White City, I thought. At his age, I supposed he still could.

'Mr Straitley, can we talk?'

I kept on walking. He followed me.

'I saw you at the house just now. I watched you through the curtains. I know you saw Ma.'

'Yes. Why did you lie to me?' We were almost at my gate. I could hear the wind in the horse-chestnut tree at the back of my garden.

Winter gave me a sideways look. Once more I remembered Joseph Apple, that quiet, unremarkable boy who had detonated so tragically ten years after leaving St Oswald's. The invisible finger, still active, started its stealthy walk across the open files of my ribcage.

'Mr Straitley. Can I come in? There are some things I need to explain.'

'You mean, how La Buckfast learnt about our escapade? Or why you left your cleaning job just as Harrington dropped the bomb? Are you even a cleaner at all, or was that just a convenient way to get me to confide in you?'

'What? What are you talking about?' He stared at me in confusion. 'What bomb?'

'You mean, you don't know?'

Winter shrugged. His look of surprise was genuine. His look of guilt had been genuine, too – but perhaps I'd jumped to conclusions. I began to wonder whether I had not misjudged him, after all.

'Look, you'd better come in,' I said. 'I'm tired, and I need a drink.'

I unlocked the front door. We went in. The scent of my house wrapped me like a well-worn blanket: dusty rugs; tobacco smoke; old books, mothballs and polish. My house smells like St Oswald's, minus the biscuity smell of boys, and it never fails to comfort me. But it was cold. I lit the fire, then found the decanter of brandy and poured us both a decent glug.

'Thanks.'

I sat on the sofa. Winter chose a chair by the fire. 'Was *that* what you were hiding?' I said. 'The fact that your mother was still alive?'

He nodded. 'I'm sorry I lied to you, sir. I don't even know why I told you that.' He looked into his brandy glass. 'But really, I mean, who *hasn't* fantasized about the death of a loved one?'

I thought about my mother at my father's funeral; the overcoats piled on top of each other; the pockets filled with socks. I thought about her that Christmas, stroking the rabbit, wearing her crown while my father watched her wordlessly. I thought about her saying: *My little boy likes rabbit pie*, and: *Don't tell him, will you?* And then my mind went back to the beach at Blackpool, and the cold wind that always seemed to be blowing there, and the grey, gritty sand, and my parents, already old, under their tartan blankets.

So many children's stories start with the death of the parents. Without our parents, we are free; free to travel; to have adventures; to develop our powers; to fall in love. The ultimate childhood hero is always an orphan: Peter Pan; Siegfried; Tom Sawyer; Superman. Do we *really* wish them dead? Of course not. Of *course* not. But boys play so many games. Cowboys and Indians. Cops and robbers. Good-guy one day, bad-guy the next, then home, for tea and sandwiches. But what did we dream, in those long-ago days, between the schoolyard and the canal? Didn't we sometimes, like Peter Pan, wish it could last for ever? Didn't I, sometimes, as a boy, wish myself an orphan?

I topped up Winter's brandy. 'So, you live with your mother?' I said.

He shrugged. 'It's not always easy. I mean – *she's* not always easy.'

'I think I know how you feel,' I said. 'It's natural to feel that way.'

'There's nothing natural about Ma. Ma's a genetic anomaly. Like the cockroach, she'll survive alien invasion, nuclear war. She's immortal. When I die, she'll be there, holding a cup of the vitamin drink she made me swallow when I was a boy. How I always hated it.'

How I always hated her.

Poor Winter. No wonder he lied. No wonder he spends all his time online, building fantasy friendships. *Sic transit Gloria mundi.* I gave a wince at the bad pun. Sometimes I worry that I don't know how to deal with emotional distress. Perhaps it's the way I was brought up, but outpourings of feeling have always made me feel profoundly uncomfortable. Maybe it's a good thing that I never married; from what I know of women (albeit not very much, most of it gleaned from Kitty Teague, or Danielle, or Mary, my old cleaner), life with them is a minefield of hormones, tears and misery.

My own mother lasted three more years after the death of my father. That's three years of multiple overcoats, of random, tearful profanity. Of cups of fishy-tasting tea while *Crown Court* or *Celebrity Squares* played silently in the background, and the other old folk (some of them lucid, others as lost as she was) would slowly settle around me like a flock of baffled pigeons, drawn, perhaps, by my relative youth and by the biscuits I always brought. By then, my mother, never a big eater, would hardly eat anything but biscuits. This caused me some concern, I'll admit – the food at the Meadowbank home, though bland, was far from inedible. In fact, it was rather better than the St Oswald's refectory, and I worried that she was starving herself, perhaps as a plea for attention. But when I gave her biscuits with a cup of much-sweetened tea, she always seemed perfectly happy, which meant that, for the sake of her health, I had to go and visit her more often than I wanted to.

I know it sounds callous. The fact is, those visits were a torture. My mother seldom recognized me; and when she did, it was not as her son, but as the man who brought biscuits. Tiny, birdlike, confused, indestructible under those layers of overcoats, she stayed alive for three more years, as the lights went off, one by one, in the haunted building.

I said: 'You shouldn't blame yourself.' By then, I wasn't entirely sure if I was talking to Winter or to some previous version of Straitley. In any case, I sounded unsure. I poured another brandy. 'I've had a lot on my mind,' I said. 'I shouldn't have come to your house. Your mother – your relationship with her – those things have nothing to do with me.'

I thought Winter looked relieved.

'But let me get this right,' I said. 'Are you telling me you *didn't* report our theft of the Honours Boards to Ms Buckfast?'

'Of course not. That's why I left,' he said. 'Apparently, they have surveillance cameras, linked to Dr Strange's computer. They caught the whole thing on camera, but you were off the premises. They said that if I'd incriminate you, they'd overlook the incident. They were very persistent.' He sighed. 'That was when I decided to leave.'

'But – won't the School involve the police?'

Winter gave a tiny smile. 'They might, except that something – perhaps a virus – got into Strange's computer. Somehow, it managed to corrupt a lot of those digital images. Including the ones of me putting the Honours Boards into my car.'

For a moment I stared at him. 'You did that?'

Winter gave a little shrug.

'Oh.'

I'd been so sure of his guilt. So certain he'd betrayed me. So certain that I'd almost played right into Johnny Harrington's hands. I felt a sudden stirring of hope, mingled with a sense of shame.

'Mr Winter, I'm sorry,' I said. 'I was so sure. I should have known.'

I explained about La Buckfast and her ultimatum. Winter listened in silence, occasionally sipping his drink.

At last, he said: 'I don't understand. Don't you *want* to retire, sir? Travel a bit, see the world? With the money they're offering – you could go anywhere you liked. You could visit Rome, Pompeii—'

'Hawaii, perhaps?' I said, and smiled. 'I think I'm too old for hula girls.'

'But you could *get away*, sir. See something more than this little town. Get a different perspective. Have *adventures*—'

I drained my glass. I knew he wouldn't understand if I tried to explain it all. And it isn't that I don't want to see Rome, or Venice, or Naples, or Carthage. But this is my world. It may be small, and yet I could live a hundred years and never come close to exhausting its infinite variety. Maybe I *do* lack perspective. But a Master of St Oswald's sees more than any tourist could. At St Oswald's, all of Life can be found in microcosm; Tragedy and Comedy pursue each other down the halls; great friendships are forged and forgotten; impossible dreams pursued; tears shed. These may not be the happiest days of our lives, but they are surely the *keenest*; days when everything cuts like a knife; days when the future seems infinite. Who would want to leave all this for the sake of a different perspective?

I must have said some of this aloud, because when I came to myself again, Winter was watching me curiously.

'Each to his own, Mr Straitley,' he said. 'But if someone showed me the door to the cage, I'd be out of it like a shot.' He reached into his pocket and came out with an envelope. 'This was in the paper,' he said. 'I was going to show it to you then. But then, things started to happen, and – well. Perhaps you should just read it for now.'

It was a sheet of newspaper, dated from three weeks ago. One item was circled in red; just a few lines, barely a squib, between a row of lonely hearts and an advertisement for a carpet warehouse.

YORKSHIRE MAN DROWNS IN CANAL

A man was found dead under a bridge over the canal in Malbry town centre in the early hours of Sunday morning. The unemployed man, Charles Wenceslas Nutter, 38, was thought to have been suffering from depression. Police say the death is not thought to be suspicious.

You never expect your boys to die. They seem to be immortal. And even though it's been twenty-odd years since Charlie Nutter was a boy, I can still see him in my mind; that pale and anxious little face, those skinny shoulder blades forever raised like hackles against adversity. And now here was his obituary – accident, or suicide? – on page 5 of a local paper, dated from over three weeks ago.

It hadn't made the *Examiner*. Perhaps Nutter's father had seen to that. But it had made the *Sheffield Scout* – a free paper, mostly given to advertising. What an obituary, I thought. A few lines in the free paper. His school reports were longer than that.

I know that bridge over Malbry Canal. The water there is three feet deep, four at most, if it has rained. The article suggests that he fell – or jumped. Depression, or alcohol? It's not that I liked him, especially. But he was one of my boys, and he – a person Harry Clarke had loved – died in three feet of water and mud, on a night in lonesome October.

I looked at the date of the piece again. Nutter had died on a Saturday night, or in the early hours of Sunday morning. Which pub had he been drinking in? There are several in the Village, though the Scholar is the most popular. I tried to think back to the day I'd seen Johnny Harrington in the Scholar. What day was that? A Friday, perhaps? Damn my failing memory. But Harrington had been edgy that day; talking on his mobile phone, then heading off through Malbry Park. Where had he gone after that call? Had he met Charlie Nutter?

'Why show me this now?' I said at last. 'Why not tell me three weeks ago?'

Winter gave a rueful smile. 'It's complicated, sir,' he said. 'There were some things I needed to check. Things I only suspected at first. But now I'm sure. All I need is proof.'

'Of what?'

'That Nutter was murdered.'

4

November 2005

Dear Mousey,

The thing about lost dogs, Mousey, is that they will always come back in the end. They run free awhile, chase a couple of cats, maybe kill a lamb or two, then slink back home for dinner. And that's why I wasn't too surprised when Poodle turned up in September, wanting to talk to me again. I'd been expecting him for some time. Well, for fifteen years or so. And for him to come back, after all this time, could only really mean one thing. Harry Clarke was dead at last. That old business was over.

Of course, we hadn't kept in touch. Things were too raw between us. But Poodle had followed my progress – my recovery years; Survivors – and finally, had followed me here, to Malbry, and a little red house in a cul-de-sac, not far from the Village.

Of course, he denied following me. 'I came back to care for Harry,' he said. 'He had no one else to look after him. Do you know where I found him? At the old people's hospice. He had no house, no possessions. Nothing but his memories.'

'Did he mention me?' I said.

Poodle gave me a venomous look. The years hadn't favoured him, Mousey. He looked old and decrepit. *Too much booze and drugs,* I thought. *He'll be gone in less than a year.*

'We never talked about you,' he said. 'I tried once or twice, but I couldn't. I couldn't let Harry know what we did. Not after all these years.'

I'd invited him inside, for fear of what the neighbours might hear, but his voice was so quiet that even I could barely make out what he was saying.

'I wanted to tell him the truth,' he went on. 'But he always trusted me. He used to write to me from jail, telling me all kinds of things. I wasn't allowed to see him. I couldn't even write to him. My father said if I ever tried to contact Harry again, they would have me sectioned.'

Well, Mousey. Imagine that. How spineless can a person be? Turns out old Poodle had lived at home ever since the trial, with regular stints in therapy. That golden summer before the trial was the only freedom he'd ever known – at least, until a few months ago, when he'd moved back to Malbry. I almost envied him that, you know. To have had Harry to himself for that time; to be with him; to be *needed* by him. And now, he was dead, and Poodle thought that both of us should put things right.

'What do you mean, put things right?'

Perhaps I'd spoken too loudly. He flinched. He never was much for shouting. Even when he was a boy, he was always the one who winced at loud voices, and cried when he had to drown the rats.

'Ziggy, we have to do it,' he said. 'We owe it to him. To Harry. He spent seventeen years under a cloud. We have to reinstate him.'

I'll admit it, I was touched. It's been so long since anyone called me Ziggy. 'Why?' I said. 'He's dead now. How can he benefit any more?'

Tearfully, Poodle tried to explain. It wasn't clear; something about Harry's ashes, and Mr Scoones, and a memorial in the Chapel at St Oswald's. It was nonsense, of course; St Oswald's would never allow it. Besides, it was impossible. I am a different person now. The events of so long ago happened to another boy. I spent seven years in therapy getting rid of the guilt of that day. My sacrifice was Harry Clarke. Don't think it was easy.

I tried to explain this to Poodle, but he was incoherent. 'He lost everything,' he said. 'Everything but this one thing. And we can give it to him now. We can give him peace at last.'

Peace? What about *my* peace? What about the life I've built for myself out of the wreckage? *I* built that, Mousey. Not Mum, not Dad, but me. And I did well. I'm a rich man. I had no qualifications, but I managed to make good, all the same. People respect money. Money gives you authority. And people fear authority – or at least, *some* people do. People who value secrecy. People who have something to hide.

I knew there was no way I could get Poodle to listen to all of this, so I pretended to listen to him as he rambled on and on. I pretended to listen, and then at last I nodded.

'OK.'

He looked surprised. 'Do you mean it?'

How very like him to say that. I said: 'I think you're right. We'll deal with it. I promise.'

His hopeful expression was almost like the Poodle of our schooldays. As if I'd given him a treat, instead of the kick he deserved. He said: 'Really? *Really?* You promise?'

'Of course.' Well, Mousey, I had to say that. I needed to buy some time to think. 'I'll have a word with Johnny,' I said. 'We're going to need him on our side.'

5

November 2005

Dear Mousey,

Getting in touch with Johnny proved more difficult than I'd thought. The new Head of St Oswald's wasn't an easy man to pin down. His phone number was ex-directory; his mobile went straight to voicemail. Even when I called him at school, all I got was his secretary, who asked too many questions and never seemed to know anything.

To be honest, it was hurtful. We'd been close for so many years, but now, except for the fifteen thousand paid into my account twice a year, it seemed that he was avoiding me. He hadn't come to see me since I moved into my Malbry home. I could tell he didn't want his wife around me any more. *She* never called me, either. Still, I'm sure that was *his* fault. Miss McRae always liked me.

Finally, I decided to call and see him in person. I went round to St Oswald's and told the secretary I'd wait. I'd brought a box of Harry's things to deliver to the Chaplain – Poodle and I had gone through them together, and I knew there was nothing in there to incriminate us. I was informed as I arrived that Dr Harrington was on a course, and that I could speak with Ms Buckfast or come back in the morning.

I didn't want Ms Buckfast. I wanted the Head, and I said so. But the secretary – a bird-eyed blonde who seemed to look right through me – must have been briefed to get rid of me, because after a wait of ten minutes or so, a red-haired woman of generous size came out of a nearby office.

'Mr Spikely,' she said. 'Can I help?'

For a moment, I almost revealed my surprise. But I've always been good at hiding things. I smiled, pulled a face at the secretary, and followed Ms Buckfast into her room.

It's funny, the things you remember. Perhaps it's the smell that brings it back; that uniquely St Oswald's smell, like cabbage, chalk and floor polish. That day it was raining, and the sound of water in the gutters and drains was like a tiny orchestra of splashing and popping and gurgling. It brought it all back, Mousey. That little room in the Bell Tower; our own form-room beneath it. The smell of the rain from the rooftops; the sound of it flicking against the glass. The way he put his hand on my leg, and whispered in my ear: *Good boy*. Not a pleasant memory, and yet it has made me who I am. A rich man. A success. You might say, a survivor.

I sat down in a leather chair and let the years wash away from me. 'Becky Price,' I said, and smiled.

'How nice of you to remember me. It must be over twenty years.'

'You haven't changed all that much.'

That was stretching the truth a bit. She's a lot bigger than she was then; more rounded at the edges. But her voice is still the same; that low and throaty contralto that used to go down so well in Church. I wondered if she'd got the job by sleeping with the boss. Probably not. I mean, why would he? Johnny's wife is gorgeous, and Ms Buckfast (what a name!) is only, at best, a four out of ten.

She gave me a smile. It brought her to five. 'It's good to see you, David,' she said. 'Now tell me, how can I help you?'

'I want to see Johnny,' I told her.

'I'm afraid that isn't possible. Johnny's very busy right now. But I can pass on a message.'

I tried a more direct approach. I said: 'Is he avoiding me? Because that would be dangerous.'

That ought to get her attention, I thought. But Becky Price just smiled again and said: 'That sounds like a threat, Dave. Can I offer you a drink?'

I shook my head. Too risky. I like to use my own crockery. The state of the mugs at St Oswald's was always suspect, Mousey. Cracks; chips; rings inside like on the stump of an ancient tree. You can catch all kinds of things from a dirty coffee mug.

Becky poured herself a cup. I admired her confidence. Then again, she must have had a pretty strong constitution to do all those things with Goldie.

'Let me make myself clear,' she said. 'Johnny isn't available. But if you want to leave a message – or anything else – with me—' Her eyes flicked to Harry's box. 'I take it you've been through the contents?' she said.

I nodded. She was pretty quick.

'Then I'll make sure it's dealt with,' she said. 'But this is a sensitive time, Dave. I don't want Johnny involved in anything that might jeopardize his work with St Oswald's. The school is already in a delicate situation. Any adverse publicity will just make his job so much harder.'

I explained to her about Poodle. She drank her tea and listened, occasionally nodding. I remember, when she was a Mulberry girl, she wanted to be an actress. From the way she reacted, I guessed she would have been a good one.

'So you see,' I told her. 'That's why I need to see Johnny.'

Becky shrugged. She isn't so much a red Flamingo girl any more. She's more like a ginger house-cat, purring by day; a killer by night.

'I've told you. That isn't possible.' She looked at me with cat-green eyes. 'You'll just have to talk to Charlie. *Persuade* him. I know you can.'

I wasn't sure what she was saying at first. But Mousey, she was serious. I'd never thought about her much, not even after what happened. She was Goldie's girl, which meant hands off and no peeking. Besides, she wasn't my type. But now I started to wonder. And to be honest, Mousey, if I'd *persuaded* Charlie, back in the winter of '81, we wouldn't have had this problem at all.

At last I said: 'I'll give it a try.'

She smiled. 'I know you will, David.'

It took me a few days after that to decide what to do about Poodle. I'd told him I was in discussions with Johnny about when to hold Harry's memorial, and for a while that was enough to keep him happy. But soon, he grew impatient, until finally, late one Friday afternoon, he turned up at my door, wanting Johnny.

'Of course. I'll phone him straight away. But he'll still be at work right now. Let's have a drink first, and talk. OK?'

He gave me a suspicious look. 'What, here?'

'Unless you'd rather go out.'

I knew what he was thinking, Mousey. He knew I was a killer. He sensed I'd given in to him just a little too easily, and he thought I might have murder in mind. I made my expression as bland as I could.

'Don't you trust me, Charlie?'

Frankly, I was a little hurt. After all, we'd been friends all this time, and I'd never revealed his secret. You'd have thought that might count for something, but apparently not to him. Fact is, he was uncomfortable being alone in my house with me.

'OK. We'll go to a neutral place. A nice pub in the Village. Somewhere we can both feel safe. I'll tell Johnny to join us there as soon as he's done at St Oswald's.'

Actually, Mousey, that suited me better anyway. I don't often go to pubs, as a rule. That meant I wouldn't be recognized. And even if I were, I thought, what could be more natural than to meet an old friend for a quiet drink?

Then I phoned St Oswald's, and asked for the Headmaster. Instead, I got Ms Buckfast.

'David, how nice to hear you.'

'I hoped I could talk to Johnny.'

She laughed. 'You are persistent, David. Johnny isn't available. But I'll take a message, if you like. Is this about Charlie?'

'He's with me right now. We're off to the Scholar for a drink.'

'I see,' she said. 'Well, I'm afraid Johnny's going to be working late. But if he can make it, I'm sure he will.'

So Poodle and I headed out towards the Thirsty Scholar. I didn't need to do much. We talked. We drank (he more than I). I paid. I knew he wouldn't turn down a free drink. Every hour I checked my phone and said: 'He should be here soon.'

But Poodle was growing impatient. 'Why isn't he here?' he kept saying.

'Don't worry. I think I know.' I explained about Becky Price, Goldie's girl from the old days. 'She's on his

Management Team,' I said. '*And* she said he was working late.'

Poodle's face broke into a smile. 'The old dog,' he said. 'Becky Price? You sure?'

'I've seen her,' I told him. 'We talked about Harry's memorial. She's going to help us set things up. She's like his deputy, or something.'

After that, Poodle seemed to relax. Somehow, the mention of Becky Price had convinced him I was serious. He babbled on happily for a while about Harry and the memorial; what hymns they'd chosen; what poetry. Then, at half past ten, I said: 'Let me walk you home, eh? You never know who's about these days.'

By then he was drunk. Not senseless, but reeling in the cold air. 'We'll walk through the park,' I told him. 'Let you get your breath back.'

Halfway through the park he was sick. I held his head as he vomited. He seemed more lively after that, talking about the memorial again.

'You've thought it all out, haven't you?'

'Harry thought it out, not me.' His eyes were wet and hopeful. 'He wrote it all down before he died.' He paused for breath, leaning against the trunk of a nearby beech tree. The fallen leaves around his feet were filled with uncanny whisperings. 'I'm so glad you're OK with this,' he said. 'I was expecting – I dunno. Resistance.'

I smiled. 'No, Charlie. You sold me. I guess I've been waiting to do the right thing.'

By then we were nearing the end of the park. Beyond that was White City; what was left of the clay pits, and, more importantly, what was left of Malbry Canal; now a stub around three miles long, bordered with weeping willows. There's a bridle path running alongside, most often used by cyclists, joggers and, in the evenings, young people in heat. At intervals, there's a walkway of corrugated metal allowing people to cross the canal. In fact, there's one just off the main road leading into White City. I led him towards it. Poor Poodle.

Think of it this way, Mousey. He was dead already. I'd given him his chance to shine. He could have had what the rest of us had. All that Survivors did for us. Instead, he chose Harry. That was his choice. *He* chose not to participate. And now he's dead, that *I* might live . . .

This is what I was thinking as I walked back along the canal-side. I met only one other person; a man in a dark-blue parka. For a moment I thought he looked at me, but that might have just been the light. In any case, I kept moving. I crossed back through the park again, and then I was home. It was easy. And the more I think about it now, the more I realize how much I needed that bit of excitement; that breath of fresh air; that moment of surrender to something bigger and braver than I. I feel as if I'm awake again, after half a lifetime of sleep. For the first time in seventeen years, I feel *alive*, Mousey.

It didn't take much. Just a little push. I don't know why I waited so long. Still, it's what happens now that counts. Living in the present. So, what next? Or should I say – who? It seems small-minded for me to stop now, when I've made such an excellent start. Harry's dead; Poodle's dead; who does that leave, Mousey?

No, you don't have to answer that. You know. He's been a thorn in my side for so long that I'd almost forgotten he was there. That he was even alive at all. Still, that could change. It can always change. Death is always waiting to strike when you least expect it. You think you're entitled to seventy years, but Death could come tomorrow. Death could come during the night, or flying through the air at supersonic speed. The fact is, no one's safe – not you, not even me, Mousey. Which is why I need to take charge of my fate, starting right here, right now. It's never too soon to tackle Death. As Straitley would say: *Carpe diem*.

6

November 4th, 2005

Headmaster, and Chairman of the Governors,

It is with sincere regret—

No, dammit. No regrets. I cannot deliver the letter now. Winter's story changes things. Damn him, why did he wait for so long to tell me Charlie Nutter had died? And why is he now so certain that the death *wasn't* an accident? Whatever his motive, he believes that Charlie Nutter was murdered – possibly for reasons connected to the Harry Clarke affair – and has promised to call again tonight, with further information.

I know. It seems unlikely. There was a time when I too would have scorned such a far-fetched hypothesis. But after the events of last year – the disappearance of a pupil, the stabbing of a member of staff and my own brush with the Reaper – I know that nothing is safe; nothing far-fetched. Under the vivid reflections of sunlight, trees and cloudless sky, the dark and lonely water awaits, and no one – no, not even a Head – can be above suspicion.

All the same, what evidence can there be to link Johnny Harrington to the death? The pink Survivors pamphlet; his marriage to Spikely's therapist; his unusual behaviour in the Thirsty Scholar close to the night that Nutter died – none of those things are enough to prove that he was even in contact with Nutter, still less that Nutter's death was linked with the events of all those years ago. And even if it were, what good would such a revelation serve? St Oswald's reputation is already badly compromised. One more hint of a scandal might finish the old place for good. And though I may be off the hook as far as the Honours Boards are concerned, the problem of Allen-Jones remains. Do Harrington and his minions have sufficient grounds to carry out their threat? With the help of the Chaplain, I think they do. In such circumstances, I cannot afford to act out any *Boy's Own Paper*-ish fantasies. I am still *in loco parentis*, and I have a job to do.

And yet, Winter's suspicions, however unlikely they may be, have reawakened my sense of revolt. The hemlock bowl, so inviting only a couple of days ago, can now no longer be considered. At least, not until my current duties have been suitably discharged. Charlie Nutter deserves the truth. Harry Clarke deserves justice. St Oswald's deserves a Headmaster who will not dismantle it piece by piece to further his ambition. And my boys deserve something more than lessons stripped of all character. No, I cannot afford to flinch, or take the easy option. Whatever Winter tells me tonight, that door is closed for ever.

I went into St Oswald's today feeling somewhat the worse for wear. Too many sleepless nights, perhaps; too many glasses of brandy. As a result, although I'd taken greater care than usual over my appearance, I sensed an odd atmosphere this morning in the Common Room. A rather too solicitous greeting from the Chaplain. A pitying smile from Kitty Teague, in the corner with Penny Nation. Could the grapevine have already spread news of my impending retirement? Or is it something more sinister?

Dr Devine was pretending to ignore me, but the nose expressed disapproval. I have to say, I'm still surprised at Devine's sudden *volte-face* vis-à-vis the management. Were it not for my Brodie Boys, I think I'd enjoy his collusion in a potential mutiny. But for the sake of Allen-Jones, Benedicta Wild and the rest, I suppose I must keep my thoughts to myself. Eric, too, was watching me from his chair in the corner. Thinking that this might be an attempt at reconciliation (he still hasn't spoken a word to me since the thing with the garden gnome), I poured myself a cup of tea and came to sit beside him.

'All right, old man?' I said affably.

To be honest, I've missed him. He's often rather difficult, but I've known him sixty years. Most marriages don't last as long. That ought to count for something.

Eric gave me a sideways look. I noticed he didn't look too well. Perhaps there's something going round. Or maybe he has missed me, too.

I passed him the biscuits. He took one. Harry's method of judging personality according to one's choice of sweets also applies to biscuits, I've found; in this case, Eric's choice (a plain Digestive) revealed his essential fragility. Eric's stomach, like Devine's nose, tends to reflect his state of mind; and when he is upset, it tends to adopt a position of sympathy.

'I heard you were taking the hemlock,' he said, between two careful mouthfuls of tea.

'Who told you that?'

Eric shrugged. Of course, it could have been anyone. But Dr Devine is high on my list. That, or maybe La Buckfast – unless he has been talking to the boys. 'Well, your informant is premature,' I said. 'I still haven't decided.'

He raised an eyebrow. 'That's not what I've heard. Besides, what good will it do to stay? St Oswald's is changing, Straitley. Might as well take the package, and enjoy the few good years we have left. Or would you rather die on stage?'

'Molière did,' I told him.

Eric made a huffing sound. 'You always were a stubborn ass.'

'Better that than a management stooge.'

He gave me a look. 'You'd better not be trying to get me involved in anything. I already told you what I felt about Harry Clarke's memorial. No reason to dig up that story again. It can only damage us all.' He finished his tea and put down the cup. 'I've lived too long in the past,' he said. 'Now I think it's time for a change.'

'What kind of a change?'

He gave a shrug. 'I thought I could move to Paris at last. Find myself a guest house. Go and see the Folies-Bergère.'

I stared at him. If he'd made a joke, then he was commendably deadpan. And yet, old Eric has always longed to go and live in Paris, an unlikely ambition that seems all the more so for the fact that his mother, aged ninety-two and suffering from dementia, needs constant attention at home, including a daily carer, which eats up most of his salary. I was suddenly reminded of Winter and his dreams of Hawaii, and of Spanish-eyed Gloria, at the door, with her rows of china dogs. *Certain people seem to project something of immortality.*

A dreadful thought occurred to me. 'Eric – is your mother all right?'

For a moment, he said nothing. Then he looked up and smiled at me. It was a bleak little wavery smile, that made him look both very old and very like the schoolboy I knew.

'Eric?' I said.

He shook his head. Then he started to cry.

It was a stroke, the doctor had said. A kind of mercy, I suppose. Eric's mother, Margery – whom I recalled from boyhood as a cheery, maternal type, with a beehive hairdo of frankly impressive proportions and a ten-a-day cigarette habit – had dwindled over the years into a tiny, rasping Tinkerbell, growing increasingly distant and fey until she had fully retreated into the snowbank of dementia, recognizing her son only on alternate days, and talking to people on the TV.

'I put her to bed on Monday night,' said Eric in a colourless voice. 'And in the morning she was gone. It must have been quick. My room's next door, but I never heard a thing.'

How very like him, I thought, to keep this a secret from everyone. Four days, he'd hidden it from all his friends at St Oswald's – St Oswald's, the place where everyone knows everything about everyone. Four days, he'd hidden it from *me*, his oldest friend, his confidant. Four days, I'd thought he was sulking over that idiotic gnome, when actually—

'Eric, I'm so sorry,' I said.

His tears had already vanished into the map of his haggard face. 'I'm not. I did what I could. Now it's my turn to live my life.' It was almost exactly the tone he'd adopted when he told me he was leaving to work at King Henry's Grammar School; almost exactly the tone with which he'd refused to speak for Harry when I was a character witness.

Stubborn; bullish; but underneath, obscurely lost and yes – *afraid*.

'When yours went so soon, I was jealous,' he said. 'Mine took over twenty years. I never put her in a home – I couldn't bear it – but all the same. You start to think they'll outlive you; that even when there's nothing left, they'll still be there, like the Albatross, just a parcel of feathers and bones, suffocating you with guilt.'

His voice had risen a little; I looked to see if anyone had heard. But the Common Room was almost empty, except for a group of Games staff talking around a noticeboard, and Robbie Roach, the historian, reading the *Daily Mirror* with a look of vacuous absorption. I'd missed Assembly, I realized. I hadn't even heard the bell. Still, my boys were used to dealing with my infrequent absences: Sutcliff or Allen-Jones would have already taken the register, and they would have gone down to Chapel alone, in more or less orderly fashion.

'Eric, don't.' I touched his arm. We Tweed Jackets don't tend to be of the touchy-feely persuasion, but sometimes one has to force oneself to make the comforting gesture. 'It's natural to feel this way. I did when Mother died.'

He nodded. 'I know. Survivor's guilt.'

That word again. *Survivor*. As if bereavement were a shipwreck. And maybe that's what it feels like, for people like me and Eric Scoones, clinging to St Oswald's as if it's the only thing still left afloat.

'I've been going through her things,' Eric went on. 'It's appalling. So many boxes of papers and clothes. I'm going to have to get someone in. You know, one of those house clearance firms. God knows where it will all end up. You see this stuff at garage sales. Personal things. Photographs. Sometimes, I just feel like setting fire to the whole house.'

'I'll help you,' I said. 'Go through them, I mean. I'm drawing the line at arson.'

I thought the flicker of a smile passed over his face. He said: 'I thought I could take them to the bonfire in the park. Just dump them on the pile and leave. Let bygones be bygones.'

I nodded. 'That's a good idea.'

'All right. We'll do it together.'

Looking back at it now, it seems such a quiet moment. An island of tranquillity on our turbulent journey. Two old Ozzies side by side, drinking tea in the Common Room. Now it looks like a scene viewed through the lens of a *camera obscura*; perfect in every detail, and yet impossibly distant. Looking back at it now, it looks like a scene from another life; perhaps the life we *could* have lived if things had somehow been different. *If* I had gone straight home after School, instead of going to Eric's house; *if* I'd spoken to Winter; *if* I'd found Harry's box in time; *if* I'd seen what was under my nose, instead of chasing phantoms—

I'm getting old. That's what it is. Old and none too quick off the mark. But I've never been what you'd call *quick*; always a bit of a plodder. The tortoise to old Eric's hare – and yet we got there in the end. *Stout-hearted boys with sharp swords win glittering prizes*. But what is the prize for Straitley? And do I really want to know?

7

November 2005

Dear Mousey,

It didn't take Johnny long to hear the sad news about Poodle. He knows all kinds of people, including the Chief Inspector and the Head of South Yorkshire Police. And he'd kept tabs on both of us, just as he had on Becky Price. Sun Tzu says: *Keep your friends close, and your enemies closer*. That's good advice, Mousey. I've followed it all my life.

He phoned me – finally – from the pub. I could tell from all the background noise. Besides, he wouldn't have phoned me from home, in case his wife overheard him. Probably the Scholar, I thought. It's pretty close to St Oswald's.

Johnny had been drinking; I could tell that from his voice. He pretends not to drink much, as a rule; but when he does, he gets angry.

'David, what did you do?' he said, by means of introduction. 'I thought you said you wouldn't do – *those things* – any more.'

Well, that *was* the arrangement. We made it several years ago. I was to stay out of Liz's way and remove myself from

Survivors, they were to pay me a salary for services to the movement. That, along with my secondary regular source of income, should have been more than enough to keep me out of trouble for pretty much the rest of my life. But Poodle had threatened the status quo. My actions were purely a reaction to that.

'I had to do it,' I told him. 'He needed to be put down.'

'Don't say that!' he hissed. There was a pause. I could hear him breathing; fast, as if he had been running. 'Listen, I'm coming over,' he said. 'We need to sort this out, right now.'

I made a pot of green tea as I waited for him to arrive. I thought it better not to offer him a beer. I rather mistrust alcohol. Alcohol's a killer. That was what killed Poodle, you know. Alcohol and stubbornness.

Johnny knocked on my front door ten minutes or so afterwards. It's only a short walk through the park, but he was already out of breath. I suppose it's the sedentary lifestyle, but at his age he ought to be careful. Heavy drinking can cut your life expectancy by twenty years – that's even more than smoking. He's thirty-eight. That would give him ten or twelve years. Not that *that* would bother me. I'm going to live forever.

I opened the door. Johnny came in. He didn't look too bad, actually, and I felt some disappointment. When he dies, his lovely wife will be a wealthy widow. And she *is* very lovely, Mousey. Some women improve as they mature.

'How nice to see you,' I told him. 'How's Liz? Give her my love.'

Johnny gave me a look, as if I'd said something ridiculous. His status has made him arrogant; I would never have been that rude.

'Would you like a cup of green tea? I've already poured one,' I told him. 'Tea's very healthy, you know. Filled with antioxidants.'

'No thanks,' said Johnny.

I shrugged and sat on the sofa. I sometimes forget that others are not as mindful of their health as I. Johnny paced up and down for a while, then turned back to look at me. He was still a little flushed. Probably high blood pressure.

'Was it really you?' he said. 'Did you really do it?'

He ran his hand through his hair, and I wondered if he'd had transplants. He's always been rather vain, you know, even when he was a boy. That perfectly straight, dark-blond hair. Mine was thinning, even then. I was not an attractive boy.

'They're saying he was drunk,' he said. 'That he fell into the canal.'

I shrugged. 'Well, yes. That *would* make sense. He *was* depressed. He had problems. He was addicted to drink and drugs. He had no reason to stay alive.'

'Did he die alone?' he said.

Stupid question. 'We all die alone.'

'Dammit! Were you with him?'

'Of course,' I said. 'I pushed him.'

'Jesus.' He started to pace again. 'Sweet Jesus, David. You pushed him.'

'*He* pushed that boy in the clay pits,' I said.

Johnny looked even more agitated. 'You *said* you'd never mention that. Oh, God. What am I going to do?'

I drank more tea and watched him pace. He really did seem quite upset. I wondered what would happen if he had a heart attack, right there. It would probably serve him right, after everything he's done.

'No one will find out,' I said. 'No one saw. If anyone comes round, I'll tell them we had a couple of drinks, that he seemed depressed, that he talked of ending it all, but that I thought he was just being maudlin. I left him to walk home through the park, and that's the last I saw of him.'

'Oh, Jesus,' Johnny said. 'Oh, Jesus, David.'

'*What?* What's going to happen?' I said. He was starting to annoy me now. 'Has anyone suggested that there might have been foul play?'

He shook his head.

'Well, that's a relief. Are you sure you don't want tea?'

Johnny ignored me. 'I shouldn't have come. Don't try to contact me again. If anyone asks where I was tonight, I'll say I was with Becky. She'll back me up. You know she will.'

'Will she?'

I thought probably she would. Maybe I was wrong about her sleeping with the boss. Not that I would have told anyone about Johnny's visit. Why would I? Still, his suspicion was hurtful. You don't behave like that with your friends.

Johnny left soon after that, without even touching his tea. I guessed I wouldn't see him again, at least not for a while. I was washing the cups and the teapot (green tea turns poisonous when it ferments, and it's never good to leave it too long), when I heard a knock at the back door. Johnny hadn't been gone for more than a couple of minutes, and I wondered if he'd had second thoughts; if he'd come back to talk to me.

But when I opened the door and looked out, it wasn't Johnny standing there. It was a ghost. A ghost from the past. And not just *any* ghost, either. Mousey, you'll never believe who it was, standing there as if nothing had changed for over twenty years—

It was *you*.

8

November 2005

Well, of course, it wasn't *you*. I know you've been dead for years. But he looks so like you, Mousey. Same hair; same eyes; even the same kind of clothes. He might be a few years older than me, but now he looks much younger. And he's lost a lot of weight since we were boys, which is why for a moment I was confused. But then I recognized the man in the dark-blue parka – you know, the one I saw the night that Poodle fell from the bridge. It was your brother – Piggy, as was – standing in the doorway, looking at me with your eyes. He was holding something under his arm. It looked like a copy of Pink Floyd's *The Wall*.

He smiled at me. 'Can I come in?'

For a moment I just stared.

'You know who I am, don't you?' he said.

I nodded.

'It's been a long time.' From the album sleeve he pulled out a Xerox copy of an old School photograph. I'd seen it before, lots of times. It came out at Harry's trial. Harry and Johnny, at Sports Day, with me in the background.

I nodded again. 'Come in,' I said. 'I'll make a pot of green tea.'

I think that, even then, I must have been contemplating murder. That album under his arm was the clue; the sleeve now spotted with age and neglect. He must have retrieved it very soon after I buried my time capsule. Maybe he watched me hide it there, from behind a burnt-out car. My treasures; the Christmas card to Harry; the list of albums I'd meant to buy; and the pages torn from my diary that I couldn't bear to burn.

'My brother liked the clay pits,' he said. 'There was always lots to do. Catching mice. Killing them. We used to look for comics, too. Things that people had finished with.' He followed me into the living room; sat down on the sofa. 'We liked to watch in secret, too. You wouldn't believe what sometimes went on.'

'What sort of things?' Even then I was wondering whether I could take him. He didn't look like a fighter, but then, neither am I, Mousey. A blow to the back of the head? No. Poison? I doubted he'd fall for that. Besides, I'm a pusher, not a poisoner.

'You'd be amazed at the number of times I got to watch people having sex. They did it in abandoned cars, or out in the open, on mattresses. I didn't like watching my brother kill mice, but watching people have sex was OK. I used to have a couple of dens I'd built from wooden pallets. Like the kind bird-watchers use, with little slatted windows. A couple of times, I saw a boy from St Oswald's, with his girl. Not like the girls at Sunnybank Park. Bright red hair, and gorgeous.'

I took a couple of beers from the fridge. Handed one to the visitor. I could see where he was leading, and I, for one, needed a drink.

'That's where I was hiding the day I saw you bury the box,' he said. 'Right up by the big rock between two of the flooded pits. At first I thought it was money, so I waited till you'd gone away. Then I dug where the earth was loose, and I found this.'

He took the album from under his arm and put it on the coffee-table. Then he drank his beer while I looked for the pages torn from my diary. Of course, they weren't there, Mousey.

Your brother looked at me and smiled. 'Of course, I had no idea what it was. I had no idea who *you* were. At the time Harry Clarke was arrested, I didn't make the connection. I thought what I had was a story, written by a sick little shit who'd buried it in the clay pits for fear that his parents might read it. But I've been making enquiries, and now I think it's something else. *I* think it's my pension fund. What do *you* think, David?'

It was blackmail, pure and simple. Simple, because what he wanted was simple enough for me to provide. He wanted money, that was all; a one-off payment of ten thousand pounds from each of the people concerned. That would ensure delivery of the missing pages; after which your brother would vanish from Malbry forever.

'I don't care about what you may or may not have done back when you were a kid,' he said. 'All that's ancient history now. I don't see the point of dredging it up. Ten thousand pounds isn't a lot. I know you can afford it.'

I looked at him in disbelief. 'How stupid do you think I am? Why should I accept your word that you won't take the money and keep coming back?'

'Because I want to live,' he said. 'And both of us know what happens to anyone who gets in your way. Trust me, Dave, I'll be out of your hair as soon as you deliver the cash.'

I wanted to believe him, you know. But Mousey, he was dangerous. Besides, with everything he knew, ten thousand pounds just wasn't enough. 'What can you buy with ten thousand pounds?'

Your brother gave a little smile. 'A ticket to Hawaii,' he said.

9

November 2005

You'd think that taking a life would have weight. Death should be something heavy. It ought to *matter*, like turning eighteen, or losing your virginity. But after that day at the clay pits, I woke up just the same as before. That's how it was with Ratboy. That's how it was with Poodle.

Poor Poodle. I never told him what *really* happened on that day. I even tore the pages out of my St Oswald's diary. I wanted him to feel miserable. I wanted him to feel guilty. After all, I thought to myself, why should *he* be allowed to forget? Why should Charlie Nutter have something that I never would?

He left me by the Pit Shaft the day we did for Ratboy. He was pretty upset, and I guess he didn't want to stick around. I was still on a high, though. The fire in the burnt-out car was still warm, and so I sat there awhile, enjoying the glow. But then I heard a funny sound coming from the Pit Shaft; a kind of croaking, slithery sound. Ratboy, climbing out of the pit, all dead and fishy and covered with mud, to take revenge on his killers. Or so my mind kept telling me, even though I didn't believe in ghosts, or retribution, or even, really, God. So I went to look. And when I got there, I found that I was half right. But Ratboy wasn't a vengeful ghost. Mousey – *he was still alive.*

He must have been tougher than he looked. That muddy water was freezing. And even though he could hardly swim, he'd managed to paddle across the pit to the side where the bank made a bit of a slope – not much, but just enough to pull himself out of the water and make a grab for a dead tree root that was sticking out of the frozen bank.

When he saw me, his mouth worked. I think he was trying to call for help. But nothing came out but a kind of squeak, as if he really were a rat.

'Shit,' I said.

I wasn't scared. But really, Mousey, I had no choice. I could hardly help him out. He would have told his parents, and Poodle and I would have been caught. I had to finish him off before he somehow managed to climb out of the pit – and he was making a decent try, in spite of those wet and slippery sides.

Ratboy must have guessed as much. He started to claw at the sides of the pit with his greasy, shaking hands.

'Shit,' I said again. At this rate, Ratboy would be out in no time. I looked around for something to use. There was an old shopping trolley nearby. It was missing its wheels, but it was still good. I started to drag it towards the pit. It was pretty heavy. I'd almost got where I wanted to be, when I heard the sound of footsteps. It was Goldie, looking alarmed, as if he'd expected to see someone else.

'Ziggy, what are you doing?' he said.

For a moment I wanted to push *him* into the water, too. Then I had a better idea.

I said: 'He wanted to *do* things. Charlie pushed him, then he ran.'

Goldie's eyes widened. 'What sort of things?'

'*Sexual* things, you moron,' I said. 'The kind of things that perverts do.'

Some kids are scared of Satanists. Some are afraid of their teachers. Some live in fear of bullies, the Bomb, or of getting cancer. With Goldie, it was perverts. To be fair, his dad was always warning us in Church about perverts hanging around the clay pits, trying to pick up little boys. And to be fair, Goldie's dad was half right. Except that the problem was never the clay pits, but somewhere much, much closer to home.

I said: 'I think we might have found the reason for Charlie's Condition.'

Goldie's eyes widened still further. 'You mean – you think he *knew* him?'

'I'm pretty sure they were meeting here. That's why Charlie kept coming round. But recently, he's been trying to change, and I think that's when things got nasty.'

In a few words I painted the scene. It actually all made sense. And finally, when Goldie looked over the side of the Pit Shaft and saw who Charlie's abuser was – a boy from the estates, no less, a dirty Sunnybanker—

Ratboy had managed to haul himself almost out of the water by then. But the clay bank of the pit was steep, and he was too heavy with water to climb. The sticking-out tree root had broken off, and now he was trying to use his hands to dig himself a place to stand. You had to hand it to Ratboy. He was pretty tough all right.

Goldie and I looked down at him – covered in mud from head to foot, only his eyes looking out at us from behind a mask of yellow clay. If he'd said a word – just one – I don't think we would have done it. But behind that mask of clay he didn't even look human, and the sounds that were coming from his mouth – wheezing, chattering, choking sounds – didn't sound human, either.

Goldie was watching him, mesmerized. I think he was playing it in his head, counting the possibilities. There were only two. One: we let Ratboy go, or—

'We can't let him go. He's seen us,' I said.

For a while, Goldie didn't say anything. He was thinking hard, I could tell. But this wasn't a piece of algebra or a Latin translation. He was out of his depth, and besides, I think he was scared of me.

I looked at the shopping trolley again. Then I looked back at Goldie.

He shook his head. 'We can't,' he said.

Below us, Ratboy was climbing the pit; digging, first a hand, then a foot, into the hard and greasy clay walls. His breath came out in jagged plumes. His fingers were crabby and blue with cold.

'We could just leave him,' Goldie said.

'What, after this? Don't be a dope.' I took his hand and placed it on one side of the trolley. The thing was heavy; heavy enough to solve all of our problems. 'No one will ever know,' I said. 'Charlie thinks he did it himself. Besides, what's one pervert more or less?'

I let that sink in for a moment. Slowly, Goldie looked at me. And then, Mousey, we counted to three, and sent the trolley down the bank, and Ratboy's eyes went wide, just once, before he hit the water—

We waited for him to resurface. But this time, he stayed under.

* * *

After that, I just went home. Watched TV, did my homework; wrote in my St Oswald's diary. But Mousey, to tell you the truth, I wasn't feeling as good as I thought. It was stupid. I know it was. But unlike the rabbits, with Ratboy it didn't feel as if my fear had found another home. Instead it had found another *voice*. Not a very loud one, but with that twang my parents hate. And that new voice stayed with me for seven whole years, Mousey, never saying very much, except the occasional *All right?* and sniffing cold air through its nose like a little animal.

But it was always in my thoughts, counting down the seconds. Like the still, small voice of God – if God was a Sunnybanker.

10

November 3rd, 2005

I'll have to kill your brother now. I hope you don't hold that against me. But I'm afraid he's dangerous. He has the torn-out pages. We must get *those* back, Mousey. We don't want anyone reading them. But it may be a good thing after all. I've been thinking of ending it, and this may give me the chance I need. Goldie's no use to me any more. Look how he was over Poodle. Look how loyal he was to me. He's always been weak. And now look – the first hint of trouble, and here he is, giving in to blackmail. And from whom? A cleaner, no less. A dirty Sunnybanker.

It doesn't take much to kill a man. A quick push over a bridge. A blow to the back of the head. You'd think it would be like riding a bike; something you can never unlearn. And yet, getting rid of your brother is proving harder than I thought. Who could have imagined that he would be so difficult? That boy I once called Piggy, who used to cry when we drowned the rats? Of course, he isn't fat any more. And he was never stupid. Careful, but not stupid, which is why he's still alive.

I paid the ten thousand pounds, of course. Goldie did, too, which rankled, given how reluctantly he always pays *my* salary. As if it were some kind of charity, instead of what he owes me. But I got my pages back, and burnt them in the fireplace, which means my mind *should* be at rest – except for your brother, Mousey, who knows what happened to Ratboy, and, remembering the clay pits and the games you and I used to play there, must have a pretty good inkling of what happened to Poodle.

A month has passed since he sought me out. Since then, I've been making enquiries. I've found out quite a lot, actually. His name is B. B. Winter. I've seen him in the Village. He lives in White City – I know the address – with his elderly mother. He doesn't drink, doesn't do drugs, doesn't seem to have any friends. A loner. He should have been easy. But, after our first meeting, he never met me alone again. He arranged to receive the cash in the coffee shop at our local supermarket, inside a bag of groceries. Ten thousand pounds doesn't take too much space. And inside a jumbo carrier bag, under a loaf of bread, some eggs and a carton of milk, it all looked perfectly innocent. I ordered a pot of tea and some toast, and he handed me the pages from my diary inside what looked like a birthday card. No one would have guessed the truth, not even if they'd been sitting right next to us.

After that, there was no need for me to see him ever again. And yet – Mousey, I kept on seeing him. One day it was in the park, walking back from St Oswald's. Another time it was in the Pink Zebra, the organic café at the edge of White City. Another time, he was driving his car, that little blue Peugeot of his, and I was on foot, and he *waved* to me. What was he *waiting* for, Mousey? Why hadn't he left town, like he'd said?

At first, I thought of arson. But Mousey, that was too risky. Your brother keeps antisocial hours, and I couldn't be sure he'd be asleep. Then I thought of lying in wait as he walked back through the park after work, but with Bonfire Night approaching, the park was always full of kids, and you could never be sure who would be there, or who would remember seeing you. Besides, your brother was careful. He didn't go out after dark. He never went to the pub at weekends. If only he'd been like Poodle, I could have caught him unawares. As he went home drunk and alone, late on a Saturday night, I could have followed him to a quiet spot and dealt with him at leisure. But he was never drunk and alone, and he avoided those places. He was like one of those rats that, if you catch them and let them go, will never let you catch them again—

And then, last night, he phoned me. Just when I thought I'd never get a chance to see him alone, he called. I almost didn't answer the phone. No one calls me late at night, except for nuisance callers. But some instinct warned me that this might just be my lucky night.

'Hello, David. It's me,' he said.

I recognized his voice at once. Quiet, not too accented, with a little occasional slur suggesting he may once have stammered. I tried to sound abrupt, annoyed. But inside, I was smiling.

'What do you want? I thought you said I'd never hear from you again.'

'Things have changed.'

'Oh, really?'

I heard the smile in his voice. He said: 'You're wondering what more I could have, now that those diary pages are gone. You know you didn't write it down; at least, not in your diary. But you're not new to blackmail. In fact, you've lived well on the proceeds.'

'If you mean Survivors—' I said.

'No, not Survivors,' said your brother.

I thought for a moment. 'You're bluffing,' I said. He couldn't know that. He *couldn't*. I'd never told anyone about that. Not even you, Mousey.

Your brother said, 'I've been watching you. More importantly, I've been watching your bank records. It isn't all that difficult. All you need are a few facts, some time and some inspiration. And what I found out is that over the past fifteen years or so, you've been receiving regular payments from an individual living in the Village. Someone we both know, in fact. Someone who kept correspondence, some dating back a very long time.'

He might still be bluffing, I thought. My paper trail is minimal. Just one letter, written when Harry Clarke was arrested. *Could* he have kept it? And if he did, how could your brother have known what I wrote in a letter seventeen years ago?

'My mother was a cleaner,' he said. 'She used to clean people's houses. She had a dozen regulars, but she also worked at St Oswald's. When she retired, I did the same.' He paused, and I could hear his smile. 'It's funny, what old people choose to keep. Notebooks, diaries, bus tickets, letters, photographs. Things you can't bear to throw away, but which pile up over the years, waiting for the inevitable. Most people never think about what's going to happen when they die. Who's going to read those letters of theirs, those notebooks, those diaries. Most people never think to destroy the things that might incriminate them. The dead are beyond embarrassment. But sometimes, something gets left behind that can affect the living.'

I tried to keep my voice level, but all the same, it wavered. I said: 'What have you got?'

'A letter,' he said. 'A letter written by you, Dave.'

I bit my lip. That letter. I think I'd always somehow known it would come back to haunt me, Mousey.

'What do you want?' I said at last.

Briefly, he outlined his plan. A final one-off payment, he said. Then, he'd be out of my life for good. I'd never hear from him again.

'You must think I'm stupid,' I said. 'This could go on forever.'

'No, it won't,' said your brother. 'You think I want to stay here? I've wanted to leave this armpit of a town ever since I learnt to walk. But I need more money for that. I don't want to have to come crawling back. Not here. Not ever.'

I thought about that for a moment. A part of me was angry and scared, but another part was grinning. Hadn't I wanted this, after all? A chance to meet your brother alone?

'All right,' I said. 'Where shall we meet?'

'Meet me by the canal bridge, tomorrow night at nine o'clock. I'll be driving. I'll park on the road. You'll be waiting on the bridge. I'll give you the package. You'll give me the cash. Then you wave bye-bye, and leave.'

I'd expected him to suggest a place like the café; somewhere safe. But he was getting arrogant. That was a mistake, I thought. Now he'd played into my hands. And the thought of meeting him on the bridge, in the place where Poodle had died, was too much for me to resist. At that time, there would be little risk of anyone disturbing us. He'd be alone, and vulnerable. I could take him easily. I knew from our games by the clay pits how sensitive he was to pain – or any form of violence. *Pathologically* sensitive, to the point of freezing up, of actually being unable to breathe at the sight of the mouse traps.

It was like a gift from the gods. Everything coming together at once. Unfinished business; loose ends; all the mess of the past seventeen years nicely, neatly swept away. Now I could see it, Mousey. A way of ridding myself, not of one, but two of my enemies. And all I had to do now was persuade Johnny to come and back me up, then to stand on the bridge at nine, waiting for my trap to close.

11

November 4th, 2005

I hadn't been to Eric's house for years: not since my mother died. And when his own mother started to show signs of encroaching dementia, I began keeping my distance, sensing that Eric wanted it so. He'd always been close to Margery; always the devoted son, and for over a decade, he'd managed to live in denial of her condition.

It had begun with the hoarding; a harmless habit at first, but which slowly became an obsession. Margery kept everything – correspondence, baby clothes, empty cigarette packs – packing them neatly into boxes, labelled in her old lady's hand and stored, first in the cellar, then under the roof, and then in every single room in the house, stacking them against the walls. Eric had tried to clear them out, but his mother's distress at his first attempt had ensured that there would be no second.

'She's just a bit set in her ways,' he would say. 'You've got to expect it, at her age.' But the fact that she was sixty-one – which seems no age at all to me now – did nothing to explain the stacks of boxes piled up in every room, or the fact that Margery would not allow strangers into the house – so that any repairs to the roof, the drains, the plumbing or the plasterwork had to be done by Eric himself, or risk a scene from his mother.

'Mother doesn't like change, that's all,' Eric used to tell me. He was no wizard at DIY, but managed to keep the house in shape – at least, until his mother's decline had forced him to bring in a carer. The first of many, as it turned out – Margery Scoones had hated them all, and unlike my own mother, who had been biddable in dementia, Margery was fiercely antagonistic; arguing that she didn't need help, accusing her carers of stealing from her; making up wildly improbable tales of abuse and even, on several occasions, actually *calling the police,* to report an intruder in her house.

Eric told me all this as we packed the boxes into his car, ready to drive them to the park. It was four thirty. The public would start to gather at six. Traditionally, the Malbry fire is always held on a Friday night, the closest day to November 5th. The bonfire begins at seven o'clock. At eight, there are the fireworks. But for now, there was no one, except for a few stalls setting up at a safe distance from the cordoned-off area around the unlit fire – Hook-a-Duck stands; coconut-shies; stalls selling toffee apples and gingerbread men. Funny, how these things never change. When we were boys, it was just the same.

Funny; I've always loved this time of year, and not just because Bonfire Night happens to fall on my birthday. At my age, I no longer celebrate the years that pass so quickly, but I've always loved the drama of the seasonal changing of the guard; the fallen leaves; the scent of smoke; the fires lit to the old gods. Of course, after what happened last year, you might have expected me to hate anything connected with bonfires, birthdays or fireworks. But strangely enough, last year's events seem even less real to me now; ghost stories told on an autumn night over hot ale and roast chestnuts.

'Thanks for doing this, Straits,' said Eric, as we stacked up the boxes around the pyre. They would burn, once it was lit. Most of the contents were paper.

'Think nothing of it,' I replied, secretly thinking of my knees. They haven't been good in the past year, and all this lifting and carrying wouldn't improve my joints a bit. Still, what price a friend, eh?

Eighty boxes later, my knees were feeling like broken glass, but at least the living room was clear. We'd made five runs to the bonfire by then. The clock on the mantelpiece said six fifteen.

'We'll not clear *all* the boxes tonight,' Eric said. 'But at last, I'm free.'

That was an odd thing for him to say. Eric is neither demonstrative, nor given to hyperbole. But losing a parent can be hard; even when the loss is marbled with relief.

'Sit down and have a drink,' I said. 'Then we can decide what to do with the rest of Margery's things.'

I have to say, I was surprised that he hadn't opened any of the boxes. Most of them had still been sealed, labelled in his mother's hand. I hoped he wouldn't one day regret the decision not to go through her effects.

'Not a chance,' he told me, when I happened to mention it. 'What would I want with old newspapers, or bank statements, or baby bootees?'

He was looking better now; we'd shared a bottle of claret, and now he lit a Gauloise, and handed me one. I knew he smoked, but he never did where people from work might see him. Eric, always wary of losing favour with the management, had long ago decided that smoking was bad for his career.

'You ought to have done the same,' he went on, taking a drag of his cigarette. 'Let the past stay in the past, instead of making a fool of yourself.'

'I assume you're talking about the Harry Clarke affair,' I said. I didn't want to argue with the old idiot, especially not in the current circumstances, but I couldn't let that pass unchallenged. 'Harry was innocent,' I said. 'That trial was a travesty.'

Eric made an impatient sound. 'He may not have *murdered* anyone. But as for the rest of it,' he said, '*everyone* thought there was something bizarre about the way he encouraged the boys in his form to hang around him all the time, even come to his house, for God's sake.'

'I never thought it was bizarre,' I said. 'He enjoyed their company. And boys would come to him for advice. There was nothing sexual there.'

'Don't be naïve,' Eric said. 'Charlie Nutter denied it because he was besotted with him. Harry denied it because he knew what would happen if he confessed. And let's face it, Straitley, it wouldn't be the first time a Master has taken advantage.'

I shook my head. 'Not Harry.'

He laughed. It wasn't a pleasant laugh – in fact, he sounded a little drunk. '*Not Harry*,' he repeated. 'God, what *was* it about that man that earned him so much loyalty? You think that because he was your friend, because you liked him, because you used to go to the pub with him, that you know all about him? How well do we *really* know our friends? How do we know what they're hiding? He was *fucking* the boy, Straits. Fourteen, and Harry was fucking him. That isn't consensual, you know. That's grooming. That's abuse. And *that's* the real reason they put him away. They knew he was dangerous.'

'Eric,' I said. 'This isn't you. This is your grief talking.'

I was trying to keep my cool, but in fact, he'd shocked me deeply. Not simply because of his use of a word I didn't even realize he knew, but because of the harshness in his voice. I'd always known he could be abrupt, but deep inside, I knew him to be a kind and sensitive person – at least, I *thought* I knew him – but as Eric had told me himself, how well do we ever know *anyone*?

Eric sighed. 'I'm sorry, Straits. It's just that I'm tired of hearing *Harry wouldn't do that. Harry was a decent man.* Even decent men make mistakes. Harry was no different.'

I looked at him. 'Did he tell you that? Because, unless he *told* you—'

'What? You think you're the only person Harry Clarke ever spoke to?' he said. 'You think you're the only person who got a little care package from beyond the grave? You got your gnome, the Chaplain got an orchid planter, or whatever the hell the Chaplain got, and I—' He broke off suddenly, turning away, and poured himself another drink. 'Anyway, it's over,' he said. 'Finally, it's over.'

I finished my Gauloise in silence. My heart was – not quite racing, but *lurching* in a peculiar way that made me feel a little sick. I suddenly remembered that I'd said I'd meet Winter after School. He had something to tell me, he'd said. Something about Charlie Nutter.

'Tell me, Eric,' I said at last. 'What did Harry leave you?'

He said: 'I never opened the box. Gloria must have put it away among all my mother's boxes.'

'Gloria?'

'The carer. Used to come in every day, make Mother's meals and tidy the house. Used to be a cleaner at St Oswald's, years ago. Maybe that's why Mother didn't seem to mind her as much as she did the others. Maybe she remembered her from the old days.'

I told you I was never quick. Always the plodder, Straitley. But now I could feel the tumblers of something falling into place; a giant, complex mechanism, groaning as it moved and turned. Gloria, with the Spanish eyes. A cleaner at St Oswald's. And Gloria's son, who wanted so badly to get away from Malbry. And Harry Clarke, who'd written to Eric just as he had written to me—

'But if Gloria put the box away among your mother's boxes—' I said.

I looked at my watch. It was past eight o'clock. The lurching sensation had become the rolling of a big ship – or a mighty Juggernaut, crushing everything in its path.

'Eric. Tell me you *didn't*,' I said, although I knew the answer. 'Tell me it's still in the house somewhere.'

Eric shrugged and turned away.

And now I could see it only too well. Eric, whose answer had always been to run away from an unpleasant reality, rather than look it in the eye, had (with my help) consigned Harry's last words – words that might have revealed the truth – to the municipal bonfire.

'Why did you do it?' I said at last. 'Eric, there might have been something in there that we could have used—'

'To clear Harry's name?' Eric gave a scornful laugh. 'Grow up, Straits, for God's sake. You always were such a bloody child. Dan Dare, and *Boy's Own Paper*. What, did you think you could solve the crime? Unmask the villain in the final act, then home in time for lemonade? What good did Harry's box do *you*? What did he leave you with but a *joke*?'

There was nothing more to say. I stood up and left without a word. Outside, the air was cool and sweet; and smelt of bonfires, and burning wood, and the bitter snap of fireworks.

Part Eight

Fides punica.
(Cicero)

1

November 4th, 2005

Mischief Night, it used to be called. The day before my birthday. Traditionally, a time put by for schoolboy pranks, and practical jokes, and the settling of scores. How many times did Eric and I fling eggs at the door of a Master's house, or hang a fish from a washing-line, or leave a turd on the doormat?

But Mischief Night is a thing of the past. Nowadays, the youngsters favour a peculiarly Americanized version of Hallowe'en, moving in gangs from door to door, demanding sweets with menaces. In the old days, Hallowe'en was the time the dead broke free. The gifts were meant to placate them; to stop them consuming the living. As I grow older, I realize how easy it is to be consumed. The dead walk in November, and they are not always kind.

We all have our ghosts. Those people we may have loved – or not, but for whom we feel responsible. My parents. Harry Clarke. Colin Knight. Lee Bagshot. And now, Charlie Nutter, whose middle name – Wenceslas – he managed to hide so completely from both his peers and his Masters during his time at St Oswald's, and whose ghost still appears as that thin, nervous boy I overlooked so easily—

And Eric. Dear old Eric Scoones, companion of my schooldays. Eric who has always been there – or at least, somewhere nearby. Eric, who, if not *lovable*, was always so *predictable*: a part of my life, just as he was always a part of St Oswald's. Why was Eric so quick to believe that Harry Clarke was guilty? What did he know – and *how* did he know? Could Harry *himself* have told him?

I did not go home straight away. Instead, I went to Winter's house. That sense of *coming together*, of tumblers dropping into place, was getting stronger all the time. Eric's words had disturbed me. His belief that Harry was guilty had been upsetting enough, but more so was the fact that he had wilfully destroyed evidence – evidence that might have helped to reinstate Harry's memory. My only hope was that Gloria might have seen something. Could it be that, in cleaning the house, *she* had looked into Harry's box? Had she mentioned it to her son? And could all this be connected with the death of Charlie Nutter?

The lights were on in Winter's house. I opened the gate, and knocked on the door. After a moment, it opened, and Gloria's face appeared in the gap. She looked both angry and a little harassed – of course, I knew her aversion to juvenile trick-or-treaters.

'Mrs Winter, good evening—'

'*What?*' she said. 'I'm not buying anything, and you're too bloody old for treats.' Then she looked again, and said: 'Mr *Straitley*? From the Grammar School?'

I nodded. 'Hello, Gloria.'

'Oh.' She seemed to hesitate. 'Come in.' I followed her into the hall, a shrine to a number of china dogs. 'What do you want, Mr Straitley?'

'I wondered if I might have a word with your son.'

Now she was looking confused. She said: 'Why? What's he done now?'

I explained that Gloria's son had been helping me with my computer skills. 'Outside his *other* duties, of course.'

Gloria looked no less confused. 'What duties? You mean at the *school*?'

And now, I suddenly realized that Gloria had no idea where her son worked, or what he did. Had he never told her? Was he ashamed of his menial role?

I said: 'We met at the Scholar. I happened to mention the challenges of being a veteran Master, faced with the march of Progress in all its electronic forms. He offered to give me a helping hand in embracing information technology.'

Gloria seemed to relax at that. She had always had a sharp tongue, but now *everything* about her was sharp; her nose; her chin; her voice, and, of course, those dark and still-expressive eyes.

'Oh, yes, the Scholar,' she said. 'He sometimes goes there after work. All hours they keep him at that bloody hospital.'

I made no comment at that, but filed away the information for later. I knew my co-conspirator enjoyed reinventing himself online, but lying to his mother seemed to be a different category of reinvention. Once more, I reminded myself that I knew very little about him, except for what he has told me – which may or may not be the truth—

'Anyway, he's out,' she said. 'What did you want him for, anyway?'

I said: 'It's not important. Unless—' I paused for a moment. 'I heard that you'd been caring for Margery Scoones up until her death.'

Gloria gave me a sharp look. 'Caring? Well, you could call it that. Mostly it was watching TV and listening to her talk rubbish. Cleaning up, if she let me. Though with them bloody boxes everywhere, all over the house—'

'One of those boxes came from – a very dear friend of mine,' I said. 'He left the contents to Mr Scoones – with a letter, I believe. I wondered if you'd come across that letter, maybe by accident.'

I was watching her carefully, on the alert for signs of unease. She held my gaze – looking, if anything, more aggressive than ever.

'What if I did?' she said at last.

I said: 'Eric Scoones was very upset. He accidentally burnt the box while he was burning Margery's things. I was hoping perhaps the letter had escaped. The last words of an old friend – I hoped perhaps you'd put it away. Put it in a safe place.'

Gloria's gaze did not flicker. 'No. I didn't tidy anything.'

'If only you knew where it was,' I said, 'Eric and I would be grateful. Certainly there'd be a reward. Probably a substantial one.'

'Sorry,' she said. 'I've not seen it.'

A long career in finding out young miscreants has made me adept at eliciting confessions. Unlike the lawmen of the real world, in which a suspect is deemed to be innocent until proven otherwise, we of St Oswald's always begin an interrogation with an apparent assumption of guilt, with which we confront the suspect in the hope that he will confess. As in certain martial arts, I find the resulting battle of wills is generally won or lost within the first few seconds of engagement, although I myself have been known to break a schoolboy's defences with a single, piercing glance.

It's a game of bluff, of course; but I am rather good at it. And although my last adversary had proved herself to be tough as nails, I left the house certain of two things. One: that letter to Eric contained something that I needed to know, and two: for all her assurances, Gloria Winter was lying.

2

November 4th, 2005

Your brother was late. It was 9.05. I'd almost given up on him. Some people just aren't reliable; or maybe they're inconsiderate. In any case, Mousey, it was rude; and if I'd not already decided to put him down, I think that would have clinched it.

He'd parked his car next to Goldie's. He got out and looked around. I could sense his caution; like a rat sensing danger, but hungry for the food in the trap. Just how hungry *was* he? I thought. And just how far would Goldie go?

Your brother was wearing a knitted cap and his dark-blue parka. *He must be older than I am,* I thought, *but still he looks younger and fitter*. Still, I didn't think he'd fight back. He never did in the old days.

He said: 'Did you bring the money?'

I nodded. Harrington just stared at him with a look of hatred. Of course, I knew he'd be furious. A menial – an *inferior* – holding us to ransom like that over something that happened so long ago. And what did he have on us?

Still, Mousey, who cared? They'd both be dead by nine fifteen.

3

November 4th, 2005

By the time I got to the end of Dog Lane, it was already a quarter to nine. The porch light was on in front of my house, and I could see a figure in a blue overcoat standing by the front door. Relief made me reckless.

'Mr Winter!' I called. 'I'm so—'

He turned; and in the glow of the lamp, I saw a familiar profile. *Not* Mr Winter, as I'd supposed, but the neat, sharp features of Dr Devine, now suffused with triumph.

'I knew it!' he said, as I approached. 'I knew you couldn't have moved those boards without the aid of an accomplice. What are you up to now, eh? And how did you talk him into it?'

I sighed and took out the front-door key. 'Not now, please, Devine,' I said. 'I've had a very tiring day. I've been helping Eric sort out some of poor Margery's things.'

The nose twitched. 'Ah, yes,' said Devine. 'I expect the fellow's upset.'

I thought his voice was rather cold – for reasons that have more to do with ambition than personality, Dr Devine and

Eric Scoones have never been the best of friends. Now, his lack of sympathy for a grieving colleague reminded me of why I disliked the man.

I opened the door, and he followed me, unasked, into the front hall. That, I thought, was bordering on rude, and rudeness, whatever his other faults, was not Devine's *modus operandi* – but for the moment, I refrained from comment. He was not in the habit of making calls, and I guessed he had a reason, which he would doubtless divulge, given time.

The central heating hadn't come on, and the house smelt vaguely damp. I took off my coat, lit the fire, turned – then saw Devine, still by the door, holding a piece of paper.

'This was in your letterbox,' he said. 'It looks like a note of some kind.'

I took the note, which was written on the back of a folded envelope. 'Of course it's a note,' I said crossly. 'And don't even *try* to pretend you haven't already looked at it. I don't know why you're suddenly so interested in my comings and goings. Or is this all just a very dull form of German trick-or-treating?'

'Straitley, read the note,' said Devine.

I unfolded the envelope. The note was only a few lines long; the writing small and even.

Dear Mr Straitley,

I'm sorry I wasn't able to speak with you this evening. I'm setting off on a trip tonight, and I was hoping to talk to you first. You've always been polite to me – which is more than I can say for anyone else on the staff. In fact, working with you has almost made my time at St Oswald's seem worthwhile.

I'll be at the canal bridge at 9.00. Be there if you want to know more. But do remember what Sophocles said: 'What a terrible thing is wisdom, when it brings no profit to the wise.' If, on reflection, you'd rather not know, I'll completely understand.

Sincerely,

B. B. Winter

I looked at Devine. 'What time is it?'

He checked his watch. 'It's ten to nine. But you're not really planning to go, are you? And on the basis of what, exactly? A note on the back of an envelope, in the middle of the night?'

'Hardly the middle of the night,' I protested.

Dr Devine just looked at me.

'It's complicated,' I told him.

Once more Devine just looked at me. I recognized an ancient St Oswald's Master's technique I often used with the Lower School.

'And *personal*,' I added, with a hint of censure.

Devine gave an expressive sniff. 'Oh, don't be so dramatic,' he said. 'How can you possibly think I don't know how you've been spending the past few weeks? I mean, you're hardly subtle. First that ridiculous garden gnome, and then all the hints about Harry Clarke, not to mention the Honours Boards, and creeping around after the Head. What did you think you were doing, eh? You might as well have been carrying a sign saying: *Rebellion in Progress*.'

I said: 'Bob Strange has cameras hidden all over the School, you know.'

'Of course I know,' said Dr Devine. 'I'm Health & Safety Officer.'

For a moment I was robbed of speech. 'You *knew*?' I said.

He had the grace to look embarrassed. 'I saw Jimmy checking the cables,' he said. 'Of course I asked Bob about it.' He gave another sniff, and I sensed that he was torn between his loyalty to the management and his personal sense of propriety.

'Bob explained,' Devine went on. 'He said it was because of last year. Said having cameras in School might have averted a tragedy. Told me if I let people know, I might be in breach of contract. The bastard. As if I would—'

I was impressed. In thirty-four years, I have never heard Dr Devine refer to a senior colleague in such unbridled terms. I thought back to the first day of term, and the altercation I'd overheard between them. *Roy Straitley knows—*

Roy Straitley knows what? Knows what he owes to St Oswald's? Knows how the management has failed in its duty towards the staff? Knows how the likes of Bob Strange will always manage to serve themselves?

'What I'm saying is,' said Devine, 'you've been keeping tabs on the Head. And if there *is* a rebellion, I want to be part of it.'

I have to say, I was impressed. In all my years at St Oswald's, I'd never seen Devine like this. It occurred to me that for thirty-four years I actually might have misjudged the man, and for a moment I almost considered filling him in on Winter's research. Then I remembered his lack of support, both for Harry, during the trial, and now, for poor, grieving Eric, and decided I was better alone. Besides, I thought, I had nothing to lose. Dr Devine still had a career. And what was the point in risking that, on a simple intuition?

'Dr Devine. I have to go,' I said, reaching for my coat. Ten minutes' walk along the canal – ten minutes' *run* – and I could be there in time.

The tumblers were falling faster now. Harry's letter to Eric. Gloria's denial of ever having seen it – even with the promise of a significant reward. Winter's mysterious double life. Harrington's expression when I saw him in the Scholar. And Eric saying: *How well do we really know our friends? How do we know what they're hiding?*

'You're not going there alone,' said Devine. 'Not after what happened last year.'

I shrugged. I suppose he had a point – last year's Bonfire Night brought not only gunpowder, treason and plot, but also the murder of Colin Knight, a near-fatal stabbing, and, of course, that ill-timed heart attack, smugly described by my doctor as 'your body's last warning to lay off the pies, the pasties, the cheese and the Gauloises'.

I said: 'Oh, lightning never strikes in the same place twice, Devine.'

He huffed. 'Statistically incorrect. In fact, *this* kind of lightning is likely to strike whenever a silly old fool sticks his neck out above the parapet.'

I ignored him and opened the door. I supposed the man was right, but I had no time to argue the point. I had no idea how long Winter would wait for me on the canal bridge. But whatever he knew, *I* wanted to hear, regardless of those tumblers dropping relentlessly in my head.

A firework rose from Malbry Park like flowers from a magician's hat; a green chrysanthemum; then a blue. A second later, I heard the sound; that faint, percussive popping. What did Winter have to say? Why had he suggested the bridge? And what did he mean, quoting Sophocles when he *knew* I was desperate for answers?

I left Devine in the doorway, not even pausing to lock the door. He started to call after me—

'Straitley! Don't be a damn fool! Straitley! I need to talk to you!'

But there was no time to hear him now. All I could think of was Winter, whose mother had cared for Margery Scoones, and Eric, who had burnt Harry's box. Could Eric have known something, back then, that might have affected the trial? Could he now, for the sake of ambition, be hiding something that could incriminate Johnny Harrington?

Reaching Dog Lane, I started to run, ignoring Devine's cries of protest. Another hatful of flowers bloomed, and I forced myself to increase the pace. This is my favourite time of year – this time of fire and falling leaves – and with my heart in its fragile state, I cannot be sure if I will see another.

But tonight was no time for fireworks. Tonight there was no time for doubt; or friendships; or nostalgia. Tonight, I needed answers. Tonight was a night for dark thoughts, dark deeds; and memories of lost boys – Scoones and Straits, and Colin Knight; and Charlie Nutter, who was one of ours, and Lee Bagshot, who was not; all of them victims, sacrificed to the spirit of dark, lonely water.

4

November 4th, 2005, 21.03

I ran from Dog Lane to the canal. Well, I did my best to run. In fact, I probably looked and sounded like one of those zombies from the old films: wheezing and shambling along the canal-side in the darkness.

If there were ghosts, I told myself, then surely this was where they should be. Perhaps the ghost of Lee Bagshot – drowned, and whose injuries, according to the coroner, *might* have been the result of a blow, or might have simply been caused by the fall. And Charlie Nutter, also drowned, albeit in three feet of water. And now something inside me protested, in the voice of Lady Bracknell: *To lose one boy by drowning may be considered a misfortune. To lose two boys, however, begins to look like—*

Murder?

I could see the canal bridge now; the place where Charlie Nutter died. There's a street-lamp on the opposite side, one of the few remaining white ones. Its light illuminated the bridge and glazed the murky water. The path on which I stood was dark: on this side of the canal I could not be seen by anyone. For a moment, I stopped, and saw two men standing on the bridge. But neither man was Winter. One was Johnny Harrington. The other was David Spikely.

21.06

The last time I'd seen Spikely, he was twenty-one, and looked forty. Now he is almost forty, and looks far younger than he did then. His hair has grown back; he looks fit and relaxed, and he has lost a great deal of weight. Even so, I knew him at once. Something in his walk, perhaps. Or perhaps it is simply the fact that, although he may forget any number of other things – his glasses, overdue library books – a St Oswald's Master never forgets a boy for whom he was once in charge.

I pressed my back into the hedge that runs alongside the bridle path. A weeping willow, leafless now, but trailing a curtain of pale fronds, served as additional camouflage. If I stayed without moving, I could remain unseen. Through the smoke of Bonfire Night, I could smell the sleeping canal; that dank and somehow melancholy scent of abandoned things left to decompose. Small sounds came from the hedge at my back; maybe a mouse or a small bird.

I listened: Spikely and Harrington were clearly awaiting someone. They stood there side by side on the bridge, Harrington looking impatient, Spikely in a gabardine coat, like a gentleman spy from a forties *film noir*. Neither spoke, and I noticed that Spikely was carrying a sports bag, much of the kind that St Oswald's boys use to carry their schoolbooks.

Was this what Winter had meant me to see? Was it an exchange of some sort? Or were they waiting for someone else with whom to conduct their business? There came the sound of a car on the road. Then, headlights swept the bridle path, and for a moment I was blind, caught like a moth in the full beam. The two men had their backs towards me, otherwise I would have been seen. But my two ex-pupils were too preoccupied by the arrival of the car to look at the path behind them; and when they turned back, the car was parked, its headlights off, and I was in darkness once more.

But I had recognized the car. I'd seen it only the other day, outside a house in White City. Most recently (and memorably) it had been used by the perpetrators of the theft of a hundred and fifty Honours Boards—

It was Winter's blue Peugeot.

21.08

Winter got out of the little car and stepped on to the canal bridge. For a moment I thought he looked my way, and I wondered if he had seen me. Should I stay hidden, or show myself? I started to move forward, but Winter gave a shake of his head. It might have been a coincidence – the turn of his face against the light – but it made me think twice, and I remained hidden in the shadows.

Clearly, Winter had a plan that involved my staying hidden there – to overhear, or to intervene? There was no way of knowing. What was the significance of the sports bag, and why had he said he was leaving? I have to say, I was feeling a little uncertain about Winter. The fact that he'd kept Nutter's death from me; his furtive, evasive manner – not to mention the letter, and the fact that he'd told me his mother was dead – well, I've been a Master for far too long, and watched too many boys attempt to get away with murder to fail to see the potential for deviousness in my young friend. And yet, I believed he was trying to help; that perhaps against his instincts, he might be putting himself at risk.

I heard him speak – his voice was low, but I heard something about money. Water affects acoustics, and the presence of the nearby canal, combined with the smoke of the bonfires, created a baffle of sound that meant I had some trouble hearing. Harrington, who was standing as rigidly as a shop mannequin, said something sharp and percussive, the sound slapping against the water. Then I heard Winter's soft reply, but not the actual words he spoke.

I began to edge a little closer to the men on the footbridge, keeping near the hawthorn hedge and trying not to catch the light. My coat was dark; and I blessed the fact that I had chosen to wear a hat. The brim was wide enough to hide the pale blur of my features; I thought that if I moved slowly enough, I might be able to come quite close without attracting attention.

Sixty feet. Fifty feet. Now I was forty feet away, and I could hear them clearly . . .

21.09

'You little shit,' Johnny said. 'You think you'll get away with this? You're lucky we haven't called the police.'

Your brother smiled. 'Just give me the cash. And thank your stars you're dealing with me. It could have been my mother.' (Oh, Mousey. I had to laugh. Piggy was still afraid of his ma!) 'My mother's no stranger to blackmail,' he said. 'And she would *never* have let you go.'

I shrugged. Piggy's ma was irrelevant. I'd deal with her later, if necessary. I said: 'So what have you got for me?'

He shook his head. 'The bag, please.' Johnny handed it over. Then your brother reached into his coat and took out a handwritten envelope. Even in that troubled light, I recognized the writing.

I've always had nice handwriting. Small, and round, and childlike. I always used a Waterman pen, with a nib that was made of real gold. And I'd taken a great deal of trouble that day, starting the letter again twice because my hand was shaking.

I took the letter. Then I said: 'Hey, wait a minute. What's that? I thought I saw something over there.'

Your brother turned instinctively. I looked at Johnny. Now was the time. From under his coat he took out an object – something I'd told him to bring along. It was an old St Oswald's rounders bat; not too large, but enough for the job.

'Look! There's someone in the trees!'

Now was the time to do it, I knew. Your brother was looking down the path. But Johnny had frozen. His face was white. Of course, I'd known that when it came to action, rather than words, he'd fold. And he had. Of course he had. Typical Goldie. All talk, and no guts.

Your brother was still looking into the trees.

I can't, mouthed Johnny, and gave me the bat.

And so I raised it, and swung it hard—

21.10

I understood what was happening just seconds too late to intervene. Winter was looking over the bridge. He seemed to be looking straight at me. Behind him were Spikely and Harrington. Then, it all happened so fast that, even if my knee had not cramped agonizingly as I moved, the whole thing would have been over before I could reach the footbridge.

I couldn't quite see the object Spikely was holding in his hands. It looked like some kind of club, I thought; short; round-ended; easy to use. And Winter was right there in his sights—

There was no time to warn him. My brain had barely any time to process what I was seeing. Later, I saw it, in my mind's eye, slowed down to a comprehensible speed, but by then it was over, at least everything bar the shouting.

Spikely raised the rounders bat. Harrington stood watching. Winter, on the parapet, was totally unprepared for the blow. As the bat swung, he half turned; saw the sudden movement and flinched away; but if Spikely had hit him then, he would have died, or been badly hurt – ready for Spikely to finish the job.

I saw it all in my mind's eye before my voice unloosed its cry. I heard the sickening sound of the blow, saw the man fall to his knees—

But Winter was not Spikely's target. Instead, as Winter turned, so did he, and smashed the polished piece of wood straight into Harrington's temple—

21.11

That was when my paralysis broke. I gave a shout – and a good one, too, in my loudest Bell Tower voice – and started to run towards the bridge. My foot slipped on the muddy path; my knee cramped again in agony. I lurched painfully to the side, and the invisible finger started to play a solo – tuba, I think, or a saxophone – along the buttons of my coat.

Meanwhile, on the canal bridge, Harrington had fallen, face-down. Winter, too, had dropped to his knees, and I thought somehow he had been hit. But as I reached the bridge, I saw that Winter was gasping for breath, as if he were having an asthma attack—

I used to have a boy like that in my form, many, many years ago; a boy of such sensitivity that he would suffer panic attacks at the sight of violence. Rugby matches; playground fights; and once, a particularly bloody staging of *Coriolanus*, during which he became so upset that he had to leave the theatre. The Old Head would have caned him for that, having no patience with what he called the *Sensitive Brigade*, but I was more sympathetic, and I'd managed to fix things somehow. That boy was Joseph Apple, and he ended badly. But he was one of mine, nevertheless, as was Johnny Harrington, and, whatever our differences – the Honours Boards, the curriculum, even Harry's memorial – I'm glad to say that my instincts remained; to intervene in defence of my boys.

With Winter helpless on his knees, it would have been easy for Spikely to finish the job he had started. But Spikely hadn't expected to see me lumbering on to the footbridge, waving my arms (as advised to do in the presence of wild animals) and shouting at the top of my voice:

'Spikely! Stop that, right now!'

5

November 4th, 2005, 21.12

There's something about a master's voice that never loses its potency. That voice took me back to St Oswald's almost as if I'd never left; the smell of polish and chalk dust; the sunlight shining down South Stair; the scent of the geraniums under the glass on the window ledge in Harry's room.

Old Mr Straitley got old, Mousey. I don't believe he ever looked young. Now he's fat and raddled and slow; not so much a lion as an elephant; small-eyed, angry, ready to charge. Another moment, Mousey, and I could have finished your brother. He was right there, at my feet. I could taste the victory. But Straitley's presence changed all that. I hadn't expected a witness. And yet, there seemed to me to be a kind of poetry in his being there; as if I'd been waiting for this all along; the final page in the diary.

'Mr Straitley. You don't look too well. You ought to take better care of yourself.'

That was true; he looked awful. Mud on his trousers; red in the face; panting like a fat dog. If only I could get close, I thought, then maybe I could use the bat. On the other hand, perhaps the best thing to do was to bide my time, then take him by surprise and maybe push him over the parapet. Besides, I was curious. What did he know? What had your brother told him?

He looked at me with those elephant eyes. 'One death may seem like an accident,' he said. 'But three starts to look like murder. Do you think they'll believe you this time? Or will you accuse someone else again, the way you did with Harry?'

I laughed. Of course, he has no idea. How could he, when I never told anyone, not even you? But Straitley went on, with furrowed brow, his voice cracked with emotion.

'Why did you do it, Spikely?' he said. 'Harry was a good man. Harry always stood up for you.'

I looked at him. He was breathless now, his eyes all bloodshot with anger. For a moment I felt sorry for him; for all his grief and outrage. It made him more human to me, somehow. It made me almost like him.

'But Harry *didn't* stand up for me,' I said. 'He didn't help me at all. I went to him with a secret – something I'd never told anyone. Something so bad it was eating me up, eating me from the inside. I trusted him. I thought he could help. And instead, do you know what he did?'

He sent me to the Chaplain. Who went right back to Mr Scoones. Because I had a problem, he said. The same one I'd had at Netherton Green. Getting too close to my teachers, he said. Day-dreaming. Making things up.

'Harry was so busy,' I said. 'He said I should talk to the Chaplain. Harry couldn't see beyond Harry and Charlie. His special boy. And so I went to the Chaplain and – guess what? The Chaplain didn't believe me.'

His hand on my leg. His breath on my neck. His hand pressing down on my shoulder. A square of sunshine on the floor, all filled with little motes of dust. The sound of his breathing, muffled by the sound of the record playing. Something by Edith Piaf, I think. Mr Scoones loved Edith Piaf. And he smelt of Gauloises and aftershave, and something bitter and soapy and sour, and when he was done he stood up and said: 'Good boy. Good boy.'

'Harry was a decent man. He didn't deserve what happened to him. What *you* allowed to happen.'

Poor Straitley. Even a decent man can hide a world of darkness inside. I don't suppose he believed me. Why did I even want him to?

'I was a child,' I told him. 'I didn't deserve what happened to *me*.'

Behind me, your brother was stirring. The panic attack – if that's what it was – seemed to be receding.

I glanced at Straitley. I realized that I'd let him distract me. Your brother was trying to stand up – and if he did, my advantage was gone. I raised the rounders bat again, and braced myself for the killing blow.

'Put the bat down, Spikely.'

Straitley sounded old, and scared. Funny to think I'd been scared of *him*. Now I know better. I'm in control. And with your brother out of the way, I thought I could handle Straitley. I might not even kill him, I thought. It would be a case of my word against his – the word of a man who, everyone knew, detested Johnny Harrington . . .

'You followed him here,' I told him. 'You'd been stalking him for weeks. You still believed he lied to the court over the Harry Clarke affair. You'd picked up the rounders bat from school. You told yourself it was just in case. But Harrington wouldn't listen. You snapped. And then, when Winter came along, you had to deal with him, too.'

'Don't be ridiculous,' Straitley said. 'Put down the weapon, and then we'll talk.'

It's funny, how you never stop being a schoolboy, somehow. Faced with my old teacher's wrath, I almost wanted to obey.

'I saw it all from the path,' I went on. 'You were completely out of control. As part of my work with Survivors, I've seen quite a number of instances of people suffering fugue states. You didn't know what you were doing, sir. I'm happy to say that under oath.'

His hand on my leg. My eyes on the wall. Edith Piaf, singing 'Hymne à l'Amour'. The scent of grass and chalk dust. The way his hand moved up my thigh. His breath on my hair. The music. And all the time, the knowledge that if it had been Harry, it wouldn't have been anything to be scared of; that if it had been Harry, then maybe I would have wanted it—

'Spikely. Put down the weapon.' I'd been so lost in memory that for a moment I barely registered that this time, the voice was *behind* me. Another voice from St Oswald's past, crisp and full of authority. 'Put down the weapon, Spikely,' it said. 'Then turn slowly, to face me. Mr Straitley may have come unprepared, but I am both armed and dangerous.'

I turned then, to see a figure there, on the other side of the bridge. A man in a dark-blue overcoat, pointing a blunt-nosed object wrapped in a St Oswald's scarf. For a moment I didn't recognize him. He'd never taught me as a boy. But then I saw that nose of his—

It was Dr Sourgrape Devine.

6

November 4th, 2005, 21.15

He must have taken the main road. In any case, I never saw him. And frankly, seeing him standing there like Horatio on the bridge, I almost doubted my sanity. Thirty-four years a Master, and I thought that I was beyond surprise. As it happens, that was because I had never before witnessed Devine in this new, swashbuckling role, brandishing a blunderbuss, or whatever it was that he had concealed behind his St Oswald's muffler—

'*Devinus, ex machina*?' I said.

Dr Devine gave me one of his looks. 'This is no time for humour, Straitley,' he said, with the look of a man exercising tremendous restraint. 'Now, Mr Spikely, put that down, and let's discuss this reasonably.'

Winter had got to his feet during Devine's intervention. Now, he stood, looking watchful, as Spikely put down the rounders bat. Harrington was moving; I felt an unexpected relief. That, too, surprised me: I had not thought it in me to care as fervently about his well-being.

'Harrington needs help,' I said. 'We need to get to the hospital.'

Spikely gave a dry laugh. 'I thought you hated Harrington.'

'He was one of my boys,' I said. 'As are you, Mr Spikely. Now give me Harry's letter, and we can go our separate ways.'

21.16

One of my boys. I had to laugh. 'You're not *in loco parentis.* Your authority over me ended in 1982.'

Mr Straitley shook his head. 'Nothing ended. You're dragging it still. Whatever this is, you can't fight it. It comes from a place inside you, which means that wherever you go, it goes too. Horace said it best of all—'

'*Caelum non animum mutant, qui trans mare currant.* They change the sky, not their souls, that run across the ocean.'

Straitley raised an eyebrow. 'It's *currunt,* Spikely, not *currant.* Curr*ant* is what you're likely to find in a slice of Christmas cake.'

I had to smile. He hasn't changed. Oddly enough, his silly joke didn't annoy me as much as it might have done when I was a boy.

On the other side of the bridge, Dr Devine was blocking my way. His arrival had startled me, but now I could see that what I'd taken to be some kind of firearm was just a blunt object, wrapped in a scarf, in the tradition of boys everywhere trying to look like gangsters.

I said: 'I never liked you, sir.'

'I know,' said Mr Straitley. 'Now give me Harry's letter.'

I shrugged and handed it over. Straitley glanced down at the envelope. For a moment I saw his expression; his sudden look of blank surprise, as if he'd been expecting to see someone else's writing.

It was time to go, I thought. Johnny may not die, of course. But even if he doesn't, I am no longer safe in Malbry. One witness I could have dealt with. But three, including Winter—

My car was parked outside my house. Ten minutes to collect my things; an hour to drive to the airport. Could I make it? Probably. Straitley was quite right, I knew. A change of sky isn't everything. But it's something. Isn't it?

I picked up the sports bag and made for the road, where Dr Devine was still covering me. Now that I was close to him, I could see that the object under the scarf was a brightly painted garden gnome, tucked under his elbow.

I should have known it was a bluff. But isn't that what being a teacher's about? A weird kind of voodoo to make kids believe that you're not entirely powerless? He raised the gnome as I approached, but I walked past him without a word, then turned around to face them both. They already looked very far away, lost in the mists of memory.

And now I could see them clearly at last; Mr Straitley and Dr Devine. They'd moved closer together, as if for reassurance. Dr Devine was holding the gnome; Straitley was holding the letter. And suddenly, I realized that the giants I'd feared as a boy looked like Ratty and Mr Toad from *The Wind in the Willows*; just two old men on an autumn night, messing about on the river.

7

November 4th, 2005

Perhaps we should have stopped him, I thought. A citizen's arrest, or some kind of a rugby tackle. But I was never a rugby man, and Devine, in spite of having proved himself unexpectedly resourceful in the matter of the gnome, was hardly a man of action.

'Why the gnome?' I said to him now. 'Any blunt instrument would have sufficed.'

'It was the first thing I saw,' said Devine, rather crossly. 'You'd run off to God knows where. The door was wide open. I went in to look for a walking stick—'

'You left my door wide open?'

'Of course not,' said Devine. High emotion, combined with the cold, had turned his nose a tremulous shade of coral-pink. 'But I could hardly let you go running off into the night without providing back-up.'

I was moved. 'Why, Sourgrape – I had no idea you cared.'

'Don't be ridiculous, Straitley.'

'Mr Straitley? Are you all right?' That was Winter, looking concerned. I suppose that both of us were looking less than wholesome. Devine looked as if he'd given blood, and I was breathing heavily. The invisible finger had ceased to dance its cakewalk on my lower ribs, but I'd lost my hat somewhere by the canal, and my hair (which needs cutting) was in my eyes and stuck to my damp forehead.

'Never better, thank you,' I said.

Devine gave a derisive sniff.

Beside me, Harrington stirred again. I'd almost forgotten he was there. I could hear his breathing now, almost as laboured as my own. I bent down to examine him – he was still only half-conscious, and there was rather a lot of blood.

'Harrington needs a doctor,' I said.

'What about Spikely?' said Devine.

'We'll call the police from the hospital. Here, help me get Harrington into Mr Winter's car.'

The next few hours were a blur. Triage; nurses; paperwork; Harrington's wife, looking stunned at the news. Winter said I'd had a shock; told them about my heart condition; insisted someone examined me while they were dealing with Harrington. Meanwhile, Dr Devine remained, in spite of my fervent protests (the garden gnome tucked under his arm), like a reluctant sentinel.

Finally, there was nothing to do but await the arrival of the police. They'd given us a little room in which to recover and gather our thoughts. Winter was looking uncomfortable, repeatedly checking his watch, while Dr Devine sipped at a cup of lukewarm hospital coffee.

Until that moment, there had been no time to inspect the letter. Or maybe I had not *wanted* to: already those tumblers were falling, inexorably, into place. And I was so tired; I wanted to sleep till the next millennium.

What a terrible thing is wisdom, when it brings no profit to the wise! Winter must have known from the start the quarry we were hunting. And he had tried to warn me against pursuing it too ardently, for fear that, like the Manitou, it would turn and tear me apart.

He saw me holding the envelope. An envelope of cheap blue bond, of the kind that Harry had used, the ink a little faded with time, and yet still perfectly legible. But the handwriting wasn't Harry's. I'd so assumed that it would be that I almost didn't recognize the childish, neatly lettered script. But I knew that writing very well. I'd marked his books too many times to fail to know it now. But what had Johnny Harrington to do with such a letter? And why would the young David Spikely have been writing to Eric Scoones?

'My mother found it,' Winter said. 'Of course, she knew what it was from the start. I told you she was no stranger to blackmail. She tried to find out what he was worth: what she could get away with. Spikely had been cashing in ever since the Clarke affair. Ma didn't see why she should have to clean old people's houses when there was a better way. She got me to investigate. It tied in with what I was doing for you. And finally, I began to see a means of getting away from her.'

I took a painful breath. 'I see.'

And yes, I *did*. I saw it now. The tumblers had all fallen silent. Eric's reluctance to testify during the Harry Clarke affair; his seven-year absence from St Oswald's immediately after the trial. His destruction of Harry's box; his decision to retire; even his words to me that night: *How well do we* really *know our friends? How do we know what they're hiding?*

'I'll get you a cup of tea,' Winter said. I could see from his face that he was worried. He left me alone with Dr Devine, still sitting stiffly in his chair, with Harry's gnome under his arm.

'Don't read it, Straitley,' he advised. 'What use could it be, after all this time?'

I started to explain. The gnome looked at me satirically. 'If we could prove that Harrington lied – that someone *else* abused Spikely – then maybe at last we could clear Harry's name. Harry could have his memorial.'

'And then what? Get Eric arrested?'

I shook my head. 'That doesn't mean—'

'Listen to me, Straitley,' he said. 'Think of what it would entail. Another scandal at St Oswald's. The Head accused of conspiracy. Another member of staff accused. The whole of that old story dragged up as if it happened yesterday. And Eric's retiring. He said so himself. Besides—' The nose twitched fretfully. 'Besides, it never happened again. Harry Clarke saw to that.'

'Harry?'

He nodded. 'Oh yes, Harry knew. Seems young Spikely confided in him. Of course, he couldn't tell the *boy*, but he dealt with it, in his own way.' Devine saw me staring, and bridled a little. 'Oh, don't look at me like that,' he said. 'Surely you must have suspected. I mean, you two were such old friends—'

'Never,' I said blankly.

My head had suddenly started to ache; my eyes were streaming. I reached for my pocket handkerchief, and found instead the conker I'd put there several weeks ago; shiny then, and glossy brown, now shrivelled to a chrysalis. I haven't played conkers in fifty years. And yet I still collect them, just as we did when we were boys, in the old days of St Oswald's.

'Did you ever play conkers, Devine? I mean, when you were a schoolboy?'

He raised his nose superciliously. 'I was Junior Champion,' he said. 'Both in Lower and Middle School.'

I have to say, I found it hard to imagine Devine playing conkers. But that was all so long ago. So much water under the bridge. David Spikely *had* been abused. All the experts said so. Could Eric Scoones have been the one? Could he have hidden this all these years?

Once more I looked at the envelope. My head was sore. The cheap blue paper tore in my hand as I fumbled it open. And in all the drama, we found that Winter had quietly slipped away, and when I looked in the envelope, I found that it was empty.

8

November 4th, 2005

Dear Mousey,

I palmed the letter, of course. I couldn't let them read it. Not because it incriminates me; I just couldn't bear their pity. I want them to remember me as something more than that sad little boy who killed things because he was afraid to live. I want them to be full of hate, and disbelief, and wonder. I want them to remember me as more than just a survivor.

I read the letter. It wasn't long. But even so, I remembered it. I remembered every word; each one chosen as carefully as in a Latin translation. *He'll read it over breakfast,* I thought to myself as I wrote it out. *He'll read it, and he'll find me. He'll find me, and he'll do it again.* And that brought it back; the fear of him; the dreadful, paralysing fear that only one thing could exorcize.

October 15th, 1989
Dear Mr Scoones,

It's been a while. I don't suppose you remember me. Even when I was a boy, I was nothing special. Perhaps that's why you did those things: because I was nothing special. And because of my history, of course, which meant no one believed me. But all that's changed. They're listening now. Everyone's paying attention.

You've seen what's happening to Mr Clarke. That could happen to you, too. I'm still remembering things all the time. And, unless you want me to remember in court exactly what you did to me, you'd better do what I tell you.

First, a cheque for ten thousand pounds to the Survivors bank account. Donations are tax-deductible. And you'd better start saving up, because you're going to be generous. You're going to pay for what you did. I'm your responsibility now.

Goodbye, Mr Scoones. You won't see me again. Except, maybe, in nightmares.

Yours sincerely,
David Spikely

Except that *I* had the nightmares. Every night, for years and years. But all that's finished, Mousey. I won. If only my dad could see me now. He never quite believed me, you know. Because of My Condition. And because my T-shirt was wet that day – you know, the day that Bunny died. He never said. But I saw his eyes. He knew, but never said so.

I tore the letter in half, then in four, then into a hundred pieces. They fluttered away like moths' wings, under the hedge, into the canal. There, Mousey. There's no going back. Those words cannot be recovered. They can never be made whole again, any more than a man's life can be made whole once it has been broken into pieces.

They change the sky, not their souls, that run across the ocean. Well, I could do with a change of sky. Maybe something blue, this time. America, Australia. No one would come looking for me. No one would care that I was gone. I've got money. I've got skills. I've got more than thirty years before I can think about dying.

And yet, the canal looks good tonight. It smells of the clay pits, and childhood. On a night like this, I could probably find a stray dog or cat to drown. Maybe even a homeless man sleeping out in a cardboard box. It wouldn't take much. It never does. Just hold his head for a minute or two. A couple of fireworks in the sky above White City. Red. Green. I stick out my tongue to taste them, the way we used to with snowflakes. I see the bright reflections on the surface of the canal. I take a step. You could almost believe a man could walk on water.

9

Monday, November 7th, 2005

It was my birthday on Saturday. Sixty-six, and still chained to the oar. If anyone had dared to tell the fourteen-year-old boy I was that I would one day *volunteer* to spend more time at St Oswald's, he would probably have given them a vicious Chinese burn, before stealing their lunch and retreating to the playing fields with Eric Scoones, to share the spoils of infamy.

Of course, in those days we both believed a friendship would last a lifetime. Now, in the light of recent events, I wonder if our friendship can. He tried to call me on Saturday night, but I was too troubled to answer the phone. We all have guilty secrets, of course. We've all done things that we regret. But if Eric abused a boy in his charge, then allowed Harry Clarke to go to jail, rather than name his blackmailer – that's infamy of another kind than the odd illicit Gauloise taken in my form-room, or failure to declare a mouse infestation, or theft from Dr Devine's stationery cupboard.

Of course, the evidence against Eric remains purely circumstantial. But if it is true – and my instincts, honed by my years as a Master, were screaming like a Greek chorus that yes, Eric Scoones was guilty as charged – then what did that say about Straitley? What price our friendship then?

I arrived in my form-room early today. Eric was already waiting for me. A bottle of claret stood on the desk, between two of my ugliest spider plants.

'Bit early for that, don't you think?' I said.

Eric shrugged. 'Happy birthday,' he said. 'I thought maybe we could celebrate.'

Of course, he must have heard the news of what happened on Friday night. The grapevine must be ripe with it now; and from his slightly awkward look, and the way he didn't quite meet my eye, I knew that he was wondering just what I knew about Spikely.

I nodded. 'Thank you. That would be nice.'

'Any word of Spikely?'

'Not yet.'

'He always was a little toad. Making up lies about members of staff. Trying to take advantage.'

'There's a change of direction,' I said, keeping my voice as calm as I could. 'I thought you said Harry deserved what he got.'

Eric looked sheepish. 'I was upset. I said lots of things I didn't mean. I hope you didn't think I was—'

'No, Eric. I didn't,' I said.

Eric gave a long sigh and sat on one of the pupils' desks. I thought that he looked very old, but I suppose both of us do. I tried to recall what else he had said, but all I could remember was that moment on Friday morning, when he had told me his mother had died. Everything that has happened since then – my search for the letter; Harrington; the scene on the canal bridge – all of that seems like a fantasy now, a story from the *Boy's Own Paper*.

'That's what happens when you get old,' said Eric. 'You fuck everything up.'

I opened the window and lit a Gauloise. With luck, the smoke would be gone before the boys began to arrive. Once more, his use of profanity – Eric Scoones, who never swears – made me feel uncomfortable. I suddenly thought of my mother, who, in the later stages of her dementia, had broken a lifetime of taboo, and started to swear like a trooper.

'You spoke about leaving St Oswald's,' I said.

Eric nodded. 'I'm tired, Straits. A nice little flat in Paris, perhaps; the Tuileries and the Folies-Bergère. I've waited for this all my life. I don't want it to be too late.'

Too late? Perhaps it is, I thought. Too late to give Harry what he deserves. Too late for him; too late for me. Too late to save St Oswald's.

'You could come and visit,' he said. 'Maybe in the holidays.'

'That sounds nice,' I told him, knowing that I never would. Dementia runs in families. Perhaps that's why I stayed here so long. An active mind dispels the fog, and I'm glad to say that my memory – in spite of certain incidents of standard absent-mindedness – is as good now as it ever was. But now that I look at him closely, I see a change in Eric. Those moods of his; the rages. The unexpected profanity. Does he sense it approaching, I thought? Is *that* why he wants to retire?

He gave me a smile; a shade too bright. 'You ought to think of retiring yourself. See the world before it's too late.'

I shrugged and put out my cigarette. 'Why bother?' I said. 'It's all here.'

We sat for a while in silence; he watching the dawn from the window. I could tell he wanted to ask what Spikely had told me on Friday night. For a moment I thought of telling him. Then I decided against it. After all, what do I know? That business ended years ago. And maybe Winter was right, after all – there are things we need not *know*, even though we may *feel* them. A man may be good in so many ways, and still carry darkness inside him. Eric is no exception. Nor was Harry – nor am I.

And so we went down to the Common Room, for a look at the morning's papers and a leisurely cup of tea. The place was already buzzing with news, and rumour, and speculation. I braced myself for a barrage of questions, to which I had only vague answers.

'Any news of the Head yet? I hear he's out of surgery.'

'Is it true you saw the attack?'

'Any idea of when he'll be back?'

Well, a head injury is never predictable; for a while, it was touch and go. Bob Strange is delighted; he gets to be Second Master while Ms Buckfast covers for the Head.

Spikely has not resurfaced, as yet. Harrington remains unclear about what happened on the bridge, and without details of a motive, the police seem disinclined to act. I can see their point, of course. After such a long time, how could I be completely sure that the attacker was Spikely at all? Devine, who recognized him, did not actually *see* the attack, and so his role as a witness seems rather less than critical – much to Devine's annoyance, as he sees himself as a memory machine of limpid, Teutonic efficiency.

However, the *Malbry Examiner* has been reluctant to let the case go. Its dislike of the Grammar School dates back to a time when the editor failed the St Oswald's entrance exam at the age of eleven, and now he never misses a chance to remind us of our mistake. The fact that the Head of St Oswald's had been assaulted, late at night, in the course of what was assumed to be some kind of assignation, was already fuel enough for the *Examiner*'s furnace, but when it was revealed that a witness had identified David Spikely – who, as it happens, now seems to be missing from his Malbry home – the speculation intensified. Add to that the death of Charlie Nutter in October, underneath the very bridge on which Harrington was attacked, and you have the beginnings of quite a promising story.

Mrs Harrington maintains that these rumours are groundless. Spikely had been a family friend. There had been no quarrel with him. They had simply drifted apart as the paths of their lives diverged. When Harrington recovers full memory of Friday's events, he will surely confirm this. Of course, we have no idea how long Harrington will take to make a full recovery – and even if he does, it may be that he never returns to St Oswald's.

The Chaplain thinks not. He isn't alone. 'My money's on Dr Blakely,' he said. 'Unless you think Bob Strange has a chance.'

'You don't think Ms Buckfast might get the job?'

'*A female Head?*' The Chaplain was outraged.

Well, I suppose he has a point. St Oswald's may not – may *never* be – ready for a female Head. And yet, Dr Blakely is too effete; for all his qualifications, he is merely a Suit with nothing inside. Becky Price is something new; not a Dragon; not a Suit; definitely not a Low-Fat Yoghurt.

I called by to see her this morning, while Blakely was taking Assembly, and found that she had moved across to the Headmaster's office – which, given her new role, makes sense. Danielle was in the anteroom, looking a little downcast. Of course, her ambition to snare a Head must have suffered a serious blow. *Call-me-Jo* Lambert, of Mulberry House, must also be wringing her elegant hands. But Ms Buckfast seems very comfortable in the Headmaster's office. I see that already she has changed the layout of the furniture, and has brought in a couple of orchids to brighten up the room, which now no longer smells of pine, but of something more subtle.

'Present from the Chaplain?' I said, looking at the orchids.

La Buckfast smiled and shook her head. 'Your friend Mr Winter, actually. It seems he's a collector.'

I raised my eyebrows. '*Winter* gave you orchids?'

She gave her Mona Lisa smile. 'We parted on more amicable terms than I would have expected,' she said. 'Perhaps, if he ever comes back, there'll be a job for him after all.'

I said: 'Really? I would have thought that with your history—'

For the first time, the smile reached her eyes. It made her look suddenly beautiful.

'History,' said La Buckfast, 'is nothing but the story of whichever side kept the best accounts. The victors write the history books. The victors paper over the truth. The early history of Europe exists almost exclusively from the perspective of the Romans. But imagine if Boudicca had had a Livy or a Plutarch on her side.'

She saw my puzzled expression and laughed. 'Oh, Mr Straitley,' she said. 'If you're going to be here at all, at least sit down and have some tea.' She poured me a mug – that's right, a *mug*. I noticed the Headmaster's china set was on the top shelf of the bookcase, where Dr Shakeshafte had once kept his collection of signed rugby photographs.

'Any more news of the Head?' I enquired, as I drank my tea. It was surprisingly good, I thought; just strong and sweet enough to stick the ribs.

'Not much, so far,' said La Buckfast. 'I'm putting together a strategy. We've made so much progress already this term. Pity to lose momentum. Still, Bob Strange is being very helpful. I think there may be a permanent job for him somewhere on the Crisis Team.'

I said: 'You seem very calm about all this. I thought you and Harrington were close.'

She looked at me serenely. 'Johnny keeps his enemies close,' she said. 'Besides, I'm very good at my job – which is, of course, to make *Johnny* look good.'

'And now?'

'I'll continue to do so,' she said. 'Johnny will get invalidity pay, and probably a settlement, too – and then, who knows? An advisor's job in London, perhaps. Something not too stressful.'

'You don't think he'll come back, then?'

She shrugged. 'We'll manage without him. Besides, it'll give him more time with Liz. You know they couldn't have children? Liz was devastated at first. Tried all kinds of treatments. But nothing worked. So now she's a family counsellor, helping childless couples come to terms with their situation.'

She smiled again and sipped her tea. Her mug, I noticed, was one of those you can have made at the print shop: a photograph of a smiling infant, with the caption WORLD'S BEST GRANDMA.

She saw me looking. 'My grandson,' she said. 'Amos. He turned three in July.'

'I didn't know you had children,' I said. 'You must have had them very young.'

'My daughter was born when I was sixteen. Her father was even younger.'

She continued to drink her tea, looking serene and beautiful. I've always said you can tell a great deal from a person's coffee mug. In this case, a whole life.

'Did you stay in touch?'

She smiled. 'When I told him I was pregnant,' she said, 'he pleaded with me to abort it. Told me no one would have to know; even said he'd pay for it all. But I wouldn't. In spite of everything – the church; my parents; the scandal – I kept my baby. I didn't tell. His family moved away, but we kept in touch. Not that I wanted to be with him – he'd shown me his true colours by then – but because I thought that maybe one day, he'd have the chance to be grateful.' She looked at the orchid on her desk. The flowers were white, veined with green. 'And yes, he's kept me close,' she said. 'Perhaps he thought I'd tell his wife. Perhaps he felt that if she knew that we'd had a child, when she never would—' She paused and took a sip of her tea. 'Johnny should have known better.'

I nodded. 'You're too subtle for that.'

'How nice of you to say so, Roy.'

Besides, a Head, like Caesar's wife, must be above suspicion. This business with Spikely, whether or not the real truth ever comes to light, has already done its damage. Harrington has been muddied by this; his gloss will never be the same again. La Buckfast, however, remains untarnished; doing the absent Harrington's job with such efficiency that, should he decide to return after all, he will find St Oswald's running much better than when he left.

Of course, there's still Dr Blakely, that over-qualified imbecile. If ever it comes to replacing little Johnny

Harrington, I would have thought that Blakely would be first in line for the top job. And yet, there is no mistaking the ease with which La Buckfast has made the Headmaster's office her own, adding bright cushions to the old leather chairs; quietly shelving the ugly prints; replacing the brown rug on the floor with a scarlet sheepskin. Well, of course, she came to us as a Rebranding Guru – and the best job she has done so far is in rebranding herself.

'I like what you've done with the office,' I said.

'Really? I thought you didn't like change.'

'It depends on what kind of change,' I said.

She sighed. 'Oh, Roy. I hope you don't think that this little change of personnel affects your impending retirement. I'm grateful for your help, of course, but from a purely financial perspective, Classics is a drain on resources. In today's world of technology, Latin has become obsolete. Only a handful of schools offer it – and besides, where does it lead? Where are the job opportunities? Where are the vital skills?'

It's an argument I've heard before from the likes of Bob Strange. We live in a world in which vocational teaching matters far more than the pursuit of wisdom, or the study of civilizations past. And yet, where would our world be without Horace, or Pliny, or Ptolemy? Those men straddled the world like gods. Their voices ring through the ages. We owe it to new generations to keep their words alive. These men taught us to look at the stars – how else could we reach for them?

I was about to answer when there came a peremptory knock at the door. It opened to reveal the girl Benedicta, looking slightly nervous. She was carrying an object that I first took to be a small radio, and which looked rather familiar, and which emitted a crackling sound.

A few seconds later, Danielle appeared. 'I told her you were in a meeting, miss,' she said, addressing La Buckfast. 'She must have snuck in while I was making tea.'

Ms Buckfast smiled. 'That's fine, Danielle.' Then, addressing the girl, she said: 'Won't you come in, Benedicta? Mr Straitley was leaving.'

Benedicta shook her head. 'Not until you've heard this.'

She held out the object in her hand. At the press of a switch, the sound of amplified voices reached us. It took me a moment to identify those of Dr Blakely and Allen-Jones. Then I recognized the thing that was not quite a radio. It was that walkie-talkie, the one whereby, according to Allen-Jones's somewhat over-elaborate scheme, Rupert Gunderson was to be revealed as a menacer of boys.

Through the speaker, Allen-Jones's voice was very clear now. '*. . . think your stance on bullying encourages victimization,*' we heard. 'I've been bullied because I'm gay, and I'd like to know where your policy of protecting people from challenging perspectives stands when it comes to protecting *me* from bullying and bigotry.'

Well, I thought, my Brodie Boys always did have a certain *panache*. Dr Blakely was fainter, but his voice was still clearly audible. He is not quite as articulate as Allen-Jones, who has, on occasion, managed to persuade me to overlook homework infractions that would, in normal circumstances, have earned him at least a detention. In fact, for a moment, Thing One was able to give vent only to a series of inarticulate *oof*-ing sounds, like someone blowing up a balloon, which finally resolved into speech.

'*Their* bigotry?' he said. 'Young man, St Oswald's is a Christian school. We have no obligation to protect or promote the so-called *perspectives* you're talking about.'

'I think you have,' said Allen-Jones. 'Your homophobic policies are directly responsible for the fact that I'm being victimized in the first place. Basically, sir, you're promoting hatred, which is a crime, according to the 1994 Criminal Justice and Public Order Act.'

Dr Blakely *oof*-ed in outrage. 'Promoting *what*?'

'Hatred, sir. Right here, in this pamphlet, sir.'

For a moment I wondered which pamphlet he meant. Then I remembered the pink pamphlet that Mr Winter had shown me, written by Johnny Harrington; published and distributed by the Church of the Omega Rose, and latterly by Survivors.

'*HOMOSEXUAL, HELLBOUND*,' Allen-Jones read the title aloud. 'Are you telling me your organization didn't produce this? Because here's the Survivors logo, right here, and—'

'That's *enough*!' Dr Blakely, inflated to capacity, almost exploded with outrage. I imagined him standing there, looking down at Allen-Jones (vaguely unkempt, with his shirt untucked, and the remnants of that Sexy Cerise glittering on his bitten nails). 'Who do you think you are, eh, to tell *me* how I should run my school? Nothing but a little queer who thinks he can get attention by stirring up trouble and making threats. Well, you might get away with that elsewhere, but St Oswald's has a moral code. We don't tolerate perversion. Do you understand?'

There came no reply from Allen-Jones.

'Now get out of my office,' said Dr Blakely hoarsely.

'Yes, sir. Thank you, sir.'

For a moment there was silence. Then came Allen-Jones's voice. 'Did you get all that, Ben?'

'Perfectly,' said the girl Ben. She turned to Ms Buckfast, who had followed the proceedings with her usual serenity, and said in a rather gruff voice: 'I thought you should know, we recorded all this. I think the *Malbry Examiner* would be happy to get an early scoop, after which I'm thinking the *News of the World*, or maybe the *Daily Mail*. Or both.'

Ms Buckfast gave a little smile. 'I don't think that will be necessary. Do you?'

'Oh, I don't know,' said Ben. 'It depends on how much support you're prepared to give to me and Allen-Jones.' She shot me a sideways look. 'Mr Straitley's been *very* supportive. In fact, you might say *indispensable*.' She faced Ms Buckfast defiantly. 'I heard he was under pressure to leave. That can't be true, can it, miss? I mean, that would be *scandalous*.'

La Buckfast's Madonna-like gaze did not falter for a moment. 'Benedicta—'

'Ben,' said the girl.

'Ben. Of *course*,' said La Buckfast. 'Mr Straitley's retirement remains his choice entirely. I certainly wouldn't put pressure on him to leave. As one of the few remaining independent schools to still offer Classics to students, I think it would be very short-sighted of us to lose one of our unique selling-points. And as for Allen-Jones, I feel sure that Mr Straitley will manage to resolve any misunderstandings – with my full support, of course.'

I felt an odd sensation in the region of my third waistcoat button. Not the invisible finger this time, but a softening, like melted ice cream. As if, after forty years of dealing with pupils in ways that, according to my Brodie Boys, ranged from benevolent neglect to callous and cruel indifference, I had suddenly acquired that most perilous of organs – a heart.

I assumed a stern demeanour. 'I have to say, Miss Wild,' I said, 'that you and young Master Allen-Jones seem to share the same deplorable love of drama. If only you had come to see *me*, instead of indulging in what I can only refer to as *shenanigans*, Ms Buckfast and I could have dealt with your problem without all this unpleasantness.'

Ben assumed a meek expression. 'Yes, sir. Sorry, sir.'

'Now you and Allen-Jones are going to give *me* that recording,' I said. 'And we won't hear any more about talking to the newspapers, or anything like that. What happens in St Oswald's gets dealt with in St Oswald's. That's the way we work here. We've been doing it for a long time.'

I smiled at La Buckfast. I noted that she, too, was smiling. Of course, this new development may not be a bad thing for her. Allen-Jones's little stunt has conveniently, and at a single stroke, removed Dr Blakely from the list of candidates for the Headship. For a moment I wondered if maybe she had anticipated, even somehow *encouraged* the plan. But that was a deduction too far. La Buckfast may be Machiavellian, but from that to suspecting that she might have orchestrated the whole thing—

No. That would be ludicrous. Wouldn't it? Of course it would.

I left with the girl Benedicta. 'I'm not leaving, Ben,' I said.

'Is that an official statement, sir? Interested parties need to know.'

I said: 'It's a promise. Will that do?'

That seemed to satisfy her. She smiled. 'I had to look up what you said, sir. *Obesa cantavit*. The fat lady sang.'

'*Did* I say that?' I prevaricated.

'Yes, sir,' said Ben.

I shrugged. 'I say all kinds of things. I don't expect pupils to *listen*.'

Arriving in my form-room, I found that Sutcliff had taken the register; McNair had filled in the absence slips;

Niu was in the process of watering my spider plants. It struck me that my boys are often at their most productive in my absence. My policy of benevolent neglect gives them the chance to think for themselves, rather than rely on me. In short, my (few) deficiencies are all for the benefit of the boys.

I opened my desk drawer to look for my packet of Liquorice Allsorts. Harry's gnome was lying there, next to the bottle of claret, a slightly debauched grin on its face. Devine must have returned it, I thought. The man is full of surprises.

I took it out and stood it on the desk.

'New supply teacher, sir?' said Allen-Jones.

'No. Just a reminder,' I said. 'A gnome is where the heart is.'

Epilogue

St Oswald's Grammar School
Michaelmas Term, November 12th, 2005

The Chapel of St Oswald's dates back to the sixteenth century. It is a listed building, much to the dismay of the Bursar, a Protestant, who sees its maintenance and repair as an unnecessary extravagance in these times of renewed austerity. I rather like it, however; its small, stained-glass windows; its buttery stone; its old oak pews, pitted and scarred by generations of scholars carving their names in secret, in the shadows.

That reminds me. I must see to reinstating those Honours Boards. Maybe somewhere less public than the Middle Corridor, but they belong to St Oswald's just as surely as I do. Maybe here in the Chapel itself, next to the war memorial, with the names of our dead boys painted in gold down the panels. Perhaps I'll talk to the Chaplain, when all of this has settled down.

Tonight, however, the Chaplain has one last duty to perform. Not as publicly as I'd hoped, but I know Harry would understand. Jimmy Watt was my partner-in-crime;

he has access to ladders as well as a full set of School keys, and Jimmy has always been helpful to those who treat him kindly. It's easy enough to open the Chapel after dark on a Saturday night; tomorrow I shall take him for a thank-you drink and a bite to eat at the Scholar. Even Bob Strange's cameras have been turned off for the evening – I told you the ancillary staff was secretly in charge of the place.

We held Harry's memorial by candlelight in the Chapel. It wasn't a large gathering. Eric Scoones; the Chaplain; myself, and, surprisingly, Dr Devine, his nose twitching with heightened emotion. I spoke a few words. We sang a hymn. And then we played the record that Harry had asked the Chaplain to play – Devine gave an audible sigh as he recognized 'The Laughing Gnome', but there was an odd look on his face, which might have been a tiny smile.

We scattered Harry's ashes on the rose bed by the Quad; a place with a view of St Oswald's and plenty of sunshine in winter. Then we shared the claret that Eric had brought for my birthday, and drank a toast to absent friends – more and more of them nowadays – using the Chaplain's silverware.

'Well, this was nice,' said Dr Devine in a slightly mocking tone. 'But really, Roy, we have to move on. We can't keep living in the past.'

'Oh, I don't know,' I told him. 'The past feels very comfortable. It's a favourite armchair, moulded to fit my dimensions. I'm getting too old and fat for ergonomic furniture.'

'I hear you've decided against retirement?'

I nodded.

'Hm. Probably wise. And Eric?' he said in a quiet voice, while Eric went to hang up his coat.

I shook my head. I knew what he meant. But I have not yet spoken to Eric about Friday night. Perhaps I never will – after all, he means to leave at Christmas. What good would it do to confront him now?

We finished our wine in a silence of flickering lights and resonances. It was a comforting silence, like that of an old married couple. Once more I thought of my parents, sitting side by side on the beach, wrapped in their tartan blankets. After a while, when the wine was gone, the Chaplain blew out the candles (in deference to Health & Safety) leaving only a single red light burning in the sanctuary.

'Time to head off, Straits,' said Eric.

Devine gave a nod. 'It's on my way.'

And so the three of us headed for home, leaving the Chapel in darkness, except for the single dull red light that shone through the mullioned windows. Above us, in the rafters, in a little stone niche too high to reach, or even to see very clearly (at least without one of those ladders), Harry's gnome watched us go; half hidden in the shadows, but laughing quietly to itself at the absurdity of it all – the tragedy and farce of it; the friendships and betrayals; the secrets and the scandals on which our little world of St Oswald's survives – minus a few Honours Boards, perhaps, but with our honour still (mostly) intact, dragging our heels like schoolboys along the rocky road that leads to the stars.

[illegible]

[illegible]

[illegible] married couple [illegible] sideways [illegible] After a while [illegible] the canals [illegible]

[illegible]

[illegible]

Acknowledgements

It takes a department to build a book, but sometimes even the greatest heroes fail to make the Honours Boards.

Heartfelt thanks, therefore, to my tireless agent, Peter Robinson, and his PA, Federica; to my editor, Marianne Velmans, and desk editor Kate Samano; to copy-editor Deborah Adams and proofreaders Dan Balado and Clare Hubbard. Thanks also to Sarah Whittaker for the stunning cover design, and to everyone at Transworld for their continuing faith in Straitley, St Oswald's and me.

Thanks, too, to Kyte Photography for the author photo, to my lovely PA, Anne Riley; and, as always, to Kevin and Anouchka for acting as my sounding board and for keeping me grounded in the real world. Thanks to all my ex-teachers, ex-colleagues and ex-pupils, who, consciously or otherwise, helped create St Oswald's. Thanks to the unsung heroes: the book reps, booksellers, bloggers and festival organizers. And, of course, as always, the readers – *you* – whose appetite for stories keeps the pages turning.

Joanne Harris is one of our best-loved and most versatile novelists. She first appeared on the scene with the bestselling *Chocolat* (made into an Oscar-nominated film with Juliette Binoche and Johnny Depp), which turned into the sensuous Lansquenet trilogy (with *Lollipop Shoes* and *Peaches for Monsieur le Curé*). She has since written acclaimed novels in such diverse genres as fantasy based on Norse myth (*Runemarks, Runelight, The Gospel of Loki*), and the Malbry cycle of dark psychological thrillers (*Gentlemen & Players, Blueeyedboy*, and now *Different Class*).

Born in Barnsley, of an English father and a French mother, she spent fifteen years as a teacher before (somewhat reluctantly) becoming a full-time writer. In 2013, she was awarded an MBE. She lives in Yorkshire, plays bass in a band first formed when she was sixteen, works in a shed in her garden, spends far too much time online and occasionally dreams of faking her own death and going to live in Hawaii.

GENTLEMEN & PLAYERS
Joanne Harris

At St Oswald's, a long-established boys' grammar school in Malbry in Yorkshire, a new year has just begun. For the staff and boys of the school, a wind of unwelcome change is blowing. Suits, paperwork and Information Technology rule the world; and Roy Straitley, the eccentric veteran Latin master, is finally – reluctantly – contemplating retirement.

But beneath the little rivalries, petty disputes and everyday crises of the school, a darker undercurrent stirs. And a bitter grudge, hidden and carefully nurtured for thirteen years, is about to erupt.

'A gripping psychological thriller . . . shows her at the top of her form'
Daily Express

'A clever story of obsession and revenge . . . another success'
Sunday Telegraph

'A delicious black comedy . . . the plot is so cleverly constructed, the tension so unflagging, you'd think she'd been writing thrillers all her life'
Daily Mail

BLUEEYEDBOY
Joanne Harris

'Once there was a widow with three sons, and their names were Black, Brown and Blue. Black was the eldest; moody and aggressive. Brown was the middle child; timid and dull. But Blue was his mother's favourite. And he was a murderer.'

B.B. is forty-two years old and still living at home with his mother in Malbry, a Yorkshire village. His social life is played out online, on a website called *badguysrock*. There, he stalks *Albertine*, with whom he shares a troubled past, and spins dark murder fantasies – especially about his mother.

As the story of his tortured relationship with his parent unravels, so does that of his blood feud with his brothers, the poignant tale of a blind child prodigy, and the poisonous truth lurking in the rotting heart of one disturbed family.

'Delivers an almighty twist in the tale . . . heartbreaking'
The Times

'An ingenious, gripping read . . . it terrified the living daylights out of me'
Daily Express

'Brilliantly written, plotted and insightful . . . beware unreliable narrators along with a huge plot twist at the end'
Mirror